lighthouse on Bleakpoint Island captured my heart, and like that lighthouse, Amanda's story is a beacon of light and hope shining on the stormy seas of life. I highly recommend this poignant and tender novel of healing, love, and new beginnings."

Katie Powner, Christy Award–winning author of
The Wind Blows in Sleeping Grass

Praise for *He Should Have Told the Bees*

"Cox is a brilliant writer, and her characters feel like old friends. With humor and a tenderness for the struggling, the novel explores what happens when people let the light in on their journey to healing."

Library Journal

"Cox's hopeful, heartwarming novel touches on complicated relationships, the value of friendship, and the impact of trauma with great heart and kindness."

BookPage

BETWEEN
THE SOUND
AND SEA

Books by Amanda Cox

The Edge of Belonging
The Secret Keepers of Old Depot Grocery
He Should Have Told the Bees
Between the Sound and Sea

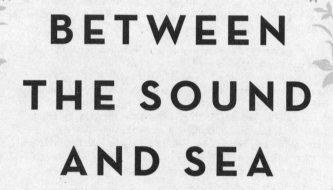

BETWEEN THE SOUND AND SEA

a novel

AMANDA COX

Revell

a division of Baker Publishing Group
Grand Rapids, Michigan

Published by Revell
a division of Baker Publishing Group
Grand Rapids, Michigan
RevellBooks.com

Printed in the United States of America

Library of Congress Cataloging-in-Publication Data
Names: Cox, Amanda, 1984– author.
Title: Between the sound and sea : a novel / Amanda Cox.
Description: Grand Rapids, Michigan : Revell, a division of Baker Publishing
    Group, 2024.
Identifiers: LCCN 2024006061 | ISBN 9780800742744 (paperback) | ISBN
    9780800745837 (casebound) | ISBN 9781493445509 (ebook)
Subjects: LCSH: Family secrets—Fiction. | LCGFT: Christian fiction. | Novels.
Classification: LCC PS3603.O88948 B48 2024 | DDC 813/.6—dc23/eng/20240213
LC record available at https://lccn.loc.gov/2024006061

This book is a work of fiction. Names, characters, places, and incidents are the product of the author's imagination or are used fictitiously. Any resemblance to actual events, locales, or persons, living or dead, is coincidental.

Cover illustration by Roberta Murray / Arcangel

Baker Publishing Group publications use paper produced from sustainable forestry practices and postconsumer waste whenever possible.

24   25   26   27   28   29   30   7   6   5   4   3   2   1

To the only man who could convince me
to go beach driving in a hurricane.
Love,
Slick

You keep track of all my sorrows.
    You have collected all my tears in your bottle.
    You have recorded each one in your book.

Psalm 56:8 NLT

Prologue

The old woman observed the young boy kicked back in the adjacent recliner, his face practically glued to that tiny screen, as it had been since his visit began. Not that she blamed him. What fifteen-year-old wanted to spend an entire Saturday stuck in an assisted living apartment with a couple of old ladies for company?

"Listen here, boy, put down that Game Boy and I'll tell you something you'll never forget."

He looked up at her, grinning. "Aw, this isn't a Game Boy. It's my new Nintendo DS, and I'm this close to beating the boss on my game." He held up two fingers, pinching at the air.

"Maybe I oughta get me one of them things. Since I can't get around on these old legs like I used to, I get bored sitting around here."

He smiled and shook his head, continuing with his game.

She glanced up at the sound of pots and pans banging in the kitchen. "What's your gramma up to?"

"Making supper for us, I think."

"Good. That means we've got plenty of time before she comes nosin' in. Now put that thing down like I said and scooch closer so

11

I can tell you something." She lowered her voice. "Something nary a soul knows except me. It's time I passed these stories down before I'm good and gone. And I've chosen you." She mined her memories for just the right tale. It'd have to be a good one to compete with a kid stuck on video games.

He gave one last baleful look at the device before setting it on the table beside him. He scooted his chair closer to hers and adjusted the blanket that had slipped off her foot before sitting back down. Sweet boy.

"It was a dark and stormy night," she began.

He groaned, looking back toward the game waiting on the side table. "A dark and stormy night? Really?"

She chuckled. "I'm not being funny. It really *was* a dark and stormy night. Way back in 1941. Now listen close, Peter, and I'll tell you how the legend of Saint-Mae was born."

She closed her eyes, concentrating on recounting the tale.

Fifteen-year-old Cathleen tied off her skiff. Adrenaline coursed through her body like the spidery tendrils of lightning dashing across the sky. The wind whipped about her head, unfurling her sodden scarf, sending it airborne until it settled somewhere over the seething Atlantic.

Hunched against the slanting rain, she jogged past her faithful light. A light that had guided her to the foolish drunk clinging to a vessel not seaworthy in even the fairest weather. A man who likely didn't merit Cathleen risking her life over. But duty had called. No matter who was at the mercy of the unpredictable currents of the Outer Banks.

She opened her eyes a tiny slit. The boy leaned in close, eyes locked on her. She had him hook, line, and sinker now.

Cathleen entered the squat stone cottage where she lived, boots squelching on the stone floor. She sidled up to the fire and added enough wood to coax the embers back to life, then she stripped out of her sodden clothes and wrapped a wool blanket around her shoulders.

She winced. *Oops.* That was probably more detail than a fifteen-year-old boy needed to hear about a fifteen-year-old girl. She continued, more mindful of the particulars she shared.

"Cathy?" Her father's voice cut through the silence. Rolling thunder sounded on its heels.

Cathleen cringed. "Yes, Da?"

"Everythin' all right? Why are you up, lass?"

"Just checking the light," she called and then pulled the scratchy wool tighter around her, sending up a silent prayer that he'd accept her answer and go back to sleep. She inched closer to the fire, aching for the heat to reach her bones. Moments later her father's snores once again echoed through the room, and the tension she carried between her shoulder blades released.

He was having a good night.

Cathleen grabbed a kettle, filled it with water, and hung it over the fire. While the water came to a boil, she rubbed her hands together, trying to turn her blue-tinged nail beds pink. Once she'd downed her tea and her fingers burned white-hot with renewed circulation, Cathleen went to her father's desk and pulled out his sacred book.

"This is our livelihood," he'd told her a hundred times. "A lightkeeper is only as good as the records he keeps."

She paused and looked at the boy. "Now, listen close. It might not sound like much, but this is the moment Saint-Mae was born."

He nodded, eyes wide.

Into the book, she poured her account of the night. How she'd woken with an inner urging to check that all was well along the coast, how she'd climbed those endless spiral stairs, chiding herself for venturing into this unkind weather without cause. That was when the light beam had glinted off the overturned dinghy being tossed about in the storm.

She wrote of the waves that had crashed over her own vessel as she maneuvered her boat. Not just anyone could have managed swells like that. Especially not someone as young as herself, be they male or female. But fifteen-year-old Cathleen had honed her skills on the water since her father had taken up his post at Bleakpoint Island when she was a little girl. Everything had been preparing her for that night. Her first solo rescue at sea.

She continued pouring her heart and soul onto the page, telling how the inebriated man had nearly capsized her when he'd grasped at the oarlocks to pull himself aboard. Though the skiff had tipped wildly, Cathleen had kept a cool head despite her knowledge that a merciless sea cared not whether it was a drunkard or a teenage girl dumped into its depths.

She'd calmed the cursing, thrashing man and coaxed him around to the stern like she'd seen her father do so many times before. And she'd saved him. Scarf and storm concealing her identity, she motored him to Ocracoke before disappearing back to her remote island home.

At the bottom of the log page, she impulsively signed a name she wished was her own. A person she craved to know but who was little more than a legend to Cathleen. A person who, if they were there, would know how to help her father.

But hadn't the night's events proven she was equal to the task life had handed her? As long as she continued doing whatever it took to conceal the fate of the real keeper of Bleakpoint Light, everything could stay as it had always been.

The girl stared at the page on which she'd poured out the events of the evening, all written in her scruffy hand instead of mimicking her father's writing as she normally did. Ever so carefully she removed her account from the precious book, leaving no trace of the torn-out page. As far as anyone knew, this rescue never happened. And that was the way it must remain.

She walked to the fire with the page in her hand. It would make better kindling than anything else. She stretched the paper toward the licking flames. "I am naught but a figment of a drunk man's imagination," she said to the empty room. But instead of releas-

ing it so that the fire could claim it, she clutched the paper to her chest, holding tight to the memory.

The woman opened her eyes to the young boy whose face was creased in concentration. "Why was she scared for her father to find out? And why did she need to keep what she did a secret?"

"That, my boy, is another story. I can tell you if you like."

ONE

OCTOBER 2007
COPPER CREEK, TENNESSEE

Joey Harris stood from her desk chair and stared out the window of her second-story office. Golden leaves dropped from the trees and pasted themselves to the damp sidewalk bordering the historic town square. Two middle-aged women chatted below, their closed umbrellas propped at their sides. If only they would move from the sidewalk into her office and write their names down in the blank spaces in her appointment book.

She stepped back from the curtain, letting it fall closed.

A shrill tone permeated the space, and she edged away from its source. What if she just ignored the call and persisted in showing up at the last planned event still in her books? Refused to accept that her services were no longer required by the inhabitants of Copper Creek, Tennessee.

Joey squared her shoulders and lifted her portable phone from its cradle. "Events by Josephina."

"Hey, honey. Just calling to check in. I've got you on speaker-phone." *Mom.* Joey let out the breath she'd been holding. Road noise and the canned voice of a navigational guidance system filled her ears.

Joey sank onto the small sofa behind her, then kicked off her heels and tucked her legs beneath her.

"Say hi to your daughter, Ronnie." Her mother hissed as though Joey couldn't hear every word.

"Babe, I'm trying to listen to that newfangled GPS woman and change lanes without the U-Haul taking out a minivan. Joey, please tell your mother I'm only capable of doing one thing at a time."

Joey stifled a snicker. "Is your trip going okay so far?"

Early that morning her parents had driven away from the house she'd helped her father build when she was only eight. How she remembered what it was like to be glued to his side, handing him any tool she was big enough to lift.

After saying their goodbyes, which hadn't been easy, Joey denied her ridiculous urge to sneak inside the trailer with her parents' displaced possessions and stow away on their fresh start.

"We're about four hours outside of St. Petersburg." It was a good sign, this lift of excitement in Mom's voice. It had been absent for far too long.

"Sunshine and sea breezes, here we come." Dad's tone was light, but Joey knew better. For years her parents had been planning to move to Florida for retirement, but not under these circumstances.

Joey ended the call and retrieved her appointment book from her desk. All those erasure marks, traces of plans that were still on, just without her help. Birthday parties. Weddings. Reunions. Graduation celebrations.

Living in a small town where everyone knew your name had its pluses . . . and its minuses. She slapped the calendar shut and stood.

She grabbed her keys and gave a parting look to the pristine space meant to communicate to everyone who walked through the door that she had an eye for beauty and detail. It was a prime location, sandwiched between a day spa and a boutique. She sighed. She wasn't ready to give up on this dream just yet, but she was starting to wonder if it was worth the fight.

Joey locked the door behind her and exited the building, inhaling the scent of damp autumn leaves. Margaret Pierce, the owner of Simple Things Bed-and-Breakfast, walked toward her, her low heels clicking on the pavement. Joey's stomach tightened.

Margaret lifted her head from her cell phone screen. She gave Joey a curt nod and chose to cross the street rather than walk past her.

Joey growled under her breath, biting back the words rushing to her lips. She'd tried to explain her family's innocence six months ago, after Margaret convinced her niece to fire Joey as her wedding planner. But if Margaret hadn't listened to reason then, she wouldn't listen now.

A drizzle started and, without missing a step, Margaret snapped open her umbrella and lifted it overhead. Joey peeled her gaze from the woman's retreating form and walked to her truck—a pearl-pink outfit with her company name decaled on the side. The thing was ugly as all get out, but her parents had been proud as peacocks when they presented it to her after she landed her first planning gig. She chuckled to herself. Dad had said she needed something practical and pretty to haul things around for her events. It was the wrong vehicle for slipping through town inconspicuously though.

She ducked into the driver's side, swiping the droplets from her bare arms and smoothing back the curls that had sprung loose from her bun. Joey pulled out of her reserved space and cruised once around the town square.

As a teenager she'd loved working alongside her father and brother, giving each of those historic buildings a facelift in preparation for the series of heartwarming movies that would be filmed outside them. Tourists and new residents alike now flocked to Copper Creek, wanting to experience that fairy-tale town they'd watched on the screen.

Too bad the people had forgotten that her father's work had been what charmed those producers in the first place.

As she drove home, she attempted to brainstorm ways to restore honor to the Harris name, but all she could see was that empty appointment book and the determined scowl on Margaret Pierce's face.

Once inside her apartment, she grabbed a ready-made meal from the freezer and popped the casserole in the microwave. While it cooked, Joey flopped onto the couch, pulling a tattered patchwork quilt over her lap. She opened her laptop and typed the name of her parents' new neighborhood into the search bar. It was beautiful. Maybe she should have stowed away in that U-Haul, after all. Despite the weight on her chest, she smiled at the mental image of taking up residence in their retirement community at the age of twenty-six and planning posh one hundredth birthday parties and fiftieth wedding anniversaries for the rest of her life.

Her search then drifted to scrolling through realty listings as she was drawn to beautiful coastal homes well out of her price range. She pictured herself standing on the front porch of one of them. In her imagination, a man appeared by her side. The preppy lumberjack wore a buffalo plaid shirt and had her ex-boyfriend Paul's face. She shook off the image. That was weird. Paul never wore flannel, nor had she ever imagined herself marrying him. What was she thinking?

She grabbed her meal from the microwave, and thankfully it tasted better than it looked.

Her cell rang. Sophie's name lit up the screen.

Joey set the cardboard tray on her side table, answered the call, and lay back, staring at the popcorn ceiling. "Hey, Soph," she said through a burden-laden exhale.

"Don't sound so excited to talk to me. You'll give me a complex."

Joey smirked at her friend's wry remark. "Don't take it personally. I said goodbye to my childhood home this morning. Mom and Dad are on their way to a new life in Florida. Plus, my business is in a rapid downhill spiral with no rescue in sight because the

Harris name makes me a pariah. Oh, and since we last talked, Paul broke it off with me for someone new."

Sophie sucked air through her teeth. "Ouch."

"Yeah, I feel like a million bucks." Joey cradled the phone against her ear with her shoulder and unwound her long brown hair from its bun.

"What happened?"

"I thought I had at least two promising events on the books, something to remind Copper Creek that I'm not a scam artist, nor am I a child of one." Joey rolled her eyes skyward. "There's this lady Cara who just moved here to open a gift shop. She asked me to help her plan her grand opening block party." Joey rubbed the back of her neck, attempting to defuse the beginnings of a tension headache. "But she stopped me on the street yesterday and said that Ada at the boutique next door said that if she used me, people wouldn't come. I know Margaret is behind this, because her B&B was almost bankrupted when—"

"Stop the train, Jo-Jo. I meant about Paul, the guy you've been seeing for eight whole months. Why didn't you call me?"

Joey huffed. "It just didn't feel like that big of a deal in light of everything else."

"What happened?"

"Last week he met this girl at the soup kitchen where his men's group volunteers, and he really hit it off with her. He felt like the right thing to do was to break things off with me before even talking to her about his feelings."

"This is the same Paul we went to high school with? Who never even bought a new shirt without taking a month to think about it?"

Joey massaged her scalp, releasing tension brought on by her heavy updo. "He said he's never felt this way about someone before. What can I say to that?"

"What can you say to that? Y'all've been together almost a year and he ditches you for some girl he just met who might not even like him back? Who does that?" Joey couldn't help but smile.

Too bad Sophie didn't live closer. She'd set all of Copper Creek straight for her.

"That's the thing though, Soph. The fact that I didn't cry or feel like throwing something . . . I . . . I just don't know what I'm doing anymore." She grabbed her casserole from the side table and stuffed a generous bite into her mouth.

"You don't think it had something to do with the lawsuit and all that mess with Margaret, do you?"

"I don't want to think that it does. But you know Paul. He's always preferred to keep things simple. And my life is not that. Not anymore."

"I vote that you pack it all up and move to Nashville. The apartment next to me is coming open in a few weeks. There would be way more opportunities to event plan here than in touristy Copper Creek. Before you know it, you could be planning parties for the biggest names in country music."

Joey set her casserole aside and sank deeper into her couch. She twirled a curl around her finger, examining the way it reflected in the lamplight. "I appreciate your vote of confidence and your chronic spontaneity, but you and I both know opportunities like that don't just happen. I would be an itty-bitty fish in a far bigger pond. Besides, at the moment, I think I'd prefer anonymity to fame. I just need to stick it out a little longer. I've still got that welcome home bash for Evelyn's son. After I ace that, things are bound to turn around, aren't they?"

"Why are you so obsessed with making things work in Copper Creek?"

Joey sat up, tucking her knees to her chest. "I . . . it's home." She picked at the nail polish she'd chipped while compulsively tightening down the squeaky floorboards in her office after a long day with nothing to fill her time.

"After everything that happened?" Sophie scoffed. "Is it really worth it? Working so hard to regain the favor of a group of people who've chosen your family as the scapegoat for all their misery?

Any idiot ought to be able to see that the bad things that happened with Harris Construction occurred after your dad sold it. There's more to the world than Copper Creek."

Easy for Sophie to say. She'd left after high school to attend college in Nashville and had never looked back. Meanwhile, Joey had jumped straight into launching her business in her beloved hometown while taking business classes at night.

A life in Copper Creek was all that was left of Joey's dreams. Growing up here had been a lot like living in one of those feel-good movies that had been filmed right outside her office windows. Joey had even played an extra in some of them. But her reality was nothing like the movies that ended with a resurrected family business and a sweet kiss in the town square. "My dad did not deserve what happened to him. Being dragged through the mud like that. I need to—"

"Fix this somehow? Joey, come on . . ." The sound of a baby cry came through the line. "Uh-oh, Liam is awake again. Sorry, friend, I better run. I know Nashville isn't what you're looking for, but think how much fun we'd have as neighbors!"

After she ended the call, Joey rested her forehead against her tucked knees.

Starting all over again? Was this really what it had come to? Eight years of building a business down the drain. Did she really have it in her to start from scratch? Did she even want to?

A few hours later, a text came through from Sophie. *"You'll probably write this off as more evidence of my so-called chronic spontaneity, but I think I found the perfect thing for you. Check your email."*

Joey opened her laptop. The subject line read "You said you wanted to be anonymous." Joey skimmed the attached job listing and eyed the grainy photograph of a lighthouse surrounded by wilderness. Sophie's scheme to get Joey to move to Nashville was absurd enough. But this? She shook her head. She wasn't *that* desperate yet. Was she?

TWO

"You'll never find me, Wally. Not today, not ever." Cay's light-filled voice floated on the wind, tickling his ears.

Walt took a right fork in the twisting deer trail through the live oaks. He might stand a chance if he kept her talking. "I almost found you last time."

"Did not. I'm the queen of hide-and-seek," she chortled, sounding a little farther away this time. He grinned. That cheater. She wasn't supposed to change hiding spots. He quickened his pace.

"If you're the queen, does that make me king?"

"More like the jester!" This time she sounded a little farther to the left.

"You moved! No wonder you always win."

No reply followed. He continued down the narrow, winding path through the maritime forest of spindly pine and live oak. He froze as darkness fell around him, sudden and thick, like someone had plucked the sun from the sky. "Cay? Where are you?"

Silence throbbed in his ears.

"Forget the game. Come out. Let's go home." He attempted to continue on the pitch-black path, legs leaden.

"Wally!" The sound of her strangled cry sucked the air from his lungs.

He fought his way forward, limbs tearing at his face, but his legs refused to cooperate. He dropped to his knees and crawled. "Please, let's just make it home." He wasn't sure if the words that spilled from him were meant to call out to his friend or to God.

Walt sat up, bumping his head on the ceiling of his boat's shallow berth. He gripped his forehead and groaned. His skin was slick with sweat. He took a few moments to catch his breath, then heaved his aching body out of bed and went above deck, out into the night.

The sailboat rocked softly, anchored in place on the Pamlico Sound. The cool breeze evaporated the moisture on his skin, causing him to shiver. He sat on the bench seat at the bow of the boat and looked up, arms wrapped around his middle, eyes feasting on the millions of pinpricks of light in the night sky. He then peered through the dark, toward the barely visible silhouette of the old lighthouse.

He wasn't sure why his sixty-year marriage had put a moratorium on dreaming of his childhood friend, but the dreams were back now, relentlessly driving him back to his old stomping grounds now that his Martha was gone.

Maybe his plan to set right the mistakes of his past wouldn't stop the haunting dreams or the ache in his chest—but he owed it to Cay to at least try.

THREE

In search of a project manager for a privately owned, decommissioned lighthouse on a remote North Carolina island. Position duration is four to six months, dependent on the time required for renovation completion. Must have a background in project management and construction. On-property living provided. Position begins November 12. Interested parties should submit applications by clicking the link below. Submission closes October 16.

Joey stared at the grainy photograph that accompanied the job listing, taking in the lighthouse tower and the overgrown shrubbery obscuring all but the crest of the roof on the nearby house.

She'd blown off the prospect when Sophie had sent it last night, but as ridiculous as the idea was, she couldn't seem to get her mind off of it. She dialed her friend's number.

Sophie answered with a groggy "Hello?"

"What in the world, Soph?"

"I'm sorry, I got about 3.5 hours of sleep last night. Refresh me on what weird thing I've said or done in the past twenty-four hours."

Joey glanced at her watch and sucked air through her teeth. It was only seven in the morning. *Oops*. "A project manager on a construction site? I'm an event planner. I deal in tulle and tiered cakes, not hammer and nails."

The sound of a yawn came through the line. "You spent your whole life working next to your dad," Sophie said. "You know loads about what needs to happen and in what order."

"I. AM. AN. EVENT. PLANNER." Joey punctuated each word by pounding the couch cushion beneath her.

Sophie laughed. "And that's exactly why this is perfect. You're a genius at getting things to run smoothly, whether it's a baby shower or a wedding with six hundred people in attendance. And it gives you some space from Copper Creek to clear your head."

Joey warmed at Sophie's unwavering vote of confidence. Even though her best friend was completely biased, compliments on her abilities had been in short supply lately. "Maybe, but . . . I don't know . . . going back to construction? What would Dad think?"

Her father had practically begged her to take over his company when he and Mom had decided it was time for them to retire. But to usurp a role intended for her brother, Trey? Never.

Event planning had been a fun way to spread her wings. To make her own mark in their booming little town. And she'd enjoyed her work—

Sophie's voice interrupted her musing. "I'm willing to bet that all your dad really wants is for you to be happy, and you're not happy where you're at. When the project is complete, you can decide if you want to return to Copper Creek."

Joey had to admit there was a certain appeal to disappearing for a little while. And to work on a lighthouse, of all things? A beacon that stood through wind and storm to guide people safely home. Being a part of making a place like that beautiful again could be the perfect respite. She took another look at the sparse description and poor-quality photograph.

"Where did you find this job listing, anyway? Are you sure this is legit?"

"It was in Kitty Hawk's community news. Remember how my

aunt Nora lives there? After my last trip, I somehow ended up on one of the mailing lists meant for locals, so I get a quarterly newsletter. I'd unsubscribe, but there is some seriously hilarious town gossip that shows up in the classifieds. There was a blurb about the planned lighthouse restoration in there too. I'll send it over if you're interested."

Joey massaged her forehead. "Sure, why not? I'll humor you."

Later that morning, Joey walked into her office, humming quietly, a piping hot chai latte from the Dancing Bean in hand. It was one of those perfect fall days, where the sky was crisp blue against the early autumn leaves.

As much fun as she'd had toying with Sophie's avant-garde ideas for course-correcting her life, Evelyn's son Jason would be home from the Navy soon and how would it look if she ran off to North Carolina and skipped out on the one sure commitment on her calendar? She wouldn't make much with all the extras she was going to throw in, but this event would be her showpiece. Her maligners would come to their senses and remember that she was the same Joey who had grown up in Copper Creek, who had successfully planned event after event without swindling a single soul out of their hard-earned dollars.

Joey swiveled slowly back and forth in her desk chair while she sipped her warm drink, enjoying everything about her tidy office. Light and airy with its mint and gold accents.

There was nothing she loved better than gathering all the little details needed for a perfect event, lining them up in neat little rows, and then causing them to dance like a room full of Victorian lords and ladies. Navigating the inevitable disasters, like a dropped cake or musicians who had the wrong date on their calendar, while the hosts and hostesses remained completely oblivious—the heroes of their moments.

Her laptop dinged. An email from Sophie, she assumed. Seconds later, she scrolled through the Kitty Hawk community newsletter, searching for information about the lighthouse.

BLEAKPOINT LIGHT GETS A NEW LEASE ON LIFE

After a recent purchase by Finnegan W. O'Hare, restorations are in order for one abandoned lighthouse. Located on a remote island near the southern outskirts of the Outer Banks, Bleakpoint Light fell into disrepair after it was decommissioned in the 1940s, following the unexplained disappearance of longtime lightkeeper, Callum McCorvey, and his daughter, Cathleen McCorvey. Legend has it that it's haunted by McCorvey's lost daughter, but O'Hare is undeterred by the potential for resident ghosts. When asked about his plans once the structure is restored to its former glory, O'Hare was not forthcoming. Stay tuned to learn more in the coming months.

Joey sat back. Ghost stories? Legends? What was Sophie getting her into?

She shook her head. It didn't matter. Cutting town to spend her winter on an island in North Carolina might sound appealing, but it wouldn't fix anything with her real life.

Two new families had recently moved to Copper Creek. Maybe they had yet to catch wind of the town gossip and would call her to plan *something*. They had children. Kid birthday parties weren't exactly her jam, but she was in no position to be choosy.

The shrill ring of her office phone punctured the silence. "Events by Josephina."

"Joey dear, I've got some unfortunate news," Evelyn's voice filled her ear.

Joey laid her forehead on her glass desktop, her makeup leaving a beige smudge. "Not you too."

"I'm afraid it can't be helped. Jason just called, and the Navy decided to keep him in Japan for another six months, so that welcome home party is going to have to wait. But you know I'll still be booking with you when the time comes."

"I appreciate it, Evelyn." Joey ended the call, stuffing down the desperation churning in her stomach. The sweet woman had warned her that Jason's return date wasn't one hundred percent definite.

Joey pressed the heels of her palms against her eyes, stood, then began pacing the length of the floor.

She sat back down to reread the article and job listing again. It was a ridiculous idea, no doubt about it, but she could always swoop back home just in time to plan that rescheduled welcome home party for Evelyn. Start fresh.

She hovered her cursor over the application button and held her breath. Chances were there were tons of far more qualified people out there vying for this opportunity. So why not go for it? It'd be a funny story she and Sophie could laugh about years later. *Hey, remember that time you convinced me to put in an application to restore a lighthouse so I could ditch my disaster life?*

She filled out the form, outlining the projects she planned and the scope of work she'd assisted her father with on various renovations, from an old theatre restored to its 1920s glamour to redoing the facades on all the buildings on the town square. Together they'd updated each one while helping them retain their historical flair in preparation for upcoming films.

She eyed the photograph and the limited specifics on what the job entailed. If the lighthouse had been neglected since the forties, whatever repairs it needed had to be extensive.

She picked up her phone and dialed her dad's number. He was silent on the other end of the line as she explained the scope of the job. A knot formed in her stomach. The more she talked, the more absurd the whole endeavor sounded.

When she finished spilling out the plans, she cringed, waiting for his reply.

His response was gentle but all business. "There's not a lot of details to go on. It makes a big difference if you are supervising cosmetic touch-ups or if there will be structural engineers involved.

And are you going to be responsible for finding the subcontractors and making sure they all have the right licensing and insurance to be doing the type of work required? What about managing the financial side of things? You need to know what's expected."

Joey swallowed hard. "Maybe this isn't such a great—"

"Joey, if this is what you've set your mind to do, then I know you'll rise to the occasion." He cleared his throat. "Because of the lack of details, I feel like this is probably an individual doing the hiring. Contractors and government entities that normally do this type of work usually have project managers on staff.

"If this is the direction you want to take, make sure to ask good questions. Pay close attention to the answers. And make sure you wait until you lay eyes on the place before signing any agreements. Talk to . . . to . . . uh, someone who's good with negotiating contracts."

She pressed her lips tight. Someone? Who? Like the son he hadn't spoken to in three years?

She ended the call with her father after thanking him for his direction. Why, despite all reason, did she still find herself drawn to this lighthouse? She propped her head in her hands and closed her eyes. *God, this might be an epic mistake, but . . . I don't know . . . something feels right about it. Help me out and close this door and lock it tight if this is going to be just one more disaster. I don't think I can handle another.*

Joey straightened her shoulders, choosing to believe that if the job wasn't meant for her, God would keep the door closed. Implementing her father's advice, she completed her application and clicked submit.

She tucked away her laptop and went outside to get some air, praying that by some miracle the old adage about watched pots not boiling would apply to her future. Maybe she should invest in marketing outside of Copper Creek. She'd rather not make long commutes, but surely Margaret's poisonous reach had limits.

As she walked toward her truck, the cool air whipped around

her, tugging her hair back from her face. She ran her fingertip along the grooves between the bricks of one of the storefronts and then stopped to peer in the window of the clothing boutique. She and her father and Trey had lovingly restored those old hardwoods and fitted new glass into the window frames several years back.

Oh, Trey. She'd thought refusing Dad's offer to take over the company would buy time. Trey would come to his senses and return to Copper Creek to take over as they'd always planned. Or Dad would fight harder to reconnect with his prodigal son. The rift in her family would heal. And things could go back to normal.

But none of those things had happened.

Joey crossed the square and sat on a bench outside of City Hall. Like a row of falling dominos, shop owners unlocked their storefronts and flipped their open signs. Maybe Sophie was right. Maybe it was time to say goodbye. If these mule-headed people couldn't separate her from the thief who had bought Dad's company and swindled them, why in the world did she feel so gung ho loyal to them?

She heaved herself to her feet. Pacing in front of the bench, she replayed her recent conversations with her best friend. Sophie who was so angry about Paul dumping Joey. Angry about the way the town was treating her. Angry. When Joey felt . . . nothing.

Well, *nothing* wasn't accurate. Disappointed. Resigned.

Shouldn't she be crying into a pint of fudge ripple about her boyfriend meeting a girl one evening and instantly ditching her? Or throwing all her belongings into boxes and not even sparing a backward glance at a town full of people who had forgotten the talented, smart, giving person she'd always been?

And yet here she was, pacing in front of a park bench, trying to find a strategy to restore the town's trust in her. Trust she'd done nothing to lose.

She headed for her truck. What missing piece did she expect to find here? Mom and Dad were long gone. Trey wasn't coming back.

Without meaning to, she found herself parked in front of her family home. A moving van was out front. A husband and wife and their three kids carried boxes inside, teasing each other as they passed. The excitement of a new beginning sparkled in their eyes despite the drudgery of moving day.

An ache swelled in Joey's chest. This was what family . . . home . . . was supposed to feel like.

She dialed Trey's number. He answered on the third ring, just like always.

"Hey, sis." The roar and rumble of heavy equipment filled the background noise.

"There's a new family moving into our house."

"Hang on. Let me get to a better spot." The background noise faded. "You okay?"

Something about that question had a way of breaking the dam of tears she hadn't known existed. She swiped at her cheeks. "I knew I could always come back here if I ever needed a soft place to land. And now . . ."

"They've talked for years about moving to Florida, Roo," he said softly.

She smiled through her tears at the childhood nickname. A double play on her once-bouncy nature and her other moniker sharing a name with a baby kangaroo. "I guess I always imagined they'd change their mind, ya know?"

Two of the kids came out of the house laughing and grabbed a couple more boxes off the truck, racing to reach the front door first. Hopefully the boxes didn't contain the good china. "I mean, it's weird, right?" Joey said. "People moving into the house we built? All of us together."

He was silent for a few moments, and then after a long exhale said, "I guess. But it's not the same for me. I've moved on. I have a new life."

His words were like daggers. Moved on from Copper Creek? Or moved on from their family? She tried and failed to keep the tremor from her voice. "Do you ever wonder how different things would be if you—" A tightening in her throat cut her words away.

"No." But she heard the doubt lacing the one-word reply, or at least she hoped she did. "Listen, sis, I know this has been tough on you, but we can't go back to the way things were. I've moved on. Dad and Mom moved on. It's your turn now."

Joey said goodbye, heart in tatters. He was right. They had all moved on. And she was left holding fragments of a life they'd loved.

The woman of the house noticed her staring and paused, squinting at Joey's pearl-pink truck with its Events by Josephina decal on the side. Not exactly the right vehicle for an impromptu stakeout. She lifted her hand in an awkward wave and pulled away with her cheeks burning.

Maybe it wasn't Copper Creek that Joey couldn't let go of, after all.

FOUR

Three weeks later, Joey's meager belongings were boxed up and stashed in her office, and she was en route to North Carolina. Apparently the owner of the property was down to two candidates and wanted to meet in person before making the final decision.

Sophie had offered an impulsive idea and then Joey had gone and upped the ante because her apartment lease renewal had come due this same weekend and she couldn't afford paying for two spaces she wasn't occupying if she happened to get this job. She was either going to return from this interview with her tail tucked between her legs with nowhere to live or she'd be staying in North Carolina for the next four to six months.

She gazed out the windshield at the Appalachian Mountains adorned in their autumn best. The farther she traveled, the lighter the weight on her shoulders seemed to become. She might be making a huge mistake, but at least she had a gorgeous view along the way. She let out a contented sigh.

Having left behind the main arteries, she navigated the twisting, hilly roads that took her past quaint towns that bordered the Nantahala River. Groups in rafts bounced along the rapids, snagging the last days of rafting before the season closed the next day.

Joey shivered. *No way.* She knew just how cold that water was in the heat of summertime. Nothing could persuade her to get that close to that spring-fed water in the autumn chill. She laughed to herself. Except maybe a calendar full of weddings. She'd probably attempt all kinds of stupid human tricks to make that happen.

She glanced at the clock on her truck's dash and did some calculations. She should make it to her hotel outside of Asheville in good time, and as long as she got on the road before the sun rose tomorrow, she'd make it on time to her afternoon meeting at an establishment called the Salty Sand Witch.

The next afternoon Joey opened the door of her Tacoma and walked to the ferryboat's railing. Alongside the Hatteras–Ocracoke Ferry, gulls floated on the gentle waves of Pamlico Sound expecting a treat to be thrown their way. Greater egrets stalked in the tall grasses of the distant marshy islands.

The wind blew her curls wild, and she pulled her light jacket tighter around her. She'd look a mess for the interview, but it was hard to care with the tang of the salt air refreshing her soul in ways she hadn't even known she'd needed.

The longer she traveled, the more convinced she'd become that she was on her way to the end of the world. Already she'd traversed a seemingly endless byway lined by massive dunes that connected the barrier islands. Heavy equipment was constantly at work, pushing back sand that had spilled onto the road. In some places the terrain she'd traveled had been so narrow that if she craned her neck to its fullest extension, she could glimpse the sound on one side of the dueling dunes and swivel her head to spy the sea on the other. The only way to get to the next island on her journey was this hour-long trip by ferry.

After that, she had another thirty-minute drive. Then she'd finally meet Finnegan O'Hare face-to-face and find out if this absurd plan of running away to a deserted island would come to fruition.

She surveyed the other passengers on the ferry. Most had remained in their vehicles. The few people who had emerged and looked over the water snapped pictures.

It was nice coming to a place when it wasn't tourist season. It felt like getting to see the Outer Banks in her true form, locals living in a committed and worn-in marriage with her, rather than overrun with tourists enamored on a first date. She assumed the scene was much different during the summer months, anyway.

As the ferry progressed, she stared over the water. Far in the distance, white crests of waves crashed over the calmer water of the sound.

She glanced at her watch. Everything was right on schedule. She might even be a few minutes early, enough time to freshen up after her many hours on the road before meeting her potential new boss. Or client? What was the right way to label this arrangement?

The Ocracoke terminal came into sight, and she returned to her vehicle. She supposed she'd be figuring it out soon enough.

A half hour later, Joey parked in a vacant spot in front of a low-slung diner tucked beyond the stretch of quaint shops.

She leaned her head against the headrest and shut her eyes tight. Why had she let Sophie talk her into this nonsense? She knew all the ins and outs of throwing together a banquet event order, but a scope and sequence of work for a decommissioned lighthouse? This Finnegan O'Hare with his sea-salt name would see right through her borrowed knowledge from working at her father's side to the frilly, tulle-and-floral center of who she really was.

She knew how to make things look pretty for an evening. But to mend something truly broken? She had serious doubts on that one.

She climbed out of her vehicle and straightened her shoulders. She was apartment-less and her stream of income was rapidly drying up—her proverbial ships were practically burnt to a crisp. If she didn't believe she could oversee this project, how was she supposed to convince Finnegan O'Hare to choose her over the other candidate? It was time to fake it until she could make it.

She took one more look at the preliminary proposal she'd put together and mentally rehearsed the main talking points of her qualifications.

On the way in, she passed a man in pressed slacks and a button-down who was pacing beside the entrance, out of place next to the no-frills diner with peeling paint. Judging by the path he'd tread in the sparse gravel, his phone conversation wasn't an easy one. Must have been some overworked executive failing at escaping for an offseason vacation.

She skirted him and entered the establishment.

"Well, speak o' the devil. It's her." The patron chatter silenced, and chairs scraped as a trio of men turned in the direction their dining companion pointed.

Joey looked behind her, hoping some other "her" was the source of this unwanted attention. But the gray-bearded men with wind-chapped skin were intent on Joey. Had word spread about her interview? Were they that scandalized by a woman project manager? It was 2007, for goodness' sake.

One of the men let out a hearty guffaw and slapped his knee. "Barlow, you're just spooked from this morning. This little filly doesn't look a bit like Saint-Mae. The eyes are wrong. Hers are brown, Saint-Mae's are the color of Pamlico Sound."

Joey scanned the room, looking for someone who might be her client, hoping with everything in her that Finnegan O'Hare was not numbered among the men at the crowded table gawping at her.

One of the other men shook his head. "Barlow came in off the water white as a sheet this mornin'. Now he's seeing ghosts everywhere he looks." The accent was Southern but not at all what she was used to in Copper Creek. Their underlying brogue pulled their words together in an unfamiliar cadence that left her straining to catch what was being said.

Joey fidgeted with the hem of her shirt and continued scanning the lightly occupied establishment. The only other customer in the joint was a gentleman in a back corner booth who seemed even older than the rest. He sat with his bucket hat pulled low while he perused the menu, as if attempting to construct a divider between him and the noisy bunch at the front table.

She checked her watch, 3:00 p.m. on the dot. There couldn't be more than one Salty Sand Witch on this island, could there?

A slim man with a slick pate slapped the table. "Nah. I'm tellin' ya boys, you've got it wrong. Saint-Mae's not a ghost. She's a mermaid. How else do you think she can save so many at sea that no human being should be able to survive?"

Joey squared her shoulders and approached the man in the booth. She cleared her throat, and he lifted his head, one bushy eyebrow hiked higher than the other.

"I'm looking for Finnegan O'Hare. Do you happen to know where I might find him?"

"Depends."

"On?" Joey shifted her feet, resisting the urge to simply get back into her truck and drive straight back to Copper Creek.

"Who ya are and whatcha want with him." The corners of his mouth twitched, and his blue eyes twinkled.

"I'm Josephina Harris. I'm here to take a look at his lighthouse project."

The man's head jerked back just a fraction, and he squinted at her. "Josephina Harris also known as *Joey* Harris?"

Her face heated. Her professional smile faltered for a fraction of a second at his use of her nickname. "Yes, sir. One and the same."

A short, gravelly laugh burst out of him. "Well, I'll be." He stuck out a weathered hand. "I'm Finnegan O'Hare. Abso-toot-a-loot-ly delighted to meet *you*. More than you know." Maybe one of her references had let the nickname drop? But why was he so confused by her introduction?

She took a small step forward to shake his hand. "I'm so pleased to meet you, and I can't wait to go over my thoughts about the rehab and see the property so I can get a better picture of what restorations are needed." She reached into her tote and pulled out a notebook and mechanical pencil along with some notes she'd made after a conversation with Trey about questions she'd need answered before formally accepting the job.

He smiled. "Hold on, now. You'd better w—"

The front door opened, and the presumed overworked exec who'd been outside strode toward them. "Well, the other project manager just declined," he said when he reached the booth. "All I have is this Joey guy who has far less experience. And he's late."

Her heart thudded like a bass drum. He'd called her Joey too. "Uh . . . excuse me . . ." She lifted her hand in an awkward wave. Had she accidentally used her nickname on the application? Surely not.

The elder of the two men held up a hand. "Finn. Finn, hold up." He gestured to Joey. "I'd like to introduce you to Joey Harris."

The man's chin dropped. He snapped his mouth closed and crossed his arms over his chest. "Joey Harris? The Joey Harris that submitted an application for the work on Bleakpoint Light? Pops, I'm not in the mood for any more of your pranks."

Joey forced a smile. "It's actually Josephina Harris, but I . . ." A nervous laugh slipped out with her words. She glanced back to the group of sea salts still going on about mermaids and ghost stories in between bites of fried fish. Maybe it would have been better if one of them was Finnegan O'Hare, after all.

His eyes traveled from her face to her feet and back again in a nanosecond. "Your paperwork said Joey Harris."

She tightened her lips in a line, drew herself to her full five-foot-two height, and extended her hand. *No way forward but through.* "Yes, sir. That's what my friends call me. And you are?" Joey left her hand hanging in the air, waiting until he clasped it.

"Finn O'Hare."

She offered him a firm shake, refusing the temptation to break eye contact through the whole stilted exchange. So he'd expected a big, strapping male Joey. Not a petite female version. His assumptions weren't her fault—she inwardly cringed—aside from the small detail of providing an inaccurate legal name on her application. She returned the appraising gaze, pretending she was sizing him up as a worthy client in the same doubtful way he saw her as the project manager.

She did have one thing going for her though—apparently she was his only option. She suppressed a sigh. Being someone's last resort wasn't exactly the experience she'd been hoping for, but it would have to do. She turned to the older man. "I thought *you* were Finnegan O'Hare."

He tipped his head. "I *am* Finnegan O'Hare . . . the original." His blue eyes twinkled in the sunlight coming through the window. "You musta been meaning Finnegan O'Hare the Third. It's an easy mistake to make. I'm sure you can understand, *Miss* Harris." He adjusted his bucket hat and gave her a sly grin. "If you were meaning my grandson here"—he jerked his thumb to the younger man—"you should ask for Finn to keep the confusion down. Folks call me Walt."

"Walt?" Her gaze ping-ponged between the two men. Finn maintained his disgruntled gaze. Walt, lively and full of zing, apparently relished this turn of events. But which one of them was she supposed to answer to?

"I go by Walt, on account of my middle name being Walter. I never did care for Finnegan as a moniker. Seemed stuffy to me." He cut his gaze to his grandson's dressy attire, as if making a point.

She smiled politely and said, "Walt, Finn, it is a pleasure to make your acquaintance, and I am looking forward to learning more about your hopes and plans for Bleakpoint Light and how I can best serve you as project manager. I'd love to go over specifics as to my past experiences restoring and preserving historic structures."

Walt nodded emphatically. "I like this one, Finn. She's a winner. Besides, it's my lighthouse, isn't it? I know we have an agreement, but I should get some say. I vote for Joey here."

"I'll take it into consideration, Pops." He glanced to the four men who had fallen silent and stared their way, necks stretched like hungry seagulls scouting for snacks. Finn gestured to the door. "It is a little lively in here. Do you mind stepping outside with me to chat a bit about the finer details?"

He spoke without a trace of warmth. She knew that tone. The moment she stepped out that door, Finnegan O'Hare the Third was going to send her packing to Copper Creek empty-handed. She grimaced and resisted the discouragement threatening to curve her spine. "Yes, sir."

She gave a final glance to Walt. He ran his fingertips over a puckered scar on his hand, a faraway expression on his face—like he was reliving the events that had put it there. But it wasn't just pain on his face. There was something wistful lacing that expression. Instead of walking out the door, she'd much rather stay and find out what weighed on Walt's mind.

FIVE

The gal followed Finn out the door, the confident set of her shoulders falling a fraction. Walt sat back against the booth and folded his menu. He was sure and certain she was full of spunk, but something must've kicked her confidence a little off-kilter. As agreed, he'd respect Finn's decision. As long as Finn discounted her because of her ability to oversee the restoration. Not because he'd expected a man.

Walt traced the raised scar that ran across his hand, thinking about the one across his chest—the one that had almost been the end of him. He wouldn't be sitting here right now, dreaming of restoring Bleakpoint Light if not for a woman. A teenage girl, to tell the truth of it. A legend in his mind all these years, but most certainly not a ghost. Or a mermaid. Or any one of the other dozens of tall tales and myths etched into the heritage of these islands.

He kept a sharp eye on Finn and Joey.

She took a step back from him, color creeping up her face. Was she about to cry? Maybe. But judging by the hands clenched at her sides, it looked to be more of an angry cry than a defeated one.

Finn gestured apologetically, but his face was set. Walt shook his head. He'd raised that boy since he was five, and though his jaw was angular and stubbled now instead of pudgy, that stubborn expression when he'd made up his mind hadn't changed an iota.

Walt slapped down enough cash on the table to cover his coffee and a generous tip and headed outside. He drew closer, and Finn and Joey's conversation died out. "Y'all ready?"

Finn turned toward him. "For?"

Joey turned away for a moment as though searching for the sea that brought the salty breeze whipping through her hair. With her back toward them, she shakily drew a tissue from her bag and pretended to blot her nose before turning back, the emotion smoothed from her features.

Atta girl. Hang in there. All is not lost yet. "To take this gal to see my lighthouse, of course."

"Pops, let's not waste Miss Harris's time."

Walt kept his focus on Joey. "Miss Harris, would you like to see my lighthouse? She's seen better days, but I don't think it's too late for her. Are you the kind of gal who can envision what could be instead of what is? I get the sense you are."

Joey nodded and stepped closer to him. "I—"

"Pops—" Finn cut him a warning glare that Walt gleefully ignored.

"Good, I thought so." He schooled the grin that was fighting to light his face at his grandson's mounting frustration. He supposed he understood Finn's worry. Walt had spent Martha's entire life insurance policy on the run-down sailboat and a deserted island adorned with a decaying lighthouse in a part of the country he'd never mentioned until recent months. And he was no spring chicken. So, to avoid his grandson putting him through a mental status exam, he'd told Finn he could oversee the hiring. But no matter what Finn thought, he wasn't going senile. He was just doing something for himself for the first time in his eighty-one years.

Finn huffed. "We were just discussing how this role may not—"

Walt swatted the air, banishing the words Finn left hanging. "I thought you said you didn't want to waste Miss Harris's time. Let's quit yakking on the sidewalk and get to it." He thumbed over his shoulder to Finn's Audi. "You can just follow us to the marina. We have to go by boat to reach Bleakpoint, of course." He scanned the parking lot and grinned. "That must be yours over there. I don't think I've ever seen a Tacoma in quite that shade."

Joey blushed and her shoulders crept higher. "That's me."

Walt slapped his hand against his thigh. "Well, *fan*tastic. We won't have to worry about losing you in the crowd."

Joey looked uncertain, probably thinking he was half out of his mind as she eyed the quiet streets.

That was all right. Let the two of them think he was a little off his rocker. He'd get away with more meddling that way.

While Joey walked to her pickup, Walt sauntered to his grandson's black Audi. Finn grumbled under his breath in his wake. Once seated in the car, Walt turned to him. "Well, speak up, son. I can't understand yer mumbling with these old ears," he said, knowing full well those words weren't meant for him. Fussing to yourself was apparently a genetic trait. The hull of Walt's sailboat had heard more than its fair share of complaints about his interfering grandson. Finn needed to keep his focus on piloting his airplanes, not Walt's life.

"Pops, is that boat of yours even seaworthy yet? What'll we do if we get out from shore and we sink Miss Harris in the sound?"

Walt bristled. "Of course she's seaworthy. How could you insult her like that?" Although the last time Finn had been in town, he'd been working on fixing a sizable leak. And a hole in the sail. But a young fella looking for work in the offseason had proven quite capable of putting the vessel right again.

Walt leveled him with his best parental stare. "And why are you so opposed to Miss Harris? You were keen enough on her before she arrived."

Finn drove the quiet streets, his incredulous gaze focused straight ahead. "I thought my reasoning would be obvious. What I don't understand is why you insist on leading her on."

"It's not leading her on. It's called *manners*, son." He shook his head. "I can't believe you were going to dismiss her in less than a minute after she's come all this way. Raised you better than that." Walt crossed his arms over his chest, grimacing at the twinge in his shoulder. "Besides, I think she'd be a perfect fit to restore that light." Walt knew down to his achy old bones that Joey Harris was the one meant for this job.

There were things that happened on that island that he'd never be able to set right, but a woman at the helm once again would shift some indefinable thing back into balance.

Finn huffed. "We agreed that you'd let me choose the project manager, and she is not it."

Walt frowned. "Sexism and ageism all in one breath. Son, you better check yourself before you wreck yourself."

The boy looked at him like he'd been sucker punched. "Excuse me?"

"You've commandeered my lighthouse project 'cause you think I'm too old and addlepated to handle it. And you're discounting Joey there because she's a woman."

Finn refocused on the road, shaking his head. "It's not safe, her being out there alone on that island. Terrible cell service. No internet. And you might call me sexist, but I call it calling a spade a spade. Those crews are likely going to be all-male teams, and you know as well as I do that it can be hit or miss with the integrity of workers on a construction team."

"Shouldn't that be up to her if she feels comfortable taking that on? Besides, from her résumé, I'm sure she can handle herself."

Finn scoffed. "The woman drives a pink pickup with 'Events by Josephina' decaled down the side. She didn't even put her real name on her application. She's an event planner, not a project manager. *That* was missing from her skimpy résumé."

Walt tipped his head side to side. "I'd say that was her one misstep."

Finn nodded along, looking relieved that they'd finally landed in agreement.

Walt schooled his grin. "It concerns me that she didn't see event planning as relevant work experience. That probably qualifies her just as much for the job as her construction experience. Maybe more."

"What?" The car wobbled between lanes when Finn jerked his gaze to Walt.

"If you had to choose between organizing engineers, architects, and work crews into an efficient workflow or a bridezilla and an emotional momma wanting to give her daughter a dream wedding, not to mention fifteen bridesmaids, caterers, musicians, florists, and a five-hundred-person seating chart, venues, plus a zillion other details that go into planning a wedding that I'd rather not fathom, which do you think would be the easier task? And be careful how you answer. Your gramma Martha, God rest her soul, was an event planner before you were born. I know the type of organizational gymnastics that woman was capable of."

Finn's tense shoulders lowered, and a hint of a smile softened his features. He was a good boy when he wasn't so wadded up with worry. "Gramma sure did a good job of keeping *you* in line." Finn cut his gaze in Walt's direction. "That's a role I'm finding to be far more intensive than I originally anticipated."

Walt grunted. "Bah, I don't need a nanny. Not yet anyway. If I had to go through the pain of losing your gramma, I figure I might as well get a little joy out of doing whatever fool thing pops into my head for as long as my old body is able. For the first time in my life, there's nobody that needs me to take care of them."

"So you decided to adopt a dilapidated sailboat and a lighthouse?" Finn grinned. "If you're looking for something pathetic to take care of, I'd've volunteered."

Walt laughed at Finn's teasing. The boy might be walking a little wounded, but he was far from pathetic.

Finn pulled into the marina's gravel lot and parked. He turned to him, the worry creeping back into his features. "Really though,

Pops, why does this lighthouse project mean so much to you? It's more than an idle hobby. Something's up you've not told me."

Walt clapped him on the shoulder and then unbuckled his seat belt. "That, my boy, is quite a long story, and Miss Harris is a-waitin'."

SIX

"I'm telling you, Soph, he hates my guts." Joey circled the parking lot as if searching for the perfect space in the nearly empty lot, stalling a few more seconds.

"He hasn't run you off yet. Hang in there. Go see the lighthouse. The old guy likes you and is rooting for you if nothing else." Her friend's voice coming through the speakerphone filled the truck cab with the comfort of an oversized sweatshirt worn on a crisp fall morning. "Now, park that snazzy truck of yours, march your rear end over to those men, and pretend Finn O'Hare is just another one of your finicky brides. You've got this, Jo-Jo."

Joey heaved out a breath as she put the truck in park. "I've come too far to give up just because he's not fawning all over my first impression."

"That's right," Sophie said. "Get your chin up and shoulders back. You're ready now. I can hear it in your voice. Call me with your good news."

Joey had been ready to make a quick escape and drive home instead of delaying the rejection that would ultimately come from this. Instead, she'd made herself call Sophie. They were always each other's first call whenever one of them needed to be talked out of a rash decision, whether it was the temptation to tuck tail and run from a grumpy potential employer or the impulse to cut their own bangs because they were feeling restless.

Joey hopped out of her truck. Air, surprisingly balmy for the first of November, lifted the hair from her shoulders. Docked sailboats bobbed in the water. The soft clink of the masts and rigging made pleasant music.

Walt lifted his battered bucket hat from his head and used it to wave her over. "Come on, Miss Harris. Let me introduce you to my pride and joy."

Still standing by the driver's side of his car, Finn unbuttoned his cuffs and rolled up his sleeves, then he unfastened one of the upper buttons of his shirt. At least he looked a fraction more approachable, but not in any better of a mood.

No matter. She was going to pull off professional Joey, despite her knocking knees, and land this job even though Finnegan O'Hare had already made her feel about three inches tall with the way he'd been looking at her. She drew closer to the men and stepped to Walt's side as they strolled down the boardwalk to the docks. "Have you always lived here?"

He smiled softly. "I grew up here. Carolina salt and sand runs in my veins. But I've spent the last sixty years living among the Kentucky hills. It's good to be back."

"Kentucky?" Joey shook her head. "If salt and sand run in your veins, how'd you survive Kentucky? That must have been quite the change."

He chuckled. "A boy will do anything for love, I suppose. At the tail end of World War II, I met a farmer's daughter at a benefit dance. I'd originally planned to come back here after the war was over, but I'd found things had . . ." He looked out over the water and swallowed hard. "Things had changed. And I had changed. So I went chasing after that sweet Kentucky girl who always had a way of making me laugh even after I thought I'd forgotten how. Though I never expected to settle down in bluegrass country, it turned out to be exactly what I needed."

They continued on until they reached the last row of docks. Walt stopped in front of a tired-looking vessel in obvious need of a little TLC. "Here she is. *Cay's Song*."

"Oh. *Wow*." Joey searched for something complimentary to say about the boat Walt seemed so proud of. "Cay? Like an island?"

Tenderness flickered in his eyes. "You could say that. You could certainly say that."

She studied him, unsure what to make of the strange response.

He grasped one of the sailboat's cables. "I know she's not much to look at on the outside, but that's on account of the work I've had done on my sleeping quarters inside."

Joey blinked. "You live on your boat?"

She sensed Finn tensing beside her. So, the grandson didn't approve of that either. Sophie's exhortation to imagine Finn as a bridezilla played in her head, and Joey covered her stifled snicker with a fake sneeze.

"Bless you!" Walt gestured to the boat. "It's quite the cozy setup. Let me give you a tour." He looked to his grandson. "Quit your glowering." Once he was aboard, he offered a hand to Joey. "Grasp this cable here. The standing rigging, it's called. And then gently step onto the edge, or the gunwale if you want to use the fancy term. Use my hand to steady yourself if need be."

She followed his instructions, wobbling a little as she went.

"Finn here would rather me be set up, fat and happy, in a retirement community," Walt said. "He's not a fan of my wild ways."

Finn shook his head, smiling wryly as he boarded. "I'd just like to know what you're going to do if a hurricane comes."

Walt leaned around the mast. "I'll do what everyone else does around here. Weather the storm as best I can. I'm not some landlubber, son." He looked at Joey. "He's just sour because some tropical storm headed for Texas is threatening to throw off his work schedule. Finny Boy hates uncertainty. You'd think he'd have chosen a more grounded career like an accountant instead of an airline pilot though."

"You're a pilot?" Joey asked. "That must be an interesting field. I bet you've got all kinds of stories."

Finn gave her a tight-lipped nod.

So much for warming him up through conversation.

"Try and overlook his grumpy mood. He's normally a fraction less persnickety when things go according to *his* plan." Walt chattered as he unmoored the boat, Finn serving as a quiet assistant, ignoring his grandfather's needling. Joey watched, mystified by all the pulleys and tie-offs the small vessel contained.

Joey clenched and unclenched her hands. She and her father and brother had worked in tandem like this. And it had always made her feel so capable. But what if she only knew how to follow and not lead? What if the respect she'd received from the men on the Harris Construction payroll had been out of respect for her father and not based on her own capabilities?

She looked back to her truck.

"Miss Harris?" Walt stood ready at the helm. "Are you ready to see my island?"

Thirty minutes later, with his passengers firmly planted on the shore, Walt lingered on the boat, watching Finn and Joey walk toward Bleakpoint Light.

If he squinted his eyes just so, with the aid of the cataracts developing on his retinas, he could so easily imagine that it was another boy and girl walking this beach. Two kids from a different era.

He could pretend the lighthouse still shone in its full glory, before the war had come to the shores of the Outer Banks and the light had gone dark. Before he'd lost the girl he loved.

Walt studied the scar that rippled the flesh between his index finger and thumb. He'd thought he'd been at peace with the mysteries she'd left him holding, but when he'd seen her lighthouse forlorn and abandoned, the decades rewound and an urgency to restore her beloved home had pulled at him like an undertow, yanking him beneath the waves.

He blinked to clear his blurring vision. No wonder Finn feared him to be going senile. He moved from the boat onto the crude dock.

He walked as fast as his stiff legs allowed, and a smile found its way to his lips. The two of them made a handsome pair. With just a little intervention . . .

"Pops?" Finn called over his shoulder.

Walt mentally shook off the movie scene playing in his mind of Finn and Joey strolling along the beach, a toddler perched on her hip with Bleakpoint Light in the background, restored and glorious. "Yep. Right behind you." He shuffled into something that almost resembled a jog to draw even with them.

Finn watched him approach. "Joey was asking about the history of the light. When it was constructed. Materials used. Any previous repairs and restorations made."

"Oh . . . uh . . . well, I don't know a lot off the top of my head. It'll take a little digging to see what's still around as far as construction records go." If only all the questions Walt had about what had happened here could be answered by things found in public domain.

Joey stepped closer to him, her hand brushing his sleeve. "Not to worry, I'm good with a shovel." She winked.

Walt swallowed the knot that had formed in his throat. "The lighthouse officially went out of service at the close of the war in '45. But it had been neglected prior to that. There's a lot of rumors as to why. I could spin tales for you, but it be naught but speculation and legend."

"So you enjoy a good mystery?" Joey asked. "That's why you bought the place?"

Walt shook his head. "I knew the family that last kept this

light, and it pains me to see their life's work in this condition. Every structure on these Carolina islands was built on a strip of shifting sand between the sound and sea. Though you're not supposed to hold on to anything too tightly here . . ." He shook his head. "Even after all this time, I can't seem to let this place go."

SEVEN

Unspoken stories swam in Walt's eyes. Joey glanced to Finn. His forehead was creased as he studied his grandfather. But she had a feeling he was driven more by worry than curiosity about the tales locked in the old gentleman's heart.

Though Finn was technically the one doing the hiring, it was apparent that it was Walt who cared about this project. "Tell me what it was like here in its heyday," she said. "What do you envision for the restoration of Bleakpoint Light?"

She tucked her hand into the crook of Walt's offered arm. Instead of continuing on the trail that led directly to the lighthouse, he veered onto a narrower path. They strolled through the maritime woods populated by thin-trunked pines, which she recognized, and squat, spindly trees that could almost pass for shrubs she'd seen populating the marshes, lawns, and woodland her entire trip down Highway 12.

"What are those trees called?" She pointed to a large specimen whose arms reached long and low.

Walt smiled. "That there would be a southern live oak."

Joey's eyebrows shot high. "Oak? Doesn't look anything like the oaks I know."

Walt nodded thoughtfully. "I don't reckon the tall oaks from your neck of the woods would fare too well here in this sandy soil and wind. But these evergreens here, God made specially so these islands could have a few good shade trees that could survive a hurricane."

Walt walked on, pointing out the flora and fauna often found on Bleakpoint Island. Though it wasn't a large parcel of land, it contained all the hallmarks of the barrier islands of North Carolina.

Finn marched along behind them, an impassive rearguard. She wasn't sure how he felt about being pushed to the back of their little group, but she didn't have much time to consider the potential ramifications of choosing to focus on Walt. She felt little hope of warming herself to the man who'd practically encouraged her to scurry on home so that he could invest his time seeking project managers he believed possessed the wherewithal to complete the job at hand.

Finn wasn't the only one with doubts. She'd known that she'd be working on a remote location. But after the long drive down Highway 12 through Hatteras National Seashore with sand from the dunes on either side spilling onto the road, she'd started to wonder what she was getting herself into. Add to that, an hour-long ferry ride to Ocracoke, thirty minutes on the road, and another long ride on Walt's sailboat to this strip of land with no electricity, no paved roads, and well water that Walt claimed was as "pristine as when God first spoke it into existence" . . . she really had reached the end of civilization.

The employment listing had mentioned that housing was included, and she was more than a little afraid to ask what that might entail on a place like Bleakpoint Island. Afraid, because even if they told her she'd be living in a tent, she was here to stay until Finn frog-marched her off Walt's island.

Reaching the end of Walt's circuitous route, they came through the clearing as he told her about the generators they had on-site to power the tools and other necessities for repairs.

There, standing like a sentinel on a strip of sandy land midway between the sound and sea, stood the stacked stone of Bleakpoint

Light. Though stunning on first impression, closer scrutiny revealed just how much work likely needed to be done on the long-neglected structure that had been battered by rain and wind for decades.

Joey pulled a notepad from her backpack and made some notes as she drew near. First thing she needed to do was vet and hire structural engineers to determine if the foundation was still good. She'd done some research over the past weeks about the restoration history of more well-known lighthouses in the area, like Hatteras and Bodie. The security of the lighthouse's foundation on this sandy soil was the most precarious hurdle they faced.

She jotted down the problem spots she identified at first glance, like the broken pane that enclosed the lantern room. Water had been getting in and likely rotting and rusting the structure from the inside out for who knew how long. The door at the lower entrance was cracked open, swollen, and lopsided on its hinges. She tugged at it and found it stuck ajar.

She turned to Walt and Finn. "The lighthouse is incredible. I can see why you'd want it preserved. But . . ." She trailed off. "It's going to be expensive. Getting the needed materials and equipment here. Hiring crews willing to come out and work in these conditions. There will surely be some surcharges built in, above and beyond the going rates in the area."

Finn crossed his arms over his chest, and his shoulders relaxed. "So, are you saying, Miss Harris, that you're no longer interested in the job now that you've seen the conditions?"

Joey propped one hand on her hip. "I want to better understand the heart behind the investment as well as your goals and expectations. Tourism? Because it is so remote, you'd likely need additional structures to house guests. Or private residence? I can't imagine you wanting to live all the way out here on your own, Walt." She stopped herself just in time from tacking on "especially at your age."

Finn dropped his crossed arms. "See? This is what I've been telling you, Pops."

So now *he's going to side with me?* To gang up on his grandpa . . . real nice.

"Bah." Walt huffed.

"You've got to listen to reason. Gramma's life insurance is already mostly spent. This will take all of your savings. I get that this place means *something* to you, but you have to think about your future. You might need that money someday. Someday when living alone on a sailboat isn't so feasible. You're eighty-one years old."

"We've been over this," Walt ground out, "I agreed to let you have some say in hiring the person who'd manage the undertaking in exchange for letting me do as I please with my money, unhindered. I just want this one thing for myself. I'm not asking you to finance it."

Finn paced. "Who do you think is going to be the one making sure you're cared for when all the money is gone and you have a pretty lighthouse but no provisions for your last years?" Finn's face reddened and he turned away. No doubt he hadn't intended on being that candid about the root of his worry, especially in front of Joey.

She stepped between them, hoping to become the buffer they needed. "Please understand I'm not criticizing the decision to restore the lighthouse. I simply want to see your big-picture vision for this place. The passion behind it." She clasped her hands in front of her. "And I want you to be prepared for the costs involved so that in the end, you are happy with the product I deliver."

One thing she'd be sure of, neither of these men would ever have the opportunity to accuse her of taking advantage of their situation. The bad reputation inherited by Harris Construction wouldn't follow her here. "Why don't you show me to the keeper's residence and I'll look around a little while you two continue your discussion in private?"

Walt's shoulders drooped as he led them a few hundred feet away where a stone cottage sat encircled by live oak. At least from the outside it seemed in fairly good condition. The squat stone structure with its slate roof had been built to stand the test of time and neglect.

Walt unlocked the rusty padlock with some difficulty before stepping back. He shrugged. "The Coast Guard locked it up after they officially decommissioned it in '45. Everything left inside is just like how they found it."

"What do you mean, how they found it?"

"We were at war, and finally after so many ships had been blown out of the water, they ordered this particular lighthouse to stay dark. But one night, Bleakpoint shone . . ." Walt swallowed hard. "Anyway, when the Coast Guard came to investigate, the keeper and the daughter were missing. The keeper's body eventually washed up along with the remains of both their boats. But she . . . she was lost to the sea."

Emotions flickered across Walt's face. Sadness, anger, confusion. She placed a hand on his forearm. "They never learned what happened?"

He shook his head and then gestured to the house. "They didn't have any family, so the place was shut up after they searched for evidence as to what went wrong that night. I hear a couple of people did upkeep on the place for short stints. Locals talked of ghosts chasing the new people off, but it wasn't that.

"Shipping lanes shifted, rendering this place obsolete. The land had been on loan to the government in a long-ago agreement. It returned into the original family's hands, but by the time it went back to them, the family had moved far inland, tired of the harsh way of this place. Here it's sat. Until now."

With that extensive preamble, she expected him to follow her inside when she pushed the heavy door open.

But Walt stayed frozen on the stoop, a haunted expression in his eyes. "I'm going to talk to Finn while you look around a bit in here." He tipped his bucket hat in farewell and left her to explore the 1940s time capsule that sat before her.

She stepped onto the stone floor, eyes adjusting to the scant light. By the door, a wool macintosh, faded by time and dust and chewed by moths, hung on a peg in the wall.

A kettle was suspended in a long-forgotten hearth. Papers were scattered on a desk in the corner. A cup and saucer waited on the table as though someone had been about to make tea and then left before they'd had a chance to fill their cup.

She stepped around the simple kitchen table and two chairs. There was one room in the back, decaying curtains splitting the room in two, a narrow bed on each side.

There were evidences on the floor—droppings and shredded fabric from the mattress and quilts—that rodents had long had run of the place. Joey shivered.

It was a bleak, utilitarian space. Would a fire in the grate and the cobwebs and dust swept away change it into something homey and comforting? She found herself longing for an inviting abode for this girl Walt talked about with a catch in his throat. A catch that he kept trying, unsuccessfully, to loosen.

"I need to know the truth."

Joey stifled a yelp that threatened to leap out at the intrusion on her imaginary fireside scene of a loving father and daughter. She turned slowly to face Finn. "I make it a habit to be honest, Mister O'Hare. The truth is what you'll get whether specifically requested or not." She softened her reply with a professional smile.

"Can you handle this job?"

"I—"

"For whatever reason, my grandfather is dead set on it being you. He likes you and . . ." He scrunched his face and massaged his temples. "And I need someone willing to look out for him. Ever since he's come back here, he's changed. I'd say it was the grief from losing my grandmother, but it's different. Something about being here on this island affects him."

"How do you mean?" She'd seen nothing of the man that gave her cause for concern. Although Walt's desire to invest so much in what seemed a pet project wasn't exactly prudent.

Finn shoved his hands in his pockets. "I catch him looking out over the water like he's searching for something that only he can see. And then there's his desperation to fix this place." Finn shook his head. "A few months after my gramma passed, he asked me to take a trip. He paid a random guy to ferry us out here. After he saw the state this place was in, he hardly spoke for two days. Next thing I knew, he'd located the family who owned it and paid way too much for it." Finn pushed back the light-brown strand of hair that drooped to his forehead from his Ivy League haircut. "I fly long hauls right now. I'm trying to get my routes switched so I can be with him on a more regular schedule, but until then, can you . . . will you make part of your job to look out for him? Keep me posted if you notice him acting oddly?"

Joey lifted a shoulder. "He seems pretty sharp to me."

Finn's brow furrowed. "Something isn't right."

Her feeling of elation at getting the job was only slightly dampened by the fact that Finn's willingness to hire her likely stemmed from thinking she would more likely accept an off-the-books role as caretaker for his grandfather than a male project manager. But it was a job, and she liked the idea of spending more time with Walt, hearing his stories. She stuck out her hand. "Yes, I can handle the job, and yes, I accept those terms."

Finn looked at her extended hand for a long moment and then grasped it and gave it a firm shake.

Before letting go, she held up two fingers. "Two more *minor* details I'd like to discuss. One, when would you like me to start? And two, the job mentioned on-site housing." She thumbed over her shoulder. "Please tell me I'm not standing in it right now."

EIGHT

Joey stood and stretched from where she'd been sitting on the floor by the coffee table drinking her morning coffee and working a jigsaw puzzle of Hatteras Lighthouse. She walked to her window that overlooked the Pamlico Sound. Thankfully, Finn and Walt had rethought their original terms and decided to provide off-site housing.

It made the most sense. In Ocracoke she'd have easy access to phones, electricity, and internet. Being it was the offseason, the leaser had given them a good deal, pleased to have guaranteed occupancy in his vacation rental for the next four months.

Joey could relate. It was going to be nice having a steady paycheck coming her way again. If she played her cards right, she might even have a decent nest egg built up by the time her job was complete, enough to return to Copper Creek and give her on-hold business one more shot. People always said that absence made the heart grow fonder. She sure hoped those words would ring true for her. For now, it was enough to have a plan again.

She'd spent the past week getting settled in the apartment and organizing her home office. Already she'd found a local with a sturdy head boat willing to ferry workers and supplies out to the site for a reasonable fee. The boat was normally used to take eighty people out at a time to fish and didn't get much use over the later fall and winter months.

She'd also hired Jerry and Renee Alexander, husband and wife history buffs who'd retired to Ocracoke, to clean up and organize the contents of the keeper's cottage.

Granted, she wasn't technically supposed to have even started work until next week, but she couldn't stop herself.

She went to her desk and checked her email for the third time that day, impatient for a response from the second structural engineering firm she'd contacted. She needed at least one more bid on the project. The first was uncomfortably outside of their budget.

Whoever she hired, they needed to know their stuff. The entire fate of this project hinged on whether or not the lighthouse foundation was viable. There was no way Walt could afford to have the entire structure moved and a new foundation laid.

After emailing two additional firms, she slid her feet into her sandals and descended the tall stack of stairs on the cedar shake stilt house to check out the variety store down the street that looked like it might have the office supplies and groceries she lacked.

She was back home an hour later with printer paper, file folders, groceries, plus a wahoo filet she'd picked up on a whim from a fish market she passed.

As she sautéed her fish in herbs and butter, she dialed Sophie to give her the promised update.

"So, how goes the deserted island?"

"Well, I'm currently on a lightly populated island, sautéing fish that was caught this morning."

"Nice." Sounds of Sophie's baby squealing filled the background. "Can I come?"

Joey laughed. "This from the same girl who tried to convince me to move to Nashville? Now you want to disappear too?"

Sophie let out a dramatic groan. "Not so much disappear, but could you bottle a little of that quiet and ocean air and send it my way?"

"It is definitely peaceful here. And warmer than I'd expected." She filled her friend in on the work she'd started and her hopes for the project.

"So you're not ready to cuss me a blue streak for sending the wild idea your way?"

Joey scratched at a series of bug bites on her ankle courtesy of her last trip to Bleakpoint in which she'd forgotten her insect repellent. She wouldn't make that mistake again. "Not yet. Give me until I get through my first month. If the mosquitos and black flies haven't carried me off, I should have a barrel of complaints on tap."

With her phone propped against her ear, Joey carried her steaming plate of fish to the deck that overlooked the sound. The setting sun turned the wispy curls of horsetail clouds shades of red, pink, and gold. "I know there are hard days ahead, full of challenges and complications that accompany restoring old structures. I didn't come here to have it easy. But it's at least a break from the problems at home."

"I hope you can get some fresh perspective on everything while you're there. The world is a lot bigger than Copper Creek."

Joey laughed. "Funny. You keep saying that, but you've sent me to a place smaller than Copper Creek, bordered on all sides by water. So I don't know if it makes the joke on me or on you."

"Point taken," Sophie said. "But I think you know what I mean. You can think through things from home without being stuck in the middle of them. Like the Paul thing. Have you processed that at all?"

Joey jerked her head back, caught off guard by the sound of her ex's name. "What's to process?" She smoothed back a dark curl that had gotten caught in the wind. "He found someone new. We weren't right for each other. The end."

Sophie's impatient huff came through the line. "I love you, but sometimes I wonder if you are intentionally being difficult."

Joey speared a bite of fish with her fork. "Maybe I'm just dense. Clarify."

"You knew he wasn't right way before he ever broke up with you. He was just a placeholder."

Joey stretched out a kink in her back. "I guess. But I was the same to him. That's why I'm not mad about him moving on. Easier to let it go."

"You're not mad about him moving on because he was safe. Safe because losing him wouldn't hurt."

Joey huffed. "Not that safe. He broke up with me, remember?"

"And you don't care. That's not normal," Sophie said. "How many things in your life are placeholders holding space until whatever it is you're waiting for arrives?"

"I don't know what you're talking about." Had she really wanted to plan events or was that just plan B to an unspoken plan A?

"You orchestrate these elaborate parties for people and make their dreams come true. You're on the edges, invisibly averting disasters your clients never know about. Always at a party without ever being *at* the party. Am I explaining it any better?"

A heron soared low over the sound, its reflection rippling beneath it in the water. Joey sighed. Was that so wrong, enjoying making memories for other people? "I don't know . . ."

"Throw parties for a living if you want," Sophie continued, "but one of these days, I hope you join the party right in front of you instead of living off of the dreams you concoct for everyone else."

Joey shrugged and forced playfulness into her tone. "If you ask me, it's much more fun in the background having my hands on all the little moving parts, sliding them into place at just the right time."

She'd done the same with the moving parts of her own grand plans once, but life had come along and knocked all the pieces right out of her hands.

Walt walked the shores of Bleakpoint Island, ghost crabs scurrying at his feet. Would he ever be able to shake the feeling that he didn't belong here?

"I'm sorry, Cay," he said to the wind.

Sorry her light had come to such disrepair. Sorry that instead of staying when she'd pushed him away, he'd chased what his sixteen-year-old self had deemed a worthy cause. Sorry it had taken him so long to return and make peace with his past.

He grabbed a cockle shell from the sand and attempted to skip it over a breaking wave, but his wrist refused to move in that smooth flicking motion like it once had. He laughed to himself. Too bad WD-40 didn't work on old joints like it did metal hinges.

He clasped his hands behind his back and continued his stroll. "You'd like the gal I have working on your lighthouse. She's got grit like you." He chuckled under his breath thinking of the pink truck Joey seemed so embarrassed about. She was softer than rough-and-ready Cay.

Barefoot. Scrappy. Favoring some boy's cast-off work pants to dresses. Her skin had been golden-hued like the sand, and her eyes the green-gray color of the Pamlico Sound. And those riotous curls. Wild and beautiful.

Walt wove through the path in the dunes, passing the lighthouse and her home, returning to his sailboat.

He was glad Finn had relented and hired Joey. She'd proven she knew her stuff, and for whatever reason, was desperate enough to take on this harebrained scheme of his. He wasn't exactly sure what was meant to become of this place when all was said and done. Hopefully the Lord would reveal it to him in due time. As it were, he imagined he understood what Noah must have felt while building an ark when nary a drop of rain had fallen from the sky.

Once onboard *Cay's Song*, he stooped into his narrow bunk below deck and stretched out, watching the stars appear through the round, salt-washed window. What if it wasn't the Lord urging him on at all? Was attempting to salve the bitter regret that had lived in his heart for decades enough of a reason to take on such an endeavor?

He was ready for the work to start. To be surrounded with noise, movement, and purpose. If he kept this up, walking around this island all on his lonesome, talking to Cay like she could talk back, he'd start believing all the nonsense stories told about ghosts inhabiting the place.

NINE

Joey had promised Finn that she'd keep an eye out for his grand-father, but over the past few weeks Walt hadn't been easy to keep tabs on. Sometimes she'd find his boat docked at the marina. Other times his slip sat vacant. She could only imagine that he was docked at the island. Or he was out fishing. Or sailing along the quiet waters of the sound, searching for whatever it was he always seemed to be searching for.

Now that she had the official reports and all the needed permits had been filed to start work, she hoped Walt Watch would become a little simpler. Surely he'd want to be in the thick of things. She couldn't wait to give Walt the good news.

She checked the time, tucked the structural engineer's report into her backpack, and then walked the quarter mile to the marina where she expected to meet Walt along with Jerry and Renee Alex-ander, who were all set to start work on the keeper's residence.

Tonight, after she returned to the house, she'd send Finn the engineer's report along with the notes she'd make today, updating the scope and sequence of work needed to restore Walt's light to its former glory. Hopefully he'd start to see that her skills stretched beyond being an unwanted babysitter.

Joey picked up her pace at the sight of Walt standing on the dock next to the Alexanders as well as the owner of the supply boat they'd hired to ferry them over along with their tools and other materials.

The waters were calm and the weather fair, making for a gentle cruise across the sound.

Renee, who had chosen a seat next to her, inclined her head closer. "Jerry and I want to thank you for taking us on. When you mentioned the house had been closed-up since the early 1940s, I couldn't resist."

Jerry leaned around his wife. "It was such a fascinating time for this area. So many Americans had no idea how close the warfront came to American soil."

"Everyone knows about Pearl Harbor, of course," Renee said, "but so few knew the true risk to our Eastern Seaboard." She clasped her hands under her chin. "And this particular island is wrapped up in all kinds of legends."

Joey glanced to Walt who stood near the helm speaking with the pilot, a grim set to his weathered face.

"I'm sure everything was thoroughly combed through many years ago during the investigations," Jerry said. "But looking through those pictures you sent us was like time-traveling to another era."

"We've long been obsessed with family histories," Renee added. "I don't know a ton about this area. My relatives hail from Kitty Hawk and northward, and Jerry's family is from Oregon, so we're not experts on the happenings at Bleakpoint. But we've heard some wild stories since we moved here. Could you imagine if we actually stumbled on something that hinted to the truth of what happened to Callum and Cathleen?"

Joey leaned close and lowered her voice. "Like you said, there probably won't be anything of significance to be found. But if you do find sensitive information or things personal to the family, please let me see them before they are presented to Walt. His grandson is worried about the toll this project is having on him, and though I think Walt seems more than able to handle himself, I did promise."

They nodded their agreement and then continued the trip with general small talk.

Walt had traded conversing with the pilot for staring over the water, crushing his bucket hat in his hands, jaw set. An expression strikingly similar to the one perpetually fixed on his grandson's face. She'd expected the mood to lighten when Finn returned to work, but it had had the opposite effect.

Once on the island, the four of them carried supplies to the house. After she went over particulars with the Alexanders and left them to their tasks, Joey met up with Walt who'd returned to the ocean side of the island rather than set foot in that old house.

He stood on the shore, hands stuffed in the pockets of his too-large cargo pants that were cinched to his waist with a leather belt. He watched the whitecaps crash on distant shoals. He started when she drew alongside him, her steps muffled by the low roar of waves and the silky sand underfoot.

"How are you feeling?" she asked. "Ready to kick off the official first day of work on your property?"

Walt nodded. "It's a good day. One that's a long time in coming."

Joey toyed with the zipper pull on her jacket, weighing whether to ask the question waiting on her tongue. Even if it wasn't professional to pry into his life as his project manager, surely it fit within the realm of the "off the books" job role foisted on her by Finn. "You seem a little down. Has something happened?"

He blinked and pulled in a breath. "Not today, gal. Not today." He crossed his arms over his chest. "You were going to tell me about the engineer's report, weren't ya? Let's have it."

"Do you want the good news or the bad news first?" she asked.

He shifted most of his weight on one leg, staring out at the waves. He turned to her, a half smile on his weathered face. "Good news first. Always."

"The foundation is actually in pretty great condition considering the age, neglect, and the shifting sand it's built upon. I've gotten a few recommendations to shore things up, but they are only preventative measures to increase longevity. Bleakpoint Light can continue standing tall, right where she's at." She'd thanked God for His mercy in that aspect. If the engineers had said that Bleakpoint had to be relocated, that would have been the end of Walt's dreams and her job.

His half smile stretched into a full grin. "That's swell, gal. Really good news, isn't it?"

She nodded. "The engineers were surprised. So many barrier island lights haven't been so fortunate."

He cupped his stubbled jaw in his hand and peered at her. "The bad news?"

"There was some damage to the ironwork of the stairwell due to the moisture getting in those broken windows. They deemed the stairwell secure enough to climb and to be rehabbed, but the rust must be addressed immediately before the corrosion worsens. Unfortunately that means the rust must be removed and the ironwork repainted. And given the age of the place, it's likely coated in lead-based paint. We'll have to hire a remediation company to come test it and deal with the removal. Same caution goes when replacing the doors and windows and basically anything that might disturb the paint. It can make for some tedious work. More expensive too."

Walt stuffed his hands in his pockets and turned toward the light. "All in all, it ain't any worse than we expected, is it?"

She shook her head. "Not much."

"Good deal."

She made a few notes on her paperwork. "I'll get together a few bids for testing and remediation and get back to you for approval before we proceed." Joey made another crack at the information Walt kept close to his chest. "So you said you were friends with the lightkeeper?"

He scoffed. "Never said that. Pretty sure he hated me. But his daughter was a school chum of mine." Walt started strolling down the beach, and Joey fell into step beside him.

"Will you tell me about her?"

He ducked his chin. "I'll never in my natural-born days forget the day I met Cathleen McCorvey. I wasn't but nine years old, but I'm pretty sure I fell head over heels the first time I laid eyes on her. She was a scrawny thing, and her grandmother had a vise grip on her arm, practically dragging her down the walk while she tugged at the collar of her pink dress. Cathleen reminded me of the time one of my sisters tried to play dress-up with one of our barn cats. Spittin' mad, she was."

Joey laughed. "And that was love at first sight, huh?"

Walt ran a hand over the back of his neck, fondness further softening his expression. "She was unlike any girl I'd ever met. I tried talking to her all day, but the teacher was a strict woman, and I didn't get in more than a lean across the aisle and a 'Hello, I'm Wally. What's your name?' before the teacher threatened me with her yardstick.

"I chased her down after school. Saw her tearing the lace from her sleeves. I asked her, 'Whadya doin' that for? It's a fine-looking dress.'"

Walt snickered. "She looked at me as if I had three heads and said, 'You ever been forced into lace? If I'm made to wear a dress, it ought not itch.' Satisfied with her de-lacing, she pulled on a fisherman's sweater that must have been one of her father's because it hung nearly down to her ankles and then she left me in the dust and kept walking."

Walt shook his head. "She was an itty-bitty thing. But tougher than nails. A couple of the bigger girls tried picking on her once thinking she looked like an easy target." Walt chuckled. "They tried that exactly one time."

Joey's heart warmed at the tenderness in his voice.

"Cathleen was the best sort. I had a real bad stutter there for a while, and that mean old Mrs. Smithers thought she could break me of it by making me recite answers in front of the class on a daily basis. This older boy liked to tease me about it any time the teacher's back was turned. The first time he pulled that stunt in front of Cathleen, she gave the kid a black eye. It was pretty embarrassing to have the smallest girl in school as my mighty defender, but I decided that if that meant we'd become real friends instead of me just being the boy who pestered her walking home from school, then it was worth it."

The rhythmic lapping of a receding tide lent music to Walt's soft drawl.

Joey touched his arm. "I would have loved to have known her. She sounds like quite the character."

"Oh, she was. And real mad that her grandmother was trying to 'tame' her. Her mother had passed away a couple years before we met. The flu, I think it was. And her father had raised her for the past several years, but he'd been transferred to Bleakpoint, and it was too remote to bring her back and forth to the village school on Ocracoke every day, so her grandmother had stepped in to help out with Cathleen through the week. A stodgy old bird, Cathleen called her behind her back. Pretty awful thing to say about her grandmother, but I think she just missed her dad."

"I imagine so." An ache swelled in Joey's heart, longing for the days when her parents had lived downstairs and her brother across the hall. And she was a grown woman out on her own now. Not a kid.

"On Fridays, he'd pick her up in his boat and whisk her away. She'd spend two blissful days in her wilderness before she'd have to come back to her grandmother stuffing her into lacy dresses."

The way Walt talked of her, Joey half expected little Cathleen McCorvey to pop her head over one of the dunes any minute and demand an account of why they'd invaded her island.

"I bet the two of you had the time of your lives exploring this place."

The playfulness in his eyes vanished. "I was never permitted to come here." Walt's lips clamped tight. He continued walking and she kept pace, but she had tread on some delicate thing and she wasn't quite sure how to mend it.

TEN

That night, Walt lay in the cabin of his vessel, reading *Twenty Thousand Leagues Under the Sea*. Neither the waves nor the narrative had succeeded in lulling him to sleep. He closed his book and shut off his lamp. Perhaps he was as tormented as that Captain Nemo, though regret not vengeance fueled Walt's mission.

His mind drifted back to the words he'd spoken to Joey on the beach. Stories about his Cay. Stories that he'd kept locked tight for decades. Not even Martha had known the half of them, God rest her soul.

It had hurt too much to dredge up memories he'd sunk fathoms deep, but Joey was so earnest and eager to fulfill his dreams for the island, he couldn't resist spilling his guts to her.

Walt rose from his bunk and went topside into the cloudless night. The moon hung low and bright in the sky. In the distance a great horned owl cried out a lonesome *who-whhooo*. Walt scanned the island hoping to spy the large bird, but his night vision left much to be desired. He shrugged and sat, thoughts drifting back to the day's affairs.

When Finn had first discovered his plan, he'd urged Walt to contact a historical preservation society to see if grants were available to offset expenses to restore Bleakpoint. But Walt had refused. As much as he craved answers, he'd promised himself to protect

Cay's secrets, whatever they might be. The last thing he needed was strangers poking their noses where they had no business.

And then dear Joey had been so excited, like she'd presented him with a fine gift, when she told him she'd hired a pair of amateur historians to clean up the keeper's residence. He hadn't the heart to tell her to find someone else. Someone who wouldn't take so much care. What if they found another fragment of information and from it spun more nonsensical stories that further marred Callum and Cathleen's legacy?

Walt blinked. Was that movement in the distance? A light shining? He stood again, wishing for the vision of his youth. In a moment whatever he thought he saw had disappeared.

He'd been ruminating too long on too little sleep about Bleakpoint's sensational tales of lingering ghosts and wailing souls at unrest. The only soul not at rest was his own.

Joey sat at her desk chair and let out a contented sigh. It had been a good day. The Alexanders had gotten a good start on the cottage. Though they hadn't found anything of particular interest, they'd done some cleaning and sorting. Joey had gotten back to the mainland in time to contact a remediation company that was set to come test the paint on the lighthouse staircase and other surfaces later that week. She had three bids in from carpenters who would take care of the new window and doorframes once the stairwell was repaired.

She typed up an email to Finn, giving a detailed rundown of bids and a proposed sequence of work thus far. She hit send and sat back in her chair, pleased with herself. That ought to go a little ways toward proving her capabilities.

Thirty minutes later his reply came through.

Sounds fine. How is my grandfather? Does
he seem okay to you? Has he said or done

anything that concerned you in any way?
Please update.

Not one word about the work she'd sent over.

She shook her head. As aggravating as that was, she had a hard time being frustrated with a man so concerned about his grandfather's well-being. She sent him an equally succinct message letting him know that his grandfather was just fine.

The next morning, Joey stopped at Murph's, a convenience store on the way to the marina, to grab one of the bacon, egg, and cheese biscuits Walt had been raving about. She'd been doubtful about the quality of gas station fare, but Walt and the Alexanders had assured her that everything was made from scratch every morning.

The woman at the counter greeted her on the way in. Joey filled a cup of coffee at the large carafe and selected a biscuit from the warmer.

She smiled at the older woman who reminded her of the southern live oaks that were all over the island, a little wind-bent and weathered. Joey suspected that, like a live oak, the woman had deep sprawling roots that clung to the ever-shifting soil of the place she called home. "Your biscuits came highly recommended."

The woman grinned, revealing that one of her incisors was missing. "That so?"

"Yes, ma'am. Walt O'Hare's recommendation."

Her grin dropped for half a second before she fixed it back into place. "Oh . . . I heard about you."

Joey swallowed hard. "Pardon?" How? How had Copper Creek's rumors found her all the way out here?

"Ain't ya skeerd of the ghosts?"

Oh, that. Joey grinned. "I don't believe in ghosts."

The woman jerked her head back and then wagged it like she

felt sorry for her. "You'll believe in 'em soon enough. The souls of Callum and Cathleen have roamed that island since the day the sea swallowed 'em up. Whether they're friendly spirits or not, I cain't rightly say. No one sticks around long enough to find out." The woman leaned across the counter and lowered her voice. "Every year on the anniversary of their deaths you can see two clouds hovering above the water, off the shores of Bleakpoint Island. One lil'un, one big'un. Folks have seen 'em other times too, but they're out there every July."

"Oh, wow," Joey replied. The woman obviously took the story seriously. She paid for her coffee and food and stepped back from the counter with a wave. "Well, I hope they'll be pleased with their home getting spruced up," she said in an attempt to appease the superstitious shopkeep.

The older woman narrowed her eyes. "You be careful, now. Things are different out here on these islands. You'll see."

Joey sobered. "Yes, ma'am. I'll see you around."

The woman nodded sagely. "I hope so."

Joey shivered at her tone despite herself and headed to the exit. As she reached for the handle, the older woman said, "Many people believed they were German spies. Helped sink that ship on purpose."

Joey froze and turned back.

"Just rumors, of course. Coulda been the other way around. Could be that the Germans got them. Killed 'em and then took over the lighthouse. Ran before they could be caught."

Joey stood with her hand still on the doorknob. "I thought Callum and Cathleen were lost at sea."

The woman scratched at her chin. "Well, now, they did find Callum's body days later, washed·up on shore, but who knows what led to him ending up in the drink." She shrugged. "Anywho, I was just a baby back then. But my parents and grandparents knew all kinds of tales. With ships being torpedoed right off the shore out there, everybody suspected everybody. 'Specially outsiders or people like the McCorveys who kept so much to themselves."

Joey crossed the room and handed the woman her card. "I've got to run, but if you'd like to tell me more sometime or if you know anyone who has more information, I'd sure love to hear it."

The woman did a double take after glancing at the card. "Event planner? I thought you said you was working on that lighthouse."

Joey gave her a coy shrug. "I'm a woman of many talents."

The woman nodded. "Well, good for you. Name's Ida, by the way. I'll call you if I turn anything up. But don't hold your breath. You'll suffocate waiting."

"Yes, ma'am. Have a good day, Miss Ida." Joey left the store with a clank of bells and questions firing off in her mind. Were Ida's wild claims merely an example of the idle speculation and rumors Walt detested? Or were they something more?

Walt was in good spirits as he ferried them across the sound. He had plans of meeting up with a buddy of his and doing some fishing. That meant she'd have plenty of time to bend the Alexanders' ears about the stories surrounding the island without fear of upsetting Walt.

Joey zipped her jacket high and sipped at her coffee, thankful it was still warm in its Styrofoam housing. She soaked in the sight of gulls and pelicans soaring across the crystalline sky. As much as she missed the Appalachian foothills of Copper Creek, this was its own slice of heaven. She peeled the foil back on her sandwich and took a bite of the flaky biscuit. Her eyes closed in delight. She wasn't too sure about the believability of Ida's tales, but the woman made a first-rate breakfast sandwich.

Walt dropped them off at the dock and motored away to meet up with his friend.

She followed the Alexanders to the cottage. Already it was looking like a new space. They'd been working on removing the dust and debris little by little, sorting items worth saving into piles.

"I'm not sure any of it has any particular historical significance so far," Renee said, "other than the nostalgia of knowing these were the very items they used. Iron cookware. Lanterns. I think a lot of it can be cleaned up and is still in fairly good condition with a little love and care."

Joey poked through the humble artifacts. She turned to Renee and Jerry. "I met a woman today who had some interesting things to say. Ghost stories." She paused. "She said the McCorveys were German spies?"

Jerry nodded. "There's been more than a few suggesting that they've seen ghosts hovering over the water. Honestly, it's nothing more than the converging of the cool and warmer currents that happens close to the island. It's all in good fun. There was a band of teenage boys some time back who ventured over here, no doubt planning some sort of mischief. I don't know if they were a little tipsy on whatever they'd pilfered from their parents' liquor cabinets or if they just got themselves worked up telling tales around the campfire, but they came back telling everyone who would listen that they'd seen someone out here. Half of them said it was a ghost. Others said it was an old woman walking the beach. Of course, out of that, more tales spun off from the original account. People started saying that there were two people out there. Then, of course, everybody started saying it was the ghost of Callum and his daughter, Cathleen."

"And what about the spy thing?"

Renee squinted in thought. "I don't know that they ever found anything to confirm that rumor as true, but it makes sense for the time period. Emotions were high during the war with all the merchant ships that were torpedoed along the coast. I can ask around if you're interested. You never know what connections might turn up."

ELEVEN

The Alexanders went out to the beach to take their lunch break. They'd invited Joey, but she decided to explore the lighthouse instead. She hadn't given things a good perusal since the engineer's assertion that it was safe to traverse those 150 steps to the top.

She shoved her shoulder into the saltwater swollen door, increasing the crack enough to squeeze through the narrow opening. Once inside, Joey pulled the small flashlight from her backpack and shined it in the dark corners beneath the lowest steps of the spiral staircase, making sure she wasn't sharing the relatively small space with something wild.

The beam illuminated the white lime-plastered walls that had grown dingy with time and rust. She traced her light along the corkscrew curls of the spiral staircase. How striking it must have been when the walls were bright and the deep navy paint fresh on the ironwork, sunlight streaming in sparkling windows in the galley unmarred by the salt film.

Later she'd get a shovel and scoop out the rotted leaves, limbs, and debris that littered the ground and clung to the corners, but for now she wanted to get the view from the top, to glimpse the domain Cathleen McCorvey and her father had devoted their lives to.

On and on she climbed. She paused for a moment to look over

the rail to the floor below. Her vision swam and it felt like the bottom of her stomach dropped out. *Note to self—don't look down.*

Her footsteps echoed in the quiet space as she continued. Had this place always felt so solemn? Surely the walls of this sentinel had echoed with laughter too, with a father and his young daughter in command.

Making things beautiful again would be simple enough. But was there any way to infuse life back into these forgotten places?

When she reached the top, she propped her hands on her burning thighs and caught her breath. She couldn't imagine having to climb up and down these stairs throughout the day and night.

Joey walked the circumference of the lantern room, around the vacant space where the Fresnel lens had once been housed. Walt had said the Coast Guard removed it when the light was decommissioned. Though the structure was no longer a navigational tool, perhaps a soft lantern glowing from within could provide a beautiful focal point for guests of the island. She pulled her notebook from her backpack and jotted down a few ideas.

She tried the small door that led to the gallery deck, but it was rusted shut. It would have to be replaced, as would the gallery deck itself. The outside metalwork hadn't fared as well as the interior. Getting the right equipment out here to install a new walk and railing would be pricey and complicated. An expense that Walt may decide to forgo, unless he had his heart set on being able to stand out there. But so far he hadn't shown any inclination to even enter the lighthouse, much less explore the gallery deck over a hundred feet in the air. She peered through one of the broken panes, glimpsing the view beyond the salt-frosted glass.

Once the new panes were installed, the panorama would be spectacular. From this height she'd have an unobstructed view of the rolling sea on one side, the winding marshes, and the gentle Pamlico Sound on the other. A feast of natural beauty, the ham-handed touch of humanity so minimal that it was easy to pretend she was the only person in existence for a moment.

Joey headed back down the stairs, paying closer attention to the condition of the plaster work as she went. Streaked with rust stains and splotched with mildew, it would need some serious TLC, or maybe it would be better to replace it. She made herself a note to research her options. Halfway down, her flashlight beam crossed a small section of chipped plaster.

She ran her finger over the uneven patch, noting the difference in texture from the rest of the wall. When she lifted her finger, a quarter-size chunk came away with it. Whoever did the repair work had done it hurriedly and without the same finesse as the original plaster mason.

In fact, she thought it might not be plaster at all but some other substance slathered over the crevice between two stones. It was gritty like sand mixed with some kind of putty maybe?

After she scraped away the flaky material, she shined her flashlight into the revealed crack. There was something in there.

She carefully worked the object free with tweezers from her utility knife—paper. Joey sat on the step. As she gently unfolded the paper, the thin waxlike coating flaked along the crease.

"The Journal of Lighthouse at" was printed in bold typeface. The adjacent blank line was filled in by small, squat scrawl that read "Bleakpoint Island."

A lightkeeper's log? She ran her fingertip over the rough edge of plaster where it had been concealed. She carefully slipped the artifact into a plastic sleeve in her project folder and tucked it into her backpack.

Eager to share her find with Jerry and Renee, she hurried down the staircase and over to the keeper's residence. Movement out of the corner of her eye caused her to pull up short. Someone or something had just disappeared into the tangle of live oak. A tingle crept up Joey's spine. "Hello? Someone there?" A lone branch waved as if saying, "This way. They went this way."

It was just a deer. Or maybe one of the wild ponies that Walt said waded the shallows to graze here during low tide in certain seasons. But she couldn't shake the feeling she had been watched. She rolled her eyes skyward. That Ida and her rumination had gotten to her.

Although it couldn't hurt to check it out.

As she approached the wooded path, a holler and resounding crash came from the direction of the keeper's residence. Joey turned and broke into a run toward the cottage. "Jerry? Renee? Are y'all okay?"

The only answer was the sound of her feet pounding the sandy, pine needle path.

When she rounded the corner, she found Jerry on the ground with Renee at his side. Joey ran to them, stepping over the toppled ladder.

She knelt beside them. "What happened?" Renee didn't answer, her complexion pallid and her eyes wide as she stared at her husband. "Renee, is he okay? Are *you*?"

Jerry suddenly pushed himself up on one elbow and rubbed the back of his head. "I'm fine. I just rattled my cage a little bit on the landing."

Renee snapped out of her trance. "You are not fine. You blacked out for a second."

Jerry lay back flat, closing his eyes. "I did not." His face creased in obvious discomfort.

"Yes, you did," Renee insisted.

"Woman, you've been working me like a dog, I was just catching a quick nap before you put me back to work." His voice came out raspy.

"Jerry . . ." Renee narrowed her eyes.

Joey rose. "Renee is right. We need to get you checked out." She stepped away from the couple and radioed Walt who assured her that he would hurry back.

Joey returned and knelt by Jerry's side, placing a hand on his shoulder. "Where does it hurt? Anywhere besides your head?"

Jerry grumbled. "Just a minor headache." But the pinched expression on his face revealed his lie.

Joey stood and stuffed her hands in her pockets. "Looks like more than a little headache, Jerry."

He winced. "Feeling a little discomfort in the ribs too, if I'm being honest."

"What were you doing on the roof?" She'd told the couple that a company was coming to tend to structural things. And now she had an on-the-job injury under her watch. Finn was going to have an absolute fit.

She mentally listed off all the things she'd need to say to assure Finn that she hadn't opened his grandfather up to a lawsuit.

Renee looked up at her. "We'd been cleaning out the fireplace and noticed something blocking the chimney up near the opening, and he insisted he get up there and take a look."

She turned back to her husband with a scowl on her face. "Oh, I am so mad at you." But the fierce yet tender way she gripped his hand told another story. "He even has a harness and straps he uses when he cleans ours at home." She gave Jerry a pointed glare. "You knew better."

"Honey, I'm sorry. Everything was going fine, but I got distracted as I was starting back down. I caught a glimpse of movement near the woods, and when I turned to look, I lost my balance." He patted Renee's hand that held his other in a vise grip.

Joey glanced to the trees and back to Jerry. "You saw that too? I thought it might be a deer or something."

He massaged his forehead. "I didn't get a real good look, but that was a two-legged creature. Not a deer." He started to rise again, and Renee pressed a hand on his shoulder. "Why don't you just lie still, at least until Walt gets here."

Joey removed her fleece vest and tucked it under his head. "Any ideas about who would be snooping around the island?"

"No telling. Could be a nosy tourist, or a local for that matter, who got wind of the work you're doing," Jerry rasped.

Two quick blasts from an airhorn permeated the atmosphere.

Joey straightened. "That'll be Walt. Thank goodness he was close. Can you make it to the boat?"

"Course I can." He stood slowly and listed like a ship with unbalanced cargo. Joey and Renee swooped in to steady him at each elbow.

Jerry blinked hard. "Ladies, I'm all right. Just a little dizzy." Joey released him but walked close beside, alert to his every step on the uneven terrain. They finally made it back to Walt who expertly steadied Jerry as he stepped onto the boat.

As they pulled away from Bleakpoint Island, Joey scanned the shoreline for signs of the vessel that would have carried the mysterious interloper onto Walt's land.

But there was no one to be seen.

TWELVE

The next morning, Joey curled onto the couch with a cup of tea and a throw blanket to cut the slight chill lingering in the morning air. She sipped her Earl Grey while the light of dawn kissed the waters of the sound, causing them to glitter.

Renee had called late last night to let her know Jerry was going to be just fine, but he'd been put on restricted activities for the next few weeks because of his mild concussion and a couple of cracked ribs. That meant the house cleanup was on hold until after Christmas, which was no big deal in the grand scheme of things. But with the work on the house at a standstill and a forced pause to wait for the remediation company to come test the paint next week, she wasn't quite sure what to do with herself.

She groaned. Should she email Finn and let him know about Jerry's accident? She'd made sure the Alexanders and all the subcontractors signed the appropriate waivers to protect Walt from liability, not that the Alexanders seemed the type to sue in the first place. And besides, it didn't really affect the overall timeline. So why hand the anxious grandson unnecessary things to worry about?

She leaned closer to her puzzle and clicked the last handful of pieces into place. Satisfied with its completion, she deconstructed it and returned it to the box and then went to the bookshelf to trade it for a puzzle depicting a marshy inlet and water birds.

She removed her project folder from the backpack sitting at her feet and flipped through the color-coded scope and sequence of work. Too bad things never went as smoothly on paper as they did in real life. She turned to the final page, the one with the final touches. The one she looked forward to tweaking as she got a better idea of what Walt really wanted Bleakpoint Island to become.

Staring up at her from the plastic sleeve was the document from the walls of Bleakpoint Light, forgotten in yesterday's excitement.

The ink had slightly faded with time, but the hen scratch was readable enough beneath the bright light of her table lamp.

December 14

Stormy seas tonight. Thick fog. Vessel spotted in the Bleak-point inlet just after midnight. A fisherman's boat foundered on the shoals. The rescue was straightforward enough. Navigating those waves is second nature to me by now. Once on board my vessel, the fishermen reported that their engine had failed, and they had gotten caught in the current. They'd been drifting for hours before getting stranded on the shoal.

When we arrived at Ocracoke, I deposited them on the island. They asked who I was and how it was I came upon them. At first I think they thought me the young son of a fisherman, but then the curls escaping from my hat betrayed me. They begged to know the woman who braved the cold and fog and waves to come to their assistance. I tugged my scarf higher, making sure most of my face remained concealed. When they wouldn't relent, I gave them the name I've come to associate with my late-night operations. And then I disappeared into the dark night where the fog swallowed me and my boat like we'd never been there. When I slipped back into the house, I was thankful my father was still at rest—free from the demons that plague both him and me.

> In the service of God and country,
> Mae

Joey set the folder down and sat back on the couch. Why did that name have a familiar ring to it?

Mae.

She was sure she remembered someone talking about someone named Mae when she'd first arrived here. She studied the note once more. It was odd that there hadn't been a year ascribed to it. Just a month and day. She did a quick internet search of records for the lighthouse, trying to ground this record in history, but she could find no record of a female lightkeeper or record of a lightkeeper's family member with that name.

And if this entry was supposed to be a part of the keeper's records, why had it been stuffed in the wall? Could there be more?

She downed the rest of her tea and then set her mug in the sink, anticipation thrumming in her veins. This was going to be an interesting day, after all. She called Walt, but there was no answer. He was probably busy working on his boat, a never-ending task.

On the way to the docks, she stopped by Murph's to get another one of Ida's biscuits. She might know something about the mysterious Mae from the hidden log. If not the truth, she'd be sure to know some associated tale.

Ida was occupied with another customer in the back of the store when Joey arrived. After a young woman rang up her purchase, Joey sat at one of the picnic tables outside and breathed in the salty-sweet air. It was cooler this morning but not cold enough to cut through her light jacket. Through the window, she spied Ida making her way to the register.

The first thing out of Ida's mouth when Joey opened the door was "I done told you snooping around that lighthouse was going to bring nothing but trouble."

Joey walked to the counter, her stomach tightening. "What are you talking about? What's happened?" Her mind spun with possibilities.

"I heard all about what happened to Jerry."

Joey crossed her arms over her chest. "He took a fall. A simple accident. He's going to be just fine."

Ida shook her head so emphatically that wisps of her white hair broke free from her claw hair clip. "No, ma'am. 'Twas the ghost of that girl and her daddy. Spooked him."

"Ida," Joey chided, "there was no ghost." There might have been somebody, but it wasn't a ghost.

She pursed her wrinkled lips. "Just because you don't believe, it don't make me wrong."

If she couldn't convince Ida that the ghost of Cathleen Mc-Corvey wasn't real, maybe she could appeal to her superstitions. "In the middle of the day? What kind of ghost haunts midday. Is that even a thing?"

Ida wagged her bony finger. "You just wait and see. Miss Ida knows all about these things. I've been around here long enough to be able to sift out the truth from the myth."

"Yes, ma'am." Joey nodded respectfully, making sure to keep anything that could be construed as mirth from her face.

Ida, seemingly pacified by Joey's solemnity, said, "I'm just trying to look out for you. Maybe you oughta quit before anything worse happens."

If Joey were the suspicious type, she'd wonder if Ida's warnings held a deeper motive aside from her superstitions.

Joey propped her hands on her hips. "I can't do that. Walt and his grandson hired me to do a job, and I aim to do it and do it well. Bleakpoint Light is special to Walt."

Ida smirked. "The way I heard it, Walt left these parts during the war. Became one of those merchant marines 'cause he was too young to enlist in the services. That is, until his ship got blown outta the water that same night the girl and her daddy disappeared. Soon as he healed up, he cut town. He didn't see and hear the things people saw and heard these many years. He's got no idea what Cain he's raising."

Joey sucked air through her teeth. There was no way she was going to bring up the log book page she'd found in the wall of the lighthouse. Ida would definitely consider exhuming it some sort of sin against the ghosts of Bleakpoint Light.

"I'll be careful, but I've still got a job to do. You have a good day, Miss Ida." Joey skirted out the door and went to the marina to find Walt. On the way, she fired off a text to Sophie. *I feel like I've slipped and fallen into an episode of Scooby-Doo. Send help.*

When she reached the dock, Walt's sailboat was absent from its slip. Scouring those old walls for potential secrets would have to wait for another day.

THIRTEEN

The shrill ring of the bedside phone vaulted Joey from eerie dreams of ghostlike figures walking on the ocean waves. She groped for the phone in the darkness and croaked out a froggy "Hello?"

"Oh, dear. I woke you, didn't I?" Renee's apologetic voice filled her ears.

Joey squinted and then put on her glasses to read the red numbers on the clock. Midnight. "Is something wrong? Is Jerry okay?"

"He's fine, dear. He's snoring away beside me, rattling the rafters."

"Um . . . okay. Did you need . . ."

"Sorry, I should have waited and called in the morning, but I got so wound up I had to call you. You see, I was lying here trying to drift off despite my husband's noisemaking when it hit me."

Joey stuck her fingers behind her glasses frames and rubbed her heavy eyelids. "Okay," she said when it became obvious Renee wasn't going to end her dramatic pause until she was sure Joey was awake on the other end of the line.

"Oh, Joey, I was so excited to tell you, and I plumb forgot when Jer took his tumble. I'm so sorry."

Joey shifted on the bed, propping pillows up behind her. This had better not be about a vintage teapot. "Forgot to tell me what, Renee?"

"I think there's something hidden under Callum McCorvey's bed."

Joey sat straight. "What do you mean?"

"Right before Jerry got up on the roof, he helped me move the bed over so I could work on the floor. Some of the stones that had been beneath the bed were loose. They made a clunk whenever I stepped on them. I was curious what kind of sub-flooring, if any, might be under there so I tried to remove one of the smaller stones. It looked like there was something metal under there. I went for my flashlight to get a closer look. That's when I heard Jerry falling. I don't know if it's anything worth being excited over, but I was lying here and got to thinking. What if that's where Callum McCorvey kept things he didn't want found? What if he *was* a German spy? What if government men who came to investigate never moved the bed but just looked under and around it? They would have never known those stones were removable."

Joey's heart beat faster. This was not the kind of thing Walt wanted to find out about this family.

"It's probably nothing," Renee continued. "But Jerry's brother is coming for a visit tomorrow so I could slip out for a bit to check it out. He's perfectly capable of making sure Jer doesn't get any wild ideas and start climbing roofs."

Joey took a deep breath. "I'll call Walt in the morning and see if he's free. I'll keep you posted."

They bid each other good night. Joey stared at the ceiling with her imagination running wild. It took all of her willpower not to call Walt and beg him to make a midnight run to Bleakpoint Island.

The next morning, Renee met her by the docks. After being incommunicado all day yesterday, Walt had thankfully answered Joey's early morning phone call.

He welcomed them aboard the supply boat, looking spry and freshly shaved. "Mornin', Joey. Renee. How's Jerry?"

Renee settled in her seat. "Oh, he's all right. Already getting a little antsy, but his brother came for a visit and they're busy watching a marathon of *Atlantic Fisherman*."

Walt nodded as he coiled a rope. "That's a good'un. If I wasn't playing chauffeur to you two lovely ladies, I might've joined them," he said with a wink.

Joey grinned and sat across from Renee. "We appreciate your sacrifice, Walt."

He swallowed hard, sobering. "Y'all mighta found something interesting in the keeper's house?"

Joey jumped in before Renee could answer. "We're not sure. Renee found some loose floor stones she wanted me to check out." No need to raise Walt's concerns over what might be nothing.

He seemed satisfied with her answer and stared thoughtfully over the water as he guided the vessel to their destination.

She might not agree with Finn that his grandfather was unfit to oversee this project, but there was something about the past that had left the man unsettled. And if Finn found out her probing had upset Walt, he'd likely shut this whole thing down.

Once on land, Joey followed Renee into the dim cottage with a couple of battery-powered lanterns. They entered the curtained-off space that had served as Callum's bedroom.

The broom was still propped against the wall from where Renee had stopped mid-task. One stone was slightly out of place where Callum's bed had once rested. "Over here," Renee said. "Help me move this larger stone."

They worked together to lift the large flat paver and slid it out of the way. Sure enough, there was a metal container beneath.

Renee lifted another small stone to give them full access to the box. "It looks like an old military footlocker."

Together they unearthed this buried piece of Callum McCorvey's life.

Renee dusted off her hands on her pant legs. "Let's take it outside so that we can see better."

Each woman grabbed one of the handles and hoisted the small trunk.

They set it gently in the grass. Renee unhinged the metal clasps and lifted the lid. Inside was a chaotic collection of loose papers and bound journals. A leather folio drew Joey's attention. She carefully extracted it from the mess. Inside were photos held in place by corner tabs. One was a faded photo of a man and a gangly teen in front of a different lighthouse, set high on a rocky cliff. Another was of a young woman and a man. Beside that was a photo of the same woman and man, but in this one she held a baby in her arms. The last one was of a girl standing in front of Bleakpoint Light.

Renee reached for the album. "May I? There could be names and dates on the back." Joey handed it over, and Renee removed the photograph of the man and the boy and turned it over. "Magnus and Callum McCorvey, Neist Point Lighthouse, Scotland, 1910," she read. "Callum and his father, perhaps?"

Joey scooted closer as Renee returned the photograph to the album and removed the next one—the man and woman gazing adoringly into one another's eyes. "May 1922, Callum and Mae McCorvey" was written in graceful, feminine script.

Mae? Joey retrieved her backpack and removed the folder where she kept the found page safely concealed in a plastic sleeve. "The same day Jerry fell, I found this in the walls." She showed it to Renee. "Could this have been written by Cathleen's mother?"

Renee held up the page next and compared it to the script on the backside of the photograph. "If this is Mae's writing on the picture, it's very different from the document."

Joey pursed her lips. "You're right. Plus Walt said that Cathleen's mother passed away before her father took the post at Bleakpoint."

Joey tucked the orphaned log back into its protective sleeve.

Renee flipped over the last two photos. The one with baby Cathleen had the same curling script as the last photo. The one with Cathleen alone had "Cathleen, age 8" written in harsh block letters. Callum's writing, perhaps?

"If it wasn't Mae McCorvey, who do you think wrote the log I found in the lighthouse wall?"

Renee shrugged. "There's not much to go on if there's no surname. No identifying year. The only sure thing is that the log was written sometime in between the time the lighthouse was first opened in 1915 and when it was decommissioned in 1945." She tipped her head side to side, considering. "Of course, it could be some reference to the local folklore about a mysterious rescuer Saint-Mae who could rescue those no one else could. Just stories, but the best ones are based on some level of truth."

Renee waved a hand over the still-open footlocker. "There could be more information somewhere buried in this box that would give you a better idea if these hidden logs are connected to the McCorveys in some way. Though you're more likely to find information revealing what led up to the night they disappeared."

Joey picked up a journal from the disorganized cache and carefully opened the cover. The name Callum McCorvey was written in the same angular block letters found on the back of the photo of Cathleen. She skimmed a few pages, then closed it and placed it back on the top and picked up another. "I'll talk to Walt and see what he'd like me to do with them before I dig any further."

Maybe something within the box would help him make sense of what had happened to his long-lost friend.

Later that evening, Walt helped Joey carry the footlocker up the stairs of the stilt house. They gently placed it in the middle of the living room.

"You're sure you don't mind me going through all of this?" Joey faced Walt, who was a little red in the face from the exertion.

"Nah, I've little interest in Callum's old things unless they're about Cathleen, and I know you'll keep me posted if you find anything about her in there." He shoved his hands in his pockets. "Cathleen was so insistent that he didn't want me or anybody else hanging around Bleakpoint. I assume he was a hard man to get along with, but Cathleen never said a word against him in all the years we knew each other."

He pressed his lips tight, his brow creasing. "If you find anything damaging to their reputation, I can trust you to be discreet?"

Joey nodded. "Of course. Is there something you expect I'll find?"

Walt crossed his arms over his chest. "They've been enough of a target for legends and ghost stories. People get obsessed with the spectacle, glorifying their tragedy when what they deserve is the dignity and privacy they always worked so hard for."

Joey could understand that. He didn't want any tidbits she might find used as more rumor fuel. "Do you want to stay, Walt? We could look through their things together."

Walt stepped toward the door. "There's still a little daylight to burn, and I need to run to the hardware store for some lacquer I special ordered." He paused in front of the bookshelf that contained puzzles, games, and books for the vacation renter's use. Walt pulled out *The Life of Pi* and held it up. "Mind if I borrow this?"

"Be my guest." She pointed to the footlocker. "I think I've got more than enough reading materials here. Are you a big reader?"

He shrugged. "I always wished I'd gotten more schooling. So now I read 'bout anything I can get my hands on."

She walked him out to his beat-up truck and watched as he pulled away.

Back inside the house, Joey heated up some soup she'd made the night before and settled in a chair next to the footlocker, hoping to discover something in the old box that would banish the sadness that lingered in his eyes when he spoke of his old friend.

Just as she was about to begin digging through the footlocker, her phone rang. Joey smiled at the sight of her brother's name on the screen. "Hey, Trey."

"You really did it. Have you settled in okay?"

"It's been eventful, but overall it's working out."

The line went silent for a few moments. "So, you're back in construction? That was . . . unexpected."

She swallowed. "Really?" Why did his gently spoken words still feel like an accusation?

"I guess I didn't realize you were interested in the field."

"It was kinda our whole life growing up. I loved it."

"Then . . ." Her brother huffed. "Then why did you say no when Dad asked you to take over the company?"

She raked her teeth over her bottom lip. They'd never discussed Dad's offer. Mom must have said something. "I think you know why."

He groaned. "Don't say it was because of me, Roo."

She smirked. "Fine, I won't say it. It wasn't just that though. I had already started working on building up my event planning company, and I never wanted to run Dad's whole operation on my own. It was a lot of things."

"Okay." Doubt laced his voice. "Anyway, I really just called to tell you that I'm proud of you for leaving that mess in Copper Creek behind. Mom said it's been rough."

Her shoulders inched up. "Well, the construction thing is only temporary. I'm going back to relaunch the event planning biz as soon as I'm finished here. I'm saving as much as I can so I have a little cushion to help get things going again."

He sighed. "If you're sure that's what'll make you happy, I'm all for it. But I can't pretend to understand."

They said their goodbyes, her heart still warring with itself. Was it absurd to believe she could restart her life after a little break? She rubbed her hands over her face. Maybe. There was plenty of time to hash out the details. For tonight, she could focus on solving someone else's mystery without worrying about her own.

Joey spent the rest of the night sorting the journals, organizing them by date. The first one began in 1936 with the last in the series beginning in 1939, two years before Callum and Cathleen's deaths. Once she sorted them by date, she skimmed through pages of tidy writing. It seemed to be nothing more than a chronicle of Callum's simple, well-ordered life on a remote island. Not the type of thing you'd feel pressed to hide away. Although, as she continued skimming through them, the last few journals appeared different from the rest. The handwriting changed, and the entries seemed progressively disjointed. But when she opened the last journal and thumbed halfway through, she found something that made her heart stall in her chest.

Some pages were crumpled, others hastily ripped out. There were large passages that had been scribbled over. If ink markings could retain the emotion of the writer, these dripped with fury. Or maybe fear. There were others with misspelled words with irregular spacing between. The ink trailed off the page in wobbly despair.

What was the meaning of these strange missives? How could they be penned by the same hand that wrote Callum's carefully documented life history?

FOURTEEN

After a long night scouring through Callum McCorvey's possessions, Joey was once again perched on the twisting stairwell of Bleakpoint Light digging for more history sealed within its walls. She'd already identified at least a dozen sections that had that same flaky appearance, ready and waiting for Joey to uncover the treasure within.

But why were these old lightkeeper logs concealed here in the first place?

The second entry she'd found moments before was similar to the first, torn from some logbook. It displayed records like temperature, tides, and winds. But then it became more descriptive, telling of a harrowing rescue of a foundered vessel caught on a shoal where the waters of the sound met the sea while a nor'easter blew. Every shift of sand created a trap for yet another victim.

The third she'd uncovered spoke of rescuing a couple of children who'd gotten themselves caught in a rip current.

Joey shook her head as she brushed away the powder her labor created. This woman single-handedly rescued these people from the hands of an angry sea. And yet there was no lightkeeper on Bleakpoint's record by that name. Joey paused. Were these actually works of fiction? The hobby of some lonely lightkeeper, writing down the legends of Saint-Mae to pass the time?

She finally broke through the hardened shell of makeshift plaster. With her trusty tweezers, she withdrew a fourth note from the walls. Squinting in the low light, she found that this one was dated February. A month after the last. It was in much the same shape as the previous three. Without taking time to stop and read it, she worked until she'd unearthed four more entries.

Ready for a short break, Joey carefully tucked all the newly found entries into plastic sleeves except for one. She descended the stairs and slipped out the door, her heart pounding in anticipation of what this next note might reveal about the enigmatic Mae.

Once outside, Joey sat beside her backpack on the step, the newest note in hand. She inhaled the fresh, salt-kissed air, but this time there was an unfamiliar acrid tang that wrinkled her nose.

Fire.

Joey stood and turned a slow circle, noticing the slight haze gathering in the air. She laid the aged paper inside the cover of her notebook and placed it on top of her bag and then grabbed the radio and jogged toward the source of the smoke.

Into the radio, she said, "Walt? Walt, can you hear me? It's Joey."

She waited a moment for a reply and hurried onward, her stomach sinking the closer she got to the keeper's residence.

She broke through the clearing to find the house surrounded by a ring of flames that consumed the dry, dead grass, closing tighter and tighter on the cottage. Though the house was made of stone, the door was not. Nor were the lodge pole supports inside.

Choking on smoke, Joey ran to the well pump and grabbed the bucket off its hook. She stripped off her shirt and soaked it through before pulling it back on. Its icy bite on her skin made her shiver. With the T-shirt collar pulled over her nose, she dumped bucket load after bucket load of water on the flames until her sides ached and her lungs burned. There must have been some sort of accelerant involved because the fire burned on despite her dousing. As she worked one portion of the circle, the untended portions burned hotter, reigniting.

She had to save Cathleen's house.

Where was Walt? Why hadn't he responded to her distress calls? She focused on the battle at hand, refusing to entertain the needling thoughts demanding answers. Like who set this fire and why. And where they might be now.

After what felt like a decade of frantic firefighting, the battle was won. Joey dragged her exhausted body to the stone landing in front of the cottage and collapsed into a sitting position.

She dabbed at her burning eyes with the collar of her shirt and attempted to swallow. As much as her body rebelled against moving another step, she needed water to quench her thirst and her fire-baked skin.

She clenched her trembling hands and stood, eyes drawn to the charred grass. No matter how much her mind resisted the idea, the burn pattern that ringed the house in a perfect circle had to have been created by human hands. But why had they only put the house in harm's way when they could have set the fire inside? Better yet, why not wait until she'd left for the day?

Ida's ghost stories and superstitions floated through her mind. She shooed them away and returned to the well pump. The water sluiced over her arms, cooling her fevered skin. Maybe she should have been more concerned about imminent danger, but if the arsonist hadn't approached while she was consumed with fighting the fire, they wouldn't come now.

After Joey had slaked her thirst, she radioed Walt again. Still no answer. Even if her radio signal failed to reach him, surely he would have seen the smoke rising over the low-slung island terrain.

Worry prickled her spine. What if the fire-starter wanted her paying attention to the house instead of their real quarry—the man behind the stirred-up dust of Bleakpoint Island and the secrets it kept.

Joey walked to the sound, senses on high alert. She scanned the water for *Cay's Song*. Instead, she spotted a small boat motoring away from the south end of Bleakpoint. Joey ran down the sandy stretch, straining her eyes for any identifiable features of the hooded person at the helm. The motorboat disappeared from view.

She checked her watch. Walt wasn't due back for two hours, so she returned to the house to inspect the interior. It was in the same organized chaos it had been the day before. She exited and locked up.

Perhaps she should return to the lighthouse to look for more of Mae's notes while she waited. It would give her something to do instead of imagining dark and dangerous scenarios.

When she drew near to the structure, her heart sank in her chest. Her notebook had blown open and the entry she'd been about to read was missing. No matter the danger to the house, she shouldn't have been so careless.

She walked in concentric circles around the tower but found no sign of the paper. What she did find was a trail of uneven footprints in the sandy soil leading away from the light. Those on the left were a distinct sneaker tread, while the right looked as though the walker had dragged their leg a bit in their hurry.

No matter how convinced Ida was that ghosts plagued the island, even she'd have to agree that ghosts did not leave footprints.

Joey tried the radio a few more times with no response. She sat with her back against the silent sentinel, keeping watch.

When Walt arrived, she radioed, asking him to come ashore.

She showed him the fire damage surrounding the keeper's cottage, walking him through everything that had happened. He didn't meet her gaze the entire time she spoke.

When she finished, he said, "We can't tell Finn about this."

She nodded in reply. Maybe it was the wrong move, but she had no desire to reveal to Finn that Walt had been unreachable during an emergency.

On the way back to Ocracoke, Walt remained pensive, eyes never straying from the horizon. She'd tried to nudge him into theorizing about who would have motive to set fire to his island, but he merely shrugged in response and muttered to himself.

Back at the marina, she eyed the docked boats knowing the trespasser wouldn't leave their boat in such a conspicuous space. She bid Walt good night and walked home in the waning light, thankful to be off Bleakpoint Island.

Walt lay in the narrow berth of *Cay's Song*, his heart pounding too loudly in his chest, reminding him of that horrible boxed-up heart under the floor in Edgar Allan Poe's dreadful story. He pushed a breath from his heavy chest. He'd lied to the gal. He'd lied to Finn.

He dragged a hand over his face. He'd lied to himself, really. Convincing himself he could make up for past failures by caring for Cay's light.

He'd been consumed by the past when he should've been keeping his promise to Finn to look after Joey. Instead, he made up stories about fishing with a friend when guilt drove him from that patch of land.

He growled. He'd gone and left his radio on board his boat, lured away from Bleakpoint by a siren's song of days gone by to the marshy shoal where he and Cay once played. Carefree kids on endless adventures until the tides of war swept away all that was bright and beautiful in their lives.

Since that spring of '43, a caul of loss had been stretched over his life and he'd yet to shed it.

First there was Cay.

Then the baby he and Martha lost.

And then his son and beautiful daughter-in-law taken too soon in a car accident, leaving he and Martha to try to fill a gaping hole in young Finn's life.

Martha.

And now Walt's foolish ploy for penance was driving a wedge between him and Finn. The last person he had on this earth.

Even recognizing the strain this venture put on their relationship, he couldn't make himself abandon Cay's light. Because until he made the past right, the darkness following him would continue snatching precious things away from him. The only way to stop it was to go back to that first mistake and do all he could to make it right.

He sat up, scrubbing his hands over his face, banishing his spiraling thoughts. Finn really would have him committed if he ever admitted the musings that plagued him in the dark watches of the night.

He sighed. In trying to make things right with his past, he'd filled his present with lies. Lies would never produce the closure he craved. Today's fire had made that crystal clear.

From now on he'd be sure to protect Joey. Fessing up about why he hadn't come to her aid today would be his first step in the right direction.

FIFTEEN

Joey woke to the sound of her phone ringing. "Hello?" The word scraped over the sandpaper yesterday's fire had left in her throat. She grabbed her glasses from the side table. Early dawn light peaked through the slits in the vinyl blinds. Did no one around here call at normal hours?

"Joey, it's Walt. There's something I need to tell you."

"Okay." Her mind created images of a toppled lighthouse or the cottage reduced to a pile of smoking rubble. "Walt?"

"Not . . . not now. Can you come meet me? There's a place I need to show you."

After she ended the call, she put in her contacts and showered. She grabbed a banana from her fruit basket on the way out the door. On yesterday's commute back to Ocracoke he'd been so stoic it scared her. And now he was so eager to talk he was calling her at the crack of dawn.

She should call Finn. Already she'd waited far too long to update him about the fire. But to leave out her concerns for Walt's current state? That was sure to rank in the unforgivable category in Finn's book.

Joey passed Murph's. As tempted as she was to stop in and grab whatever breakfast sandwich Ida offered up, she was in no mood for more of her warnings.

A rogue thought took her captive, causing her pace to slow. What was it that Ida had said about Walt?

"That is, until his ship got blown outta the water that same night the girl and her daddy disappeared. Soon as he healed up, he cut town."

The way Ida had spoken made it sound like Walt had been mixed up in their disappearance somehow.

He'd asked Joey to be discreet with anything he'd found about the McCorveys, but maybe those old lighthouse logs and Callum's journals were more than he'd anticipated her finding. Did Walt have secrets on Bleakpoint too?

She shook her head to clear it. It didn't make any sense for him to sabotage his own project.

And, besides, he'd been out fishing with a friend.

Albeit a friend she'd yet to see.

Again, her imagination attempted to fill in the incomplete picture with improbabilities. Still, there was definitely something odd going on with Walt. She'd sure love to know why he hadn't answered her distress calls.

She headed to the marina and down the dock to Walt's slip. He stood on the boat with his back to her, polishing the gunwale, oblivious to her approach.

She grasped the standing rigging. "Permission to come aboard?"

He started and turned, a sad smile on his face. "Yes, ma'am."

She stepped onto the gunwale and then over the lifeline, the boat softly rocking with her motion.

"Well, now. Look at you. You're moving like a seasoned sailor now."

She laughed. "I'm finding my sea legs."

"The weather is fair and the water like glass. Mind if I take you somewhere to talk?"

"Not at all." How could she mind sailing on quiet waters, taking in all the untouched beauty.

Walt worked the sails while Joey tried to decipher the connections between all the lines and pulleys. Such small adjustments altered their course.

They headed in the opposite direction of Bleakpoint Island, deeper into the sound, away from the Atlantic. She turned back, facing the shrinking lighthouse. What untold stories had it witnessed? Heroic rescues? Tragedies? She itched to get back to the island to garner more of her secrets. But today Walt had some of his own to confess.

Another twenty minutes passed, and Walt carefully pulled alongside a makeshift dock. Sand, sea oats, and live oaks their only company. He tied off the boat and gave her a hand as she stepped onto the wood planks.

She followed behind him. "What is this place?" And why had he felt the need to sail all the way out here to confess whatever it was he needed to tell her?

Walt rubbed a hand over the nape of his neck and then turned to her when he stepped off the dock. "I told you I was meeting a friend to go fishing yesterday. But I wasn't. I was here when I shoulda been there. With you. On that island."

Joey pressed her lips tight together, searching for a way to respond to Walt's distress. "It's none of my business what you do with your time. Why make up something that wasn't true?" She joined him on the sand.

He smiled and shrugged, lending him the look of a schoolboy caught skipping class. "In a word, Finn."

"Finn?"

"I know he has you reporting back to him on how I'm doing. I couldn't have you telling him I was going off on my own, wandering around lost to time and nostalgia. Not with me promising I'd stick close by you. And now, with the fire and everything." Walt gazed at the water in the direction of Bleakpoint Light, though it wasn't visible from this vantage point. "I'm an old man who's not much good at playing superhero, but having someone else around deters a person from trying things they ought not to, you know. I shoulda been there." His features crumpled. "How long am I destined to repeat my mistakes? You coulda been hurt or worse."

Joey placed a hand on his shoulder. "But I wasn't. Everything is okay. We can go forward from here and do better." Joey gave him a wry smile, hoping to lighten Walt's mood. "So, Finn put me up to keeping an eye on you, and he put you up to keeping an eye on me. He thinks us both incompetent fools."

The twinkle returned to Walt's eyes. "No. You're the incompetent one. I'm just senile."

"Oh, well. That's *much* better." She sobered, suspecting there was more to this rendezvous than Walt had shared. "So why have you been coming here instead of staying at the lighthouse?"

He resumed walking, taking a narrow trail through the twisted live oaks that looked like they'd been created by animals instead of human hands. "I feel like I'm trespassing."

She followed, wishing she could read his unexpressed thoughts. "It's yours, Walt. You literally own an entire island."

He stopped and faced her. "No matter whose name is on the deed, that island will never be mine. I'm only taking care of it for her since she can't."

They continued on until they reached the end of the trail. He stepped forward and moved aside, revealing a stunning view. Rolling dunes in one direction, endless marsh threaded by twisting streams in the other. "This here was ours. Mine and Cay's."

"Cay?"

"Most knew her by Cathleen, but Cay was what I always called her."

Joey glanced back in the direction of the dock even though the trail obscured it entirely from view. "Your boat?"

He nodded. "Was named for her and the songs I used to play on my twangy mouth harp to coax smiles out of her. You asked if Cay in the name of my boat referred to an island, and it's funny, but until that moment, I hadn't realized just how well my shortened version of her name fit her." He grew quiet. "But she was different when she was here with me."

Walt continued walking past the end of the trail and Joey ambled alongside him, the loamy soil soft beneath her feet. In the distance, egrets stalked in the marshes, their feathers stark white against the golden grasses.

"We discovered this place the summer we turned ten. Her dad had given her a skiff with a little outboard motor. I had gotten a job at the marina helping out, and this old guy let me borrow one of his old boats to tool around in if I took care of upkeep. Anything I didn't bring home to help out the family finances went into that gas tank."

Joey's eyes widened. "When you were just ten you helped with the bills? Came way out here all by yourselves?"

He nodded. "Times were different then. We claimed this little marshy stretch as ours and traipsed all over the place. Some days we fought Blackbeard. Other days we were the pirates. We'd huddle up beneath stick forts drawing maps of our newly claimed land."

Joey looked over the beauty surrounding them, and it wasn't hard to picture young Walt and Cay tooling through the winding inlets. "Why didn't you buy this place instead?"

His expression was so wistful it made her heart ache. "Would've if I could've. It's federally owned."

The silence stretched between them, interrupted only by the lonesome call of mourning doves.

"What happened between you two, Walt?"

He blew out a long breath and scratched his jawline. "Cay was about fourteen, I guess, when she moved to the island full-time. Her grandmother passed away, and Cay dropped out of school. She said her father needed her at the lighthouse.

"I tried talking her out of it. Told her she could stay with my family, but she wouldn't listen. Bleakpoint swallowed her right up. She became the wild thing her grandmother tried to keep her from becoming. Not in a bad way, mind you. Parts of her came alive in ways I'd never witnessed before. But she became more isolated. And we started to grow apart." He tilted his head. "No, that's not accurate. She grew away from me. I never moved. Leastways, not at first."

Joey placed a hand on his forearm and squeezed.

"As I got older, I started working longer hours with a local fisherman. Cay and I became like ships passing in the night. We'd leave little notes for each other in a hollowed-out tree. We'd meet up when we could. Then, of course, the war came, and that changed everything again.

"I was only sixteen, so they wouldn't take me in the service. I thought about lying about my age to enlist. Some of my friends did. But my granny had put the fear of the Lord in me about lying from the time I was a little thing. I got scared of what might happen to my immortal soul if I ended up getting killed fighting after lying to get there. Soon enough I found a new way to serve. The merchant ships would take sixteen-year-olds without batting an eye."

Was Walt ready to share his account of what had happened the night his ship went down? The night Cathleen disappeared? She clamped her lips tight to keep her avalanching questions from interrupting Walt's confession.

"Cay and I got into a big ol' row about that one. She was so angry at me for putting my life in danger when I could be safe at home. I don't guess I blame her. We'd watched dozens of ships burn in the night at the hands of German U-boats."

Joey couldn't imagine voluntarily climbing aboard an unarmed ship knowing it could likely be blown out of the water. No wonder Cathleen was angry.

"I hadn't seen her for weeks and she'd stopped leaving notes in our tree. I was about to ship out, so I ventured to Bleakpoint to say goodbye, not wanting our last words to be angry ones. I knew better though. She was forbidden to let people come to Bleakpoint."

Joey and Walt stopped on the crest of a small rise.

"When I got there," he continued, "I discovered her and her father arguing outside the lighthouse. Cay was pulling him toward the house, and Callum was struggling against her. Gone was the strapping man I'd occasionally see on Ocracoke back when he'd pick Cay up from her grandmother's. He looked angry and, I don't know . . . lost. A thin and sickly feral thing. I got closer to help, but Cay yelled at me to stay back, that I would only make things worse." Walt wrapped his arms around his middle and stared at the grass poking up out of the sandy soil at his feet.

"After getting him inside, she came back out and ripped me a new one for coming when she'd told me not to. I asked if he was drunk or something, 'cause that was the only thing that remotely made sense of the scene I'd just witnessed. She shoved me and told me to mind my business." He shook his head. "Goodness, she was strong for someone so small. Near-about knocked me off my feet." He swallowed hard, the hint of a smile dissolving. "Told me that I already had decided to go and get myself killed so I might as well leave her to tend to her own problems.

"I was never sure if she was more angry I'd witnessed her father in the state he was in or that I was risking my life when I didn't have to." Walt cleared his throat a few times and stared over the vista. Finally, he said, "Last time I ever saw her." His brow furrowed and he ran his thumb over the scar on his hand.

In that moment it wasn't images of Cathleen and Walt that played in Joey's mind, but the sounds of her father and brother yelling and the squeal of tires as Trey left. She clenched her hands at her sides. If they could hear the pain and regret in Walt's voice, would they change their course?

Walt swiped quickly at his cheeks before turning back to her. "I don't know if I can ever forgive myself. Whatever was going on with her father, she should never have been left to face it alone. No matter how hard she pushed me away, I should have stayed."

SIXTEEN

When Walt and Joey returned to the marina, they found a figure pacing in front of Walt's slip.

Walt spat out some unintelligible word before turning to Joey. "Finn wasn't supposed to be back for another week. Did you tell him?"

Joey shook her head. "I didn't." But how she wished she had. Her brief tenure as the project manager of Bleakpoint was about to end.

Silence as thick as a thunderhead hovered over the trio as Walt docked the boat.

When all of them had their feet back on dry land, Finn rounded on them. "So, when were you going to tell me?" His gaze bounced from Joey to Walt.

She wasn't exactly sure which something he was referring to, but there was no way she'd provide more ammunition than he had on hand. Joey smiled sweetly. "As I mentioned in my last email, there are far less renovations needed than I had thought at first glance. I thought you'd be pleased."

Finn narrowed his eyes. "My schedule changed, and I thought I'd come see how things were going. I found you two gone, so I asked around to find out when you might be back. I met a fascinating woman named Ida who gave me a whole earful of what Joey here has so conveniently left out of her updates."

Joey's eyes fell shut. *Stinkin' Ida*. She stepped between Walt and Finn. "Don't tell me you believe Ida and her ghost stories."

Finn didn't seem to notice her, his gaze was angled toward his grandfather, who had turned slightly away from his grandson and looked over the lapping waters of the sound. Some might see an elderly man avoiding the heat. Joey saw a soldier readying for battle.

Finn huffed and focused on Joey. "Trespassers? Fires? Accidents?" He ticked off each item with his fingers. "Did I get anything wrong? Miss anything?"

Joey opened her mouth and closed it. Either Ida had been a little more accurate than normal or Finn was good at sifting between fact and fiction. "There's been some unexpected happenings. But you can't take Ida's words to heart. She blows everything out of proportion and then embellishes it with tall tales and nonsense."

The tiniest spark of humor flashed in Finn's eyes before the reigning anger snuffed it out. "Neither of you have said a word about any complications. An accident on the job? We could get sued. And did you call the police about the trespasser?" He cleared his throat and folded his arms over his chest. "I'm sorry, let me rephrase in order to make sure I'm giving an *accurate and unembellished* representation of the situation. Did you call the police about the *arsonist* on your property, Pops?"

Walt harrumphed. "Wouldn't do no good if I did. Nobody cares about the goings-on at that little stretch of land that lies between jurisdictions. Besides, no real damage was done."

Joey stepped closer to Finn. "We aren't getting sued by Jerry and Renee. They carry their own insurances, and I have all the appropriate releases signed and on file if you'd like to see proof. Jerry freely admits that he was on that ladder of his own volition." Notwithstanding, the Alexanders were some of the kindest people on the planet.

Finn paced. "I said that I would be hands-off on all of this as long as everything went smoothly, but the more I hear, the more I know that decision was a mistake."

Joey's heart thudded hard in her chest. He couldn't shut this down. He wouldn't. Not when this meant so much to Walt. Not when there were still so many questions left unanswered. Finn didn't know the heartbreaking way Walt had lost Cathleen Mc-Corvey or the regrets he was still trying to make up for all these years later.

Joey propped her hands on her hips. "You gave your grandfather your word that you would support this project as long as you got to oversee the hiring of the project manager."

Finn opened his mouth to speak.

Walt stepped to Joey's side. "It's my money paying for it, son. Not yours."

Finn scrubbed a hand over his face and his stance softened. "I'm not trying to fight you. I'm just worried about you, Pops." He looked to Joey. "And I don't want to needlessly put anyone in danger on our account." He shoved his hands in his pockets, his bottom lip disappearing. "I have next week free. Let's get to the bottom of who's been hanging around there and why. If we can effectively deal with that, I'll leave you both in peace to finish this project without me. Okay?"

Walt agreed, and Joey had no choice but to go along with the plan even though she was less than thrilled to have the skeptical Finnegan O'Hare hanging over her shoulder while she worked.

After grabbing a quick lunch at a small deli, Finn, Joey, and Walt made a trip to the island to show Finn the evidence of the fire and let him look around. As they drew alongside the Bleakpoint dock, an odd heaviness settled in Joey's gut that had nothing to do with the Reuben on rye she'd had for lunch.

It was like walking into a room that though nothing visible had changed, you knew someone had been there. Someone uninvited. She looked to Finn and Walt, but if they felt the same foreboding, they didn't show it in their demeanor.

She rolled her shoulders to release the tension. She was just catching hold of Finn's worry. Whoever had been lurking on Bleak-point had had ample opportunity to do her harm and further vandalize the property. But they hadn't. They were just . . . seeking . . . something. She bit down on her lip, trying and failing to sort the scattered pieces into a coherent picture. The fire was a distraction, not destruction. But a distraction from what exactly?

Finn and Walt worked together to tie off the boat and then the three of them walked single file down the trail with Joey bringing up the rear, still trying to figure out what someone could want with the abandoned island.

The image of the interior of the lighthouse and all its hidden logs flashed in her mind. And the one that had been missing, blown away after the fire. At least she'd wanted to believe it was just missing . . .

She edged around Walt and Finn and broke into a jog. "The lighthouse," she said by way of explanation as she hurried ahead. Why she felt such sudden urgency, she wasn't quite sure. If her hunch was right, she was too late.

It was a punch to the gut when she squeezed through the door and shined her flashlight along the pockmarked plaster where, she was sure, documents had once been hidden. Someone had been quite busy in her absence.

Walt and Finn came in behind her.

"Whoever set the fire must not have liked the fact that I was finding Mae's lighthouse logs."

"Logs?"

She turned to Walt whose face was creased with confusion. Joey sighed. "While I was working, I found lightkeeper logs hidden in the walls signed by someone named Mae. Incredible stories of heroism. I was trying to figure out who she was and her connection to the island before I brought it up to you. I know you've had enough of all the idle stories about this place."

He nodded slowly. "I see."

"And now they're gone. I should have found a way to stay the night after the one went missing. I'd convinced myself it blew away."

Walt patted her on the back. "I know you're upset, gal. But I don't mind a bit about those old logs. They were somebody's story, and it's sad to have lost them. But maybe they meant something special to whoever found them. I just hope whoever did this is satisfied and will leave Cay's light alone from now on."

Finn pulled out his phone and started taking pictures of the walls.

Joey turned to him. "What are you doing?"

He raised his brows. "Cataloging the damage. Obviously we can't prove what, if anything, was taken. But this needs to be recorded." He stared at Walt and Joey, shaking his head. "How else are we going to report this if we don't have anything to show?"

Walt stomped outside, grumbling under his breath.

Joey shrugged. "There might not have been anything for them to take. And we've got to have all this old plaster sanded down anyway. No real damage was done to anything except the grass from the fire. Like Walt said, I can't see the authorities staking the place out."

"We won't know unless we try. You still have some of the logs, right? Can I take a look?"

"They're back at the house."

"I'd like to get a few pictures of those as well."

She started to protest again, but she wasn't in the mood to waste her breath.

She and Walt walked Finn over to the house where he took pictures of the burned grass. Joey stepped inside the house, and as she'd expected, everything was as it should be. They had to get a new door for the lighthouse so that it could be locked up as well.

"Look what I found!" Finn's voice rang out in the quiet. Joey hurried outside. He had a small rectangular container delicately pinched between two fingers. "Lighter fluid. This could have our arsonist's fingerprints on them."

He sounded so serious, she had to fight to keep from laughing. He sounded like a *CSI* superfan who'd watched a few too many episodes.

Although, it did give her the creeps knowing that, even now, someone could be watching from the woods trying to see what they were up to. Though Joey couldn't shake the feeling that whoever did these things didn't have malicious intent, she was becoming less and less annoyed that she'd have Finn's extra set of eyes watching her back.

SEVENTEEN

That evening, after Finn had gotten his fill of scouring Bleakpoint for clues, he followed Joey to her rental. She led him to the living room where she kept the binder of log entries and Callum's footlocker. "Nothing was taken from the house that we know of. There's no sign the lock was tampered with."

She handed him the notebook that contained Mae's notes. "The lighthouse has been here, unlocked, all these years, apparently left undisturbed. But then we show up, I stumble upon those logs, and things begin to happen."

Finn opened the binder and glanced through the handful of pages in their protective sleeves. "Maybe it was the local interest articles that came out after Pops purchased the place that drew the unwanted attention. And I'm sure he's been gabbing with his old buddies about what he wanted to do with the place."

Joey almost blurted out the fact that she didn't think Walt actually had many friends around here anymore, but Finn was already worried enough about the man.

"Any information about anyone who might still have a vested interest in the lighthouse all these years later?" Finn asked. "Anyone who could be harmed if things from the past were revealed?"

She shook her head.

Finn took a few pictures of the entries. "My grandfather has been very tight-lipped about his sudden obsession with this old lighthouse. Until my grandmother passed away, I had no idea he'd grown up in these parts."

Had Finn ever expressed genuine interest in Walt's project or had he always made him feel like an irresponsible child? Questions she wanted to ask but didn't feel it was quite the right moment to challenge her sort-of boss. Instead, Joey acted on the hospitality skills her mother had ingrained in her. "Can I offer you something to drink?"

"Some water would be great, thank you. And then I promise I'll leave you in peace."

Out of courtesy, she encouraged him to take his time before going to the kitchen to fill a glass. When she returned, he crossed the room, meeting her halfway, and took her offering.

The latest puzzle Joey had been working of the Outer Banks coastline snagged his attention. Hovering over the array of pieces scattered across the table, he spied a corner, the same piece she'd hunted for this morning and somehow missed. He snapped it into place. Joey stuffed down her annoyance. The man needed to work his own puzzles and leave hers alone.

Finn straightened his stance and took a long drink of water. "Anything else you can think of that's missing?

"There's the log that went missing the day of the fire. I'd just started to read it when I put it down." She shrugged. "At first I'd thought that it had blown away, but now I'm wondering if the trespasser set that fire so they could check out what I had been up to. The dusty mess I left behind gave them all the clues they needed to start looking for the ones that remained."

Finn set the glass on a coaster and edged toward the door. "I better head on down to the station to show them what we have so far. I know you and Pops are probably right, that no one is going to put much stock in what I have to say, but maybe curiosity about the rumors will be enough to get someone at the station to pay attention."

She gave a humorless laugh. "Walt will be thrilled to have more gawkers on hand."

He dropped his gaze. "I have to make sure he is safe. That you're safe. I care far more about that than airing old secrets." He reached for the door handle. "I'll get out of your hair." He lingered for a second. She'd seen the same look in his eye when he'd snapped photos of the logs. He might not admit it, but this whole thing had his curiosity sparked. If she could make friends, or become allies at least, it might help her and Walt's case in the long run. She could not get sent packing to Copper Creek. Not yet.

She gestured to the metal box. "Stay. You can get a closer look at the logs. I've also been reading through the journals in Callum's trunk to try and see if there is anyone still living who might have some sort of vested interest in the secrets of Bleakpoint Island. Some connection to the family or otherwise."

He released the handle and took a step toward her. "I've already intruded enough on your evening."

She shook her head. "I picked up fish from the market this morning. I've got some veggies in the fridge to go with it. Plenty for two."

Finn shifted his feet. "Well, I . . ."

"The station will be there tomorrow."

He pulled a small object from his pocket, fidgeted with it a moment, but put it back before she could figure out what it was. "I could stay a little while. Some fresh-caught fish sounds pretty good in comparison to the peanut butter crackers left over in my suitcase." The corners of his mouth twitched. "I was a little too furious to do any shopping after Ida filled me in on her version of what had been going on. Of course, her version included the barnacle-encrusted ghosts of Callum and Cathleen McCorvey setting the entire island on fire."

Joey shivered at the mental image. "Gross. I wonder what her deal is."

He cracked a smile. "She's a character."

Joey moved toward the kitchen. "You are welcome to join me, or you can start looking through the journals and things."

Finn followed her. "I'm not much of a cook, but I can at least chop vegetables."

She retrieved zucchini, yellow squash, and bell peppers from the fridge and placed them on the counter by the sink, then pulled out a knife and cutting board for him.

While he washed and chopped the veggies, she seasoned the fish, finding an easy, quiet rhythm with this man who seemed so adverse to her participation in Walt's life. After he finished sprinkling on the seasoning she'd set out for him, he lined the spice containers up in a row, all the labels facing him.

He caught her watching him as he tossed the vegetables in olive oil and seasoning in a large mixing bowl. "Did I do something wrong?" He cringed, looking at the bowl. "Too much spice?"

"Not at all. I was just thinking that it was nice to get to know you a little. Face-to-face."

"Oh?"

"What I mean is that Walt has talked about you a lot."

Finn sucked air through his teeth.

"Good things." *Mostly*. "I mean, obviously you two don't see eye to eye on his latest project—"

"Obsession."

She waved the comment away. "Tomato, toe-mah-toe. I get the sense that the man would walk through a hurricane for you. And getting to know Walt, I admit, has made me curious about the person he is so deeply fond of."

Finn smirked. "So, I'm another of your puzzles?"

"More like keep your friends close . . . your enemies . . ."

Finn nudged the bowl toward her and then crossed his arms over his chest. "I am not the enemy."

She shrugged playfully. "First impressions being what they were, you'll have to overlook my mistake." She tensed. This whole exchange was starting to feel a little too flirty. Being friendly to get on his good side was one thing, but this might be crossing a line.

He lined up the knife and the tossing utensils on the chopping board and then braced his hands on the countertop, glancing her way. "In that spirit, mind if I ask you something . . . um, personal?"

She took the bowl of veggies to the waiting sauté pan, turning her back to him. Yikes. This "get to know you" thing might have been a mistake. "Sure."

"Why the career switch? Event planning didn't work out?"

She dumped the contents of the bowl into the pan and let the sizzle fill the silence for a few moments. "It's not so much a switch as a chance to reset my life a little bit." She pushed the vegetables around. "Things were slow with my business." *Understatement of the year.* "And this was a good change of pace that gives me a chance to reevaluate some things. Figure out if the path I've been on is the one I want to stick with." Hopefully that was enough information to keep him from probing any deeper. He'd likely be less than thrilled to find out her dad's construction company had been wrapped up in small-town scandal. She turned back to him and offered a smile and a shrug.

He nodded, expression pensive. "I admire that—you recognizing that you needed a reset and taking the break. Life can be weird. The way one path leads to another and leaves you wondering how you landed where you did."

"Yep." She wasn't sure she deserved half of the credit he gave her considering this adventure had been more a last-resort, semi-impulsive leap than the thoughtful move Finn described.

Later, after they had eaten their fill and cleaned up, they retreated to the living room to look through Callum's journals. She chose a seat across the room though there was plenty of space beside him on the couch.

She was embarrassed to admit she'd enjoyed the company of the Finn she'd met over dinner—a version of him that didn't fret over his grandfather's life choices or look at her like she might be half incompetent. They'd maintained friendly banter with ease, but it disturbed her how easily she'd slipped toward borderline flirty with someone she didn't like very much.

Needing an outlet for her nervous energy, she crossed the room to her jigsaw puzzle, finding the last of the edge pieces and putting it in place. "Keep your *enemies* closer," she muttered the reminder under her breath before she returned to her seat.

"Pardon?" He looked at her, the quizzical set to his brow disarmingly adorable. *Adorable? Ugh. Focus, Jo-Jo. The guy is a threat to your project and insensitive to his grandfather. Nothing adorable about that.*

She gestured to the metal box. "I've been looking for any connections to the family and the island other than Callum and Cathleen. Someone besides them who would care about the lighthouse and its revitalization. I haven't found any connections yet, but I want to show you something really strange that I noticed and see if you can make anything of it."

She pulled out the earliest journal and opened it to the first page. "Most of the journals look a lot like this one." After she showed it to him, she placed it back in the row of journals and pulled out a book three-quarters of the way through the chronology. "Now in this one, you can tell it's still Callum's handwriting, but the writing gets shaky about halfway through, like there's a tremor in his hands." She turned the brittle pages with care. Deeper into the journal she opened the book fully. "Now look. The tremor seems worse. Most of the journal keeps going like this, and by the end it's almost hard to tell it is his handwriting at all."

"That's not that uncommon as a person ages," Finn said, "for your hands to lose steadiness."

Joey shook her head. "Not when you're in your forties. Your grandfather mentioned seeing Callum once right before he died and said he looked unwell. Maybe intoxicated? But I don't know that that fits the handwriting issue you can see here."

"What do the next journals look like?" Finn shifted forward in the seat, eyeing the stack of books.

She pulled out the last three. "These get really strange. Inconsistent spacing between the letters. The spelling gets weird too. In the earlier journals, he never misspelled words." She showed him a few examples. Then she pulled out the next in order. "Most of these are illegible, and the ones that weren't were hard to follow. The sentence structure isn't right, and a lot of the entries dropped off in the middle of his account. Some of the pages were torn out. It's obvious Callum was struggling, but he kept writing. The last journal is the worst. A lot of ink blots and scribbles. Odd drawings."

Finn studied the journals. He absently stroked his square jaw with his thumb, and his brow pinched in concentration.

She'd seen a similar look on Walt's face when trying to piece things together. If Walt had looked anything like his grandson at that age, he'd been a heartbreaker. She swallowed hard. *Nope, nope, nope. Not going there.* Sure, Finn was an objectively handsome man. But what did that matter? She was here to complete a job, not to get distracted by some guy that was completely wrong for her.

She walked back to the jigsaw puzzle and worked on sorting the pieces into color-coordinated piles while he studied Callum's memoirs.

She heard Finn set the journal on the coffee table, so she turned back to him.

"If these are Callum McCorvey's journals," he said, "it's surprising that he wasn't deemed unfit for duty." He flipped back and forth from the first page to the last, comparing the writing. "I wonder if we could get ahold of his lightkeeper logs from that time? Compare the writing. Surely if he hadn't been able to keep his records, he would have been removed as lightkeeper?"

"You would think. I mean, this wasn't exactly a low-pressure job. People's lives were in Callum's hands."

Sorrow filled Finn's gaze. "Looking through this journal, it's like watching him lose himself little by little. And his daughter, Cathleen, what did that put her through?" The emotion in Finn's voice made her wonder if he was talking about something a little closer to home. He continued, "And Callum was pretty young. His forties, you said?"

"My best guess according to a childhood photo we found in an album from that box."

Finn stared at it.

"I'm not sure what all of this means," Joey said, "but I bet this has something to do with why Cathleen became so protective of Bleakpoint Island."

EIGHTEEN

The next morning, Joey woke longing to follow up on the headway she and Finn made in uncovering the truth about Callum and Cathleen, but first she had an appointment with an abatement company to take a look at the paint inside the lighthouse.

She dressed for the day and made some coffee, then returned to her bedroom where her Blackberry rang on the nightstand. Sophie's name lit up the screen. She answered and put it on speakerphone so she could continue getting ready.

"Hey, Soph." She sat in front of her wicker vanity to tame her sleep-mussed curls.

"You're still alive. I was beginning to wonder."

"Sorry, it's been . . . a little wild." Joey filled her in on the found logs, the fire, and Walt's revelations. "And then Walt's grandson showed up unannounced and I hadn't told him any of this, and the version he was introduced to was provided by dear Ida. You remember her, right?"

"Uh-oh."

"Yep. By the grace of God, I still have a job . . . for now. Since Finn plans to stick around and monitor Walt and me." Joey rolled her eyes. "I'm trying to make friends. I made him dinner last night and showed him some of the artifacts we found. I actually think he's interested in helping figure out the missing pieces of Callum and Cathleen's disappearance." She sipped her coffee. "We got along a lot better than I thought we would." So much so that she found herself smiling, wishing for a repeat of the evening.

"He's hot, isn't he?"

Joey choked. "How did you get that out of anything I just said?"

Sophie cackled. "The way you said it."

"You're full of it."

"So, he's hideous? Not at all attractive?"

"That's irrelevant. He's my sort-of boss-slash-client. And did you forget this is the same guy who didn't want to hire me because I'm a woman. Whatever glee you're poorly attempting to contain, quash it."

"He never actually *said* he didn't want to hire you because you're a woman."

"Didn't have to."

"No matter what he said or didn't say, I've been your friend since first grade. I know when you think a boy is cute just by the way you say his name. Besides that, your defensiveness is quite telling."

Joey put on a headband, inspected her reflection, then took it back off and tossed it into a drawer. "I'm here to do a job. Be a professional. Prove myself. Not get a date. But, yeah, I'll admit I find him slightly less abrasive after getting to know him a little."

Sophie snickered. "Also, Walt is your boss-slash-client, not the handsome grandson. Send me a picture. I want to see this guy."

"Why would you think I have a picture of him?"

"Take one today and send it to me, you goof."

"You've got to be kidding me. What am I supposed to say to him? 'Smile for the camera. My best friend wants to see what you look like.'"

"You'll figure something out. Do you think he likes you too?" Sophie sighed like a lovesick teen. "Of course he does. How could he not?"

Joey burst out laughing. "What is your obsession? Get a baby-sitter and go out on a date with your husband. Or go rent a rom-com from Redbox. Butt out of my nonexistent love life." Joey leaned close to the mirror, double checking that her moisturizer was blended at her jawline. "Don't forget. I just got out of a long relationship."

"*Paul?*" Sophie snorted. "That's the lamest excuse I've heard yet."

"Fine." Joey slouched against the back of her chair. "Finn is hideous and a chauvinist jerk and I have no interest in him. Satisfied?"

"Nope. Send me a picture."

Joey dabbed concealer under her eyes, hurrying through the final steps of her morning routine. "It's all about the looks for you, huh?"

"Sure, why not. Have some fun. Go on a date if the opportunity arises. Live a little."

"Because uprooting my life and moving to an island for four months isn't living a little?"

"It's a start," Sophie quipped. "This adventure is made for seizing the day. Living in the moment. Go where the wind takes you."

She glanced at her watch. "Speaking of the moment, I've got to run. I'm about to be late for my appointment this morning. And you, my friend, are in desperate need of a night out. Call your husband and leave me alone."

"Say hi to Finn for me."

"Bye, *Sophia*." She swiped on a light coat of mascara and then grabbed her keys on the way out the door. She wouldn't make it to the marina on time if she walked.

She met Walt, Finn, and the two guys from the abatement company at the dock. They ferried over in the rented supply boat.

Once they were underway, she leaned close to Finn, hoping that their passengers wouldn't overhear. Without meaning to, she inhaled the clean scent of his cologne. *Get out of my head, Sophie.* "Did you make a report with the police?"

He shrugged. "Yeah."

"And their response?"

A corner of his mouth lifted. "Was pretty much what you and Pops said it would be. But"—the lopsided smile dissolved—"it was important to get everything on file. That way, if anything else happens, we have record of it."

He made a fair point.

Since it didn't take long for the abatement team to obtain their test samples, Walt volunteered to ferry them back so that Joey and Finn could stay and finish their work.

She returned to the lighthouse. Finn patrolled the area, looking for signs that anyone might be around. Joey combed the walls of the lighthouse with a flashlight in hopes that some log might have been overlooked. But their thief had been thorough.

She returned to the keeper's residence to continue Renee's work, sorting the cleaned items into the labeled weatherproof totes. She wasn't quite sure what Walt would do with Callum and Cathleen's things. Besides Callum's footlocker, it was all so utilitarian.

Joey walked into the part of the room Cathleen would have occupied. There was nothing to indicate the girl had inhabited the space. No hairbrush. No clothes. A simple iron bedframe and a small square table were the only things in Cathleen's compartment.

Callum's hadn't been much better, but on his side of the room there had been shaving implements and a comb. Clothing. The footlocker.

The first time she'd laid eyes on the utterly barren state of Cathleen's bedside, the hairs on her arm had stood at attention, and it had a similar effect on her now.

"Joey!" Finn's voice rang out through the quiet. She rushed to the open doorway. "Joey!" The second call sounded closer and a little breathless.

She headed in the direction of his voice. "Finn?"

He broke through the clearing of live oaks and relief washed over his features. "You're okay?"

"Yeah? You?"

"I saw someone. Couldn't tell much about them. I was too far away, but they walk funny. With this odd, shuffled stride."

"You couldn't catch up to them?"

"That's what was weird. It was like they just disappeared."

Joey crossed her arms and lifted an eyebrow. "You believe in ghosts now too?"

He scoffed. "No. But whoever it was is good at hiding. Sneaking around. So that's why I hurried back here. I . . . I was worried they'd circled back to you somehow."

"I haven't seen or heard anything." Joey surveyed the winding paths through the twisting live oaks and rolling dunes. There were plenty of places to hide. Especially if you were more familiar with the place than the people pursuing you. "Well, from what you described, they sure don't sound like much of a threat."

He raised his brows. "Sure. No threat at all. They just creep around starting fires and stealing things."

She lifted her hands in surrender. "Okay, okay. Point taken. What now? Call Walt? The police?"

"Let's look around a little. See if we can flush them out of their hiding place."

Joey pointed to the marshy coast. "There's only one way to travel to an island. We might have more luck finding a boat than a person." She described the small motorboat she'd seen fleeing the island a few days ago.

Whoever their trespasser was, they certainly knew Bleakpoint's secrets. Including her hideaways.

NINETEEN

The following day brought rain and gloom, and there was no work scheduled for Bleakpoint, so Joey made a quick call to a family-run historical society in Frisco that specialized in local lighthouses.

The second call she made was to Finn. "Are you busy?"

"No." The reply was gruff and clipped, even by two-letter-word standards. Maybe this wasn't such a good idea.

"I found a museum that has lighthouse logs from Callum's tenure in their archives. Wanna check them out with me?" She cringed, anticipating another sharp reply.

"That would be great. Pick you up in ten?" This time the tenor of his voice was reminiscent of sunlight breaking through storm clouds.

So, she *had* found a fellow puzzle solver. "Sure."

Ten minutes later on the dot, he was knocking on her door. He lifted his keys. "I'll drive."

She grinned and shrugged into her raincoat, hoping to minimize the effect of precipitation on her curls. "I don't mind taking my truck."

A muscle twitched in his cheek and humor glinted in his eyes. "Like I said, we'll take mine."

"I can't believe you don't want to be toted around in my pink pickup." She grabbed her bag.

"It certainly is eye-catching," he said as he stepped outside.

As they pulled out of the drive, she asked, "Is everything okay?"

"Sure. Why?"

"You sounded . . . less than happy when you answered the phone."

The lines around Finn's mouth tightened as he stared out the windshield. "Pops and I . . . we just . . . we aren't seeing eye to eye on some things right now, that's all. So, how did you find the museum?"

"My cleanup crew from the house, Jerry and Renee, recommended it. When I told the curator that I was working on revitalizing Bleakpoint Light, I could hear her excitement, especially when I told her about having some of Callum's journals in my possession."

"She's actually going to let us flip through the logs?"

Joey patted her bag. "I bartered a peek at a couple of his journals for that privilege."

Finn's brow furrowed. "Which ones?"

"Two of his earlier ones."

The furrow relaxed.

"It felt wrong bringing the latter ones. Like I was exposing him somehow," she said. "Something about those words, those markings, feels so agitated. Frightened."

"Like the writer was making a desperate grasp for a part of himself that was slipping through his fingers?"

"Exactly."

He tightened his grip on the steering wheel. "I researched conditions that cause changes in handwriting when I got to my room last night. . . . It was bleak. Dementia, brain tumor, schizophrenia. I know you shouldn't internet diagnose anyone, but whatever was going on with him was severe."

They grew quiet for the rest of the trip.

Joey was consumed by thoughts of Callum and Cathleen alone on that island. Callum in some undiagnosed state of decline.

Cathleen powerless to stop it. All on the cusp of a war that threatened the barrier islands off America's shores.

An hour later Finn parked in front of a nondescript building with a sign that read "Lighthouses of the Carolinas." As long as they had those keeper logs, this trip would be worth it. Finn held the front door open as Joey walked through.

The interior contained row upon row of tidy displays in glass cases. The museum was the very picture of the term *hidden gem*.

"Hello there. Welcome to Lighthouses of the Carolinas." An older woman of small stature shuffled to meet them. "I'm Maude Jenkins, head curator."

The small space looked in need of only one, but Joey wasn't about to challenge her on it. "Hello, my name is Joey. We spoke on the phone."

Maude's brown eyes grew sharp and bright. "You're the one with Callum McCorvey's journals?"

"Yes, ma'am. They're not mine to hand over, but I have permission to show them." Not *technically* true. But Walt had allowed her to mine the artifacts for information about Cathleen's death, so she chose to believe the information trade she'd worked out with the woman fit Walt's parameters.

"First, let me show you"—Maude cast an appraising eye at Finn who stood slightly behind her—"and your handsome fella around." Joey's face heated. She wasn't quite sure how to correct whatever assumption Maude had formed about the two of them. He certainly wasn't her fella. Her boss—not exactly. Supervisor? A sort of . . . enemy? Not anymore. Friend? Possibly.

Finn and Joey obediently filed in behind Maude as she walked them through the set of three rooms, showing them old photographs and artifacts from life as a lightkeeper on the barrier islands of North Carolina. There were displays of the more well-known and centralized lights with longer histories than Bleakpoint, like Hatteras, Currituck, Bodie, and Ocracoke. There were others about various life-saving stations and river lighthouses located in between.

Everywhere she looked she saw heroic stories of the people who faithfully watched over those ever-shifting shoals. No where did she see anything about a woman named Mae.

As Maude tottered through the rooms, she chattered on. "My great-great-uncle was a lightkeeper for most of his life. I'd come visit him and his family in the summers. It always seemed a grand and adventurous life. And when everything went automated, it was a way of life that went right out of fashion. I didn't want it to be forgotten. People should remember the brave men who kept the coast safe. She walked them to one corner of the room. "And then World War II came to our back door. Not many people realize just how close the war was to American shores."

"Can you tell us more about that?" Joey asked. That time period was right in line with Walt's claim of when something shifted in Cathleen's life.

Joey approached one of the displays, perusing grainy, black-and-white photographs of men on horseback. Beside that photo was a depiction of a foundered tanker, black smoke billowing over the waters.

"It was a harrowing time. Lighthouses, the very thing we'd come to depend on for protection, illuminated the silhouette of the merchant ships ferrying supplies to Europe. By the time the military got around to changing things, the Battle of the Atlantic had shifted."

Finn studied the grainy photograph. "My grandfather was on one of those ships. He was too young to join the military, but they let him on the merchant ship. It was struck by a torpedo."

Joey placed a hand on his arm. "It's a miracle he survived."

Finn turned to her, his expression pensive. "It's not something he talks about, but when I was a boy, I stumbled upon old articles either he or my grandmother had saved. I pestered him to death with questions until he finally told me what I assume was a tame version of the story. He was the lone survivor, but for a few days everyone thought there were no survivors because of a local journalist's misunderstanding."

In the last room, Maude hurried them past most of the other items in the display case. "Now before we get to those lightkeeper logs, let me show you the crowning glory of this museum. Sadly, it's too damaged to be read, or even handled. It's not much to look at, at first glance. Most other places don't really want it. It's just an old journal, after all." She smiled slyly. "Unless you look closer."

Joey walked to the case. Inside was a small book, swollen and warped by water damage. She squinted her eyes to decipher the faded lettering handwritten in dark ink across the clothbound book. "The Harrowing Adventures of Saint-Mae." She turned to Maude, the name Mae resounding in her mind like a cymbal. "What is this?" Could this record of Saint-Mae's exploits somehow be connected to those lost keeper logs?

"Haven't you heard of Saint-Mae since you've been here? She's Ocracoke's lady of the water. She'll come to the stranded. The forgotten. The lost. The ones beyond even the Coast Guard's reach. Saint-Mae appears and rescues those no one else can." Maude looked up at her. "Course those are just the tales we tell. Any foggy morning on the water, you'll have a fisherman come back swearing up and down he saw Saint-Mae rowing on the water. I'm guessing this little book is where it all started. Some writer out there wrote some tall tales, passed them around, and a legend was born."

Joey sat across from Finn at a diner down the street from Maude's museum.

Finn drew a whirlpool in his blob of ketchup with a french fry. "Did you notice what I noticed about Callum's light logs?"

Joey nodded. Thankfully an older couple had come into the museum, leaving Finn and Joey plenty of time to comb through the logs for inconsistencies without Maude's prying. They'd scanned the same dates that corresponded to the changes in Callum's journal writing.

"I saw traces of a shaky hand there for a while," she replied.

"But as the pages progressed, the writing got better instead of worse."

He lined up the condiment bottles, arranging them smallest to tallest. "Yep. And the records became increasingly concise, and they remained well-written instead of misspelled and gaping like the journals."

"I'm no handwriting expert. The writing looked a lot like his, but it wasn't, was it?" She added more ketchup to her plate, purposefully setting the bottle out of formation with the rest of Finn's condiment parade.

Finn shook his head. "The slant was a little different, and the letters became shorter and rounder in his later logs. Nothing like his journal entries from that same time period." He slid the ketchup back into alignment, oblivious to her attempt at aggravating him. She disguised her grin by taking a drink from her water glass.

"Cathleen?"

He ate another fry. "He asked his daughter to scribe for him, I guess."

"So, she was keeping his decline a secret."

"Maybe not at first. Neither of them likely knew what was in store for Callum's future. She was just a faithful daughter trying to assist her tired father. And she ended up swept in a rip current of his disease, not knowing if she should fight it or let it carry her far beyond where she planned to go." The sure tone in which he said it made her wonder what currents Finn had gotten caught up in during his lifetime.

Joey's heart ached. "Imagine the changes in his mood and demeanor that would have occurred. Cathleen facing that alone. They didn't understand things like dementia or whatever his affliction was like they do now."

Finn took a long drink of his sweet tea. "I guarantee that's why Cathleen kept Pops away from Bleakpoint. She couldn't have anyone else knowing. Not if she wanted to keep the only home she'd ever known."

But had Bleakpoint been her haven or her prison?

Joey took a bite of her chicken sandwich. "That old water-logged book has me thinking about another piece of the Bleak-point puzzle."

"Yeah?"

"Maude called it a book of stories. A collection of the legends of Saint-Mae an anonymous writer compiled. What if the words we found hidden in those walls were just new stories. A second volume. Or originals."

"Why hide them though?" Finn wiped away the dot of mustard at the corner of his mouth with his napkin.

Joey shrugged. "I don't know. I'm spinning tales as we sit here. Grasping for connections that likely aren't even there."

"As interesting as this is, I think we need to focus on the here and now," Finn said. "We need to find out who was trying to keep you from unearthing those stories."

Joey leaned against the booth. "If they're just stories, then why would anyone want to stop them from being read?"

"If either Cathleen or Callum were mixed up with German spies like some of those rumors suggest, I could see a family member being eager to keep anything hinting to that past in the past."

"Even after all this time?" Joey asked.

Finn shrugged. "All people have now are tall tales that people take with a grain of salt. Facts, now that's something else entirely. Would you want people knowing that your great-great-uncle helped the Germans take American lives?"

Considering the guilt by association she'd faced in Copper Creek, she thought maybe Finn's theory wasn't all that implausible.

TWENTY

Walt took Joey and Finn to the island the day before Finn was set to head back to Charlotte for work. Walt brought a book and a lawn chair and set himself up on the beach while they spent the afternoon going over the walls of the lighthouse with a fine-toothed comb one final time before the abatement company arrived to begin removing the lead-based paint from the stairwell.

Finn sat on the step as Joey inspected the last section of the wall with her flashlight. "I wish I'd figured out who has been hanging around here before I had to go back," he said.

Joey sighed at the return of "helicopter Finn" and clicked off the flashlight. "Since the incident with the fire, Walt's been sticking closer. He felt really bad about not being there with me." She sat beside him. "Besides, going forward, there will be large work crews present. Whoever's been lurking isn't that bold."

"I'd feel better if I were here . . ."

Over the past few days, she'd started to forget the way he'd secretly commissioned her and Walt to look after each other like they were a couple of tweens left home alone for the first time—equally likely to be just fine or to burn the house to the ground. "I know you care for your grandfather, and in all your protectiveness you mean well, but—"

"Are you two ready to head on back?" Walt called out from down below. "The sun's position in the sky and my rumbling stomach are telling me we'd better go sooner than later."

Finn and Joey trudged down the stairwell. This had been a complete waste of time.

Walt cast a glance between them and tugged at the brim of his bucket hat. "If there's anything else y'all want to get done, better hop to it and let's skedaddle."

Joey crossed her arms. "No, I think we're all done here. Besides, Finn needs to get on the road to Charlotte bright and early tomorrow." She gave him an obviously forced smile, hopefully communicating the conclusion of their interrupted conversation.

Wordlessly Finn left them to retrieve Walt's camp chair from the beach. Then the trio made a slow trek across the island, past the lighthouse and the keeper's residence, and then through the grove of live oaks.

When they reached the marina, Finn helped Walt tie off the borrowed supply boat next to his sailboat. "Pops, next time I'm in town, maybe we can look for a house for you. If you really are intent on a permanent move all the way out here."

Walt gestured to *Cay's Song*. "You're all worried about my finances and harping on about being practical when I got this boat for next to nothing. It works double as shelter and transportation. Now you want me to sink money into a house?" Walt harrumphed. "I'm going for dinner. Stop by before you cut out of town . . . if you want." He strode away with Joey and Finn still standing in the boat.

"Uh." Finn shifted his feet. "Sorry about that. I just thought it would be nice to be able to stay with him when I was in town instead of having to hunt down a hotel room every time. I'm trying to get things in place so that I can be here with him more."

Joey smirked. "Because you think an octogenarian living alone on a rickety sailboat is an epically poor decision."

Finn opened his mouth to protest and then closed it, following after Joey as she disembarked. "I purposefully didn't say that this time."

She looked back at him. "You didn't mention that you wanted to be able to stay with him either. That might have at least gone down a little smoother."

When the dock widened, he fell into step beside her. "What happens if he loses his balance? Falls? Hits his head on the way down and lands in the water? I know he's in great health now. But what if that changes? What if he needs care and he's sunk everything he has into an old, abandoned lighthouse that has no way of making a return for him?"

The plea in his voice made her heart stutter-step. "You've put a lot of thought into everything."

"I'm not always like this." Finn looked sideways at her as they strolled the marina boardwalk.

She hardly knew him. Had no way of gauging the person he was or what facet of himself he referenced. Joey raised an eyebrow in question.

"Focused on profitability. The idea that Pops should only invest the kind of cash he's planning on the lighthouse if he plans to make it back somehow."

"Those aren't bad things, you know." They were solid, practical. "And you're right, the sailboat is not going to work as a long-term housing solution for him."

His shoulders relaxed a fraction at her words, and the lines of his face softened.

"But . . ." She paused for effect. "Even though he's on up there in years, he's still strong and healthy. He's your grandfather, not a wayward toddler. It's not fair to treat him like one."

Finn took a seat on a bench that overlooked the sound. Joey sat on the other end. He fidgeted with a slim gold band before clenching it in his fist, hiding it away. *A wedding band?* She'd never noticed Finn wearing a ring.

"When Pops said he wanted to do something for just himself, I thought maybe that meant buying a boat and fishing more on Cannon Creek Lake. Or taking up a new hobby. Not that he doesn't deserve to do whatever he wants for once." Sorrow stole over his face. "Right when he was getting ready to retire, my parents passed away, so he kept working so my grandmother could stay home and take care of me. Then, shortly after I moved out on my own, my grandmother's health started declining." Finn scrubbed the back of his neck with his hand. "The man has sacrificed an awful lot to ensure I never wanted for anything. Seeing him like this, so focused on a part of his past I never knew anything about. Spending money with no thought for the future—it's so different from the man I've always known. It scares me."

He opened his hand and stared into his palm where the ring rested. "He's looked out for me my whole life. Through the good decisions." He closed his fist tight again. "The mistakes." He sighed. "Now it's my turn to do the same for him."

Joey wanted to ask him about the ring, but instead she asked, "Do you really feel like his mental faculties are declining?"

Finn stared over the water for several moments. A chorus of hungry gulls filled the silence. Something had shifted in the man beside her. The overprotective grandson had faded. As had the intrigued treasure hunter. He was just a guy trying to figure out what was best for the person he loved most. "He seems sharp. But something's definitely different. It feels like he's so far away even when he's right next to me."

Joey scuffed the bottom of her shoe against the weathered wood. "He's grieving your grandmother, so there's that."

He looked up at her, hopeful. "Maybe it's easier to focus on this project than deal with how much he misses her."

She nodded. Walt had a lot of pain in relation to his past with Cathleen, but it was at least more distant. "Have you asked him about his childhood? Bleakpoint? Cathleen?"

"I've asked him why the lighthouse means so much to him," Finn replied. "But he didn't give me much other than to say that history mattered. That preserving the past had a value I was apparently ignorant to."

"Did you ask him about the lighthouse in the same tone you used when you told him he might need his head examined?" She smiled to soften the edges from her statement. Did this man have any subtlety? Any grace in his communication with his grandfather? Or did the pair of them always use their words like blunt force blows? "Maybe you should ask again. Be interested, not worried. He might surprise you with all he has to say."

Finn's gaze jerked to her, hurt evident in his eyes. "He's talked to you about why this project means so much?"

She shrugged. "I know there's more to it than what he's told me. But he has a lot of regrets, and this is his last-ditch effort to make things right."

Finn swallowed and the hurt in his eyes eased. "I get that."

"Show him that you care about more than dollars and cents." She nudged him with her shoulder and then tapped her temple. "And sense. For whatever reason, this lighthouse, that island, has made the steady grandfather you've always known throw practicality to the wind. Instead of letting this push you two apart, let it bring you closer. Take the journey with him."

TWENTY-ONE

Walt sat staring out over the water with a book in his lap. *The Old Man and the Sea*. He related to his latest reading selection far more than he'd like to admit. Desperate pursuit of something that could not succeed. Really though, how long could he go on living out of a sailboat? Finn wasn't wrong. Not that he'd admit it to the boy.

He turned his attention from the water at the sound of footsteps on the boardwalk. Finn headed toward him, hands clasped behind his back. "Hey, Pops." The look on his face reminded him of a long-gone day during which young Finn confessed he'd put a dent in Walt's red pickup.

"Hey, yourself."

Finn drew closer and gestured to the empty space on the bench. "Is that seat taken?"

"Nope."

Finn sat. "I always liked *The Old Man and the Sea*."

"It's a sad story."

"I guess. But what always grabbed my attention was Santiago's determination and passion," Finn said.

Walt shifted on the bench, angling toward him. The indignation that had been simmering in his gut since yesterday settled. "Even though the old man gets back to shore with nothing but a pile of bones to show for his effort?"

Finn nodded. "Even if."

They sat in silence for a few moments. Walt tried to make sense of Finn's sudden change in demeanor. It had been some time since he'd seen this side of him. Walls had gone up when that boy's mess of a marriage crumbled. Walls that blocked his better qualities from view.

Finn wrung his hands in his lap. "I know why the old man wanted that fish so bad. It's all there on the page. But there's so much of your life I don't understand, Pops, and that's my fault. I haven't made the effort to learn why this project means so much to you, and I'm sorry."

Walt attempted to smile at him, despite the embarrassing quiver in his chin. "Don't you need to go, son? You've got quite the drive ahead of you, and I don't want you speeding."

Finn slapped his thighs and made to stand but then he relaxed against the bench. "Before I go, tell me one story about growing up here."

Finn had never asked about his childhood. This had Joey written all over it. Walt's heart softened. She was something else. "My family came to Ocracoke in '35. Times were hard, and my father managed to get a job in Roosevelt's WPA. He constructed dunes and planted seagrasses to stabilize the ever-shifting terrain. We'd lived in Raleigh up 'til then, and this place felt like a deserted island by comparison. All those connecting bridges didn't exist back then. We had a couple private wooden toll bridges, but nothing compared to now. Even the mail came by boat." Walt noted Finn's patient expression and knew he'd probably waxed on in his nostalgia a little too long for a grandson on a time crunch.

"It must have been quite the adjustment for you," Finn said.

Walt leaned back against the bench and stretched his legs out, easing the ache that had been building in his joints. "I was a regular fish outta water. I didn't know a thing about the ocean and its tides or how to set crab traps or make new friends when nearly all the ones I had in Raleigh I'd had since birth. But then I met Cathleen McCorvey. Before I knew it, the salt and sand and marshland was in my blood like it was in hers." He turned to him. "I didn't realize it at the time, but she was my first true friend. All the others I'd had before were because of proximity. My parents knew their parents. Cathleen became my friend because she chose me."

Finn put a hand on his shoulder. "Cathleen meant a lot to you, didn't she?"

Walt nodded and stared at his worn, liver-spotted hands. Hands whose aged appearance sometimes still shocked him. So many years had passed without his permission. "I really let her down when she needed me most. And I might be as foolish as Santiago doggedly fighting his marlin in *The Old Man and the Sea*, but I've unfinished business by way of Cathleen, and restoring that lighthouse of hers is as close as I can get. Maybe you don't understand all my whys, Finn. But surely you can understand the pain of unfinished business."

The boy gave a succinct nod. "I do." He swallowed. "I have to head out now, Pops, but let's talk more next time I'm in town."

Walt gave Finn a firm pat on his shoulder. "Safe travels, son."

"Yes, sir." He stood and took a few paces before turning back. "I'll miss you." He put his hands in his pockets and looked at the wood beneath his feet. "I . . . I want to explain about what I said yesterday. When I mentioned buying a house, I wasn't trying to get you to get rid of the boat. Or say you shouldn't have it. I was imagining the future and thinking about spending more time with you here. But you're happy with how things are, so if I want to spend time here, I need to make the investment." He dipped his chin in farewell and strode down the boardwalk to his car.

Later that evening, Walt headed to Joey's place with a key lime pie from the corner café and one of the diet colas he'd seen Joey drink on occasion. He'd planned on flowers, but the meager selection at the market was hours away from being counted trash can fodder. Hopefully the gal had as big a sweet tooth as he did.

He climbed the steps to the stilt house and rapped on the door.

When Joey answered, he gestured to her face. "I didn't know you wore glasses."

She smiled. "Only as a backup for contacts when I'm settling in for the evening."

"Oh," he said as he took a step back. "I'm so sorry I bothered you."

She shook her head. "Not at all."

For a half second, she reminded him of Cay with her dark curls bouncing with the movement.

"I was just sitting here in the living room getting a little work done. Come on in."

Walt stepped inside, heat rising to his cheeks. This had been a silly idea. She'd think him an old fool making much of nothing, but there he was holding a whole pie and a twenty-ounce soda with nowhere to hide it. "I brought this for ya." After a pause, he added, "As a thank you." He held out his offering.

She took them, her head tilted. "No thanks necessary. I'm loving the job."

"No, not that. Though I am grateful. I meant for whatever it was you said to Finn. I know you had something to do with him coming to talk to me this morning."

A smile lit her face. "He did? I'm so glad."

They stopped at the living room, which was cluttered with papers. She blushed. "I've got some things spread out everywhere in here. Let's head to the kitchen. I think I might need a little help eating that pie."

Walt followed her, but his gaze lingered on the various stacks around the apartment. "That stuff is all things you've found at Bleakpoint?" Part of him wanted to ask if she'd found anything noteworthy. A bigger part of him was terrified of what Joey might have discovered about the girl he'd loved.

"Some of it. Some is research." In the kitchen, Joey put the pie on the counter and got a knife out of the drawer. "What variety do we have here?"

"Key lime."

"Yum. One of my favorites."

Walt swallowed hard. "What kind of research you doin'?"

Joey slid the knife through the whipped cream decorating the top. "The journal entries or logs or whatever those pages I found from the lighthouse are, they don't have any dates, so I thought that getting to know the history of these islands might help me ground them in time." She passed a slice to Walt and stuck the tip of her index finger in her mouth to remove the bit of pie that she'd gotten on her finger. "That pie is the real deal."

He warmed, pleased she liked the gift. He took a bite of his pie, and his lips puckered. "Woo-wee, that's tart!"

She laughed. "That's how you know it's a good key lime, if the first bite gives you a little shock." She opened the soda, poured it into two glasses, and passed him one.

"You little booger. I brought all this as a gift for you, not for me to gobble up."

She shrugged and gave him one of her winsome smiles. "The best gifts are the ones you can share with someone, you know."

"I guess I can't argue with that." She and Finn would make such a good match. Her natural joie de vivre would be good medicine for the boy after all he'd been through. And Finn really was a good man—when he didn't let fear serve as his guide.

He glanced over his shoulder toward the living room and then looked back to Joey, nerves thrumming. "I know quite a bit about the history in this area. At least the part of it I lived. If you'd like me to take a look at some of those papers, maybe I could pick up on some hints."

Joey chewed her bottom lip. "Are you sure? I mean, it might not have anything to do with Cathleen and Callum. It might not be anything but stories someone stuck in those walls long ago. More legends and myths. And I know all this stuff with Cathleen isn't easy for you, which is why I haven't asked you to look at them. I didn't want to get your hopes up. Or your fears up. You know, if this was all nothing."

"Shucks, I'm tougher than I look."

She eyed him doubtfully. "All right then. We better finish our dessert first. If I get key lime on those old documents, Renee will skin my hide."

"Deal." He chuckled and clasped his hands, trying to cover up the way they'd started to shake. He wasn't halfway restoring Cay's lighthouse, so he couldn't go halfway on facing potential hurt. It just wouldn't do. If it was Cay sitting across from him, she'd call him a big fat chicken. And she'd be right.

After they finished the pie, they went to the living room and sat in the two spaces not occupied by books and papers. Joey passed him an aged page inside a protective sleeve. "This is the first one I found."

He pulled his specs from his shirt pocket and perched them on his nose. He stared at the words, trying to make sense of what he was seeing. He lifted his gaze to Joey, blinking back the moisture gathering in his eyes. "That there was written by Cay's hand."

Joey pressed her hands to her cheeks. "You're sure?"

"I'd bet my two-bit life on it." An ache twisted in his chest. "Remember all those letters she'd leave me in that tree?"

Joey slumped back against the couch. "We've got to get those stolen keeper logs back."

TWENTY-TWO

Joey stepped onto the shores of Bleakpoint two weeks later for a final walk-through with the remediation crew before signing off on the project, just two days before Christmas.

After a quick holiday visit with her parents at their new home, she'd be back next week as another company was scheduled to install the custom glass. Once all of the broken panes were replaced, she'd be set to get the interior fully refurbished.

Walt came to her side. "It's coming along, ain't it?"

"Sure is." She reviewed her upcoming plans with him. If only those plans included a way to recover Cathleen's stolen pages. But that had come to a stark dead end. And she wasn't any closer to learning why Cathleen had signed her writings with Mae instead of using her own name.

She had her guesses, but Joey was determined to stick with facts. Cathleen and her father had been subjected to enough speculation.

Walt pointed up to the galley walk. "What about that? When are we replacing the walk?"

Joey chewed her lip, Finn's disapproving face flashing in her mind. "It won't be cheap. The custom ironwork. The equipment that will be needed for the install. Getting that equipment to the island."

Walt had crossed his arms over his chest as she spoke and had begun to work up a scowl. "Don't let Finn get in your head. I've money enough to get Cay's light completely restored. None of this half-done stuff and nonsense."

"It's an expensive fix for something that isn't very necessary." Joey grimaced. That did sound an awful lot like Finn.

But instead of the resistance she'd expected, Walt's weathered face softened with a wry smile. "Is any of this necessary? This scruffy island with its old light sits at the junction between nowhere and the end of civilization. If I did nothing to the place, no one would notice any more than if I made it into a paradise draped in every luxury. In the grand scheme of things, it really doesn't matter much at all." He scrubbed a hand over his face and looked out toward the sea. "But it matters to *me*." His eyes grew watery. "I can still picture it like it was yesterday. I'd be on the water, helping my boss bring in our catch. I'd lift my binoculars whenever her light was in view, and there she'd be, standing on the landing, gripping the rail, waving. Other times I'd catch her looking out to the sea like it called to her. Even though I was too far away to see her expression, I could feel it in my soul. The sea beckoning that wild-spirited girl. I half believed she could sprout wings and soar off that tower and out over the waves."

Joey stepped closer to him, placing a hand on his arm. "Do you know yet what you want to do with the place? Any thoughts at all?"

He turned back to her with sadness clouding his eyes. "I just want to make things right." He scrubbed a hand over his face. "But I can't. I can't bring her back. Can't go back and undo leaving her. Can't make her laugh again." He turned his gaze on her. "It's a fool's errand I'm on." The slight quiver of his chin seared her heart.

She put her arm around his shoulder and squeezed. What words could she offer to this depth of pain? She who still lived with the constant refrain of her own what-ifs. Regret had a power she hadn't learned how to conquer yet.

But maybe she could find a special way to honor his lost friend. If Walt somehow made peace with his past, surely Finn would agree that no dollar amount could be placed on that.

Later that evening, Joey sat across from Walt in her living room. Renee had discovered a small hidden compartment in the desk from the keeper's cottage that she'd brought home to refurbish. A log matching the ones found in the lighthouse was inside the compartment along with a photograph of a woman. The name "Mae McCorvey" scrawled on the back.

Walt held the folded page with the same tenderness. "This might be the last thing of hers I ever get to read." He unfolded it gently and patted his shirt pocket. He looked at her sheepishly. "Forgot my reading specs."

Joey scooted forward in the chair. "I could read to you if you'd like."

He hesitated, but then handed it over.

He'd likely prefer the privacy of reading it himself, hearing the words in Cathleen's voice instead of hers.

"These old eyes aren't what they used to be."

She nodded and began to read.

April 1941

I stand on the galley walk, looking over the ocean, pretending I am alone. Bleakpoint's beam, my only companion. Only when the keeper sleeps can I breathe easy. In his waking hours, I do not know how to explain to him that the world he thinks he lives in is not his reality. Sometimes I play along and let him believe that I am my mother, Mae, even though I am an unimaginably poor substitute. My father has always said she was the bravest person he'd ever known. But I am just a lonely and scared girl, handed far more scattered pieces of my father than I can hold together. If the true Mae were here, I'm sure she'd know what to do.

What illness makes you see someone not for who they are

but for who you wish they were? He is like a time traveler whose body is stuck in the present while his mind travels places I cannot follow. Why is his past so much clearer than his present? Day by day his memories of me slip away like sand on these shapeshifting Atlantic shoals. Swept off to someplace else and churned together by crashing waves until he can no longer sift through it all to find me. Little by little I am forgotten, even though I'm right here.

I wonder if I'll ever know what it is to love someone like he loved his Mae. The closest thing I know to this kind of love is what I feel for this light. This island. But that is not the love of a husband and a wife.

Sometimes I see the way Wally looks at me and I wonder what could be. My friend who is brave and kind and loyal. But I will never know. Because the moment he starts looking at me with love in his eyes, I . . .

"I'm sorry. I can't make out the rest." Water damage had diluted the ink into dark smudges.

Walt wiped at his eyes. "It's all right, gal. I know how it ends." He chuckled softly. "I know exactly what she did whenever she caught me daydreaming about a future with her. She'd convince me she had a huge fish on her line, stealing her attention from me, only to lose the catch every time. Or she'd cut out running through the live oaks, playing a game of hide-and-seek that I could never win.

"Even so, I knew she felt something for me," Walt continued. "It was her father who kept her distant, wasn't it? She talks about him like he's out of his mind."

Joey glanced to Callum's metal box that was tucked beneath the end table. Should she tell him their conjectures? "Finn and I have looked through his things. We're not experts, but—"

Her ringtone interrupted. The screen showed Finn's number. "That's Finn now. I should probably see what he wants. Tell him about the latest find." She picked up her Blackberry and answered. "Hello?"

"Hey, Joey. Did I catch you at a bad time?" There was an energy in Finn's tone that she'd not heard before.

Joey glanced to Walt. "I'm sitting here with your grandfather. Renee found a keeper's log in a hidden compartment of the family desk. It talks about Cathleen's concerns about her father's mental state. I was about to share our suspicions about Callum."

"Oh . . . okay." He paused. "Call me back after he leaves. I have some news, and I'd rather have this conversation when he isn't listening to your end of it."

Her pulse quickened. "Will do." Walt looked at her curiously as she set the phone back down on the coffee table.

"He didn't want to interrupt. I'll call him back later."

"Is it about the lighthouse project?" he asked.

"I think so," she said even though she had no idea. Why didn't Finn want Walt in earshot of her replies? It took everything in her not to shove the poor guy out the door to find out what was behind the lift in Finn's voice.

"I wouldn't have minded. It is my project, after all. I have vested interest." Was it her imagination or was that grin of his a little sly? Like he suspected that the call was of a more . . . personal nature. *Oh dear.*

"I'm with you on that one. But I'd left you hanging with what we've found out about Callum. Or what we suspect."

He raised his bushy gray eyebrows. "And?"

"From looking through his journals, Finn and I think Callum must have suffered from some sort of condition that caused his mental state to deteriorate. Possibly some form of early-onset dementia."

Walt swallowed hard. Joey reached for his hand. An anchor to hold him fast. He looked up, moisture gathering in his eyes. "Why'd she think she had to bear that alone?"

TWENTY-THREE

After Walt returned to the marina, Joey fixed herself a glass of ice water and went out onto her back porch to sit under a canopy of stars, still troubled by the pain Walt carried. If only there was some way to help him find peace, but she couldn't rewrite history any more than he could.

She picked up her phone and ran her thumb over the raised buttons. Just as Walt had taught her how a shift in the winds could predict a storm, she sensed Finn's call brought with it more than a casual chat.

She pressed her lips together and dialed his number.

"Joey?" He seemed winded.

"Yours truly. Are you all right?"

"Oh, yeah. Sorry. I was just finishing up my run before you called."

A run? The only way she could see herself running was if the fabled ghosts of Bleakpoint Island were on her tail. "Want to call me back later?"

"No, no. I'm good. Great, actually. Pops doing okay?"

"Yeah. It's been a day. Like I said, Renee found another of Cathleen's logs. From the way Cathleen talks about her father, it sounds like you were right about him suffering from dementia. There was a picture of her mother with the log, so I'm guessing she took on Mae as a sort of pen name for her rescue efforts." Joey stood and paced idly back and forth across the porch. "Reading about Cathleen's experience with her father was hard on Walt. Knowing that not only did Cathleen bear this burden alone but that she hid it from him when he would have done anything to help—"

"I quit my job," Finn blurted.

She stopped pacing and sank onto a deck chair. "What?"

"I quit the airline, and I'm moving to be near Pops. I should have done it weeks ago. I'm starting to get that this is so much more than a passing fancy with an old lighthouse." Finn grew quiet.

Joey's pulse pounded in her ears. This was it. This was the part where she would be told that her services were no longer needed. "So, what will you do?"

"Private charters. They don't offer the same stability as a commercial position, but now I can be there for Pops while this lighthouse is finished. And for whatever comes next."

"I . . . I know he'll be so glad to have you near."

His wry chuckle came through the line. "I hope so. He was really proud of the job I had. And knowing him, he'll suspect I'm trying to babysit him."

Joey shut her eyes tight, bracing herself. She should be used to being told her services were no longer needed. But this stung. Bad.

"Can you do me a favor?"

"Uh . . ." Her voice came out craggy. She blinked and cleared her throat. "Yeah. Sure."

"Can you keep an eye out for available housing? I want to keep this under wraps until I have everything settled as far as a place to stay and employment details mapped out."

She looked through the large picture windows into her living room. It wasn't home exactly, but she hadn't expected to have to leave it so soon. "There's the house I'm staying in, of course. At least, you know, for a temporary solution. I can check if they are open to something more permanent."

Silence throbbed in her ears for several long moments and then Finn coughed. "I don't think sharing the house is the best—"

"No!" She spat out the word like it scalded her tongue. "I'll have vacated the premises, of course. I wasn't implying that we should—"

"So, what? You're quitting? Is my presence *that* intolerable to you?" His voice held equal parts humor and hurt. "I thought—"

"Quitting?" She blinked rapidly, trying to find the missed turns in their conversation. "No. But you hired me because you wanted someone to look after Walt's well-being and to make sure he wasn't being taken advantage of. With you here . . ."

"I need you to stay."

I need you . . . When was the last time someone had said that to her? Joey swallowed hard, longing for the ability to rewind the conversation so that she could hear those words from his lips again.

"Pops would never forgive me if I took over your job. And I don't want to give him the slightest impression that I'm here to stick my nose in. I've made enough mistakes on that front already. I just want to be the supportive grandson. I need you as the project manager."

"All right. Sure," she managed to squeak out. Her pulse returned to something less tachycardic. She wasn't losing her job. Just her mind. Or maybe her heart. Whatever it was, she'd better get a handle on it quick before Finn noticed. Thank goodness this conversation wasn't happening face-to-face. "I'll be on the lookout. When are you hoping to move?"

"A few weeks, if possible. I need to finish up my agreement with my airline, and I'm working on getting a buyer for my condo. Shouldn't be too hard. My area in Charlotte is currently having a housing boom."

"It's too bad you can't make it for Christmas. I know Walt would have loved it."

"I know. I tried to get my schedule changed . . ."

She sighed, picturing Walt spending the holiday alone. "Maybe

I should cancel my trip to my parents. It is a pretty long trip to take just to turn around and come back."

"Pops will be all right for a couple days, and I'll make sure we have a good long phone call. If you have a chance to see your family, don't miss it." From the ardent way he spoke the words, she could feel how much he regretted not having the time with his grandfather.

"If you're sure, in regard to the property hunt, is there anything in particular you want me to look for? Location? Size? Rent? Buy?"

He rattled off his preferences while she jotted them down on a scrap of paper.

"This is good, right? Me moving there?" he asked, uncertainty coloring his tone for the first time since the conversation began. "I won't badger Pops to move off his boat or give up his project, but I'm putting down some of my own roots so that if anything changes, I'm there."

Her mind replayed Sophie's accusations that Joey lived her life as a spectator to other people's dreams, and she thought of all the work Finn must have put into becoming an airline pilot. Work that he was setting aside for the sake of someone else. Dreams were elusive things. "Walt won't like you giving up your life. Especially if he suspects that you did it because you're worried about him."

The line was quiet for a few moments. "It's flying that I love. I'm not really giving anything up, aside from company health insurance and a steady paycheck." He laughed under his breath. "You know . . . the perks of corporate employment."

"The flexibility of self-employment can't be beat though."

He cleared his throat. "My life was pretty all over the place for a season. To be honest, I spiraled after . . . well, after some life things. My job gave me structure I needed. That I've come to rely on. It's a little scary giving that up."

She tried and failed to picture the version of Finn that he described. What did spiraling mean for someone who always seemed as put together as he did? That he had a few hairs out of place?

Finn sighed. "Seeing Pops, the regrets he has, I don't know. I just don't want to have any remorse where he's concerned when all is said and done. I need our relationship to be good more than I need anything else. I'm actually getting excited about the move. I think I need this change more than I realized."

Change was coming Joey's way once again, whether she was ready for it or not.

Though she was reluctant to risk a run-in with Ida, Joey headed over to Murph's the next morning before she raced off to catch her flight to Tampa. The bulletin board was the unofficial hub for community listings.

"Be right with ya," Ida called from the kitchen as the door chime announced Joey's entrance. Didn't that woman ever take a day off?

Joey scanned the multitude of items posted on the corkboard. Lost pets. Found pets. Services offered. Services needed. She tore off a few tabs with phone numbers for For Sale by Owner listings and a couple rental properties. Now to make a quick exit.

She rounded the corner and crashed into the very woman she was attempting to evade.

"Land sakes. Where's the fire?" Ida blinked, registering who she'd collided with. "Oh, it's you. You probably do have something on fire." She gave Joey a cheeky smile.

As frustrating as Joey found the woman, if anyone knew about someone having enough of an interest in the island to steal hidden documents, it would be Ida. "You know everyone around these parts. Far more than an outsider like me." She batted her eyelashes. "Do you happen to know anyone around here with a vested interest in the island?"

Ida slapped a hand to her chest. "Oh, honey. Everyone, and I do mean everyone, is curious about that place. They want to know what really became of Callum and Cathleen McCorvey." She lowered her voice to a conspiratorial whisper. "And did Cathleen have something to do with the death of her father? Some say he kept her captive and she did what she had to do to break free." Ida wriggled her shaggy eyebrows. "They found his body. Never did find hers."

Joey blew out a breath, trying for more patience. "I meant something more than idle curiosity and tall tales. Anyone have a personal connection?"

Ida drummed her fingers on her thigh. "Nothing springs to mind. Why do you ask? What did you find?" Ida inched closer like a hungry hound eyeing steaks on a grill.

Joey took a step back. "Nothing."

If word hadn't gotten around about the missing pages from the lighthouse walls, all the better. "Just trying to learn more about the history. The *real* history." She held her palms out. "Just the basic boring facts," she added before Ida could jump in with another dramatic retelling of island lore. "Let me know if you think of anyone who knew the McCorveys or anything like that."

Ida's gaze landed on the real estate tabs in her hand.

Joey stuffed them in her pocket.

"Making a permanent move?"

Joey checked her watch. "I'd better run or I'll miss my flight. Have a Merry Christmas." She rushed out the words as she made for the exit before Ida had the chance to inquire further. If Finn wanted to keep quiet about his move, Ida couldn't catch a whiff of it. Walt would know the whole story before Joey had time to make it to the docks to hand him his Christmas card.

TWENTY-FOUR

Three weeks later, Finn was back. Joey was eager to show off the progress they'd made since he'd last visited. The stairwell was repaired and repainted. The walls of the lighthouse were prepped and ready to be replastered. Once the interior was complete—navy railing against the white interior walls with accenting brass hardware—the place would look like a dream.

Walt and his new friend Karl left them on the island to go fishing. Karl was a red-cheeked fellow a little younger than Walt who'd recently retired to Ocracoke. The two older men waved goodbye as they motored off in Karl's fishing boat.

Joey turned to Finn as soon as they were out of sight. "So, the closing on your new place is coming up quick."

He gave her a wry smile. "Yep. It's a fixer-upper, for sure. But I think it has potential." The crosswind ruffled his hair. Joey noticed it was lighter and a little wilder without the product he normally used. He looked so much more relaxed than she'd seen him before. A change that made it difficult to focus on the actual conversation at hand. She had half a mind to snap the photo of him Sophie was still pestering her about.

She wrangled her own wind-whipped curls into a messy bun, attempting to redirect her thoughts in a more productive direction.

"Your house could use some updates, but the view alone will be worth the asking price, I think."

Finn laughed, shoving his hands in his pockets. "Pops is going to have a field day harassing me when he sees it. I guess I deserve it after the way I went on about his run-down sailboat."

"What goes around comes around," she said with a grin. "If you're hiring to have any work done, let me know what you need, and I can make some recommendations. I've gotten to know a lot of the local companies. Who's most reliable, best pricing, and whatnot."

He glanced at her as they made progress in their hike to the lighthouse. "I was actually going to ask you about that. Would you want to oversee my house renovation? Unless you think it will interfere with your work here."

She had to admit that his offer was tempting. Unless Walt gave her some clue of how he'd like to use this place, there weren't many modifications left to be made. Taking Finn's offer could prolong her stay, hopefully giving her enough time to make headway with the unknowns in Cathleen's story. "Have you told Walt about the move yet?"

Finn's gaze shot to his feet as they continued. "I'm looking for the right moment. Not sure how he'll take it."

She nodded in understanding and motioned to the lighthouse. "I'm pretty close to wrapping things up here. Renee has cleaned, sorted, and organized the artifacts from the house. I have a company coming to make a few minor repairs to the slate roof and install new gutters. And in a couple more weeks, the interior of the lighthouse should be complete." She shrugged. "It'll be touch-ups from there. If your grandfather wants this property to be inhabitable, I could see about putting in a bathroom with a composting toilet. There are some really unique ways we could make this off-the-grid house livable. But if he wants it more as a monument to days gone by, there's no need for those updates."

Finn slowed to a stop, and she followed suit. "I've tried asking about his hopes for the place, but all I get from him is that he wants to make things right. And when I ask him what that looks like, he says, 'When I know, I'll know.'"

"Well, if that isn't clear—"

"As mud." Finn laughed as he finished her sentence.

Joey pointed to the lighthouse. "He mentioned wanting to get the galley walk replaced so that it's accessible."

Finn's brow creased. "Does he want to go up there or something? Can he even manage those stairs with his knees?"

"I don't know. As of yet he's barely set foot inside the keeper's residence or the lighthouse."

"That man is something else." Finn crossed his arms over his chest. "Do you have anyone lined up for the galley walk?"

"There's a company located on the mainland that specializes in ironworking that I've been consulting with regarding the stairwell. They've offered to come out and give an assessment free of charge."

Finn gave a nod. "Okay, then. Here's what I'm thinking. Since Pops won't give us a straight answer, dream up a couple of scenarios on how this place could be used in the future. Draw up estimated costs for those modifications whether it is modernizing the keeper's residence, building new buildings, or simply restoring the place and leaving it alone. All of it keeping within the original budget that Pops has for the project. We'll present the options and let him make final decisions on what he wants."

"I can do that." It would take a little bit of legwork to draw up various plans that Walt might not even want, but that sounded better than waiting while the clock ran out on her contract. "Do you want to go up in the lighthouse? The new glass has been installed and that view is incredible."

"Sure."

They circled back to the lighthouse and climbed the stairs, both slightly winded when they reached the top.

Finn pressed a hand to his chest. "Whew. Those lightkeepers

must have been in good shape. I run every day, but that still got my legs burning."

"No kidding. But you have to admit the view is worth it."

They stood side by side and turned a slow circle. A 360-degree view of the sound and sea, a narrow strip of sand running in between. Dunes on the ocean side, maritime woodlands and marshes on the other. This land was wild and free. An untouched paradise.

"That might be the most beautiful thing I've ever—" When he turned to her, his words cut away and he swallowed hard. "Seen."

She took a small step back, not sure what to make of the way he looked at her. Was it anything more than an overflow of the emotion roused by the natural beauty around them?

She'd seen hints of this look before—when they'd made a new discovery about Cathleen's life or unraveled some bit of the McCorvey story. But they'd been so fleeting it had been easy to dismiss them as nothing more than Sophie getting into her head.

She turned away from him, gesturing to the ocean waves. "It's like being in a different world." It was only natural that two single people such as themselves might feel some sort of attraction, but that didn't mean either of them should act on it. She was here to get a job done, and according to the mysterious ring Finn carried—and hints Walt had dropped—Finn had some baggage he wasn't quite ready to work through.

He touched her shoulder, startling her from her thoughts. "There's a red boat heading our way."

Joey turned to where he pointed, then gasped. "It's the same one from before." They peered out the window, watching its approach. Instead of driving around to the cove they suspected the trespasser had hidden in before, the boat headed straight for the place Walt normally docked.

Joey turned to Finn. "What do you think they want?"

There was tension in his jaw, causing a muscle to twitch in his cheek. "Best if they don't get the chance to disembark before we find out." He hurried down the stairs and Joey followed. At the bottom of the lighthouse, she grabbed the battery-powered nail gun sitting on top of the toolbox.

They made it to the dock just ahead of the boat. Joey strained her eyes. What sort of person were they up against? The figure sat hunched, a hood shadowing their face from view. "Let's see if they're willing to talk."

Finn looked at her and his eyes widened. "What are you going to do with a nail gun? Coerce them?"

Her cheeks heated. "I don't know. I panicked. I thought, you know, we might need some backup. Or something . . ."

He stifled a snicker. "Well, the battery pack is missing, so a lot of good that will do."

So it was. She managed a smile despite her frayed nerves. "Knew I should have grabbed the hammer."

He shook his head, laughing under his breath. But the momentary lightness disappeared from Finn's face as the vessel drew alongside the wooden gangway. Finn straightened his stance and crossed his arms over his chest. "Can we help you?" he asked over the growl of the motor.

Either the pilot couldn't hear or they'd chosen to ignore the warning in Finn's tone.

The person stood, the tall lanky form unfolding and the hood falling back to reveal a young man who looked to be in his late teens. He took a shuffle-step forward, a rope in his hands. "Mind helping me tie off?" His voice was low and quiet. He tossed the rope and Finn caught it.

"First we'd like to know your business here. This is privately owned property. We've had some issues lately with *someone* having unauthorized access, you see."

The kid cut the motor and faced them. His stance was defensive, but his eyes reminded Joey of a hunted animal.

She hid the useless nail gun behind her back, wishing she could drop it and the ground would swallow it.

The kid's gaze darted from Joey, to Finn, and back. "I'm sorry. That . . . that's why I came. To say that I'm sorry." He took another shuffle-step forward, a walking cast on his foot hindering his stride. "I have something I need to return." He lifted a backpack. "Permission to come ashore? Please?"

TWENTY-FIVE

"This was a terrible time of day to go fishing," Walt's friend Karl said after they'd put down anchor. He grabbed a couple of cola cans from the cooler and passed one to Walt.

Walt laughed as the boat bobbed on the gentle waves. "Fine. I'll admit it. I wasn't really fishing for fish."

Karl popped the tab of the can and took a long swig. "If you're a fisher of men, you ought to know this soul has already been caught and is safe and secure with Jesus."

"Good to know, but I wasn't fishing for souls either. I needed an excuse to leave so that my grandson and Joey could get a little time to themselves without me underfoot."

Karl placed his cola in a cupholder and kicked back in his seat, cradling the back of his head in his clasped hands as he stretched out his legs. "Ah. Now I see. You've used me as an excuse so you can play Cupid." He raised his eyebrows. "Matchmaking is a dangerous game, my friend."

Walt grinned. "I'm not matchmaking exactly. Just providing them a little time to get to know each other one-on-one. What will be will be."

"Sure," Karl said.

"Tell me you didn't catch the way they kept sneaking glances at each other when they thought the other wasn't paying attention."

Karl sat up and grabbed his drink. "I don't know anything about that. Didn't you say the other day that things had been a little rocky between you and your grandson? I'm not sure meddling is going to do you any favors. He can likely manage his love life without assistance."

Walt scoffed. "Don't be so sure. Nearly a decade later, he's still hung up on that ex-wife of his. They got married for all the wrong reasons, so that wasn't a great start. Add to that that they were too young and immature to deal with what life dealt them." An ache throbbed in his heart. "Not that any marriage knows how to handle losing a child. But they were just eighteen."

Karl's eyes widened. "Eighteen? That's a tough hand to be dealt."

Walt stood and stretched, looking to the lighthouse. "He and Joey might not be 'meant to be,' but she's good for him. I'm getting glimpses of the old Finn. And if a little time together on that old island reminds him that there is still life to live, then my foolhardy plan to rehab the place will be worth something. I can't go back and take the chances I missed. But if I can encourage Finn to start taking chances again . . ." He shrugged.

"What about you?" Karl asked. "You've still got to live life too. To take chances."

Walt bristled. "I sold everything I own, bought a fixer-upper boat and an entire island. Sounds chancy to me."

Karl waggled a work-roughened finger at him. "Yeah, but was that 'cause you were living in the present or chasing the past? There's a big difference."

"You don't know a lick." Walt growled good-naturedly, side-stepping the ring of truth in Karl's words. "Wait 'til ye're my age. All I got is past. The future is but a blip."

Karl busted out in laughter. "I'm nigh on seventy."

Walt sat back down and crossed his arms over his chest. "Ye're just old enough to *think* ye're old. Wait 'til ye're eighty." He'd had a fella tell him the same thing on his seventieth birthday and thought he'd try the line out on old Karl.

His friend shook his head, still laughing. "You're somethin' else, Walt. And maybe you're right. But the way I look at it, as long as you've got enough breath in your lungs to blow these Carolina skeeters away from your face, then the good Lord still has something in store for you earthside."

"Oh, yeah? What's He got in store for you?"

"Well, for today I reckon He saw fit for me to spend the day with this old codger I met down at the market and remind him that any decent fisherman knows not to go out this time of the day if he wants to make a good catch."

Walt glanced in the direction of Bleakpoint. The sun glinted on the water. "I don't know. Might be just the right timing for the kind of fishing I'm doing. He blinked and rubbed his eyes. Was that a boat tied off at the dock? He raised his binoculars. A small, vacant vessel bobbed in the water. Three people stood a few yards off, obscured by the foliage. "We need to get back. They could be in trouble."

"Walt, Finn can handle his love li—"

"There's an unfamiliar boat at the dock, and I don't have a good feeling about this."

With his feet on terra firma, the kid opened the backpack and held out a three-ring binder to Joey.

She passed the useless nail gun to Finn who gave her an incredulous look before he shrugged and set it on the ground.

The kid took a tiny shuffle-step forward in his walking cast. Again, his hood slid back, and he pulled it lower around his face. He couldn't be more than sixteen or seventeen. "This is for you."

She glanced at Finn. The temper of a disgruntled honey badger came to mind. *I guess I'm playing good cop.* "Pardon the lack of introductions. We were caught off guard by your arrival. I'm Joey Harris, the project manager here on Bleakpoint. Like my friend Finn here said, we've had some trouble on the island so we're a little on the jumpy side." She paused. "And you are?"

The kid's eyes darted around like he was scoping out escape routes. "Just . . . here. Take this. Please." He shuffled forward again, pushing the folder into her hands. "I'm sorry for what I did. At the time I thought I was doing the right thing, but I read them, and this isn't the kind of thing that should be forgotten. Even if it means I lose everything."

Joey took the binder from the boy's hands and opened the cover. Page after page of Cathleen McCorvey's writing carefully tucked into protective plastic sleeves. "*You* took them? Why?"

The boy edged back toward his boat. "Doesn't matter. You've got them back." He quickened his pace.

"Hold it right there." The authority in Finn's voice made Joey jump even though she wasn't the one it was directed toward.

The boy froze. He glanced to the boat, back at Finn, and to the boat again. Anguish passed over his face. That wiry kid would have been gone in the blink of an eye had it not been for that walking cast.

"You've trespassed, stolen property, and I'm guessing started a fire that could have been devastating to the property or injured someone," Finn continued. "And you expect us to let you leave without explanation? What's your name, kid?"

The boy's face crumpled. "P-Peter."

Finn crossed his arms over his chest. "Peter, what?"

She wanted to signal Finn to throttle down. The kid was obviously petrified, and he had brought the stolen log pages back. No lasting harm done. But then again, she did want answers, and Finn's tone was all they needed to hold the kid in place.

Peter dropped his chin and his shoulders slumped further. "H-Hall." He wrapped his arms around his middle, making Joey want to step in and give him the hug he so obviously needed. "P-please don't call the cops. I know I should have never done the things I did. And I brought the stuff back. Everything. I promise—" He swallowed, looking like a spiky seed ball from a sweet gum tree had lodged in his throat. "I promise never to set foot on this island again. Just . . . please don't report this."

Joey glanced to Finn and saw concern briefly soften the hard set of his jaw. She stepped between them. "Peter, can you help me understand why you did what you did? And why you're back now?"

He lifted his chin, his eyes searching hers, the tiniest ember of hope flickering to life. He released the vise grip around his middle. "I love this island. I know it's not *mine*, but it's been abandoned forever, and so no one cared that I came here. When I saw work happening, I panicked. I knew this place was going to get torn to pieces just like before. Condos or, I don't know, turned into some sort of tourist destination."

"Before?" Joey motioned to the dock. "Why don't we all have a seat and you can tell us more."

He edged back from them a fraction. Joey could feel the weight of the stories he kept locked tight in the emotions that played across his face.

She gently turned the plastic protected pages. "You've taken such good care of these, Peter. Thank you." They now had dozens of entries to scour for clues to the truth. "We think that the writer was a childhood friend of the man who bought the property. We're so grateful to have these back."

The sound of a motor broke the tenuous thread that held him in place. Peter hobbled away. She expected Finn to make him stop again, but instead he watched him leave, his brow furrowed. In less than a minute, the boy had unmoored his boat and sped off in the opposite direction, sure to be hidden in the twisting marshy estuaries in mere moments. Karl's fishing boat moved their way at a fast clip.

She turned to Finn. "You let him go."

"So did you." He shrugged. "He's just a lost kid. And he returned what he took."

She chewed her lip. "But why take them in the first place?"

Finn shrugged. "He said he was worried about the place becoming a tourist locale. I guess he saw your interest in them, and I'm sure he knows all the old stories about this place. Maybe he was trying to scare you off?"

Walt called from the boat. "Are you two okay?" Finn picked up the nail gun from the ground, and they walked to him.

Walt's eyes roved over them like he was assessing them for injury. They widened at the nail gun in Finn's hands and the binder in Joey's.

Joey smiled. "We got Cathleen's stolen papers back."

"It was just some kid," Finn added.

"I don't think he'll bother us anymore," she added, hoping she was wrong.

Karl laughed. "So not the romantic afternoon you were hoping for, Cupid?"

If looks could kill, Walt's glare would have incinerated Karl on the spot.

Uh-oh.

TWENTY-SIX

That night, Finn and Walt sat on the sectional sofa in Joey's living room.

Joey was seated between them, with Peter's binder on her lap. She opened the cover and turned the protective plastic pages. "He took really good care of these. I'm impressed." She looked over a few more pages. "They all seem to be in order by months too." She went back to the first entry. "Ready?"

Finn nodded and Walt made some unintelligible reply that Joey took as affirmative.

Over the next hour she and Finn traded turns reading, trying to find anything that confirmed Walt's belief that these were written by Cathleen's hand. Walt needed no convincing.

As they read stories of rescuing boats stranded on the shoals and braving storms that ripped the coastline, Walt's eyes shone with pride. And when they read the other entries, written by a lonely girl who felt that she was erased, bit by bit, as her father's memory faded, his eyes glistened with unshed tears.

Finn closed the binder and rubbed his tired eyes. "We'd better call it a night."

Walt sat straight and blinked as though emerging from a trance. He looked at his watch. "We have a little more time, don't you, Finn? Enough time to finish?"

Finn stretched. "I'm exhausted, Pops. I know you are too. Maybe it would be better to face whatever is in these final logs after a good night's sleep."

"Do you think I'd sleep a wink, lying there knowing Cay's last words still waited?" Walt quipped. "You head on out if you want. Joey and I will finish up."

Finn checked his watch again, gave Joey a sidelong glance, and settled back in his spot on the couch.

Joey opened the notebook.

January 19

From the lighthouse galley, I saw the explosion on the Atlantic. That sized vessel had to have been a freighter full of supplies making its way to Allied Forces. But what happened? Surely not the enemy. Not this close to American soil. I know Pearl Harbor, just last month, was American soil too, but that seemed worlds away to me. This is my back door. It must have been some sort of accident. I hope.

Walt propped his hands on his knees, staring at the space between his feet. "I remember that night. My mother's knickknacks were jarred right off the mantel. We learned later that it was *The City of Atlanta*, just seven miles away. Sunk by a U-boat. If you didn't believe it before, this note proves it was written by Cay."

Joey nodded in reply and turned to the next entry.

March 21

Radio broadcasts speak of events an ocean away but don't breathe a word about the ships I've seen burning just off Bleak-point's shore. Does the rest of America have any idea what goes on here? How much longer can the threat be denied? When German boots make prints in our golden sand? Or, I should say, what was once golden. Now it's slick with oil, tainted with wreckage. Bodies. Can't they send forces to protect the ships? Or at least the innocent civilians trying to make passage?

I do what I can, looking for the few survivors under the cover of darkness. But it's not more than a drop of salve on a catastrophic wound that won't cease its bleeding. In the chaos and confusion, I'm hardly noticed. If anyone reads the official logs, it will be my father recorded to be out searching and not I. There's too much panic, fear, fire, and smoke for any person to soundly confirm or deny his presence.

Father remains much the same. Strangely, these terrifying times have calmed him, and I've been seeing more of the man who raised me than I have for quite some time. We were surprised by a visit from his supervisor yesterday. The man gave no indication he noticed anything amiss as he gave my father the new radio equipment that we're to use if we see any suspicious activity.

I thanked the Lord for His mercy with the supervisor. But is it wrong to be thankful for succeeding another day in this deception? Surely I did not receive the Lord's help in that. But then I think of the story of Rahab, and I'm not sure how to parse it all out. Is deception allowed if it's for a good cause? And what counts as a worthy enough cause to merit a lie?

Walt growled. "Foolish girl. Trying to hold all that trouble in her own two hands. Trying to protect her father. Keeping watch as if she was the only thing standing between the Nazis and American soil."

Joey stared at the words on the page, feeling the full weight of them. "I wonder if it was more about her trying to hang on to the life she'd loved." Hadn't that been why Joey refused to take charge of her father's company? And why she'd stayed in Copper Creek even after all the people she loved had left? Because it would have been like hammering nails into the coffin of the family life she was supposed to have had. "Being a lightkeeper was ingrained in her father's identity. And hers. I think she was doing everything she could to keep from losing him completely."

Walt clenched his hands into fists resting on his knees. "But she did lose him. And I . . . I lost her. If only I'd known."

Joey put her hands over his. "It wasn't your job to save her either though."

Walt looked away. "If not mine, then whose? Who else in the world was going to have her back? I've replayed our lives over a thousand different ways, asking myself what if I'd done this or that." His words were so garbled by emotion that she could hardly make them out. He grabbed a tissue from the side table and blew his nose with a resounding honk. "I thought I was doing some brave thing by going off to sea, but the braver thing would have been to stay when the girl I loved needed me."

Finn had been so quiet Joey had nearly forgotten he was still there. Finally he spoke, "Would you really undo it all if you could? If saving her meant erasing everything. Your life with Gramma, Dad, me?"

Walt loosened his clenched hands and stared at them as though they held a mystery. He shook his head. "Regret is a strange animal, son. It makes you create alternate realities inside your head with hindsight as your guide. You long for those imaginary outcomes until it's a sickness. But there's also another side to regret. Remembering its pain made me love your gramma more fully, embrace every moment with your dad and with you. Take nothing for granted. Because I knew how much it cost to get it wrong."

Slowly he traced a thumb over the scar on his hand. "I should've died the night my ship was hit. Sometimes I have this dream that it was her who saved me. Swimming my wrecked body to shore. But it couldn't have been. When I came to in the hospital a week later and asked after her, my mother told me that Cathleen and Callum McCorvey died the night my ship went down." A tender smile softened his features. "I like to think it was her spirit comforting

mine as my life teetered in the balance. A sign she forgave me."
He shrugged. "I don't think that pans out theologically, but the
dream has always brought me comfort, nonetheless." He gestured
to the binder. "What else does she say?"

Joey turned the page and began to read.

June 20

I've fought wind and waves on stormy seas and near-about
lost my life on more than one occasion. Anything to keep my
father's secret and his post at Bleakpoint secure. But nothing
has filled my heart with more dread than the command we've
just received. Not because of the enemy threat off the coast of
my beloved home, but because my own father might unwittingly
play accomplice to the Germans lurking beneath the surface
of the sea. I just don't understand why this order has come
now. Because the trade routes have shifted? The bombings
have nearly ceased anyway. Is this simply phase one in shutting
down this old lighthouse? I knew it would come one day, but
never thought so soon.

They say the light that used to save souls from the ever-
changing shoals now illuminates the silhouette of merchant
ships being targeted by the German U-boats. In our unpopulated
area, we are near-about the only light source, and it's simple
to eliminate it and give ships safer passage through our area. I
understand. I do. But will my father? That shining light has
always been something I could point to, to prove to him everything was all right. Even in his worst moments.

I am trapped between two miserable options. Confess the
problems my father has been having and tell them I've been
forging documents and functioning as the principal keeper of
Bleakpoint Light. Or continue. For two years I have devoted
my life to these waters, rescuing countless souls. I've inadver-
tently become something of a legend. Devoted daughter by day.

Saint-Mae by night while he sleeps. Does it really matter who completes the task as long as it's done?

The more time that passes, the more I know giving up my life at this lighthouse is the right choice—and the harder it becomes to abandon the course I've chosen. What will happen to me when the authorities find out how long I've forged official documents? And what of my father? They'll think him insane.

My father told me once that the day he was no longer capable of keeping the light burning, he'd just as soon walk into the sea and let it swallow him whole. I believed him then, and I believe him now. And as I watch him lose more of himself, little by little, I know that I am not ready to let my lightkeeper father go. Nor am I ready to lay Saint-Mae to rest. So I hang on a little longer, hoping a better answer finds me.

I continue this false life that feels more true than the one I am supposed to be living.

Walt stood and paced. "I remember the lighthouse beam right before the torpedo hit." He pinched his lips tight until they nearly disappeared. "Fool that I was, in that split second before everything was blown to bits, I thought that burning beacon meant she'd forgiven me. Loved me even."

Joey clasped her hands in her lap. "I don't think we'll ever know her state of mind that night, but I don't think she hated you for leaving. Not really."

Finn sat back against the couch. "She was just scared. Her father was forgetting her, day by day. She kept her true identity hidden. And she thought there was no way you, the person who knew her best, could make it back alive."

Walt paused his pacing. "I wouldn't undo these past sixty-five years, Finn. But if there was one thing I could fix, it would be the way we parted."

TWENTY-SEVEN

"How's Walt doing today?" Joey asked Finn as she cruised down Highway 12, one hand on the steering wheel. On her day off, she had gotten a permit to do some beach driving. But what she had not planned on was Finn inviting himself along.

"You know how he gets with me," he replied. "He said he needed to work on his boat. Alone."

"You're sure you shouldn't have stayed behind? Pushed him to talk through it a little bit? It's been a week." Hearing Cay's hardest moments all lined out on paper had been hard on the man, but surely he needed to open up at some point.

Finn gathered the paperwork she'd left on the dash that had shifted when she made a turn. "Sometimes a body needs some time alone to sort everything out." He tapped the cockeyed stack against his thighs to straighten them and then tucked them in the crevice between the passenger seat and center console. "At least Pops and I do. So, when he told me to go with you, I listened."

"He told you to come with me?" She wasn't sure what to make of that slight sinking sensation that came with learning Finn joined at Walt's urging instead of originating from the man beside her.

He shifted in the passenger seat. "He was worried that you'd get stuck on the beach. It happens to a lot of tourists, and it's pricey to get towed."

She shot him a glare that she hoped thoroughly conveyed her annoyance. "I did my research. I've got my tire pressure gauge in the glove box, and I know the right amount of air to let out so that I don't get myself into trouble. I didn't ask for assistance."

He shrugged sheepishly. "I told him you'd be fine." Sunlight glinted off the smooth surface of the gold ring he rolled between his fingers. Something he seemed to do whenever the situation grew tense. "I wish you'd just told me if you didn't want me to come." Was that a tinge of hurt in his tone? So maybe he hadn't come just because Walt told him to.

She sighed. "I sorta just flashed back to our first meeting. I thought we'd finally gotten past that, and your statement about being worried about me—"

"*Pops* was worried about you," he interjected. "I didn't even know getting stuck was a thing. I've driven on Florida beaches many times, and apparently it's nothing like here. But he schooled me on the finer points of beach driving before he let me leave this morning. The man should make instructional videos."

They chuckled over the thought, but then Finn grew quiet. He was still fidgeting with the gold band, but when he caught Joey looking his way, he closed his hand around it. Maybe today would afford an opportunity to unearth the significance of the talisman he carried.

He gave her a wry smile. "I don't think Pops's nudging was all about the beach driving. He's gotten it in his head that you're a good influence and knows your time here is limited. I think he's trying to keep you around me as much as possible."

She laughed lightly in response, though she didn't feel it. What was her problem? She wasn't seriously interested in Finn. Was she? Why did it sting every time he hinted that he was by her side at Walt's behest and not his own? She shrugged it off. She wanted to be project manager of Bleakpoint Light, not of Finnegan O'Hare's life. But that didn't mean she wasn't curious. "You seem to be doing just fine on your own. I don't think you need my influence."

Finn gazed out the passenger window. "I went through some things right out of high school. Kind of lost myself there for a while." He glanced at her with a sheepish expression. "A long while. Pretty much up until I quit my job a few weeks ago. Weirdly, it feels like I'm coming out of a fog. Seeing life in a different light."

She nodded. "Just when you think you finally figure out what you want from life, life goes and flips the script on you."

Finn didn't reply for several minutes. Finally he said, "Pops isn't wrong. You have been good for me. You have a way of making me see that I was existing over these past several years, not living."

Joey squeezed the steering wheel tight. How could she do that for another person while still struggling to fully dive into her own life? Existing on the sidelines of the party, as Sophie claimed.

She was about to attempt a deeper dig into Finn's past when she noticed someone just ahead cleaning up trash in one of the beach access parking areas. Someone with a walking cast on his left foot.

She braked, slowing the truck to a crawl as her heart rate quickened. "It's Peter." They hadn't seen the kid since he disappeared from the island a week ago, and there were so many things she was dying to ask the teenage boy who had so carefully preserved Cathleen McCorvey's words.

"Are you sure it's him?" Finn asked. He certainly looked like a different kid in his white T-shirt and red ball cap, focused on a task instead of skulking under an oversized hoodie.

"One way to find out." She parked and rolled down the window. "Peter?"

The boy stiffened and then turned in the direction of Joey's voice. She waved and smiled, hopefully conveying friendship and not creepy-stalker-ready-to-pounce-on-her-prey. "It's me. Joey. From the lighthouse."

He stared at her, garbage bag clutched in one hand, trash grabber in the other.

She got out and hurried over to him. The passenger door closed, and footsteps sounded behind her. "We read the stories," she said.

Peter took a small shuffle-step back. "Like I said, I'm really sorry for the trouble I caused." He glanced over his shoulder and lowered his voice. "Please. Please don't report what I did. I know I don't deserve to be let off the hook for trespassing and taking things." He swallowed hard. "And the fire." He dropped his chin. "But I can't get in trouble again."

"Again?" Finn asked as he drew to Joey's side. She shot him a glare signaling him to drop the accusation from his tone.

Peter's face crumpled a bit, and he turned away from them. He heaved out a breath that could be heard over the ambient wind and waves, then he stepped closer, his voice coming out a raspy whisper. "That other time, I didn't do anything wrong." He lifted his booted foot. "Caught in the wrong place at the wrong time with the wrong people. I had no idea my old friends from home had planned to do what they did. Didn't deserve to take the fall for them either, but I did. And I know I deserve punishment for the stuff at the island, but if you turn me in, it will go on my record. I'll lose everything. I'll never get out of this place." He lifted the trash grabber. "Can't you count this as time served for the crimes I actually did commit. Please?"

Joey's heart clenched at the ache in Peter's voice. It wasn't up to her, but how she wished it was. She glanced at Finn, relieved by the compassion softening his features. Gently, she asked, "If you knew what it could cost you, why did you do it?"

Peter stabbed at the sand with the trash grabber. "I . . . I've lost a lot over the past few years, and when I thought I might be losing that island too, I . . . I panicked. It was so stupid." His gaze darted over their shoulders. "I need to get back to work. Like I said, trouble is something I can't afford."

"I can't thank you enough for returning the letters, even knowing it could make things worse for you," Joey said. "The man who bought the property cares about protecting the island's history, so I'm trying to collect all the stories I can for him. The notes inside the lighthouse walls belonged to a friend of his who died during the war. Bleakpoint was her home. I was hoping to learn more about your connection to the island since it seems to mean so much to you too."

A look of confusion passed over Peter's face. "A couple of years back, my great-grandmother started talking about that island. Telling me stories. Later, when I was forced to move to Ocracoke, going there helped me feel close to her again. And then I read those stories you found, and they sounded an awful lot like the ones Nana Kit used to tell me. And I wondered if what she'd told me had been true." He glanced behind him again. "Look, I don't want to be rude, but I'm supposed to meet up with my supervisor at my next location in, like, five minutes, and I'd best have something in my bag to show for my time."

"Hang on one more second." She jogged to her truck and grabbed one of her cards while Finn waited with Peter. She passed it to him. "When you're done for the day, will you give us a call?"

TWENTY-EIGHT

Walt sat in a back corner of the deli with the papers that Joey had given him about potential plans for the island laid out across the booth. Head spinning with thoughts of the past instead of the proposed future, he returned the project outlines to their folder and took a long draught of his tepid coffee.

As much as he had hoped that restoring Bleakpoint Light would give him some sort of closure, this whole ordeal had forced him to relive every mistake he'd made with Cay. From this vantage point of sixty-five years in the future, every wrong turn he'd made with her blared like a neon sign.

His sleepless nights aboard *Cay's Song* had become endless replays of the past. And when he finally slept, he dreamed of making critical decisions in an attempt to alter the course of his and Cay's history. But every night he'd wake, trapped in a fixed existence in which the past could not be undone.

Was that why he had such a hard time envisioning a future for the lighthouse? Because if he had to move on, he had to finally accept the ugly ending to their story.

He'd been convincing himself that he'd let her go for decades. After his many months of recovery, he'd boarded another merchant ship and made harrowing journey after harrowing journey, burying his grief in work and sea spray. And when that was done, he buried himself in Martha's ample love and ready affection.

Walt smiled to himself as his thoughts turned to his grandson. Unlike himself, Finn seemed to be truly learning to make peace with his past. He'd overheard him and Joey talking about his plan to move here. Pleased as he was, Walt hoped the boy wasn't making a mistake on his account.

He smacked the front of the folder with his scarred hand. That lighthouse still had life left in her too. He just had to figure out what it ought to look like. He reopened the folio and thumbed through the options. There was a certain appeal to Joey's idea of creating a one-of-a-kind event venue. Cay's island certainly would make a breathtaking backdrop for a wedding, the joining of hands and lives on those pristine shores. A place of coming together instead of tearing apart.

Or the isolated world of Callum and Cathleen could open to embrace families coming to spend a week away from all the hustle and bustle of real life in a place that was tucked away from the rest of the world in the wilderness, where they could play like he and Cay once had.

He stared at the last proposal, a historical site dedicated to the lives of Callum and Cathleen. Would Cathleen have wanted their lives on display for all to see? She who worked so very hard to keep her father's struggles a secret? Who saved others under the cover of night, never taking credit for her heroism?

She'd hate that.

But it didn't change the fact that she deserved recognition for the way she'd risked her life for others time and time again.

Walt paid his bill and walked outside, his thoughts returning to Finn and his plan to move here.

When he'd bought the island, he'd expected to spend his twilight years alone with only occasional visits from his workaholic grandson. He hadn't minded Finn's rare visits when Martha was still alive. But he couldn't deny that the past several months had been awfully lonely. And when Walt's decisions caused strife with Finn, he'd feared he might lose the little time they shared. But the mettle of their relationship had been tested and there was still something left.

He had Joey to thank for that.

With any luck Finn would wake up to the fact that Joey was quite the catch. He'd seen the little sparks between them when they'd worked together figuring out the clues Cay had left behind. And he loved seeing lightness return to his grandson's spirit. He wondered though, had Finn revealed his past to her yet? He wished he would.

Joey's pickup pulled into the lot, flecked with salt and sand. She waved out the window. "Hey, Walt! Chip at the marina said we might find you here." She parked the truck and she and Finn hopped out. Joey's cheeks were tinged pink, and both had hair tousled by their beach-driving adventures. "We saw Peter," she said. "He told us that the entries from the walls were the same as the stories his great-grandmother told. There must have been someone else that Cathleen confided in. We're going to talk with him more tomorrow and he said he'd share what he knows about his great-grandmother's life. Maybe she knew what really happened the night Cathleen disappeared, or at least has a good idea."

Walt nodded, not having the heart to diminish the excitement in her eyes.

He might not know exactly what happened to Cathleen McCorvey that night, but neither did anyone else out there. The stories that Peter's relative told were a coincidence. A conflagration of the legends transformed into bedtime stories with just enough similarity to those documents for the boy to believe them to be one and the same.

Cathleen McCorvey had always been an island unto herself.

Later that evening, Walt and Finn walked to Joey's house. Finn had a sack of groceries in his arms.

"So, Joey here said she'd teach you how to cook, eh?"

Finn nodded, shifting the paper sack. "Yeah. I . . . I can't live off diner food from the Salty Sand Witch forever. I . . . I'm moving here, Pops. I bought a house. It's not much to look at yet, but . . ."

Walt raised an eyebrow at him. "You sure you know what you're doing? It's an awful big change from what you're used to."

Finn shot him a nervous smile. "Which is why Joey offered to teach me to cook."

Walt nudged him and winked. "You could just keep coming over to Joey's."

"*Pops*," Finn warned.

"What?"

"Seriously, you're not upset about me moving here?"

He'd never confess that he hadn't been too keen on the idea when he'd first overheard the plan. "Why, no. Not if you're sure it's what you want. I know Joey will be happy you're around. She seems to have taken a shine to you despite you being a royal pain in the rear."

Finn shot him a good-natured glare. "I'm here because I want to be near you. Joey's likely leaving here in another few weeks, unless you decide on a plan that will keep her here the full six months."

Walt shrugged. "She might be persuaded to stay. You never know. I know you like her."

Finn gave a resigned sigh. "Sure. She's sweet and kind. Gracious. Truthful."

"Good-looking?" Walt grinned.

"Pops!" Color crept up Finn's neck, and he quickened his pace a fraction.

Walt forced his legs into a couple of shuffle-jog strides to catch back up. "What? Ain't she?"

Finn chuckled. "Well, yeah."

Walt dropped the smile and put his hand on Finn's shoulder. "Have you told her about Cassie? The baby?"

Finn scrunched his face and shook his head. "Hasn't come up. She doesn't want to hear about all that mess. Besides, it's ancient history."

"That ancient history has influenced a whole heck of a lot of your life. Besides. I'm not thinking about her wanting to hear it, I'm thinking about you needing to tell it. Uncork that bottled-up stuff and let it air."

They climbed the steps of the stilt house. Walt rapped on the door.

"And take it from me," Walt continued, "that Joey is a good listener."

As Walt was finishing the statement, the door popped open. "Why, thank you, Walt. I knew my ears must've been burning for a reason. Glad to hear that it was compliments not cutdowns." A surprising hint of bitterness flavored that last bit.

"I can't imagine anyone having a harsh word for you, gal. And if they do, give 'em my number and I'll set 'em straight."

Joey's musical laugh filled his ears. "I might just take you up on that. Come on in, guys. Finn, you found everything on the list?"

"Yes, ma'am. Ida says hi, by the way."

Walt entered with Finn following in behind.

"You went to Murph's for ingredients?" Joey asked over her shoulder.

"She was at the grocery, shopping with another lady."

"Ah." She took the bag from Finn's arms and started laying everything out on the counter.

Walt settled on a barstool across from Finn and Joey as they worked together in the kitchen. Some sort of shrimp dish seemed to be on tonight's menu.

Joey glanced up at him from chopping some tiny purple onions. "Have you had a chance to look over the proposals?"

Walt nodded. "I have but . . . I don't know . . ."

"Any that we can rule out or any you're leaning more toward?" Walt's chest tightened. "Still thinking."

Kindness radiated from Joey's gaze. "No worries. I was just wondering. I'm excited about this final phase of the project." She refocused on her cooking tasks. To Finn, she said, "Oh, I think that's probably enough pepper. You don't want to overpower the shrimp."

Finn looked up at her, brow creased in worry. "Did I ruin it?"

She grinned. "Nah, I like a little heat." She turned her attention back to Walt. "What was it like here when you were a kid? Different, I imagine. Care to entertain us with tales of the past while we cook?"

Walt braced his hands on his knees. "Anything in particular you want to know?"

Joey scrunched her face in concentration. "Hmm, we've read a little about Cathleen's point of view of the battleground off these shores. What was it like for you? Your family?"

Though a lifetime had passed since, it was funny how quickly he could pull up those memories. Like bookmarks in an oft-read tome.

"It was some wild times. Seeing ships burning in the night. The sounds." Walt shook his head. "The sand slick with oil. Pieces of ships washing up on shore. Wrecked lifeboats. Bodies."

Joey's head jerked up. "Bodies?"

Walt squeezed his eyes shut, banishing the gruesome picture that flashed in his mind. "Yeah."

"Weren't people scared?"

"Sure. But the Outer Bankers are a tough lot. They lived way out here in a place that almost felt like a separate country in a way. They were used to hard living and harsh realities. Natural disasters. Catastrophic shipwrecks off these shores certainly weren't a new thing. Most people, even if they were scared and suspicious, kept their heads down and kept on with living." He cocked his head to the side. "Strangely, one of the things that made the reality of war set in wasn't the torpedoes but having certain places restricted for civilians and all the government men showing up. Like I said, this place was so far removed from the rest of the country that we weren't used to people telling us where to go or where to be." Walt shrugged. "So, sure it was really scary. But then it became almost normal. I wonder if the kids in Europe or the Pacific who had war knocking on their door felt the same way. Scared and uncertain, but also trying to go on with life as usual."

"It's wild that I never learned about this in school. Other than Pearl Harbor, World War II was always talked about as something that happened far away."

Finn had abandoned his food prep entirely. Unexpected warmth invaded Walt's chest at his grandson's rapt attention.

He continued. "People were urged to keep it hush-hush. Loose lips sink ships and all that. There were mounted patrols and trigger-happy watchmen. Even the locals would pitch in trying to help find survivors from the freighters and oil tankers."

"And after seeing all of that, you wanted to get on board those same ships?"

Walt stood and walked to the large windows facing Pamlico Sound, remembering what it was to be sixteen. "I was tired of watching everything happen without being able to do a durn thing to make it better." He scoffed. "And I was young and dumb enough to look at the wide blue yonder and feel like disasters were things that happened to other people. Not fearless *men* like me." He came back to sit at the stool. Finn and Joey worked in quiet harmony. Like two pieces of a puzzle that fit together. But maybe he'd worked up this connection in his mind because Finn favored him in looks, and Joey, with those dark curls, reminded him of Cay. "It sure didn't take long for reality to catch up. I wasn't fearless, and I wasn't much of a man yet either."

TWENTY-NINE

The next day, Peter's eyes roved over the laminate menu like a starved creature surveying a feast while he sat across from Joey and Finn at the diner.

When the server came, he mumbled that he'd like a double-stack cheeseburger, fries, and a chocolate milkshake. He looked at Joey apologetically, and she gave him a reassuring nod and ordered the same. His curved posture straightened a little.

Finn handed over his menu and ordered a side of fries. "I don't know how you're going to eat all of that," he said to Joey. "We had lunch an hour ago."

She nudged him under the table and gave him a pointed look. "Just watch me." She'd never be able to compete with a teenage boy's appetite, but she was at least going to try to put Peter at ease.

She turned her attention to Peter. "I was intrigued when you said that the stories you read were familiar to you. Stories your great-grandmother told you, right? Did she ever tell you where the stories came from? Or how she knew them?"

Peter fidgeted in his seat. "When my mom was alive, she and my gramma would take me to Nana Kit's retirement home. One day she started telling me stories, but only when I was alone with her. It was our special thing. Then she got real sick. She kept telling me the stories, even in front of my mom and gramma, but she seemed confused and acted like these things weren't stories. Like they'd actually happened to her. It made my gramma Mae real upset."

The name Mae collided with Joey's heart, making her pulse quicken.

"Gramma Mae stopped the visits. She said it was too much for Nana Kitty." Peter blushed, then cleared his throat and resumed speaking, his tone suddenly half an octave lower. "That's what I called her when I was little. Everyone called her Kit, and I guess I turned Kit into Kitty, so . . ."

Joey ducked her chin in an attempt to hide her grin. The obvious affection he had for his great-grandmother juxtaposed with his attempt to come across as grown was just too cute.

The server brought over their milkshakes and Finn's Coke. After she walked away, Peter resumed his story. "Mom snuck us in to see her a few more times, but then Mom's cancer got too bad. Mom said she didn't know if Nana's stories were true or not but that my great-grandmother was in a lot of pain and telling the stories seemed to bring her comfort. I dunno." He shrugged and took a sip of his milkshake, then aimed a hopeful glance Joey's way.

Oh. He thought that her not reporting him to the police was dependent on the information he was able to share. She rushed to alleviate his distress. "Thank you for sharing what you know, Peter. You don't have to worry. As long as you don't trespass or take anything else that doesn't belong to you, we're not going to file a report." She looked to Finn, knowing she'd definitely spoken out of turn.

Peter nodded but slumped in his seat.

Finn propped his elbows on the table. "You mentioned some previous trouble you were mixed up in. Enlighten us."

Ugh. Finn and his cursed practicality. It made sense to make sure the kid wasn't a repeat offender, but Peter sure seemed like a good-hearted kid who loved his great-grandma.

"Before my mom died, I lived in Hatteras," Peter said. "Beautiful land that had been in our family for years and overlooked the sound. After she died, my stepdad sold it to a developer. Our house was torn down and a bunch of vacation rentals piled on top of each other took its place. Mom would've been heartbroken to see it." Moisture shimmered in the kid's eyes. He dragged his forearm across his face. "I got the stupid idea to go back one night and see the construction site. Met up with some kids I knew from my old school, told them how angry I was. I guess they got the wrong impression of what I planned 'cause they brought spray paint." Peter ducked his chin, his focus on the laminate table. "Cops came, they ran. I fell and messed up my ankle real bad. They found me. I even had paint on my hands from trying to take the paint can from a buddy of mine." He sighed. "I was given a bunch of community service and told it won't go on my permanent record as long as I don't get another strike against me. But . . ." He swallowed hard. "I know I did wrong on Bleakpoint Island. A lot more wrong than I did at that construction site. And I know I don't deserve for you to just let me go like nothing happened, but if this goes on record, I could lose my scholarship. And if I lose that, I'll never make it out of here." He chewed the corner of his lip. "I know it doesn't excuse what I did, but I thought I was about to lose that island like I lost my mom's house, and I panicked. I'm so tired of the important things in my life getting erased like they don't matter."

Joey's heart twisted at the sorrow and pain in Peter's voice. She glanced at Finn, relieved to see that compassion had softened his expression.

"I'll talk to my grandfather," Finn said. "But I don't think he'll mind if you visit the island on occasion. Maybe you could just give us a heads-up if you plan on being there?"

Peter lifted his chin, his expression wide-eyed and hopeful. "I can do that. Just tell me who I should call. That's . . . thanks . . . really . . ." He took a deep breath, and his eyes closed, the tension smoothing from his face.

Finn drew his mouth in a tight line. "I *would* like to talk to your father though."

"No!" Several people in the diner turned their direction at his exclamation. He lowered his voice. "He's my stepdad, not my dad, and it shows if you know what I mean. He'd just as soon report me himself. I'm three months from turning eighteen, so can we please leave him out of this?" His hands clutched his milkshake glass.

Joey reached across the table and gave his tensed forearm a squeeze.

Finn held up a hand. "I hear what you're saying, but you're obviously going through a tough time, and I don't feel right about not letting someone in your life know what's been happening at Bleakpoint. Someone who can check in with you and help you stay on track." The pain reflecting in Finn's eyes caught Joey by surprise. "I promise the decisions you make in these next few years can set the course for your life. And you need people in your corner. Trust me. I've been there."

What Joey would give to be sitting alone at this table with Finn right now. To discover what lay beneath the conviction in his voice. But it was Peter she needed to rescue in this moment. "Your grandmother? What if Finn spoke with her instead of your stepdad?"

Peter raised his gaze to meet hers. "Better her than him. But I haven't seen her since she and my stepdad got into it at my mom's funeral." He bit his lip and shook his head slowly. "I'm sure she'll be thrilled to hear how great I've turned out. And that I've been trespassing on the same island my great-grandmother carried on about."

"You said her name is Mae?"

"Yeah."

"Did you notice how all the notes in the wall were signed Mae?" Joey couldn't hold back her curiosity. "Do you think they are connected to her somehow?"

Finn squinted in thought. "Can't be. The entries were written in the early forties. That would have to have been his great-grandmother's time, not his grandmother's."

Joey propped her elbows on the table and leaned forward. "But maybe his great-grandmother knew Cathleen McCorvey and her connection to the name Mae. Maybe Peter's great-grandmother named her daughter Mae to honor her friend."

Peter fidgeted in his seat. "I don't know about all that, but I suppose you can ask her when y'all tell her about what's been going on with me. Just a warning though, she may not be real thrilled with you asking her about anything that has to do with that island."

Finn's brow creased. "Do you know why?"

"I think she was just scared Nana was getting confused. Mixing up reality with myths and legends. People around here believe all sorts of stories. Some real, some a little out there. But for Nana Kit"—he sucked air through his teeth—"spreading rumors and gossip—always a big no-no in her book. And that's putting it lightly. So I guess when she started talking about those old stories and about Bleakpoint, it scared Gramma—like she was losing her mom. I guess it's tough, feeling like you're losing your mom—whether you're fifteen or in your fifties."

THIRTY

Joey parked in front of Finn's new stilt house. She'd promised to stop by and help him put together a plan to remodel after finishing up her day at Bleakpoint.

She was happy to consult with him on preparing a place he and Walt could someday share. Though it was across the street from the sound, it would still have an incredible view.

As she was about to exit her truck, an unfamiliar number lit up her phone screen. "Hello?"

"Hi, there. Is this Josephina Harris with Events by Josephina?" The Southern drawl coming through the line dripped with molasses.

Who in the world? Joey straightened in her seat. "Yes. Yes, it is."

"Wonderful. My name is Lacey Nichole, and my family and I just spent the weekend at the most *darling* bed-and-breakfast. The moment I stepped into the town square, I knew it was the place I was destined to be married. My fiancé is a musician up in Nashville, making a name for himself and all that. But I just want my weddin' to be somethin' simple and sweet, and Copper Creek is everything I want."

Nashville? Musician? Did Sophie have secret connections she hadn't spilled? Joey attempted to collect her swirling thoughts as Lacey prattled on. "You know, nothin' real fancy. About eight hundred in attendance."

Joey choked. "Oh, okay." Not what she'd define as simple, but an event with that number of attendees would certainly resurrect her business.

Lacey squealed, and Joey pulled the phone back from her ear. "So you'll do it? Cara said you were the go-to wedding planner around there."

Cara? She racked her memory. Joey switched ears and rubbed the one Lacey had squealed into. "I'm sorry, did you say Cara recommended me?"

"Yes, ma'am. The lady with that adorable gift shop? Said you were the only one she knew of that could handle an event of that size."

Oh. The newcomer who'd felt so bad about not using her for her grand opening soiree when old-timers threatened to blacklist her. Joey smiled at the hint of vindication shooting through her.

"We're hoping for an October wedding, which I know is a bit short notice," Lacey continued.

Joey pulled her calendar out of her bag. February. "Eight months is doable." Her mind had already sprung into action, cataloging all the vendors that needed to be booked.

"Could we get together and meet before I leave town?"

That put the brakes on her racing thoughts. "Lacey, I'm honored you called, but I'm actually working on something out of town at the moment."

"Oh, that's okay, honey. I can come another time."

An odd blend of anticipation and dread churned in her middle. This wedding was exactly what she needed to return to Copper Creek. She glanced toward Finn's house. But was that what she really wanted? "I'm about to go into a meeting. Can I call you back?"

"Shoot, yeah. No rush. Although I guess it's a little rush with the time crunch." Lacey giggled. "Boyd and I can't wait to tie the knot."

Joey promised to call as soon as she had a chance before saying goodbye and exiting the car with her legal pad in hand.

She crossed the street and began taking notes on the issues she identified with the house. The front deck that overlooked the sound sagged a little bit in one place. That would need to be addressed sooner than later. She continued walking the perimeter of the house, ideas for autumn centerpieces competing for her attention as she noted drainage issues in the modest yard.

Finn came down the set of stairs, looking relaxed in a fitted T-shirt and ball cap. He lifted a hand in greeting. "I didn't hear you pull up." He motioned to the notepad in her hand. "I have the home inspection notes inside. Save you some time."

She nodded. "I'll take a look, but I like to make my own assessments before I look at someone else's work." She flipped a page on her legal pad. "I'll hurry and wrap this up so I can get out of your hair."

"I only meant to save you some work." He lifted a shoulder. "I'm in no hurry for you to go."

Was that a hint of longing in his voice or just an echo of her own heart? She volleyed the wayward thought and pursed her lips. "I'm just surprised you wanted a girl for a job like this."

His face reddened. "You're never going to let me forget that, are you? I was worried about Pops's entire project being a disaster no matter who took it on. And I'll admit I was a little thrown, and I shouldn't have assumed you were a man. Because it doesn't matter. But you not being the person I expected paired with my worry about Pops—" He tugged at the brim of his ball cap, adjusting it slightly. "Let's just say you didn't catch me in one of my finer moments." He winced.

She held up a hand, laughing. "Just giving you a hard time." Joey wriggled her eyebrows. "And maybe I feel a little victorious, having won you over. Going from last resort to first pick is quite the career jump."

He shoved his hands in his pockets and stared at the ground.

"Won me over is an understatement." A soft smile curved his lips as he lifted his chin to meet her gaze. "You'll impress me even more if you can get Pops to settle on how he wants to finish out the lighthouse project."

She shook her head. "I'm starting to think he'll just leave it as is. But I'm sure the two of you can figure things out without me if he ever decides." In another couple of weeks, she'd have technically completed the four-month contract. Then she'd be free to return to her hometown and prove herself once again to Copper Creek via Lacey's huge wedding.

Finn nudged a piece of gravel at his feet. "Do you think you . . . I mean would you consider extending your contract if Pops did make a decision and it needed a little more time? Or maybe you're in a hurry to get back . . ."

As much fun as she'd had pouring herself into Walt's project and Cathleen's mysteries over the past several weeks, she couldn't afford to pass up the opportunity to plan this wedding. With the business she'd bring to the town through all the visiting wedding guests, how could they still look at her like she was the enemy? And why hadn't she thought of marketing herself as a destination wedding planner for Copper Creek? It was genius. She looked at Finn. "You're here now. As long as you keep an open mind and don't let fear dictate how the two of you talk through issues, what do you really need me here for?"

Finn stepped closer and took her hand, causing her heart to stutter-step. "You're good at your work. Excellent, in fact. I'm sorry for the times I minimized your role. I underestimated you, and I underestimated how important this project is. I understand now, and I'm sorry." The vulnerability in his eyes and the earnest tone of his voice pricked her heart. Thoughts of Copper Creek all but vanished.

She squeezed his hand before releasing it, the warmth of his touch lingering. "Well, um, thanks. It means a lot to hear you say that." She glanced back to the house, needing a little space to process what she was starting to feel for her boss-slash-client-slash-supervisor-slash-friend. "I'd better get to work on writing up notes for your project before it starts getting dark."

After she'd finished up her walk-through, she took a seat at a barstool at the island in a kitchen that begged to be brought out of the 1970s. Finn pulled a couple of colas from the fridge and sat across from her.

"The biggest expenses are going to be the repairs to the decking," she told him. "I'd get on that quick, because as of right now, the current structure can stay. But if you leave the issues unaddressed for much longer, they're going to compound the problem and you'll end up having to replace the entire thing." She tapped her pen on her notepad. "Another expensive ticket item is making the house wheelchair accessible. The ramp system won't be cheap. But that is something that probably can wait." She gestured to the walls and sucked air through her teeth. "This burnt orange and olive wall paper on the other hand . . ."

"Sure makes a statement," he finished before popping open his can.

She laughed. "That was kinder than what I had in mind. I say we start peeling now."

Finn grinned, but then the humor faded from his features. "Pops would have a fit if he knew I was building a ramp for him, much less entertaining the idea that he won't be living out the rest of his days on that boat of his." He shrugged. "And who knows. Maybe he will. But if things ever take a turn, I want to be ready."

Joey warmed at the tenderness in his voice. "When it is all said and done, I hope he'll feel loved knowing that you made it a priority to help him live out some of his dreams and remain close. That's a beautiful thing."

Finn absently turned the cola in his hand. "It's nothing when I think about how that man has been there for me through thick and thin. He and my grandmother, recent empty nesters, ended up having to cancel all their retirement plans and start all over again as parents when mine passed away. Raised my hardheaded self, and Lord knows I didn't make it easy. Especially when the teen years hit." He rubbed his jawline. "Even through my lowest moments, Pops was so understanding. I guess he knew a thing or two about choices you wish you hadn't made and things you wish you had control over but didn't." He forced a laugh. "I'm just as bad as he is. Clinging to things I wish I could undo or do differently but can't."

Joey picked at the tab of her drink, making a metallic *tink*. "Do you want to talk about it?" She didn't want him to feel like she was prying, but she couldn't deny the curiosity she felt about the man who fidgeted with a wedding ring he never wore.

He gave her a pained look. "Not particularly. But looking at Pops in his eighties still carrying his regrets"—he swallowed hard—"maybe I ought to give the talking thing a try."

He gripped the can until it emitted a resounding crack. She put her hand over his clenched one.

He stared for a few moments at the place her hand rested and then began. "I fell hard for a girl in high school. A girl that I was convinced would never notice me. But she did. And when she did, she became my whole world. Friends, sports, family. I dropped it all for Cass. Pops and Gramma tried telling me to be careful. You know, not awaken love before its time. To take things slow. As you can imagine, my seventeen-year-old self thought I knew better. Thought I could handle my life without their interference." He grimaced. "Cass ended up pregnant at the tail end of our senior year. I was scared, of course, but I loved this girl, and I was so sure that even though this wasn't how I planned to kick off my adult life, that it would all work out fine. Because I thought . . . I thought Cass loved me like I loved her. Maybe she did . . . or maybe marriage was a way for her to feel better about the choices we'd made. I don't know.

"I proposed. She said yes, even though her parents didn't approve. The minute we were both eighteen, we tied the knot at the courthouse. I got a job making decent money. It wasn't flight school like I'd planned, but I had the girl of my dreams, and we were going to have a baby. Life might have been happening out of the order I had been raised to do things in, but we were going to make things work."

Finn fell silent, the ache holding back his words throbbing in Joey's ears. He lifted his gaze, unshed tears glistening in his eyes. "We lost the baby when she was thirty weeks, a little boy. Doctors couldn't explain why."

The tremor in his voice tore at Joey's heart.

"She moved back home with her parents. And I was left sitting alone in an apartment, one-half of our living room turned into an empty nursery." He scrubbed his face with his hands and sighed.

"I'm so sorry," she said. How she wished she had something more substantial to say, some way to ease his pain.

"Pops and Gramma were by my side when my matchstick life toppled, even though I'd spent the past six months acting like the north end of a southbound donkey. I'd rejected their counsel and acted hateful when they tried putting boundaries in place," he said. "I was free to go back to my original plan, to attend flight school. But I didn't feel free. I was drowning in emotions too big to handle, so I worked so hard I didn't have to feel them anymore. At least that's what I told myself."

"And now?" she asked.

He lifted a shoulder. "I think I am finally ready to stop punishing myself for the choices I made as a teenager. Forgive mistakes God forgave a *long* time ago. And I want to give back to Pops what he gave me. Patience. A listening ear. Kindness. I want to help him find the closure he's after. In his own way and his own time, supporting him right where he's at.

"I know I didn't go about things the right way at the beginning, but you have to understand that I was seeing a side of my grandfather I'd never witnessed before. I thought I was losing him. But

I was really gaining a side to him I hadn't been privy to before. And you're the one who helped me see that."

Did that mean her work here was done? One family restored. Maybe it was time to return to Copper Creek and reestablish her family's reputation. Because if she couldn't have her own family back together, at least she could have Copper Creek and the memories it held.

THIRTY-ONE

A couple of days later, Joey, Finn, and Peter boarded the ferry to Hatteras in Finn's Audi. They'd finally wrangled Peter into choosing a Saturday to make the trip to see his grandmother.

Joey turned around in her seat to check on him. The kid looked like he was on his way to get booked at the police station instead of to visit the grandmother he hadn't seen in months. He shifted his long legs that were folded at odd angles to keep from kneeing her seat.

"I wouldn't have minded sitting back there," she told him. "I'm much shorter than you. Plus, with that walking cast, you can't be at all comfortable."

He shrugged. "I'll be in enough hot water as it is. If I got caught making a lady ride in the back seat . . ." He sucked air through clenched teeth.

The way Peter acted about this visit, meeting Gramma Mae might be something akin to facing down a hurricane. Then again, maybe he just hated the thought of disappointing her. "So you were close with your grandmother?" Joey asked. "Before you moved to Ocracoke?"

"Yeah. She lived nearby. I could bike over. And when Mom got sick, she was always there helping her. My stepdad didn't handle all that real well."

"She doesn't come to Ocracoke?"

"Nah. My stepdad told her she wasn't welcome at our house at Mom's funeral, and I guess Gramma thought she ought to respect that." Peter huffed. "My momma was a good woman but not so great at picking out men."

Joey twisted the end of her curl. "That must have been tough. A fight happening on that day."

She glanced back at him.

He picked at a cuticle while looking out the window. "Gramma wanted me to live with her. My stepdad refused. I guess he won the argument because I've been stuck with him for the past year. All he cares about is having access to the money my mom put aside to help with raising me. Not that it's all that much." Peter ceased his assault on his cuticle and wrapped his arms around his middle.

"You said your mom's house was family property, right? Your grandmother didn't own it?"

"No. My grandma is actually my bio dad's mom. He decided being a husband and father was too much for him, but thankfully Gramma Mae still wanted a grandson. Or, at least, she used to."

How painful, knowing that someone he cared so much about hadn't fought harder to remain a part of his life. At least that was how Joey would have felt had she been in his size 10 sneakers. "I'm sorry."

Peter made some soft, unintelligible sound in reply.

In an attempt to lighten the mood, Joey turned to Finn. "I can't believe you didn't want to take my truck."

He snickered. "If four-wheel drive isn't required, I'm not going to be caught dead in that eyesore of a vehicle. I didn't know they made them that color."

She smiled. "For the record, it wouldn't have been my first choice, but it was a gift from my dad when I started my event planning business. A free truck is not the sort of thing you turn your nose up at just because the color isn't your favorite."

Finn shot her a doubtful look. "If you say so."

"It was his way of giving me his blessing about starting my own thing instead of taking on the family business."

Finn glanced her way again as he pulled into the ferry line. "Why didn't you? You seem to love this type of work."

She shrugged, the nonchalant action incongruent with the stabbing sensation in her chest. "It wasn't my place. It was supposed to have gone to my brother. He and Dad had talked about that transition since he was a kid. But then he and Dad had a falling out. I felt like if I accepted Dad's offer, Trey wouldn't have a reason to come back. I guess I also thought that if I said no, my dad might try harder to repair their relationship. He sold the company instead."

"Did it bother you that your dad didn't plan on selling it to both of you?"

She shook her head. "You'd have thought it would, but it didn't. I preferred being the shadow that followed my big brother around instead of the main one in charge. I'd probably still be project managing for him if he'd stayed." She stared out the window, sifting her thoughts. "I think . . . I think Events by Josephina was my attempt at proving to myself that I could do something on my own. Something that was totally mine." And still somehow her business had gotten tangled up with Harris Construction. But Lacey's wedding could change all of that.

She still hadn't told Finn what had happened with her father's business after it sold. She glanced back at Peter who had a troubled past of his own. Maybe it would help in some small way to let him know that she understood what it was to be innocent but believed to be guilty. "When Dad sold the company, he sold it to a new guy who had moved into the area. Said his background was in construction. Turns out there was a reason he'd moved towns. He'd bought Dad's company with stolen funds on incomplete jobs in another state. The work he actually completed in Copper Creek was poorly done, costing homeowners and business owners thousands to get it redone correctly. And others didn't even get their jobs started. He took their money and cut town, off to find his next victims."

Finn tapped his thumb against the steering wheel, a solemn look on his face.

She went on. "Even though the only thing Dad did was unknowingly sell to a thief, the Harris name was attached to the business and people blamed him. Maybe they thought he made a quick buck selling the company, not caring how the new person would treat them. Maybe the name Harris left a sour taste by association.

"People canceled their events with me," she continued. "They snubbed my mother in the grocery store. Sent anonymous letters to my dad. Even attempted to sue him because the other guy skipped town and my dad was the one still around. It didn't go anywhere legally, of course. But those things take a toll. My dad had been proud of his good name." She stole another glance at Peter who was listening with rapt attention. "It's a big reason I wanted this job here. To get out of the mess for a little while."

With all the cars in place, the ferry motored away from the dock. Finn remained quiet by her side, and she wished she could read his thoughts. She'd hoped that by now she'd have built up enough trust with him that he wouldn't doubt her integrity. He rolled down the windows letting the crosswinds blow through the car.

She turned to him. "Maybe I should have mentioned it sooner. I just . . ."

"Didn't want to give me another reason not to hire you?" he finished with a crooked smile.

"Something like that."

"Anyone who's spent even a little bit of time knows that you take way too much pride in your work to take on a job you couldn't finish well."

Unexpected moisture welled in her eyes at his kind words. She looked out the window, even though her view was blocked by the ferry's tall cockpit, and blinked back tears. Too bad the very town she'd grown up in hadn't been able to recognize that. "Thanks." The word came out raspy.

"For?"

She looked at him. "For saying that. For trusting me with your grandfather's project."

He smirked. "I don't know if I should get a thanks for that. Pops strongarmed me, and you earned the trust."

She shrugged. "I had the trust of the people of Copper Creek and did nothing to lose it, but they still turned on me."

"They're stupid," Peter said from the back seat.

Joey turned in her seat. Peter's eyes blazed.

"I feel that way sometimes too," she said. "But they aren't stupid. They're hurt. That guy did some real damage to the people there. One woman, Margaret, almost lost her bed-and-breakfast. That house has been in her family since the 1800s. Others lost thousands of dollars. And while I've had my share of frustration at people's unwillingness to see reason, I've carried the blame they put on me too. If I would've said yes to my dad, none of this would've happened to them. When people are hurt and scared, they aren't always able to reason through things well. They can't see past the pain and fear."

Peter crossed his arms over his chest and leaned back against the seat. "It's still wrong."

"Sure." And maybe it was time to kick the proverbial dust from her sandals and move on. Or maybe it was time to hold her head up high and remind them what she was made of.

Joey unbuckled her seat belt. "This view might be commonplace to you, Peter, but it's still brand-new to me, so I'm going to go to the rail and see what I can see."

Finn followed suit. "The new hasn't worn off on me yet either."

"It'll never wear off," Peter said. "Not in a million years."

The three of them exited the car and stood by the rail, pointing out shoals and stalking marsh birds. Finn pulled a gold band from his pocket, clenched it in his fist for a few long moments before dropping it into the gray-green waters of Pamlico Sound.

His eyes found hers, and she offered a gentle smile. She wasn't quite sure what that act of release meant to Finn or what turn in the conversation had led to this moment, but it sure seemed a weight had dropped from his shoulders when that ring hit the water.

It was a feeling she craved for herself, but she hadn't quite figured out which facet of her life she needed to let go of and which to hang on to.

THIRTY-TWO

After they disembarked at the Hatteras terminal, Peter guided them on the route to his grandmother's house. His rhythmic heel taps on the rubber floor mat gave away his jittering knee.

How were they going to navigate the conversation with Mae from telling her about Peter's misadventures on the island to nudging her into talking about what she knew about the place? Joey suspected that none of this conversation was going to come easy.

Finn parked in front of a small white cottage in need of a fresh coat of paint. It was nestled in a grove of live oaks. Sunshine filtered through the leaves, speckling the house with shadow and light. It was far enough from the main thoroughfare with all the packed-in rentals that it felt like it was all to itself.

She turned to Peter. "Ready?"

He made some noncommittal utterance and flipped his hoodie over his head. Poor kid was nervous as a cat in a room full of rocking chairs.

Joey exited the vehicle as a woman who looked to be in her mid-sixties stepped out onto the front porch. "You'd better turn yourselves around. The rental property is the next driveway."

Finn stepped closer and gave a friendly wave. "Hello. Are you Mae?"

"Who's asking?"

Joey shot a glance over her shoulder at Peter. His shoulders crept higher.

"You didn't tell her we were coming?" she hissed.

"Um."

Finn pushed Peter to the front of their group. "Wrong move. Fix it, dude."

He shot Joey a "somebody save me" look and then called out, "Hey, Gramma. It's me, Peter."

The woman peered at him, her eyes growing wider by the moment. "Sakes alive. It *is* you. Who are these people with you? Who have you brought to my door unannounced?" She tugged her housecoat tighter around her.

"Our apologies, ma'am," Finn said. "We didn't realize our visit was unexpected. We'd be happy to come back another time."

She harrumphed. "I haven't seen that grandson of mine in near-about a year. You folks wait here while I freshen up a bit." She struck a match and lit a series of citronella torches lining the porch, then she disappeared into the house but was back a moment later with a damp cloth in her hands. "Peter, wipe down the chairs. We don't want your guests sitting on cobwebs and dust." There was a sternness in her voice, but her watery eyes gave away how affected she was by the sight of the boy she obviously adored.

She looked at Finn and Joey who were now congregated at the foot of the porch steps, shooting each other uncertain glances. "When Pete finishes up the chairs, feel free to take a seat. I'll be out in a jiffy." The woman disappeared back inside, and Peter went to work wiping down the rocking chairs. Joey and Finn joined him on the porch.

Finn crossed his arms over his chest. "You seriously didn't tell her we were coming? What if we came all this way and she wasn't home?"

Peter didn't look up from his task. "I called once and she didn't answer," he mumbled.

Joey's mouth dropped open. "Voicemail?"

His hood fell back revealing red-tipped ears. "I don't do voice-mail."

Finn and Joey exchanged a look of commiseration. What was the deal with the rising generation and their aversion to voicemail?

Finn shrugged. "Maybe the saltwater taffy will at least sweeten her disposition."

"Oh! I forgot about those." Joey jogged back to the car and retrieved them from the center console. Joey's parents had taught her never to show up empty-handed at someone's home. Hopefully Mae liked taffy as much as Peter said she did, because they were going to need all the help they could get.

Time ticked by. Peter, Finn, and Joey sat side by side, the chairs creaking softly as they rocked. Joey studied the writing spider in the eaves who worked diligently on its web.

"Do you think she forgot about us?" Finn asked.

Just then the door swung open and Mae stood before them with a loaded tray. She was dressed in a pair of slacks with a button-down blouse tucked in. Her leather mules clacked as she stumped across the porch. "Sorry to keep you folks waiting. I've got some coffee for the grown-ups. Cream and sugar are there so you can fix it the way you like it." She leveled a look at Peter. "Chocolate milk for you, young man. I made it just the way *you* like it. Extra chocolate, whipped cream on top."

Peter groaned. "Gramma, I'm nearly eighteen. I drink coffee all the time." The corners of his mouth twitched upward.

Mae scoffed. "I told you when you were knee-high to a grass-hopper, no coffee at my house until you are officially an adult. I stand by it."

She and Peter laughed quietly, some story from their shared past somehow wrapped up in the moment. Mae placed the tray on a small table and straightened. "Now mind yer manners, Peter, and introduce me to your friends here."

Fidgeting with the cuff of his hoodie, he said, "This is Finn and

Joey. They . . . uh . . . they've been doing the work on Bleakpoint Island."

Joey stole a look at Mae who stiffened at the name of the island. "That's the place—"

"Nana Kit started talking about all the time," Peter finished. "Yeah. Finn and Joey, this is my grandmother, Mae." Finn and Joey stood and shook her hand, each expressing how nice it was to meet her.

Joey handed her the box of taffy. "A little thank-you for taking the time to chat with us."

Mae arched a brow. "How nice." Joey understood the confusion. What kind of guests didn't call ahead but brought gifts?

They settled back in their seats while Mae busied herself handing out steaming mugs. Once they'd been served, she sat, hands propped on her knees, peering at them over her glasses. "It's been nigh on a year since I heard from you last, and here you've turn up out of the blue with people I've never met." She raised her drawn-on eyebrows. "Where's that stepdad of yours anyway?"

Peter shrugged. "Work."

"Rick doesn't know you're here?"

He shook his head.

"You in some kind of trouble?" She pursed her lips. "Besides that nonsense you got yourself into up near your old place." She glanced to the walking cast on his foot.

Peter cringed.

"Yeah, I heard about it." She scoffed. "How big do you think this island is?"

"I didn't—"

She held up a hand to stop him. "I know you didn't. Knew that afore you said it, 'cause I know you."

Peter's face reddened, and he jerked his gaze away from her. How much harder would it be to tell her of his exploits on Bleakpoint after her unwavering vote of confidence?

Peter started fidgeting with the cuff of his hoodie again, fingers trembling. "I did do something else though. Joey and Finn here said that I had to tell somebody in my life what had been going on with me, and I didn't want it to be Rick."

Mae's gaze darted to each of them, and Joey made sure to keep her expression calm and open. When no one said anything, Mae's attention refocused on Peter. "Go on, then. Spill it."

He heaved out a breath. "When I lost Mom, I didn't just lose her. I lost you and Nana Kit. I . . . I was really alone. You know how Rick is—about as good company as a fence post, and that's on a good day. I didn't have anything better to do, so I walked around and picked up odd jobs around the marina. Working on boats and such. This old guy lets me take one of his older boats out as partial payment." His gaze darted to his grandmother and then back to the floor. "You hear a lot of chatter, people coming and going, tales people tell to entertain the tourists and whatnot. But at one point, I heard the name Bleakpoint Island and remembered that that was the same place Nana Kit told me stories about."

Joey snuck a glance at Mae, her expression growing pained.

Peter continued, "So I started going there. After school. On the weekends, I told Rick that I was going to a friend's house, but I spent nights camping on the island, walking around imagining the stories Nana Kit told. Or sitting beneath that old lighthouse imagining what it would have been like to be called upon to put my life at risk to save another. Even though I didn't live there, it became mine." He glanced at Finn and then Joey, an apology in his soulful brown eyes. "But then people started showing up and work started happening on the island. I panicked. I'd lost Mom. I'd lost the only place I'd ever known as home. Then I lost you and Nana Kit. I couldn't lose that island. It was the place I went to pretend nothing had changed. That you and Mom were waiting for me to return home. It made me feel close to Nana and the stories she told.

"I hung around out of sight, trying to figure out what the plans for the place were. And then Joey found something in the lighthouse and seemed really excited about it. I knew that if what she found answered even one of those questions people had about that old island, nothing was going to hold back the tourists." Peter paused, his face crumpling. "So I, uh . . . set a fire as a diversion to get a look at what Joey had found."

"You wha—" Mae interjected, but Peter barreled on, seemingly determined to get the entirety of his story out.

"It was one of Nana Kit's stories. When I stepped inside the lighthouse I saw where Joey scraped away the plaster between the stones. I came back later and worked until I had uncovered every last note. And I stole them."

"Oh, Peter." Mae pressed a hand over her mouth.

He dropped his chin. "I know it was stupid, but it felt like even if I lost the island, I'd still have a little piece of it all to myself. But when I read them, I knew what I'd done was wrong. I mean, I know stealing is wrong. But I guess I thought the action was all right as long as it was for a good cause—taking what belonged to Nana Kit.

"But if those stories were real, if someone did all of these brave things, they needed to be recognized, not hidden. So I mustered up some courage of my own and brought them back." Peter lifted his chin, resolve glinting in his eyes. "The letters or journals, whatever they are, they were signed with your same name. They were the same as the stories Nana Kit told. Do you know why?"

THIRTY-THREE

Walt strolled the island he and Cay had once claimed as their own. He stilled when the breeze washed over his face, imagining it carried her laughter like it had when they were children playing hide-and-seek. Cay always had a solemn bent to her, so he'd made it his unspoken mission to coax laughter out of her every chance he got.

One thing that could get her going without fail was his attempt to play the mouth harp he'd won in a high-stakes poker game one day after school.

His tongue found where he'd chipped his front tooth, making it slightly uneven with its pair. He'd been sitting on the sand of this very island, around a small campfire they'd built, attempting to play this newly acquired instrument. He'd positioned it wrong in his mouth and caused the flexible metal tongue to collide with his tooth. It smarted, but he barely felt the pain over the song of her laughter. "That's what you get," she'd told him. "The preacher done warned you boys that gambling was a sin."

He'd given the mouth harp to her on their last shared day on the island. He'd pressed it into her hand wishing it was a ring and a promise. But he dared not ask a question he already knew the answer to.

Walt shut his eyes tight, but the memory played like a picture show projected on the insides of his eyelids.

Cay withdrew her hand, confusion wrinkling her brow. "What's this?"

He shoved his hands in his pockets to hide their shaking and attempted a smile. "You know what it is."

She peered up at him, her Pamlico-green eyes holding the tiniest spark of humor, a joy that had been missing for far too long. "It's that ridiculous instrument you play." She held it out to him. "So play me somethin'."

His eyes roved over her, committing her to memory. Heaven and earth, she was beautiful. Wild as the marshes. Faithful like the barrier islands between a roaring sea and a placid sound. "Keep it safe for me, Cay. Keep it and remember the laughter it brought on the days I'm not here to do it."

All traces of humor dropped from her face. Her chin quivered. "What are you saying, Wally?"

"They need men on those freighters, and they've said they'll take me. I ship out in a couple weeks."

Her eyes widened in fear for a fraction of a second before they narrowed into slits of steel. She pressed her palm to his chest. He could feel the cold metal harp between them. It might as well have been a dagger.

"You're lying. Take it back." Whether she meant his words or the harp, he couldn't say.

"It's done, Cay. I have to go where I'm needed. And as much as I want that to be here with you, you've made it clear it's not." He swallowed, trying and failing to rid himself of the tightness growing in his throat. "I'll come back for you. I promise. And if things have changed, maybe the two of us—"

"Go on, then," she rasped. "Get yourself blasted into fish bait. Why should I care more about your two-bit life than you obviously do?" She squeezed the harp tight in her fist and then shoved him hard enough to make him stumble back. "Go!"

"Cay, please. I love you."

Her chest rose and fell as she gasped for air. She chucked the harp as hard as she could, and it disappeared into the sound with a plunk. "Well, I don't love you."

All sound was sucked from his ears save for the reverberation of her words, colliding with his heart, mirroring the rippling water where she'd sank the harp.

"Goodbye, Cay." He managed the whisper before he backed away, the anger on her beautiful face forever sealed in his mind.

Walt took a shuddering breath. Even then he'd known she hadn't meant those words. That it was hurt and fear talking. Fear he better understood from this side of things. Day by day, she was losing her father and with it her island home. And at the same time, she lost the boy who made laughter reign despite her world of trouble. The boy who was supposed to remember her even if the whole world forgot.

Walt continued walking the winding path until he reached the old, knotted tree. He ran his hand over the bark. "There you are, old friend. So glad to have finally found you." He had tried to locate it on his previous trips, but time and change had thrown him off course. He'd begun to wonder if the tree still stood.

He peeled away a piece of dead bark blocking the oblong hole in the trunk. How many notes had they passed in that hollowed-out space? Messages tucked into a tin can. A few words of greeting, or plans to meet up, or a poorly written but heartfelt verse about the sand and sea and sky.

Walt stepped closer and pulled the mini flashlight from his hip pocket. What if he'd somehow missed the old tin message can on that final trip? Not likely, but it was fun to look.

Not long after he'd healed from his injuries, he'd come back with the hope that there might be a final letter from her. Something, anything, to hold on to. But he'd found the hollow empty as their last goodbye.

He used a stick to poke through the decaying leaves and twigs.

His pulse quickened at the metallic sound that met his ears. Could it be?

He reached carefully inside and grasped the old coffee can. When he tilted it to work it out of the hole, a clank rang out. Not only was the missing can back, but there was something inside it.

He took a step back and let out a cry as his foot found a sinkhole between two roots. With no way to catch himself, he fell back. There was a sickening crunch and pain shot through his leg. An otherworldly sound rushed out of him along with all the air in his lungs. White-hot pain radiated up his leg.

He lay still for what felt like half a century, trying to force air back into his jarred lungs.

Propping himself up with an elbow, he inched his way into a sitting position. He attempted to wrest his ankle free, biting down on the inside of his cheek in a futile attempt to manage the pain. When spots blipped in his vision, he ceased the effort. After he'd won the battle to remain conscious, Walt assessed his situation.

His ancient rear end was alone in a wildlife sanctuary with about four hours of daylight left. His ankle was broken or severely sprained, stuck between two roots, and swelling by the second. No way to call for help. Hadn't even bothered to mention to Joey and Finn or Karl where he was going.

His only glimmer of hope was that Joey might eventually think to come looking for him here. But how long would it take to find him if she happened to remember how to get to the nondescript island?

With only his light jacket to shelter him from the mid-February wind, it was not going to be pleasant when the sun went down.

He shut his eyes tight, breathing through the pain. After he had a while to process the predicament he was in, he remembered the object that had started this mess. He looked about, trying to discover where it had landed after his fall.

He finally spotted the tin can on his left, behind him in the weeds. He lay down flat on his back and reached. His fingertips brushed it, scooting it farther away. He groaned, a melding of pain and anguish. What was in that can?

Who else would have known about the tree they used as a capsule for their messages to one another?

Just out of reach, the thing mocked him. Withholding yet another mystery he was powerless to solve.

Walt propped himself on his elbows, looking for something to extend his reach. If he was going to be stuck here until he returned to the dirt the good Lord formed him from, he was at least going to find out what was in that blasted tin can. In front of him, he sighted a forked stick that might be long enough to knock the can back into his reach.

With another groan he sat up, scooting forward as far as his aching joints and injured ankle allowed. Oh, to have the flexibility of his youth restored. He reached, hand trembling from the effort and the blinding pain radiating up his leg. He didn't permit himself to relax until his hand found purchase on that gnarled stick. "Ha!" he yelled out, fueled by elation.

He lay back down and carefully nudged the canister close enough for him to get a solid grip. It took a few maddening attempts before he achieved the desired angle, but he finally had that rusty vessel in his hands.

He panted with the treasure clutched to his chest until the black spots ceased to cloud his vision.

When he twisted the lid, it came away with little resistance. Nestled in the bottom was that same mouth harp he'd been reminiscing about earlier. And there was a note.

Hands shaking, he unfurled the small scroll covered in Cay's tidy, squat handwriting. He blinked hard and moved the page far enough away from his face that his vision cooperated.

Wally,
I've failed you in so many ways, but this was the worst. I wanted to save you. I thought I'd done enough, getting you to

shore, but you had the pallor of death after losing so much blood. If I had known what I know now, that I was too late to save my father, I would have stayed by your side. But I'd left him to come to your aid, and help was on the way for you. When I saw the report in the papers, that all on board your ship perished, I near-about lost my mind. Did for a while, I suppose.

I shouldn't have been able to find you at all that night. Among the wreckage, the chaos, the dead. It was an impossibility that makes no logical sense. My only thought was that the Lord was allowing me this one chance at redemption.

After all, it was me who got you into this mess. Keeping you distant when all I really wanted was to be held. Not trusting you with my secrets when I should have.

Please know my father meant no harm that night. He thought he was doing his duty making that light shine in the darkness. If you blame anyone, blame me. I was given a second chance and, somehow, I botched even that. I should have never left your side.

I don't know why I'm pouring this out. My words come far too late to do you any good. I suppose it's a beggar's attempt to salve her guilt. But you and my father are at least together in heaven. It is I left below, bound to forever drown in my regret.

Yours,
Cay

He turned the letter over. The other side of the page was covered in typography. It was a copy of the same article his mother had kept and he'd later inherited. The local journalist had reported that all the men aboard Walt's ship had been lost. They'd gotten the death toll wrong by one.

Walt returned the items to their home and hugged it tight to his middle. Was this some sort of pain-induced hallucination? Nothing about this made sense. From the mouth harp that had been thrown into the sound to a note that came after Cathleen McCorvey was supposed to have died at sea to the words he read saying she'd rescued him that night. All of it impossible.

The moment he'd seen Bleakpoint Light illuminated that fateful night, he'd had one moment of idiotic hope that she was signaling her undying love, beckoning him back. And then the world exploded, the torpedo's impact launching him into the sea.

Over the years he'd had strange dreams about Cay finding him among the wreckage, helping his half-conscious form onto floating debris.

But he'd thought them only figments of his imagination, invented by his shattered heart.

After the debacle with the light, locals had labeled Callum and Cathleen postmortem as German spies. And now he held the proof that said it wasn't true. Proof that Cathleen McCorvey had lived beyond that fateful night. But where had she gone?

He squeezed his eyes shut, praying that rescue would come sooner than later. That he'd have the chance to discover the truth behind the piece of Cay's puzzle clutched in his hands.

THIRTY-FOUR

Mae sat staring at her grandson, emotions flickering over her face. Peter had not dropped his daring gaze, a new side of him appearing before Joey's eyes. A glimpse of the steady and bold man that Peter could someday grow into. He repeated his question. "Gramma, do you know why your name matches those logs from the lighthouse? They were from the early 1940s. Things about rescues at sea and World War II."

Her mouth worked but no sound came. She shook her head. "Peter, dear, it's a coincidence. Mae is a common name. You're bright enough to know I wasn't alive in the 1940s."

"I know that, but what if Nana named you after someone she knew or something. The stories in the lighthouse walls—they sounded so much like the ones she started telling me. She must have told them to you too."

Mae stood and straightened the items on the coffee tray. "My mother was very sick when she started all that nonsensical talk. She's filled your head with stories. Legends and gossip that muddled together in her weakened state. If she has any connection at all to that island, she went her entire life up until then not saying a word about it. Now you've taken to trespassing and setting fires in order to protect a fantasy, egged on by inventions from a sick woman's addled brain."

"But she started telling me those stories a long time before she got sick," Peter interjected. "She said she needed to pass them down to someone, and she chose me."

Mae flicked her wrist. "Excuse me if I am far less interested in discussing old legends and the fact that I share a name with someone who wrote hidden messages before I was a twinkle in my momma's eyes and a little more invested in hearing how these fine people plan to handle your misdeeds."

Finn cleared his throat. "Ma'am, all is forgiven. We simply asked that he let us know ahead of time if he plans to make a visit to the island, and obviously to not take anything without asking."

Joey glanced at Peter who had dropped his chin and retreated back into his hoodie. A metamorphosis in reverse.

"It's obvious Peter is struggling," Finn went on. "And it seemed irresponsible to sweep it under the rug without letting someone who cares for him know what's been going on." Finn shifted his gaze from Mae's face to the porch slats between his feet. "We've all been there, during those growing-up years, trying to find our way as we become adults. I don't know if it was the right thing to do, coming here and sharing this with you, but I do know that I couldn't leave him standing on the side of the road that day picking up trash looking like a ship without harbor."

Mae sat back down, her posture softening. "I'm sorry for being snappish. I've been told I get that way when I'm upset." She gazed lovingly at her grandson, ardor building in her voice. "I'm upset that my former son-in-law kept Peter away. I'm upset that Peter has been caught up in situations neither of us is proud of. I'm upset that my mother's fever dream stories were all he felt he had to hold on to when I was just a ferry ride away." She blinked rapidly and sniffled. "Peter, I'm sorry I didn't fight harder for you when Rick told me you didn't want me in your life anymore. He said you were angry with me about not being there the day your mother passed. And maybe you were. But I shouldn't have let that keep me away." She pressed her hands to her cheeks, eyes shut tight, and then tried to stem the tears rolling from her eyes.

The poor woman had gone from a lioness with its hackles up to a puddle of mush in the span of a minute. Joey put a cautious hand on the woman's knee, hoping she wouldn't switch back and swat away her offer of comfort.

Mae removed one hand from her cheek and gave Joey's a squeeze. "I can't undo the time we've missed," Mae continued, looking at her grandson. "Peter, can we start again? I want to be a part of your life whether Rick is in agreement or not. I've tried to respect your mother's wishes, but you're about to be a man and not a minor. You get to decide."

Peter snapped his head up from where he'd been staring at the ground. "Mom's wishes? What are you talking about?"

"The fight at her funeral started because I said something about you coming to live with me, and Rick said that, on her deathbed, your mother insisted that I was not to be a part of your life. That she wanted him to raise you. It went against everything she and I had talked about when she learned that her cancer was terminal. But then we'd had an argument shortly before she took a bad turn . . ."

Peter looked as though he had swallowed something bitter. "You believed him? He just wanted to get his hands on the money Mom put in a trust for me. It was supposed to go to you to relieve the strain of having another mouth to feed." Peter glared. "He'll be turning me out the moment the clock strikes midnight on my eighteenth birthday and I 'cease to be useful to him,' as he's so fond of telling me. There won't be any money left in the fund. He's making sure of that."

Joey's heart clenched in her chest at the resigned sadness in Peter's voice. Lost. Feeling abandoned. Misunderstood. Suddenly it wasn't Peter sitting there but her brother, Trey, after the fight with their father.

Mae grumbled. "Let him keep the money. I don't give a rat's

hind leg about that. I got enough to get by. Come home to me, Peter."

The teen sighed. "I'd like to, but I have to finish up this semester at school, and then I've got to finish up my community service. But after that . . . if you'll still have me . . ."

Mae got up and pulled him to standing and then into a tight embrace. "Of course I'll have you. I've been miserable lonely without you."

Joey leaned around the pair to catch Finn's attention.

She gave him a nod of encouragement. He'd been right about pushing Peter to talk with his grandmother. The peace washing over the two of them could be felt in the air, like a warm breeze blowing in from a gentle sea.

Joey rose from her seat and motioned for Finn to follow her to her car. "Let's give them a minute." They'd become the trespassers on this private island.

"Mission accomplished," Finn whispered when they reached the car.

"Except the part about her answering where her name came from."

"It's probably just a coincidence like she said."

Joey scrunched her nose and leaned against the passenger door. "I don't believe in those. She's trying to shut down Peter's questions about the place for some reason."

Finn's eyes widened. "For some reason? Ha. Yeah. That's a real mystery. He nearly set fire to a historical landmark and stole artifacts. All Mae cares about is the kid staying out of trouble."

Mae, suddenly appearing to remember that a couple of strangers had tagged along on this past-due reunion, called out from the edge of the porch. "Bless you two for bringing Peter home to me. If there is any way I can repay you . . ."

Finn placed a hand over his heart. "Trust me when I say getting to witness your reunion is more than enough thanks." There was a thickness in Finn's voice that made Joey do a double take.

Was that moisture in his eyes? If it was, it was gone in an instant. Peter gave his grandmother a hug and trotted down the stairs to the waiting car.

"We weren't trying to rush you," Joey said.

Peter shrugged. "She's taking the ferry over next week. We'll have time to talk more then."

Mae stood at the porch, grasping the support beam, a wistful smile lighting her face.

"Hey, Gramma?" Peter shielded the sun from his eyes with his hands, looking back at her. "Do you really not know anything about where your name comes from?"

Joey expected the woman to switch the subject again, but instead she said, "I can't say I lived up to it, but my mother once told me I was named for the bravest woman she had ever known."

THIRTY-FIVE

He was flat on his back, floating in the sea. Freezing cold yet burning hot. Like someone had stoked a fire inside of him that seared his innards but refused to warm him to the skin. A small but calloused hand squeezed his.

He turned his head, looking for her. She tread water beside him, gripping him tight.

"I knew it was you."

Damp curls clung to her solemn face.

"The island legends were more than legends, weren't they? You're the one they call Saint-Mae."

She gripped his hand tighter.

"I should've never left. I should've fought harder for you."

She shook her head.

"Everyone said you'd died. But you didn't, did you?"

Her hand loosened a fraction and he attempted to squeeze tighter, but she kept slipping through his fingers like she was made of sand.

"Where did you go? Why did you let me believe a lie?"

Cay released her hold on him.

"Don't go. Please don't leave me here alone."

She offered a sad smile and dove beneath the surface of the water.

Walt blinked heavy lids. The unforgiving solid ground lay beneath him. The stiffness in his old limbs returned along with the throbbing pain. He shivered in the cold wind despite the fevered heat radiating in his bones. Walt stared into the night sky, still haunted by that oddly comforting dream.

He attempted to count the million pinpricks of light to pass the time and still his thoughts. He searched for the North Star. Anything to orient him to the here and now instead of the past, no matter how much pain he currently suffered.

He reached, his hand bumping the tin can that had rolled from his chest. He was not a heartsick sixteen-year-old just blown clear off a foundering merchant ship, rescued by the girl he'd loved. He was a broken and bruised eighty-one-year-old man.

And he was going to die out here. Alone.

THIRTY-SIX

"You haven't heard from him at all?" Joey wrung her hands as Finn paced the marina boardwalk.

"No. Karl said he went out alone yesterday. Hasn't seen him since."

Joey groaned. They had gotten home from Hatteras late yesterday and had each gone to their respective homes, planning to update Walt the next morning.

But the next morning they'd arrived to an empty slip.

"What should we do?" she asked. "Call the police? Coast Guard?"

Just then, Finn's cell phone rang. "Hello? . . . Hi, Peter. . . . I really can't talk. . . . Oh. Well, yeah. Actually, that would be fine. Would you mind a couple of extra passengers? . . . Okay. See you in a few. . . . Yes, that's right. Ocracoke Marina." He tucked his phone in his pocket. "Peter wanted permission to visit Bleakpoint. He's going to ferry us over."

Joey nodded. "Walt probably just went out yesterday and maybe lost track of time and decided to dock there for the night instead of risk coming back with the sun getting low. It's not the first time."

Finn massaged his forehead. "I told him that this wasn't safe—going off without anyone knowing his plans. I don't care what he says, it has nothing to do with age. It's just normal safety measures. Why does he insist—" Finn's voice cracked, cutting off his words and she stepped to him, wrapping her arms around him, holding tight.

Despite the dread weighing her middle, she summoned her best calm-the-nervous-bride voice. "We'll find him, and he'll give us that gruff, annoyed grunt he does when he realizes we were worried sick. But deep down he'll know that he needs to do a better job communicating, because that's what you do when you love someone. Even if it is annoying. And when he sees how worried you are, he'll understand. Even if he won't admit it."

Finn rested his cheek against her head. "Thanks," he choked out. He took a few deep breaths and released the embrace. "I have a habit of clinging to the absolute worst-case scenarios my mind creates, and I can't see anything else." He ran a hand through his hair. They both turned at the sound of an approaching boat. Peter stood at the helm of a boat bigger than the one they'd seen him in before. He waved and then expertly guided the vessel alongside the dock so that they could come aboard.

Finn gave him a crooked smile. "You didn't hijack, or boatjack . . . or whatever you call it when it's a boat?"

"Piracy?" Joey offered.

"No siree. I was with my boss when you called. He let me take his bigger boat out since I was going to have you two along. Where's Mister Walt?"

Finn explained, and Peter's face creased with worry. Once they were past the wake zone, he accelerated. Thankfully the winds were calm, and Pamlico Sound was smooth. Peter passed Finn and Joey each a pair of binoculars. They scanned the area for any sign of *Cay's Song*.

But when they reached Bleakpoint, no boat was docked at the usual spot. They continued on, scouring the shoreline, but found no signs of him. Peter docked the vessel, and they all came ashore, just in case Walt was somehow here without transportation.

Joey looked inside the keeper's residence while Finn searched the lighthouse. Peter limped along the nearby trails. All of them calling his name with no answer. Joey met Finn in the stretch between the lighthouse and the cottage. His face was pale. "Where else would he be? Why isn't he here? He should be here."

Joey chewed her lip, positivity failing her. "Maybe we somehow passed him and he's already back?" she said weakly.

"I think it's time we alert the authorities. Let's get back in cell range so I can make the call."

Peter joined them. "Can you think of anywhere else he could be?" he asked.

She searched her memories of their shared conversations. Her racing heart slowed. "I think I know where he is."

Finn and Peter turned to her, relieved.

"I . . . I mean I sort of know where he is."

"What does that mean?" Finn's tone was clipped.

She looked toward the sound. "One time he took me to this island. He said it was a place that he and Cathleen explored when they were kids. He told me that he goes there often. It's where he was when the fire happened and when Jerry fell from the roof. That has to be where he is now."

Finn stared over the waterway. A waterway dotted with marshy islands that went on forever in either direction. "Which one? Which way?"

"Well . . . uh . . . well, I know that when he took me there, he left the marina in the opposite direction of the one he takes when he comes here."

"Okay . . ." Finn turned back to her. "Anything else?"

She hugged herself. "It's part of the national seashore. It took us about thirty minutes to get there from the marina."

Finn pressed his fingertips to his temples. "That's a huge search area."

Peter stepped between them. "I know the area she's talking about. I can take you."

After a quick stop at the marina to get help, Finn, Joey, and Peter were out on the water again. Fanning out in their wake were other locals who'd heard about Walt's disappearance.

"This was what Pops loved about growing up here," Finn said. "If a garden was getting weedy because the family was sick, they would wake up to a pristine vegetable patch and a basket full of the harvest on the front porch. Or if someone saw a dog wandering and knew who it belonged to, they'd take it back home and put it in its fence." Finn nodded. "I know a lot has changed since his childhood, but if he could see this, the way people still look out for each other here, it would please him."

Joey continued to scan the area with the borrowed binoculars as Peter carefully motored among the marshy islands. "If that's true, why didn't Cathleen think she could count on the people to help with her father? Why were they so quick to label them as spies?"

Finn shrugged. "People didn't understand dementia then like they do now. They'd probably have thought him mad. Besides, with the war at people's doorsteps, I can imagine emotions were running high. People were suspicious. So was she." He lowered his set of binoculars, a faint tremor in his hands betraying his frayed nerves.

Joey wrangled her growing concern. This would all work out fine. They'd find Walt. He'd change his wandering ways. And she'd help him finish his project and find the closure he craved, laying his memories of Cathleen and her father to rest. They'd demolish rumors with facts.

Peter rounded a bend, then pointed. "There! There's a boat over there."

Finn stepped closer to the bow. "It's his."

Peter slowed and maneuvered his vessel next to Walt's where it was securely moored to the makeshift dock. Finn vaulted over the opposite side, splashing through the shallows. "Pops! Where are you?" In a blink, he had disappeared into the live oaks.

Joey looked to Peter, her gaze traveling to his booted leg. "You'd better stay. I'm going to check the boat over and then help Finn search."

He nodded, his face set like granite. He posted an orange-and-black flag that Joey guessed was a distress signal to anyone passing by.

She carefully stepped from Peter's boat onto *Cay's Song*. Everything seemed undisturbed. Even Walt's cell phone, basically useless out here, rested on the console. The boat bobbed merrily on the lapping waves like all was right in the world.

Please. Let that be so, she prayed.

She disembarked and hurried along the trail from the dock, stopping when it split into several directions. In the distance, she could hear Finn calling out. Should she follow his voice or spread out and choose another path? What had Walt said about this island? That this place was his and Cathleen's playground. That he had once known every inch of this land like he knew the lines on his own palm.

Which way? It wasn't an eloquent prayer, but it was a soul-deep cry for help. Something nudged her to take the left path. Divine intervention? Maybe. Maybe not. But it was all she had. She took the trail, lightly jogging. *Guide me. Guide me.* She prayed the words with each puffed exhale. She came to another fork in the trail. A strange assurance washed over her to turn right instead of left. Normally she'd talk herself out of following such impressions. Convince herself that it was all in her head. But she didn't have time for that now.

She crested a small hill. Just ahead a figure lay on the ground near a twisted tree. "Walt!" The scream rolled out of her as she ran closer. He didn't stir. Her already racing heart slowed to a heady pounding. "Finn! Finn, I found him!" she yelled at the highest volume her body had the capacity to produce. Then she stuck her finger and thumb between her lips and gave an earsplitting whistle like her father had taught her to get his attention over the sound of the heavy construction equipment.

Walt still hadn't moved. She walked closer, tripping over a metal coffee can. She nudged it away with the toe of her shoe and knelt next to him. She gently jostled his shoulder. A barely audible groan wheezed from him. He was alive. She felt for his pulse. Weak and thready. His skin was hot to the touch. It was then she noticed the fine sheen of sweat on his brow. She stood straight and yelled for Finn again, wishing she'd thought to bring the air horn from the boat.

She continued to assess Walt, noticing his foot trapped in a hole, wedged in by two roots. She heard the sound of pounding steps and Finn tore out of the copse of trees, clutching his side, his eyes wide with fright.

"He's alive," she said, "but we need to get him help. Fast."

THIRTY-SEVEN

Joey gently tapped on the door to Walt's recovery room.

"Come in." Finn's voice sounded haggard and raspy.

Though he was exhausted and in desperate need of sleep and probably a shower, his face lit up at the sight of her. "I thought you were his nurse."

"How's he doing?"

He stood stiffly, his face growing more serious. "They've been getting a lot of fluids and strong antibiotics into him over the past day and a half. They say the pneumonia is starting to respond. And he's going to need to have a little hardware added to that ankle to repair it, but they're waiting for him to stabilize before they book him for surgery." Finn rolled his shoulders. "He hasn't really been fully conscious. Waking up here and there, thrashing about, talking about some coffee can. Most of it unintelligible. His heart rate kept spiking, so they've kept him sedated. I don't know . . ."

She lifted a bag. "I brought you some things. Toothbrush, toothpaste. Some shampoo. Deodorant. There's clothes too. Not exactly high fashion and I guessed on the sizes, but . . ."

"You're a lifesaver." The sincerity in his voice made heat rise to her cheeks.

She shook her head. "It's just clothes and stuff."

He stepped to her, resting his hands on her shoulders. "It's more than just clothes. You found Pops. And before that you . . . you . . ." He trailed off, looking into her eyes in a way that stirred to life feelings she'd been working very hard to ignore over these past weeks.

And maybe he felt the same about her. But now was not the time and place for either of them to make declarations.

She stepped back from him, lowering her gaze. "I'm glad that I've been here, that I've gotten to play a role in your and Walt's story, but I don't think I should be the one getting the credit. I could have never orchestrated the way things have come together with the project. With you and Walt making peace with each other." She'd thought she had been running away from a frustrating situation when she'd left Copper Creek. But what if God had been nudging her down a trail, using a not-so-great situation to help her find her way here, for such a time as this? It was possible, right?

Finn smiled softly. "Then thanks for being you. For sharing your kindness and compassion. And expertise."

She ducked her chin, cheeks growing hotter. "I can sit with him if you'd like to freshen up. Or I can get out of here." She raised her gaze to meet his. "I came to let you get a little rest, not talk your ear off."

He was still looking at her like she was the coming dawn after a dark night, but he stepped back. "All right. A guy can take a hint. I'll get a shower and brush my teeth."

"I wasn't hinting—"

"After I get a little nap, I'll bring us some decent coffee and you can talk my ear off all you want. As long as Pops isn't up, 'cause I'm sure I'll get some kind of earful when he comes to. He's been saving up his word count while he's been out."

She took his humor as a sign that either Walt really was on the mend or poor Finn was semi-delirious from exhaustion.

On the way out, he turned around one more time. "If I haven't said it enough, Pops was right and I was way wrong about not wanting to hire you."

She waved him out the door before settling in the seat Finn had occupied. She prayed for Walt's recovery. And then she was left with the agitating quiet, interrupted only by an occasional beep from the monitors and muffled pages over the PA system. She looked to the ceiling tiles overhead. Nothing to occupy her thoughts besides dissecting her feelings for Finn.

She glanced at the poster of a cell phone with a diagonal line through it, then she glanced at her phone. No bars. Wouldn't work even if she wanted to rebel and call Sophie for advice.

To escape thoughts of Finn, she engaged her captive audience. "Hey there, Walt. You're going to be okay." The only answer was the beeps of the monitors. "I knew it would take more than a little mishap like that to keep a guy like you down." She shifted and sat longways, propping her feet up on the short vinyl couch. "I've been itching to tell you about Peter's grandmother, Mae. She says she has no idea about her mother's connection to Bleakpoint, but that can't be right.

"Think about it," she continued, "Peter says his great-grandmother told him detailed stories about the island. And then she named her daughter Mae. It seems to fit so well. What if Mae is Cathleen's daughter, named after Cathleen's own mother? That makes Peter her great-grandson. It would fit so well, except for the fact that Cathleen died when she was sixteen." Joey sighed and picked a fuzzball from her T-shirt. "I wish I could solve this for you. If only we'd been able to talk to Peter's great-grandmother. I know she's somehow connected. Knew Cathleen or something."

Walt moaned, and Joey turned to him. His eyes fluttered and his weathered hands clenched the blankets covering his legs. "The c-c-c-c . . . the c-can." His hands moved over his legs like he was searching for something. "Dropped it." His eyes fluttered open for a moment and then shut. The tension in his face relaxed and he was still again.

She stared at his still form, trying to make sense of his words. She gasped. The can.

Joey grabbed a small notebook and pen from her purse and jotted a note to Finn.

Finn,

I'm so sorry that I had to run, but I figured out what has Walt so troubled when he wakes. I'm going to get it and bring it to him. I'll be back tomorrow. See you soon.

Joey

Hopefully Finn wouldn't be too angry she'd left Walt unattended. After all, there were nurses caring for him in ways Joey couldn't. And this would help Walt in a way only she could. She folded the note, wrote Finn's name on it in big block letters, and then propped it up like a miniature tent on the rolling table beside the hospital bed.

She pressed a kiss to Walt's forehead and then hurried out the door.

Once she was in her car, she dialed Peter's phone number. Just when she was sure that he wasn't going to pick up, he answered. "Hello? Joey? Is Mister Walt okay?"

"He's hanging in there. Listen, I need a favor."

"Sure."

"Do you think you could find your way back to the island where we found Walt?"

"Yeah, no problem."

"Will you take me?"

"Of course. Call me when you get to Ocracoke, and I'll meet you at Walt's slip."

She hung up the phone and drove as fast as she dared for Hatteras to catch her ferry.

Peter picked her up at the marina, and they headed out, making their way quickly to Walt and Cathleen's island. Peter had no trouble finding the place. He easily pulled his small boat next to the dock, now vacant after Karl and another local fisherman returned Walt's boat to the marina. She disembarked with Peter limping close behind. Joey paused a moment at one of the forks in the twisting trail. Which way had she gone before?

"It's left," he said from behind her.

She hesitated.

"If we've come to get what I think we've come to get, you need to turn left."

"You stayed on the boat when we found Walt."

"You said he was talking about needing an old coffee can, right?"

She took the trail to the left. "Yes, but—"

"Trust me." He passed her, taking the point position.

As she hiked onward, Peter said, "Not quite sure what to make of all of this, but six months ago, I came to this exact island and put an old-timey coffee can in a hollowed-out tree."

She stopped short. "Hold on. What?"

Realizing she was no longer following him, he ceased his hurried pace and went back to her. "One of the last times I saw her, my great-grandmother gave me a map of the waterways and a map of this island. Both were drawn on this old, yellowed paper. She asked me to bring this can and leave it in the tree marked on the map. Under no circumstances was I to tell anyone about it or open the can."

Joey stared wide-eyed. "What was inside?"

He gave her an incredulous look. "How should I know? You saw how fierce Gramma Mae is, and she's got nothin' on Nana

Kit. I've done some dumb stuff lately, but I know better than to ever cross my nana."

She leveled a stare that she hoped would pry the truth out of him.

"I'm not kidding. I didn't look. And I don't know how I feel about taking you to it now, other than I know if Mister Walt is that upset about losing the coffee can, then it must have been meant for him."

"And you remember the way there?"

"Sure do."

She motioned him forward. "Lead on, Pete."

The kid moved pretty fast even in that walking cast of his. No wonder he had been so good at hiding from them on Bleakpoint.

Before long they were standing in front of the twisted tree where Walt had fallen. They searched the ground that had been disturbed by the first responders who had contributed to Walt's rescue effort.

Finally, she glimpsed a rusty red can hidden in the yellowed grasses. "I found it."

Peter came to her side. His mouth forming an O when she removed the top.

"What?" she said. "I didn't make any promises to anyone. This is all connected to Cathleen McCorvey. One way or another." When he made no move to stop her, she reached inside and found a small metal device and a note.

"That's a mouth harp," Peter offered in answer to the confusion that must have been on her face. "That same one used to sit on Nana Kit's bookshelf."

She unfurled the small scroll. Her pulse quickened as she read the words. She looked at Peter. "Cathleen McCorvey lived. All this time everyone thought she died, but if this note is true, she didn't die that night." She shook her head in wonder. "All this time Walt blamed himself for her death, for not being there when she needed him most, and she lived."

She carefully rerolled the note and put it back in the can with the mouth harp. "I'd give anything to have talked to your great-grandmother before she passed and find out how she knew Cathleen McCorvey."

Peter tilted his head. "You can talk to her if you want. I mean, you might have to get past Gramma Mae to make it happen, but Nana Kit's still alive. She lives at a rest home over in Swan Quarter."

THIRTY-EIGHT

Joey parked in front of the hospital a couple of minutes before 8:00 p.m. Her mind still whirred from Peter's revelation. She thought back through all their conversations and the way he'd talked about the woman in the past tense. Talked about how she had gotten terribly sick, how they'd been separated by circumstance, but he'd failed to mention that she recovered. Could she be the missing and presumed dead Cathleen McCorvey?

All of that could be sorted out later. The first item on the ticket was to return the canister with Cathleen's strange letter to Walt. No wonder he was so worried about the thing. She entered the elevator and got off on his floor, then hurried toward his room.

"Ma'am, visiting hours are over," called a nurse. The woman's authoritative tone caused Joey to skid to a stop. She momentarily contemplated the potential consequences of disobeying the order. Then Finn exited Walt's room.

"I have it! I found what he's been looking for."

He smiled, shaking his head. "You're something else, Joey Harris." He strode to her and took the tin from her hands, eyes filled with wonder. "This is what he's been going on about?"

She nodded. "Wait until you see what's inside."

Finn approached the haggard-looking nurse who was likely at

241

the tail end of a too-long shift. He peered at her with those disarming blue eyes of his and glanced at her name tag. "Miss Lively," he said softly, "I know hours are over, but my friend here went a really long way to bring this back for my grandfather. Could she please give this to him?"

Her eyes widened. "Is that the thing he keeps asking for?"

He nodded. "We think so."

She pinched her lips tight and motioned for them to go on. "Make it quick. And have a little amnesia about who gave you permission if anyone stops you. I'm on my way out, and my relief is on her way up the elevator." She winked. At Finn. Not Joey.

When they were out of earshot of the nurse, Joey released the snicker that had been building in her chest. It came out as an unflattering snort. "I think you have an admirer."

He grinned, shaking his head. "Whatever. Being nice can get people much further than they realize. Or so I'm learning." He opened the door for her, and she walked to Walt's bedside. She lifted one of his hands and gave it a gentle squeeze. "I found your missing treasure. It's here, safe and sound." She nestled the can against his body and laid his hand on top. His fingers twitched and moved slightly against the metal. The tension around his eyes relaxed.

She turned to Finn who blinked rapidly and swiped his face with his sleeve. "Thank you," he said.

They sat down on the small couch, and Joey filled Finn in on the contents of the canister and what she'd learned about Peter's involvement in placing it in the tree at the behest of his great-grandmother. And the fact that his relative still lived. Once she had spilled all the latest, she leaned back against the couch, realizing for the first time that day just how exhausted she was.

He pulled out his wallet and handed her a plastic card. "Take my hotel room. Pops's allowed one overnight visitor so I can stay. It's too late for you to be driving the whole way back."

She shifted on the uncomfortable seat, the vinyl squeaking with her movement. "There's no way you'll be able to sleep on this thing. I can get my own room."

He pushed the key card back to her. "Not likely. They're probably all booked up, which is why I got a room as soon as I arrived even though the only time I've even been in it was to shower and take that nap this afternoon when you came."

She grimaced. "Sorry about leaving. I hope I made the right decision."

He glanced at his peacefully resting grandfather and released a breath that relaxed his shoulders. "No doubt about that. Please take the room. I'd rather be here anyway."

"If you're sure," she said as she stood. "When was the last time you had a decent meal?"

"I got a sandwich from the cafeteria a couple hours ago."

She propped her hands on her hips. "And that qualified as decent?"

He quirked an eyebrow. "Decent is a generous description."

"We'll probably both feel better if we get a full stomach before we turn in. How about I scout out somewhere with late hours, and I'll bring it back. We can eat in the atrium, because I have a feeling they won't let me back in here until visitor hours open again."

Joey returned half an hour later with takeout from a Thai restaurant. Finn met her in the lobby, and they found a vacant table in the atrium.

"How's Walt?" she asked.

"About the same but resting much better." He opened his container and his eyes closed appreciatively at the savory sweet aroma of pad thai.

"See, better than the sandwich. Am I right?"

He grinned. "So right."

She pointed to her red curry. "Feel free to trade if you'd rather have mine. I wasn't sure what you'd want, but pad thai seemed a pretty safe bet."

"No, this is perfect. Thanks."

They ate in companionable silence, neither of them having enough energy for words.

After they finished, he said, "Thank you. I needed that."

She nodded. "No problem. I'd better let you get back to that tiny couch you insist on occupying. Get all the rest you can." She moved to pack up the empty foam containers, but he placed his hand over hers, causing her to freeze in place.

"Don't go yet. I mean, if you need to go, that's fine. But don't rush off unless you want to. I . . . I could use the company."

She checked her watch more to give herself something to do than to ascertain the time. A quarter past ten. *He wants my company.* Not because Walt encouraged it. And not because solving Cathleen's mystery demanded it. "Sure. Okay. Yeah." A smile stole over her face, and with it came a burst of energy from some hidden reserve.

After the trash was tossed, they strolled around the atrium and then ventured outside, following signs to a nature trail that turned out to be little more than a sidewalk through some flower beds. The string lights overhead and the frog serenade lent it the charm it might have otherwise lacked.

His hand kept bumping hers as they walked. *He might as well take my hand before we both end up bruised.* The instant the thought blipped through her head, his hand enveloped hers. He shot her a questioning look.

She laced her fingers through his even though she wasn't sure this was wise. Was he falling for her in the same way she'd been trying not to fall for him? And what of her plans to return to Copper Creek? Their hands fit together but could their lives? *Stop it. Take Sophie's advice and hold the cute guy's hand.* Still, she'd give anything to know what had caused him to make that move just then.

She glanced up at him. "So, you think we should visit Peter's great-grandmother?"

"I think we have to," he said. "It's like the final piece of the puzzle that will make everything make sense. But we'll have to find some way to get Mae's blessing."

Joey grinned. "Can we get away with saying a man's life is hanging in the balance and that talking to Nana Kit is the only way to save him?"

Finn chuckled softly. "I mean, it's a bit of a stretch, but . . ."

"Under the circumstances . . ." She shrugged.

"Exactly." He tugged her to a stop and faced her. "Under the circumstances."

There was a heat in his gaze that made her stomach flip. He stepped closer, leaning in. How she wanted to close that gap. To forget the questions clanging in her mind and just kiss him. But reality kicked her hard in the shins. She released his hand and backstepped. "I'm sorry. I can't." She turned away.

"Joey, wait." The anguish in his voice froze her to the spot.

She faced him. "You're exhausted and wrung out. And I'm not thinking clearly either." Despite her words, she took a step closer.

"Actually, I'm thinking more clearly than I've—"

"And . . . and . . . I've got a wedding." The last bit burst out as a frantic grasp for anything practical to dissolve the very impractical impulses drawing them together like a pair of magnets.

He blinked twice. "You're . . . you're getting married?" Confusion and hurt clouded his features.

She scrunched her face and shook her head. "No." Good grief. She sounded ridiculous. "I have a wedding to plan. A dream job in Copper Creek, after the lighthouse is done. Maybe. I don't know. And you . . . you're still trying to figure things out with your past. And your life is here, with Walt."

The confusion on his face dissolved. "I'm all for making plans. But sometimes I think we—I, at least—use plans as a wall to keep myself safe. I don't have to worry about taking a chance on what's right in front of me because my eyes are on the safe route I've already charted."

She clasped her fingers together in front of her, wringing them. "I might know a thing or two about that."

He drew nearer and scooped her hands into his, his gentle grip steady and calm.

She gazed up into his eyes. Who knew the color blue could hold that much warmth? Her study of him dropped to his lips. She leaned in the slightest fraction.

"And that ring I used to have?"

She pumped the brakes on her heart. "Yeah."

"I carried it with me to keep the pain fresh so I wouldn't let myself get hurt again. But the more I've thought and prayed about everything, though I definitely have actions I wish I hadn't taken, it's not giving my heart away that I regret." The wind snagged one of her curls, and he tucked it behind her ear. "Pain makes for a horrible shield. So I'm letting it go."

Thoughts whirled. Questions she wanted to ask. Facets of their individual lives she craved to piece together before she made another move. "What changed?"

"You." He said the word like a sigh of relief and cupped her cheek in his hand.

She tossed aside the mental file folder she was already assembling on the pros and cons of long-distance relationships, clutched the front of his bargain store T-shirt, and found his lips with hers.

Joey entered Finn's hotel room, pressing her cool fingertips to her heated cheeks. She leaned against the closed door, her legs feeling like the bones had been replaced with jelly. She pulled out her Blackberry.

Soph, are you up?

> Of course. Liam never sleeps, and it's only
> 11:30.

So it was. It felt like she'd lived two weeks in the span of a day. She clenched her teeth and typed.

> Call me when you get him settled.

She set the plastic shopping bag from the pharmacy on the nightstand, then grabbed the toothbrush, contact solution and case, and face wash she'd picked up on her way to the hotel. The toiletry items she'd brought Finn earlier were lined up on the counter from smallest to tallest. She snickered. Even when the man was exhausted, he couldn't help himself.

Joey squeezed the travel tube of what she thought was toothpaste but froze when translucent gel oozed out instead of the normal minty green. She caught her mistake just before it plopped onto the bristles.

She squinted at the tube. The yellow tube. *Antibiotic ointment? Really?* She grimaced. Maybe she was more distracted than she cared to admit when she'd walked into the store, her lips still tingling from that kiss. The corners of her mouth stretched upward against her will. She leaned against the wall and groaned. She was not supposed to be happy about this. Embarrassed? Maybe. Worried she'd allowed her heart to run away with her? Sure. But not this buoyant feeling in her chest.

After she brushed her teeth with borrowed toothpaste, she checked her phone to make sure Sophie hadn't called yet, then jumped in the shower.

Under the steaming spray, Joey pressed the heels of her palms to her eyes. This was not good. Despite the growing feelings she'd been having for Finn, she'd promised herself not to give in. His life was here with his grandfather. And she had a chance she couldn't pass up to repair her family's name in the town she'd always loved.

Joey towel-dried her hair and put on the oversized North

Carolina T-shirt she'd found on sale at the pharmacy, wearing it like a nightgown.

She plugged in her phone and pulled back the covers on the bed. They were rumpled from where Finn had napped earlier. Laying her head on his pillow, she caught the scent of his shampoo. Joey covered her face with her hands, thinking about how long she'd spent sniffing shampoos to pick a masculine scent he'd like. *Yeesh.*

Growing feelings? What a joke. She was two steps from head over heels. After Paul, she'd promised herself not to entertain the idea of any relationship unless it could be with someone she actually could see herself spending her life with.

The kiss had been a mistake. But why did doing the wrong thing feel so very right? Her eyelids grew heavy, the adrenaline that had kept her going through the final hours of the day dissolved like mist.

Joey jerked awake at the shrill ring of her phone, then answered with a groggy "'Lo?"

"Oops. I woke you, didn't I? Sorry I took so long. Liam fought sleep like a UFC fighter. Mark's working overtime, so . . ."

Joey scrubbed her face hard trying to wake back up. "No worries. It's been a wild couple of days, and I sorta just crashed." Joey filled her in. The potential wedding planning gig in Copper Creek. Finding Mae. Walt's disappearance and rescue. The coffee can with Cathleen's note.

"No wonder you fell asleep waiting on me."

Joey groaned. "And that's not even why I called you."

"You have something bigger to tell me than all of that?"

"I kissed Finn. Technically, I'm not sure who kissed who first but—"

A sound halfway between a squeal and a giggle came through the line, forcing Joey to pull the phone away from her ear. "This is fantastic."

"It's really not."

Sophie quieted. "Oh no. Is he actually married? That's why he always had that ring? Joey . . ." There was a disapproving quality in her friend's tone.

"No, no. He's single. Has been for a long time."

"Oh!" Her friend's sudden switch from disapproving to sunshine made her sound like a cartoon character on a sugar high. "So you two have some things to talk about, but there's time enough for that. So why do you sound so wrung out? He's a bad kisser?"

"No." Her face flamed. That *was not* the problem. At all.

Sophie chuckled. "Well, that's a relief. So . . ."

Joey blew out a shaky breath. "I . . . I think what I feel for him is something real, Sophie. He's loving and persistent and curious. He values family like I value family. And . . . well . . . he's not bad to look at. But what if he just kissed me because he's sleep-deprived and scared about his grandfather. Stress makes people do strange things. Things they wouldn't ordinarily do. And his life is here. I've got that dream of a gig in Copper Creek."

"Whoa. Slow down. You don't have to have a ten-year plan on paper just because the two of you kissed."

"Well, no. But I shouldn't have kissed him until I'd mapped at least a little of my future plans and examined the contingencies."

Sophie snickered. "Well, when you say it that way, it does sound so much more romantic than stolen kisses in the night."

"Sophie . . ."

"I'm not saying you should just do whatever idea pops in your head, but I know you enough to know that's not even a concern. I don't think that kiss with Finn was as spur of the moment as you think. My guess is that you both had your defenses down just enough to be vulnerable and take a chance. Dial back the overthinking a smidge. Don't miss out on what might be a great thing just because you don't have everything cataloged and accounted for in that binder you wag around. No more spectating."

THIRTY-NINE

Walt ran his hand over the rough metal of the old coffee can. He blinked bleary eyes. The beep of a monitor filled his ears.

He turned his head sideways. Finn lay scrunched on that short couch with a hospital blanket pulled up to his chin, snoring away. His hair stood up at odd angles and was flattened in other places.

He smiled, remembering the boyhood version of Finn who raced down the stairs in the morning begging Martha for blueberry pancakes.

He couldn't feel the pain in his leg anymore, so they must have him on some strong meds. But, whew, did his chest feel heavy. He coughed, trying to rid himself of the awful weight. Finn stirred beside him. *Drat.* He hadn't meant to disturb him.

"Pops?" Finn sat up.

"Still kickin'," he croaked like an ailing bullfrog.

Finn stood and came to his bedside. "It's good to see your eyes again."

Walt coughed again, and Finn held up a large cup of water, positioning the straw so that he could quench his parched mouth.

After a sip, Walt said, "You found my treasure."

Finn raised an eyebrow. "That ratty tin can? You have Joey to thank for that. And that kid, Peter."

A ghost of a smile tugged at the corners of his mouth. "Our arsonist-trespasser?"

"Yep."

Walt chuckled, sending himself into yet another coughing fit. Boy howdy, did his chest hurt.

"You've got pneumonia pretty bad, but it's responding to the medication," Finn told him. "You oughta be feeling more yourself in a day or two and then we gotta get that leg fixed. You did a number on it."

"Figured." He attempted to catch his breath. "Listen, I'm sorry. I shoulda told you—somebody—where I was going."

Finn sighed. "I know I aggravate you to no end with my worry, but I love you and I'd like to keep you around for a good long while."

Walt suppressed the laugh rising up in his chest, knowing it would just make him start hacking again. "Pretty sure I said those exact lines to you the day you got your driver's license. My, how the tables have turned."

Finn shrugged. "For the past sixty years, you had Gramma to keep you in line. You looked out for each other and told each other where you were and when you'd be coming home. I'm sure now that she's gone, it feels kinda odd for the boy you raised to be trying to take on that role. I didn't mean to patronize, but I know I did sometimes. It's just that everyone needs someone looking out for them." The boy gave him a sheepish smile. "I do."

Walt tugged his blanket higher. "I call and check in on you sometimes, sure, but that's not the same as what you're talking about, Finn. Who's been looking after you?"

Finn let out a humorless laugh. "Trust me, if I didn't show up for work when expected, somebody would've backtracked to where they last saw me."

"That's not the same. Work only cares what you can do for them. I meant somebody who cares about you."

"Well, now that we're close, we can be that for each other, Pops," Finn said.

He huffed. "In my personal opinion, I think you ought to let Joey-gal take on that role. She's got more energy than me." He expected Finn to rebuff his romantic nudging, but instead, a lazy grin crept over his face.

"Uh-oh," Walt said, glee warming him. "What's going on? Spill it, son."

Finn ducked his chin, smiling like a shy schoolboy. "Nothing. And besides, she's going back to Copper Creek as soon as she finishes up the lighthouse project. She's got some big wedding on the books."

"Why do you think I've been taking my sweet time deciding what to do with my place?" Walt winked. "I'm trying to give you two young fools time enough to see what's right in front of your eyes. If y'all blink, you might miss out on the love of a lifetime." He was caught off guard by the moisture welling in his eyes. He swiped it away.

"Pops?"

He laid his head back against his pillow, wheezing slightly.

"Can I ask you something?"

Walt nodded.

"I hope I don't sound harsh saying this, but there's things I just don't understand. You and Gramma were married sixty years. You always seemed happy."

Memories of Martha flashed in his mind. The accompanying pang in his chest had nothing to do with illness. "We were. I miss her every day."

Confusion wrinkled Finn's brow. "But . . . but now you're here, giving everything you've got to restore this old lighthouse of Cathleen's, this girl who was just a blip in the timeline of your life by comparison. You're not trying to do something in Gramma's memory but this other girl's. You've barely talked about Gramma all this time."

He'd wondered if his exploits had hurt his grandson. "The reason I took that first trip here was because my heart couldn't take living in that house without Martha. As far as this ridiculous mission I'm on . . . the difference between my life with Martha and that blip as you called it, is that with your grandmother I can honestly say our relationship, though imperfect, was one without regrets. I'll miss her until my dying day, but our past doesn't haunt me like mine and Cay's does. All I have left of my friend is regret. I know what I actually need isn't a bright shiny lighthouse but to forgive myself. But I don't want to. I'd rather take action. Fix something in my power to fix."

A look passed over Finn's face, one Walt knew meant he was trying to figure out whether to speak what was on his mind or not.

"I read the note inside the can," he said finally. "Cathleen lived?"

Walt squeezed and released his hands trying to get his fingertips to warm. "I can't make sense of it. I went back to that island after I was released from the hospital. I checked our tree, and it was empty. And that mouth harp, she chucked it into the sound the last time I saw her. It should have been lost forever." He reached for his water, and Finn steadied the straw.

"We know how the tin can ended up in the tree."

Walt choked on the water.

Finn leaned him forward, slapping him on the back as if that was going to accomplish something.

Walt collapsed against his pillow, lungs on fire. "What did you say?" he rasped.

"Peter's great-grandmother asked him to put the can there. He's the one who helped Joey find the tree again. The way Peter talked about his great-grandmother, we thought she'd passed away, but she's alive, Pops."

Walt attempted to follow what Finn was saying but the thoughts refused to connect. Was this a product of his illness? "Peter, the boy who'd been snooping around Bleakpoint? He put the tin can in the tree with my old mouth harp and the note from Cay that was written after she was supposed to have died?"

"According to Joey."

Walt blinked hard to clear his blurring vision. "Who's his great-grandmother? Her name?"

"Mae and Peter call her Kit."

He studied his grandson's face. "She couldn't be her. Could she?" He squeezed his eyes tight and then blinked rapidly, trying to organize his thoughts. "I'm not making sense, am I?"

Finn shrugged. "Anything feels possible at this point."

Walt shut his eyes again. "All this time." Years flashed before his eyes, years in which he'd mourned a girl who hadn't died, dragged down by the weight of his guilt. But how could he be angry at the one who had spared his life? "You'll go see her, won't you? Peter's great-grandmother? You'll tell me if it's her?"

"You don't want us to wait until you're well?"

"Life is short, Finn. We have a chance now, and we'd best not miss it." He gave Finn a pointed look, hoping he'd catch that he was talking about more than just the chance to talk with Peter's great-grandmother.

He ducked his chin and a little color rose in his cheeks. "I kissed her."

So Finn *had* caught his drift. "Who? Nana Kit?" he teased.

Finn snorted. "Joey. I kissed Joey."

Walt grinned. "'Bout time. Now what?"

The joy dropped from Finn's face. "I . . . I don't know. It was just a kiss."

Walt scoffed. "It better not be just a kiss. It better have meant somethin' to ya. If you were toying with that girl's heart, I'll tan your hide. You're not too big for a good whoopin'."

Finn quirked an eyebrow. "Maybe not. But you're in no condition to be dishing one out." He dropped the mischievous smirk. "I don't know how it will all play out with Joey. If she'll stay. If she'll go. But when I shut my eyes, I can see a life with her, and I haven't had that feeling in a really long time. And I'm trying to have the courage to lean into that and not away."

"You're coming along all right, I reckon." Walt winked. "Took you long enough though. Say, where is she now?"

"My hotel room."

He fixed a glare on Finn. "Excuse me?" The number on his heart rate monitor jumped.

Finn's eyes widened in panic. "No. Pops, no. I've been here the whole time. It was too late for her to drive back. I didn't. I wouldn't've. That's not . . ."

Walt relaxed. "Glad to hear it. I want you to live in the moment and all that, but for a second there, I thought you took me to heart a little too much." He coughed and pressed a hand to the ache in his chest. "All this gabbing has me worn plumb out. I'd better get a little shut-eye before the nurses come to prod me again."

Walt grasped the old coffee can in his hands and closed his eyes. "And I don't need a babysitter 24/7. When the hour's decent, take Joey out for breakfast and talk things out."

"Yes, sir." Finn chuckled.

Walt fully relaxed into his pillow and prayed. *Thank You, Lord, that I'm still living and breathing. That I'm getting to witness Finn come out on the other side of his dark days. Thank You, Lord, for Joey who's just stubborn and sweet enough to straighten us all out.*

He closed his silent prayer with a whispered *amen* and allowed sleep to sweep him away to dreams of what was to come.

FORTY

Joey woke and stared at the unfamiliar light fixture above the bed. She sat up, taking in the generic decor typical of a coastal hotel. The evening came rushing back to her. She covered her eyes with her hands. That kiss. She rolled over and grabbed her phone. One missed call from Finn. She accessed her voicemail.

"Hey. Hope I didn't wake you. Pops has been up and talking and has cleared me to give him a few moments of peace, as he so kindly put it. Can I take you to breakfast? Call me back and let me know. No pressure."

She let her phone fall to her lap. Could he take her to breakfast? Like as a date or as two exhausted adults in need of better sustenance than hospital food? Hopefully the second, because she couldn't possibly be going on a first date with Finn in yesterday's stale clothes.

She called him back and made plans to meet him downstairs in twenty minutes. After slipping on yesterday's jeans, she tied the oversized T-shirt in a knot at her hip, giving her nineties flashbacks. She piled her curls in a messy bun and pinched some color into her cheeks. This was as good as it was going to get.

Finn arrived in the lobby looking about like she felt, with part of his hair standing on end. He'd apparently tried to flatten it with water, but it had vigorously resisted his efforts.

"It's not far. Do you want to walk?"

She nodded and they headed out the door and down the sidewalk, balmy air lifting her spirits further.

Something about the two of them going on this sort of date in yesterday's clothes made her smile inside. First dates were normally full of pretenses and obsessing over putting the best foot forward. This was none of those things. For all she knew, he didn't even think of this as a date. Just as the thought flickered through her mind, he took her by the hand.

"Did you sleep okay?"

"I did. Thanks for letting me use your hotel room. I never would've made it all the way home."

"Glad to. It was good to be there with Pops when he woke. The more cantankerous he gets, the better I know he's feeling. It's a better barometer than the monitors they have him hooked up to."

She glanced at Finn, raising her brow. "So, now he knows that Cathleen lived?"

Finn nodded. "He does. He asked that you and I meet with Peter's great-grandmother as soon as we can arrange it. He doesn't want us to wait."

"I'll call Peter later," she said.

He guided her to a small diner. "Some of the nurses recommended it. Said the waffles were to die for."

The host led them to a booth in the center of the bustling establishment. They settled across from each other, perusing the extensive menu. When the server came, they both ordered coffee and water. Joey ordered waffles with a side of bacon and Finn asked for a southwest omelet. Meals settled upon, Joey could no longer hide behind the guise of reading the menu. They had to talk about last night. She grabbed her water and took a sip.

"So, about that kiss."

She choked.

"Sorry." Finn smiled weakly. "Bad timing."

"The kiss?" she croaked.

He winced. "Not for me, I hope not for you. I meant about making you choke. I've gotten really bad about timing my comments lately. I almost made Pops asphyxiate."

"Oh." She pinched her lips tight. "Not literally, I hope."

"Thankfully not." He was quiet for a few moments as he stared at the table. "Anyway, what I was trying to say was it's been a really long time since I've let anyone that close. Kissed anyone like that."

I would not have guessed that. She fanned her face with her menu and looked up to the air-conditioning vent. Somebody needed to turn that thing on.

"I don't know what last night meant to you, but I wanted to be up-front about what it meant to me." He ducked his chin for a moment and then lifted his gaze back to hers. "I hadn't planned on that kiss last night, but I'd be lying if I didn't tell you I'd been thinking about that, wanting that, for a while now."

Joey swallowed back the knot tightening in her throat. *A while* meaning the past few days or longer than that?

He took a sip of his coffee, his expression growing somber. "I don't know what I'm trying to say other than that I've got some junk from the past I'm still sorting, as you know, and it's only becoming clearer to me the more I'm around you."

"Um. I'm sorry." Maybe she would prefer the veneer of a first date. This was downright painful.

He ran a hand over his face. "No. Um . . . I'm trying to thank you for being who you are. I'm just doing a really bad job at it. What I meant was I started falling for you, and it scared me to death. That fear made me do a little soul searching. You made me see that I hadn't healed like I thought I had. I'd just shut parts of myself down and locked them away. I won't pretend that I'm walking around baggage-free, but I want to be. I'm sorry if that's all too much. I mean, I know it's too much for the typical first date. But we have a little history to go on, anyway."

She smiled. All they had was history. Digging through the past regrets of other people, trying to restore a broken story.

"Anyway, I just wanted to be up-front with you," Finn continued. "I know you have your own life that you're wanting to get back to. And I'm here with Pops. I don't know if our lives fit together." He reached across the table, and she tucked her hand into his. "But I do know that I feel home when I am with you, Joey."

The server arrived with their meals, and Joey let out the breath she'd been holding, thankful for the blessed interruption in order to collect her thoughts. She gave autopilot replies to the server's inquiries as to whether everything looked okay and if they needed anything. *What to say? What to say?* Finn had poured his heart out. Could she risk the same?

The server left them alone again, and Finn's gaze locked on hers.

"I . . . I . . ." She gulped. "I don't have the history that you have, Finn. But I have this weird habit of helping everyone else's dreams come true without considering my own. I convince myself I'm living, but I've actually been in this holding pattern. Like if I stay steady in one place, stick to the plan, then the things that are missing from my life will somehow find their way back to me. You make me want to forget all that. It's scary."

He grinned, cutting into his omelet with his fork. "So, it's settled. We're terrified of each other."

Laughter bubbled up in her middle and infected him. They cackled a little too loudly, drawing the attention of their booth neighbors.

They attempted to stifle their noise. "Sorry. I don't even know why I'm laughing," she said.

"Me either." He gasped, trying to catch his breath. "I'm guessing a delightful blend of stress, fatigue, and uncertainty?"

"Probably."

"What do you say we see where this goes? You game?"

She cut a bite from her waffles and stabbed it with her fork, then lifted it in mock toast. "Here's to living in the moment."

Finn nodded. "No regrets."

Or maybe there would be some regret, but they'd both come far enough along to realize that any regrets that might come along the way provided an opportunity to grow.

FORTY-ONE

Two days later, Finn, Peter, and Joey made their way across Pamlico Sound on the ferry to Swan Quarter. Though Mae's blessing for the meeting with Nana Kit had been laced with reluctance, she'd told them she was all for helping Walt find closure and peace as long as it wasn't at the expense of her mother's well-being.

Joey glanced in the mirror on her sun visor, checking on Peter. He was looking out the window with his headphones over his ears. Joey turned to Finn who sat relaxed in the driver's seat as the ferry carried them along.

"Walt gets out in a few days. He can't stay on that boat." A corner of his mouth twitched. "So far I've avoided saying 'I told you so' to the man even once."

"Wow," she said in mock admiration.

"I wish I had that ramp we talked about ready to go." He sighed. "I never dreamed I'd need it so soon."

"My rental has a ramp on the back entrance. Walt could stay with me."

Finn shifted in his seat, thinking. "I don't know how he'd feel having to depend on you to care for him. Me, on the other hand, he'd probably say turnabout is fair play."

Doubtful. Walt wouldn't want anyone fussing over him. "We could trade spaces."

Finn's brow creased. "You'd give up your nicely furnished rental to take on my renovation nightmare?"

"Nightmare?" She smiled. "I'll probably just have a lot of dreams that I'm stuck in a seventies disco. I reckon I could subject myself to such torture, but only for Walt's sake."

He slapped his hand to his chest like she'd dealt him a heart wound. "Only Walt? What about me?"

She shrugged. "He's my one true love. But since the age gap is a little much, I'm settling for the grandson."

Finn snickered and reached for her hand.

"What is going on between you two?" Peter said from the back seat. "You didn't forget that I'm back here, right? 'Cause this is getting weird."

Joey's face flamed. She hadn't *exactly* forgotten he was back there, but she'd definitely thought he was in his own world with his headphones blasting. She started to pull her hand away, but Finn squeezed it tighter, giving her a conspiratorial wink.

While Finn focused on the disembarking process, Joey turned to Peter. "What music are you listening to?"

He shrugged. "Casting Crowns. A CD Gramma gave me. It reminds me of when me and Mom would go to church together. It's been a long time since I've been." At the tremor in his voice, she released Finn's hand and shifted to fully face Peter. He had his bottom lip trapped between his teeth, and the rims of his eyes had turned red.

"What's wrong, Pete?" she asked.

He lifted one shoulder and removed his headphones and left them resting around his neck. "I'm just thinking about how I felt back then. Before everything got messed up. And now I don't feel like that same kid, and I don't know how to go back."

The ache in his words collided with the pain she carried. That craving to turn back her life to the way things once were. To a family before it had been fractured, to a time when her town still felt like a fairy tale. A childish desire that she needed to put to rest. It was past time to leave behind the "if onlys."

"I'm not sure going backward is ever the answer. We learn what we can from the hard times and keep moving forward."

Peter looked up from pulling at a loose thread on his hoodie. "Yeah. But lately I feel like I'm walking in the dark. Alone."

Joey nodded. "I know that feeling."

Finn spoke up beside her. "But even the darkness will not be as dark to you. The night will shine like the day, for darkness is as light to you."

Peter bit his bottom lip. "Um? Okay."

"It's from Psalms," Finn said. "My gramma used to quote that one when I was scared of the dark."

Joey smiled at him before turning back to Peter. "I think it means the things that look so dark and confusing to us are not that way to God. So even if we feel overwhelmed and like we've lost sight of the path ahead, we can still trust He's there beside us. Guiding us."

She rubbed her eyebrow, trying to get her thoughts in order. "You don't have to become the old Peter to find your way because . . ." She warmed at the mental image playing in her mind of Walt's lighthouse and the joy she found in preserving the past and giving the broken-down places new life. "Because God meets us right where we're at. And maybe things in our lives get broken down and beaten up along the way. The good news is restoration work is kind of His specialty."

Why had it been so hard to trust in that truth for herself? Maybe because when her brother and her father had their falling out, instead of trusting God to redirect Trey, Dad had attempted to force him back to the path he'd forsaken. Because he was afraid.

And ever since Trey and Dad parted ways, she'd let fear have a say in the direction of her own life.

Fear of getting it wrong.

Fear of getting herself so far off track that she'd never find her way back.

She didn't need to be the puppet master pulling all the strings, making sure everything ran in perfect order.

She glanced back at Peter. He sat relaxed, the tension gone from his face, headphones back in place. Hopefully the reminder she'd needed had been a comfort to him too.

Half an hour later, Finn parked the car in the lot of Swan Quarter Retirement Living. Just behind them was Mae in her navy sedan.

Joey's phone rang. She checked the screen. Lacey Nichole. She cringed and silenced the overdue phone call. Now was not the time.

Behind her, Peter unbuckled his seat belt. "Well, here goes nothing."

Joey was the caboose in the single-file line of visitors walking down the hallway to Nana Kit's room—a line led by a grim-faced Mae.

Mae stopped in front of room 43. "If my mother shows the least sign this meeting is too much for her, I'll shut this little rendezvous down faster than a hammer on a mousetrap. She's been through some health scares this past year, and I can't have her being overtaxed."

Joey, Finn, and Peter answered with a chorus of "Yes, ma'am."

Mae gave a succinct nod. "I'll let her know you all are here, then I'll step outside and let y'all have the room. But I'll be right outside this door."

Mae slipped inside. Joey waited, nerves jangling like a skydiver readying to launch herself from a plane. The lightkeeper logs tucked in her backpack were possibly about to be returned to the hands that penned them over half a century prior. Tales of courage and grit. Of sacrificial love. Of loss.

Joey wiped her damp palms on the legs of her jeans.

Mae stepped out. "She's ready for you. I told her that Peter was here to visit and he'd brought along a couple of friends looking into the history of Bleakpoint Light." Mae huffed. "Lit up like a Christmas tree at the mention of that place."

They stepped inside, Peter leading the way. He bent and hugged the white-haired woman in the rocking chair. A patchwork quilt covered her lap despite the stifling air of the room.

"Nana Kitty, it's good to see you again."

She patted his arm with hands twisted by arthritis. "It's been too long, my boy." Her voice was wispy like fog over water.

Joey's heart dropped. This woman looked aged compared to Walt. But maybe he'd simply been blessed with better health.

"I know. My stepdad would never bring me. And Gramma Mae—"

"Thought I was too sick for company," she lamented.

"Yeah. And I know it upset you when I hitchhiked that last time." Peter stepped back. "These are my friends, Joey Harris and Finn O'Hare. They were doing some work on that island you used to tell me stories about. They found notes hidden in the walls of the lighthouse, keeper logs about rescues at sea. I told them they sounded just like the stories you told me. Down to the little details. They've been trying to find out who wrote them and why they were hidden away like that, and I thought maybe you could help."

A girlish smile broke over the woman's face, and she pressed her hand over her heart. "You found them."

Joey removed the notebook from her backpack and handed it to Peter who placed it on Kit's lap. She opened it to the first page, then fumbled with the plastic protected pages, but the delight on her face was evident.

Joey stepped closer. "Are these yours? Are you Saint-Mae? Cathleen McCorvey, rather?"

The woman looked up at her, moisture in the corners of her blue-gray eyes. "I wish I was."

Joey's heart dropped.

"I'm not either of those people. But I guess you've figured out by now that they are one and the same. That Cathleen McCorvey was the legendary Saint-Mae. The stories of what she did are sometimes wilder than the legends."

Finn knelt in front of the woman. "Can you tell us how you knew her? How you came to be in possession of the coffee can you asked Peter to put in the hollowed-out tree?"

Kit set her gaze on her great-grandson, her expression turning steely. "You didn't tell them about—"

"No! No, ma'am. I kept my promise. A man named Walt found it, said the mouth harp inside belonged to him."

Finn placed a hand on the notebook. "Cathleen McCorvey was a friend of my grandfather. They used to play on that island and leave each other notes."

Kit clasped her hands beneath her chin. "Oh my, this has gone even better than I ever hoped it would. It's like Cinderella in reverse, except instead of a glass slipper, it's a mouth harp in an old canister." A raspy sound of glee slipped out of her.

Oh boy, this Kit was a character.

"Do you mind if we back up a little so you can fill us in on the finer details?" Joey asked. "We know Walt and Cathleen were good friends. We know her father had struggles, maybe with dementia, and she hid it. We know there was a misunderstanding between Cathleen and Walt that separated them when he took a job on a merchant ship. Then there was a mishap with the lighthouse and Walt's ship was hit. And somehow in the middle of it all her father drowned at sea. And we thought, like most people, that Cathleen had died that night too, until Walt found that can. And then Peter told us it was you who had him place it inside that old tree?"

Kit wiggled her arthritic hand toward a loveseat under the window. "Sit a spell, and I will tell you a story you'll never believe."

The three of them scrunched into the small space like clowns cramming into a clown car.

"One morning in the late spring, maybe early summer of 1942," Kit began, "I had gone out to feed the livestock at my farm in New

Bern. I near-about had a heart attack when I found a teenage girl curled in the corner of our barn. She slept so soundly, my clattering about hadn't roused her. I thought for a minute that she'd up and died.

"Though I was a little terrified at the prospect of an intruder squatting in my barn, being I was living alone with my husband off at war, she looked so bedraggled and innocent that I turned myself around, went to my kitchen, and whipped up a whole mess of eggs and biscuits. Poor dear. I knew that whatever her story was, it had been a hard-lived one.

"She was still sleeping when I returned, so I left a note with her food asking her to come up to the house when she woke. I expected she'd sneak off, but an hour later, while I was hanging my laundry out to dry, she slunk to me, skittish as a barn cat, empty dishes in hand. She introduced herself as Cathy and apologized for trespassin'. She asked if I could use a farmhand, as if it wasn't obvious I needed help by the shabby state of the place. But I didn't have a spare dime to my name.

"She said she was no stranger to hard work, and if I could let her sleep in the hayloft and allow her a share of the food we grew, she'd be grateful. Instead, I showed her into my spare bedroom and asked her to stay and help out until my husband returned home from the war." Kit paused. Her eyes fell shut for a moment and she sighed. "As it turned out, he never did make it back, and Cathy stayed on with me for about fifteen years.

"She didn't breathe a word about who she really was or how she ended up in my barn that morning. But a couple of years into her stay, when I got the notice that my husband had been killed in action, Cathy started telling me these fantastic tales about rescuing people at sea and her secret identity and the legends people told about her.

"At first, I thought she was just making stuff up to help me pass the quiet evenings when the work was done and my grief near-about swallowed me whole. But when she told me about Walt and how she lost him, I knew. The longing and regret in her voice. It felt just like *Romeo and Juliet* retold."

Kit cleared her throat and motioned to a water glass on the nightstand. "Peter, honey, I need to wet my whistle."

Peter jumped into action, and the spell Kit had woven with her words momentarily dissolved.

"What happened to her? Is she still alive?" Joey had scooted so close to the edge of her seat, she about fell onto the floor.

Kit held up a hand as she finished her drink and then continued. "About fifteen years after I lost my first husband, I started seeing a man from church. I guess Cathy got the idea that we were getting serious so she up and disappeared one day.

"I think she was worried I'd ask her to move on and left before I got the chance. She left behind a few odds and ends, that note and harp in that old tin can. I hung on to them for years hoping she'd come back for them, but she never did.

"Right before I got real bad off with a bout of pneumonia paired with some heart issues, I caught a glimpse of an article about Bleakpoint Light. That a man named Finnegan W. O'Hare had bought it with plans to restore it. I couldn't believe my eyes. I just knew it had to be Cathy's Walt or one of his progeny. She had to have been wrong about him dying."

Mischief danced in her eyes. "Did I mention how much I hate the way *Romeo and Juliet* ends? So I sent Peter on my mission. I just knew that if this was Cathy's friend, he'd find that old can and learn the truth about what had become of her."

Joey tilted her head. "You couldn't have had Peter just give it to Walt?"

Kit shot her a look that questioned Joey's sanity. "And if it was some other Finnegan who happened to have W for his middle initial? I couldn't risk handing that over to some stranger looking to make a buck off Saint-Mae's island."

Joey couldn't argue with that. She'd been around long enough to get a taste of the way people clung to the legends and folklore around that place. Pair that with tourist opportunities? "You still haven't heard from her in all this time?"

She gave them a sly look. "I get a Christmas card every year from the same address. Same photo every year. Simply signed with a C. I've tried writing her back, but she never answers. I know it's her though, letting me know she's all right. She never did lose that stray cat way about her." She waved her hand. "Over there in the top drawer, Peter. You can grab the one on the top of the stack."

Peter obeyed her request and brought Kit the greeting card.

"I think in a lot of ways she's still running," Kit said. "I looked into it, the history of everything, some years back. Cathleen Mc-Corvey, in that old forgotten record, is still listed as missing. Things weren't as organized back then as they are now, especially out there on the Banks. Because she was little more than a forgotten file, all she'd needed was to go back to the town she was born in, which was somewhere up in New England if I recollect, to get her birth certificate to get all the paperwork she needed to start fresh with her old name.

"Nobody outside of Ocracoke would have ever thought to connect the thirty-one-year-old woman with the missing teenager who'd been presumed dead decades prior. Even the locals didn't really care about solving that anymore, anyway. The ghost stories were enough to keep them sated."

She handed Joey the envelope. "I think she's still there. She was in December, anyway. When you get there, I think you'll see how she ended up in Knotts Island."

FORTY-TWO

A week later, Walt was settled into Joey's rental. He felt bad for having ousted her from her house, but she and Finn had conspired against him.

Finn walked into the living room and handed him a cup of coffee.

"I need to get out to the boat," he told his grandson, "make sure she's doing all right. I'm too cooped up in this house."

Finn busted out laughing. "You're cooped up in this house but not in that tiny cabin on your boat?"

He shrugged. The boy had a point. Maybe it wasn't the house. Maybe it was being taken care of like a decrepit old man that made him tetchy.

A little while later, Finn headed out to pilot a short charter flight. Thank goodness. Walt settled himself in front of the television and turned on a western.

Not ten minutes went by when the doorbell rang. He hoisted himself up and hobbled to the front door with his walker and walking cast. Joey stood on the other side of the door with what he suspected was a key lime pie concealed in a white cardboard box. Peter stood beside her.

Walt pointed to the boy's booted leg. "Now we match."

Peter smiled. "Hobbling around like old Blackbeard, we are."

"Aye, matey. Is that pie I spy, Joey-gal?"

She grinned. "Lead me to the galley, and I'll serve up some slices to you scalawags."

He stumped into the kitchen with the aid of his walker, Joey and Peter in his wake.

"What's Finn up to today?" she asked.

"Oh, I finally ran him out from under my feet. Did he send you over to coddle me? Make sure I haven't fallen and can't get back up?"

She opened her mouth and then closed it, choosing to answer with a shrug.

He huffed and then lowered himself into one of the kitchen chairs. Peter sat across from him. "Make yourself at home," Walt said to Joey.

She laughed lightly. "Strangely, I do know my way around this kitchen pretty well." She served them each a piece of pie and joined them at the table.

He took a deep breath. "I've decided how I want to finish out the lighthouse project. It's a bit of a combination between a couple of the plans you presented me. I know it might be a long shot and a waste of time and money, but I'd like to try and see what comes of it." He gestured to the file folder on the kitchen island. "Bring that over here, would you, Peter?"

Peter stood and grabbed it. Walt spread out two of the plans and showed Joey the circled elements on each he'd like to incorporate into the finished property.

She smiled at him, the expression a little uncertain. "I really like what you've put together, but it's no small undertaking. It will take some time." What was behind the worry on her face? She'd proven herself more than capable.

He shrugged. "I know. But this feels like the right thing to do."

Joey nodded once, tucking the pages back into the folder. "Yes, sir. You're the boss." She peered at him. "Before you kick off this big plan, do you think you should contact her?"

The envelope with Cathleen McCorvey's address was on his bedside table, mocking him every waking moment.

It didn't seem real that Cay could be alive. That it was possible to travel up her walk, ring her doorbell, and see the woman he'd mourned for over sixty years. "I want to go see her. But not until I can walk to her door by my own locomotion, even if I do have this boot on my foot. Maybe it's silly, but a man has his pride. The last time she saw me, I was a strapping young thing."

Joey patted his forearm. "She's aged just like you have, Walt."

"Maybe so." Apparently, he'd never quite outgrown the desire to impress Cathleen McCorvey. He turned his attention to Peter. "If I haven't said it yet, thank you for bringing that tin can back to the island and for helping Joey here find it after I dropped it."

Peter's shoulders crept toward his ears. "I would've just given it to you if I'd known it was meant for you. Nana just told me to put it in that tree, nothing else."

Walt waved the words away. "Bah. Don't apologize. It was one of the great thrills of my lifetime finding that thing in our old tree. Well, until I went and banged-up my ankle. That was not so thrilling."

The boy cracked a small smile.

"Say, do you still have the maps she gave you?"

Peter nodded. "I kept them safe. I could tell they were special."

Walt rubbed at his chin, feeling the whiskers scrape his palm. "Cay and I drew them."

Peter leaned forward. "Really? They're so detailed. Accurate too. Y'all could've had careers as mapmakers."

He and Cay had thought of themselves as a regular Louis and Clark duo back then. "It was our little world. Some of it imaginary, but all of it was real to us." He shut his eyes, seeing her dark curls bouncing as she ran down the trail in front of him, racing to her skiff. What he wouldn't give to go back. Relive one more day with her. Time and tides had pulled him on. And her too. Flotsam and jetsam.

But against all odds he'd been given another chance to tell Cay the things he'd been too scared to say back then. For all he knew, he was going to meet her and her husband and a whole passel of kids and grandkids. Great-grandkids even. He hoped so, for her sake. "Joey-gal, how soon do you think you can get those plans finished with the lighthouse?"

She squinted in concentration at the pages he'd given her. "Honestly, the lighthouse just needs a few small details. The new structure you want is straightforward enough as long as there's no snags with permits. The adjustments to the old house will likely be the biggest challenge, just because anytime you are working with existing structures, you have to work around what's there. But that house has strong bones, and I'm quite fond of restorations." Light bloomed over her face. "I've just had an idea. I need to make a couple of phone calls and get a few things in the works. Do you guys mind if I run? Peter, you can stay here with Walt or come with me. Whichever you'd prefer."

Peter stood. "I'll get the maps and bring them back. They should be in your hands."

FORTY-THREE

Later that day, Joey's hands trembled as she dialed Lacey's number. What was that old saying? Better one bird in the hand than two in the bush? And Finn had said that it was the chances you didn't take that you tended to regret the most. But what did you do when faced with the choice between two chances?

"This is Lacey."

"Hi, Lacey. This is Joey, um, Josephina, with Events by Josephina, calling you back." She tightened her grip on the phone. She had to take a chance on the choice that would cost her the most to lose.

"You've been a hard woman to reach, Joey." Despite the way she'd been putting her off since their first chat, Lacey's voice was still full of honey, giving every sign that she was the picture of an ideal client.

"I apologize for leaving you waiting. I had an emergency situation, but still, I should have reached out sooner."

"Not to worry, sugar. We'll hit the ground running with this planning thing and be just fine."

Joey pinched her lips tight and then forced out her next words. "I'm really sorry to do this, but as much as taking you on as a client would be a dream come true for me, I've had an opportunity arise out here in North Carolina, and I can't pass it up."

Lacey was quiet for several moments, and Joey braced for the ire she deserved. "You could do the bulk of your work long distance, couldn't you? And swing into Copper Creek in time for the big day?" Her voice wasn't pushy, simply questioning.

"Lacey, ordinarily I would. But what I've got going on here requires my full attention. And that wouldn't be fair to you. Not when it's your wedding day." Joey gave her the contact information of a few local wedding planners whom she trusted to make Lacey happy and ended the call with well-wishes for the bride and groom. Then she let out a long breath. She'd done it. She closed the open door.

She didn't know what was next after she finished this project, but for once, that was freeing instead of frightening. All this time she'd been focused on restoring the Harris family name in Copper Creek. Not that she'd mind getting that deserved vindication. But what was a name without the family that bore it?

The next call she made was to her father. "Hey, Dad, how would you feel about coming out of retirement to help me with a little restoration-slash-addition project to a 1940s lightkeeper's cottage?"

His chuckle coming through the line warmed her. "How did you know?"

"Know what?"

"That I was just complaining to your mother this morning about how restless I've been feeling."

Mom, who must have been listening in, said, "Please take him off my hands for a week or so. This adjusting to retired life is not for the faint of heart." Joey laughed at her mother's teasing. Her father was accustomed to working from dawn to dusk, six days a week. It had surely switched up their marriage dynamic. "You can come too, Mom. I have a place y'all can stay."

Her father chuckled. "I think she has some sort of girls' cruise planned with some of her new friends. I might be struggling, but your momma is thriving."

They made plans for him to come in two weeks. He sounded genuinely excited to help on the project. Joey just hoped he'd retain that enthusiasm once he realized the full scope of the plans she had in place. She then dialed one more number and hoped her brother would answer.

The next evening, she arrived at her old digs to make dinner for Walt and Finn. She was pleasantly surprised to see that Peter was there too. While she layered the lasagna ingredients she'd prepped earlier that day, he and Walt played a game of chess. The maps Peter had returned were spread out on the coffee table, held flat by paperweights at each corner. Once dinner was baking, Joey joined them, studying the intricately drawn maps of the marshy islands, including Bleakpoint with a miniature lighthouse indicating its location. Then there was the other map—a detailed rendering of Walt and Cay's island, labeled with the places that had been special to them. Her eyes caught on one marker that read "Blackbeard's Treasure," indicated with a red X. She turned to Walt who was studying the chessboard. "Imaginary treasure, right? You didn't seriously find Blackbeard's cache?"

Walt wriggled an eyebrow. "I'll never tell."

Peter grinned. "If it was there at one point, it's not now. I checked just in case." His cheeks reddened.

Walt chuckled as he slid a pawn into play.

She watched the game progress. Walt won the first, so Peter set up the board for a rematch. Joey sniffed, savory scents of tomato sauce, oregano, and baking cheese wafting in the air. "I'd better go check on the food. Peter, you better watch yourself with that ol' pirate you're playing against. I've heard he's gone head-to-head with Blackbeard."

As she was walking to the kitchen, Finn entered the front door. He snaked an arm around her waist, pulled her to him, and planted a quick but soft kiss on her lips. He looked down at her, want filling his gaze. "I didn't realize you were coming over this evening."

Walt, having spied them from his seat in the living room, called out, "Welcome home, Finn. We've got *company*." The smile in his eyes belied the chastising tone.

Finn released the embrace and let out an embarrassed laugh. "Hey, Pete. Pops."

Peter lifted a hand in greeting, but his eyes were focused on the chessboard, intent on outfoxing his opponent.

Finn put his messenger bag down by the door. "I'm going to go help Joey in the kitchen."

She grabbed his hand and tugged him with her.

"Might as well order takeout. The food'll be burned," Walt grumbled.

Joey laughed at his teasing as she donned an oven mitt and removed the lasagna from the oven. She placed it on a trivet and gave a chef's kiss. "Perfecto."

"So, now that there are no worries about burned food . . ." He pulled her close and lowered his lips to hers, letting the kiss linger longer than the peck they'd shared at the front door.

She'd heard of firework-inducing kisses, but this was more like being steadily warmed by a sunrise over the building waves of the Atlantic. She released a contented sigh against his lips.

A part of her still urged her to run, that she was falling too hard and too fast for this not to be a sure thing. But what person with any sense ran from a sunrise?

She stepped back. "I'd better finish up the salad."

"Let me help."

She got the bowl of lettuce from the fridge along with some vegetables that needed dicing. He grabbed a knife and cutting board. While he rolled his sleeves to his elbows, washed up, and started chopping carrots, she sat at one of the barstools. "Good day at work?"

"Yeah. I had a few private flights today. Happy people headed on vacation. And a businessman who needed to make a quick trip home to smooth out some wrinkles in a multimillion-dollar deal he's working on. Those last-minute gigs always pay really well." He looked up from his work. "And how are things coming with your latest scheme?"

"Both Dad and Trey are coming in two weeks to work on Walt's plan. Building materials are ordered and en route. Everything is scheduled to be ferried over. Walt's fishing buddy is helping out. Renee and Jerry are going to work on the lighthouse project. I think Peter may even do some of the display descriptions. He's shown me a few things he's written, and I think he'll do a great job. I'm waiting on a permit for the new structure."

Finn stopped chopping. "So . . . your dad and your brother? Do they know they're both coming?"

She gave him a clenched smile and shrugged.

"You sure that's the best idea?"

"No. But neither of them would've come . . . so . . ."

"You're going to *Parent Trap* them?"

She shrugged. "None of the more conventional methods like telling them, 'Hey, don't you think it's time to bury the hatchet?' have worked so far, so they are at the mercy of my machinations now."

Finn grabbed tongs and clacked them in the air like a feisty crab before tossing the salad. "Uh-oh. I guess they're in for it, then."

"Maybe it's a bad idea bringing them together to work on my project," Joey said. "Manipulative even, knowing that while they are both angry, neither will want to hurt the baby girl of the family they both adore." She propped her hands under her chin in an innocent Shirley Temple pose. But then she grew serious. "Walt and Cathleen's story changed me, Finn. I'm taking a big chance that might just blow up in my face, but I've waited long enough to do something. At least now I won't be wondering sixty years later if I missed a chance I should have taken to help my family."

Mischief kindled in Finn's eyes. "I'm hoping this also applies to . . . I dunno . . . other areas of your life?"

Her heart swelled. The way he made her feel was uncharted wilderness. She lifted one shoulder. "I'd say the other areas of application are a strong maybe."

Bleakpoint Island had warmed her up to the promise of wilderness as she'd unfolded its mysteries. Now it was time to dive into her own unknowns with anticipation instead of dread.

That evening, gathered around the table with Walt, Finn, and Peter, she had to admit that this whole adventure had gone majorly off course from the sequence of events she'd charted when she left Copper Creek. Along the way she'd uncovered buried heartache and regret. Time lost that could never be regained. Brokenness. But she'd also witnessed hope, second chances, and even restoration. She had to believe Bleakpoint Island wasn't finished with her mending quite yet.

FORTY-FOUR

Joey checked her watch. Her dad had been a half hour away when he'd last called. That meant he should be pulling into Finn's driveway in fifteen minutes. Trey stood a little ways away, making notes on the packet of papers she'd printed off for him detailing the work to be completed on Bleakpoint. She'd tasked him with overseeing the cabin build and the updated dock system to better accommodate guests.

While Trey worked on those aspects of the project, she and her dad were going to focus on the restoration and modification of the existing keeper's residence. That way her dad and brother would be working adjacent to one another, but neither under the authority of the other.

Trey looked up from his work packet. "I'm ready to take a look at the site. You said you were waiting on someone . . ."

Joey swallowed the knot forming in her throat. "Yeah, um. Dad."

Trey's face went slack like she'd slapped him. Then his expression hardened. He opened his mouth to speak but seemed to think better of spewing venom on his little sister. He took a step toward his car.

"Trey, wait," she said, following after him. "I'm sorry. I should've told you Dad was going to be here, but I knew you wouldn't come, and this has gone on long enough. Somebody has to stand up and tell the two of you to swallow your pride and work through whatever it is that y'all are fighting over. I miss you. I miss our family."

Trey ran a hand through his hair, making it stand up on one side. "Does Dad know I'm—"

She pinched her lips tight and shook her head.

"He won't work with me."

"You don't know that. Give it a chance."

Trey took a shaky breath, and she caught his flinty expression crack a fraction. She stepped closer. "You're not still the twenty-one-year-old who ran off angry after a fight I'm fairly sure neither of you remember the finer points of. And he's . . . he's still Dad. I know he hates what happened between you two. Wishes he had the chance to undo the things he said."

Trey looked away. "I can't deal with it if he starts in on me. Criticizing my every move."

She crossed her arms over her chest. "I know Dad didn't handle things in the best way, but I don't think calling you out for not showing up for work because you'd been out barhopping with your friends all night and hooking up with any girl that would have you is *quite* the same thing as criticizing your every move."

He turned back, hurt reflected in his eyes. "I'm embarrassed of the way I left, Roo. That's the real truth. Thinking I was being a man when I was really just a kid trying to prove myself to anyone watching. Prove that I knew better than my old man who was trying to control my life."

She went to him and wrapped her arms around her older brother, squeezing tight. "Tell him that. I think you're both hanging on to the embers of that fight because you're not sure what you have left if you don't." It was the same reason she'd hung on to Copper Creek. Because, to lose her hometown might mean she'd lose that dream world where everything magically got put back together the way it once was.

Trey stepped back from the embrace. "I'm doing really well for myself, and I'm proud of the man I've become. If he starts treating me like I'm that same immature kid I was . . ."

Just then, their father's truck turned on the street, drawing nearer. She moved between her brother and his car. "Trey, please." Still, he looked poised to run. On foot if he had to.

But then the rigidity in his shoulders collapsed and hope swelled in her middle.

Their dad pulled into the drive, parked, and exited the car. He stared at Trey, eyes like saucers.

She hurried to him and grabbed his hand, squeezing tight, and his gaze broke from Trey and found hers.

"I asked Trey to help me, and he came. That's great, right? The Terrific Trio, back on the job together. I couldn't finish this job without the both of you." She prayed she had not made a mistake.

Dad stared at his son like he was afraid that if he blinked, he'd be gone again. His eyes grew red-rimmed. "Trey, son, it's real good to see you." The words came out as little more than a hoarse whisper that tore at Joey's heart.

Trey gave a nearly imperceptible nod. "You too, Dad."

"I'm sorry." A choking sob squeezed out of her father's chest as he took a stumbling stride forward. The pages fell from Trey's hands as father and son closed the gap between them. One moment they had been two crumbling stone statues, and in a blink, they were transformed into living things, far stronger than stone, holding each other up.

Tears streamed down Joey's cheeks. She was sure they'd been more likely to come to blows than to a place of reconciliation. She couldn't wait to tell Walt how much he'd inspired her.

Five weeks into the final phase of the Bleakpoint Island project, the end was in sight. As excited as she was to see everything come together, Joey knew it also marked the end of something she had been dreaming of for years.

After Mom heard the news that Trey and Dad were reunited and working through their issues, she decided to drive up after her cruise, making the family reunion complete. It felt like days gone by with Mom making them sack lunches and long hours working alongside her brother and father. Everyone under one roof, even if it was Finn's borrowed house. There had been more than a handful of tense moments, but they'd found their way through them.

It was the most fun she'd had in a long time. Doing work she enjoyed, no longer under the pall of her brother and father's broken relationship. And though this arrangement was only temporary, it felt as though they'd been given the chance to rewrite the ending to Harris Construction.

Joey walked through the nearly completed work on the keeper's residence, which was being updated into an off-the-grid, eco-friendly home complete with running water and electricity. Then she headed over to the new construction that was taking place down a winding trail. This build was an off-the-grid cabin, simple, small, but functional.

Trey had done a great job getting the project under way. She hadn't expected him to stay this long, but he'd said he had a good group of people running things for him in his absence and that he was long overdue for some time away.

How she'd miss him when he was gone again. But now they had the promises of Christmases and Thanksgivings spent together as a mended family.

After walking through the cabin, she returned to the lighthouse where Peter, Renee, and Jerry scrubbed and cleaned everything until the interior of the lighthouse nearly sparkled. She climbed the winding staircase, looking over the displays as if seeing them for the first time. Each lighthouse log had been framed and hung in the order it was written. Every few steps another act of courage was displayed.

At the top she walked the circular path around the lantern placed inside. Not the type that would guide lost ships home but one that would put off a warm glow, a gentle reminder of its history.

She stepped out onto the newly installed galley deck. The sea air tossed her hair. A little ways in the distance, Walt's boat bobbed on the water. She waved and imagined him waving back the way he had once greeted Cathleen.

It was nearly time for that trip to Knotts Island. Walt's physical therapist told him he was almost ready to trade the walker for a cane. A form of assistance Walt had deemed dignified enough for reuniting with his long-lost friend. She couldn't imagine caring about such things in her eighties, but this was Walt's story and she wasn't about to judge.

In the interim, Joey had done a little digging and found that there was indeed a woman by the name of Cathleen McCorvey still living on Knotts Island. She'd even scrounged up a brief article about the woman's retirement that noted her many years serving first as a lifeguard and then decades as a lifeguard instructor. She itched to meet the woman with or without Walt.

"Hey, Joey?" Peter's voice beckoned her back inside.

She closed the door tight behind her and walked down the stairs, where he met her, moving much easier now that he was rid of his walking cast. "What's up?"

"I meant to give this to you earlier." He passed her an envelope. "It's an invitation to my graduation. It would mean a lot if you and Finn, and Mister Walt could come. Gramma Mae will be there. Who knows about Rick."

She threw her arms around Peter and gave him a tight squeeze. "We wouldn't miss it." She put the envelope in her back pocket. "Have you thought about what's next for you?"

He smiled shyly and shrugged. "I have an academic scholarship to UNC–Charlotte."

"Seriously? That's impressive."

A tinge of red crept into his cheeks. "I want to major in history. Maybe teach. Or write. I'd like to uncover forgotten bits of history, the stories that most people don't know, and save them from being lost to time. I don't know if that's a realistic plan or whatever, but it's what I'd like to do."

"I think you'll do just fine as long as you don't resort to trespassing, piracy, or arson," Joey said with a wink.

He ducked his chin and laughed. "No, ma'am. I've learned my lesson. I can promise you that."

She placed a hand on his shoulder. "I'm really proud of you, Peter. You've found your footing, and I can't wait to see where the path leads."

FORTY-FIVE

Walt stood in front of the mirror and straightened his tie. He had to admit he looked pretty decent for an old guy who'd nearly kicked the bucket two months ago.

"You 'bout ready, Pops?" Finn called from the living room. "Need a hand with anything?"

"Coming." He hadn't meant to sound gruff. But he was well past the point of needing help getting himself presentable. In fact, he was coming through physical therapy with flying colors. He eyed the walker and the cane side by side near the bedroom door. He chose the walker.

Finn looked up in surprise at the squeak-step, squeak-step sound on the vinyl flooring that announced his arrival. Didn't your PT clear you to ditch that thing a week ago?"

Walt shrugged. "It's been raining, and Pete's graduation is on a football field. Then there's the wet pavement."

Finn held up his hands in surrender. "Whatever you think is best. The last thing I want is you reinjuring that ankle, but all I've heard about is how decrepit the walker makes you feel and how you don't really need it but the doc is making you. And you've been busting your tail in therapy to rid yourself of it."

"It's raining," he grumbled.

"You said as much, but it wasn't raining yest—"

"Are you ready to go or what? We're going to be late if we loiter around gabbing when we should be going."

Finn stood and brushed the wrinkles from his suit pants. "I'm ready. Joey ought to be here in a minute. Thought we'd go together."

Walt jumped on the opportunity to shift Finn's attention to something besides his recovery. "And how's that going?"

An irrepressible smile bloomed on Finn's face. Walt couldn't help but smile with him. It had been so long since he'd seen the kid this happy.

"It's good. We're good. Taking things slow."

Walt scoffed. "Don't take 'em too slow. She'll be heading back to Tennessee before you know it. Better let that woman know you're serious about her."

Finn crossed his arms over his chest. "My life is here, and I don't know if that's what she wants."

"She won't know what you're hoping for if you don't tell her. Even if she says no—"

Finn held up a hand. "I'm trying, all right. You know better than anyone that I once thought a girl I loved wanted the same things I wanted. The pain of loving someone more than they loved me will always be fresh in my mind. And I'll own up and say it. I'm scared to death of the way I feel about Joey. And even more scared I'll tell her and she'll leave anyway. Last I heard, she had a wedding to plan after she finishes this. But like I said, we've stayed away from the future talk and just enjoyed what we have now."

"Sometimes you gotta bite the bullet and do the thing that scares you. Ask the girl to stay."

Finn crossed his arms over his chest. "Uh-huh. All I want to know is if you're taking your own advice."

Walt sputtered. "What are you talking about?"

"Don't think I forgot about what you told me when we first found out Cathleen McCorvey is still alive. You wanted to wait until you ditched the walker. And then you punished yourself in therapy to get to that place, and now that you've accomplished the goal, you're holding back."

"That's not . . ." He wasn't a liar, and he didn't know how to respond without telling a whopper. He huffed and checked his watch. "Where is that girl? We're gonna be late."

"We've plenty of time. You're just trying to get out of this conversation." Finn stepped to him. "You've found out there's still time to get closure on something that's been haunting you for years. Not everyone gets that chance. Don't miss it."

"I'm not making some declaration of love to the woman, Finn. It's true she once had my heart. But your grandmother filled that empty space, and we made the most beautiful life. I'm sorry if all my wrestling with the past ever made you doubt that."

Finn nodded. "I understand. You regretted how you left things with Cathleen. Felt responsible. What a blessing that you're able to get answers and understanding on this side of heaven. That doesn't always happen. So, finish this fourth quarter while there's still time on the clock, Pops."

The doorbell rang. Finn walked to the door and greeted Joey with a quick kiss. Walt shuffled to the kitchen for a glass of water to give them a moment. Young love was a fleeting thing that ought to be savored.

He wavered for a moment and returned to his room to trade the walker for the wooden cane.

When he reappeared, Joey said, "Ready to go?"

"As I'll ever be."

Finn gave him a nod, pride brimming in his eyes. The kid was going to make him blush. Walt grabbed the envelope on the entry table and shoved it into Finn's hand. "Here. You were about to forget Pete's graduation gift."

Joey had stepped back from the group to take a quick call from her parents who let her know they'd made it safely home. She sure was going to miss that brief sweet window in which they were all under one roof. A tattered family patching itself together again. They might not all live in the same town, but now they had the promise of holidays spent together.

A few paces away, Walt, Finn, and Mae gathered around Peter, taking pictures of him grinning in his off-kilter mortarboard.

Imagine if he'd ended up facing his graduation day alone. She pressed a hand to her heart. *It's good to be home.* The thought stopped her in her tracks. That's what made home, home wasn't it? The people? She smiled. Bleakpoint Island was supposed to be a brief pit stop on her journey to get her life back in order. But it had become so much more.

So many things had transpired that hadn't been a part of her original plan when she'd taken this job. Helping Walt and Finn mend the misunderstandings between them. Helping Peter reunite with his grandmother. And then there was Cathleen's story. And hers.

They took Peter to a steak dinner at his favorite restaurant and then they were off to ice cream. From there, he piled in his grandmother's car and said goodbye. Now that he was officially eighteen and a graduate, he planned to stay with his grandmother for the summer. Joey smiled as she waved them off. How wonderful that they could share this precious time together before Peter officially launched out into the world.

Once they were out of sight, Finn drew closer to her. "I want to make sure Pops gets in okay, but do you mind waiting?" he whispered. "There's something I'd like to talk to you about."

She nodded, but the nervous way he looked at her made her want to change her mind. Joey paced the gravel parking area and checked her reflection in the parking mirror of her truck. The Events by Josephina decal had started to peel. She poked at the raised edge, resisting the itching in her fingertips to pick at it. She pinched the vinyl between her nails.

"What are you doing?"

She spun. Finn looked at her questioningly.

"The decal is coming off. It was bugging me."

He nodded and stepped closer. He'd removed his tie and jacket. The sleeves of his blue shirt were rolled up and the top few buttons undone. There was a look in his eyes, a mingling of hope and fear. Tenderness and want. A look that marched in cadence with her own heart.

She gestured down the road. "Should we walk? There's a trail not far. You get great sunset views."

He nodded.

They walked a ways, and she took his hand in hers. "You're quiet," she said. "What's on your mind?"

He laughed under his breath. "A few things."

"Good things?"

He nodded thoughtfully but didn't say anything else. Her thudding heart was more than adequate to fill the silence. Was this the part where he told her he wasn't ready to move on, after all?

They left the road and strolled the boardwalk trail that ventured out over the marshes. Still, he didn't say anything. She tugged him to a stop. "Finn, please, what is it?"

He turned to her, taking her other hand. There was a tremor in his hands, and she thought she heard the pounding of his heart, but it was probably her own pulse in her ears.

"There's something I want to ask you." He grimaced. "Or tell you. We said we'd take things slow and see where they went. But forget that nonsense." He took a shaky breath. "Despite my best attempts at maintaining my overly cautious MO, I can't stop thinking about you. Admittedly, at first my mind was consumed with all the ways we could go wrong." One corner of his mouth lifted. "But now all I see are all the ways it could go right." He released her hands and angled slightly away from her, running his hands through his hair, making his carefully combed style stand wild. "And I'm embarrassed to say that that still scares me half to death." He faced her again, a new determination in his gaze.

"Okay. Here's the facts. I know I have no right to ask this of you, but the truth is I don't want you to go back to Tennessee when you're done here. In fact, I hate that idea. Like really, really hate it. If you need to go back and plan that wedding and every possible celebration Copper Creek can hold, I'll respect that and not say another word about it. But I couldn't let you leave not knowing how I feel. What I want."

She pinched her lips tight. In all the nerves of attempting to reunite her brother and father and get Walt's plan off the ground, she'd never fully explained that she'd canceled that plan—not delayed it.

She grabbed his hands, tugging him back to fully face her. She'd never seen the man so undone, except for when Walt was missing. She squeezed his hands. "I think I need to better explain to you what's waiting for me in Copper Creek. So that you understand."

He seemed to have stopped breathing.

She squeezed his hands again and smiled. "Nothing."

"Nothing?" His voice faltered and hope lit his blue eyes.

"Copper Creek was a place. My business was something to fill my time. Just one way to exercise my God-given talents. And I thought I needed to regain my town's approval before I could move on with my life because that place was all I had left of a life I'd lost. But you—" The tightness in her throat cut away her words. "You're more than a place and time. You're the chance I want to take, Finnegan O'Hare."

He wrapped his arms around her, lifting her, spinning in a circle. A shrieking laugh escaped her at his unexpected move.

He sobered. "Seriously?"

She laughed and pulled him close. "Seriously," she whispered as her lips brushed his.

FORTY-SIX

Walt shifted in his seat, rehearsing what he'd say to Cay, as Finn drove down a long driveway and parked in front of a light blue cottage with white shutters. Walt understood just how Cathleen McCorvey had wound up settled on Knotts Island. It was a lot like Ocracoke in a way. Not exactly convenient to get to the required ferry rides, but it had a similar quaint, world-unto-itself feel.

Walt wiped his damp palms against his trousers.

"Do you want me to come with you?" Finn placed a hand on his shoulder.

Walt shut his eyes tight and shook his head. "I need to do this on my own." He opened the car door, and Finn passed him his cane from the back seat.

He traveled down her walk, holding his posture as straight as his joints, stiff from travel, allowed. A reunion over sixty years in the making. Would she even believe who he was when he told her?

He knocked on the door and then shuffled back, careful not to trip. The last thing he wanted was her opening the door to him sprawled out on her porch like a drunken spider.

A woman answered the door, gray-haired and wiry in a button-down blouse and Bermuda shorts. He smiled, and his mouth went dry. That was his Cay. Beautiful as ever in her wild marsh girl way.

"Can I help you?" Her tone was clipped, and her expression guarded.

He nodded once, blinking back the moisture gathering in his eyes, trying to resist the way his mind attempted to wind back through years and memories and lost time between them. "I . . . I hope so. You're Cathleen McCorvey?"

She edged backward, poised to shut the door. "Who's asking?"

He swallowed, trying to wet his mouth enough to form words. "My name is Finnegan Walter O'Hare. But my best friend Cay always called me Wally."

Her eyes flashed wide in shock and then narrowed. She shook her head. "He died."

"He didn't." He pulled the mouth harp from his pocket and gave it a twang.

Seemingly against her will, a wondrous smile stretched her life-weathered cheeks. She pressed a hand to her chest. "How?"

"The article you saw was a misprint. They corrected it, but—"

"It was too late."

He nodded. "I'm sorry about your father."

That haunted, shuttered look returned.

"He was sick, wasn't he? Dementia maybe?"

She had the look of a warrior ready to defend her post, even unto death. "How do you know about my father? No one—"

He pointed to two rocking chairs on her porch that overlooked a field. "I don't mean to be presumptuous, but could we sit? I've had a bit of an accident recently, and this ankle of mine troubles me if I stand too long."

She nodded and they each took a seat. She kept shooting him sideways glances as if expecting him to have vanished when she wasn't looking.

He gripped the armrest, unsure of how to proceed. Of how she'd feel about what he'd done. "I . . . uh . . . when my wife, Martha, passed away, I was an unmoored ship, and I found myself drifting back to our old stomping grounds, caught in a current

I'd thought I'd learned how to navigate. But the truth was, I was still tore up about the way I left you, and it took over my every thought. I . . . I bought Bleakpoint Island, and I've been restoring your light, Cay. We found some of your father's old things he'd hidden away . . . that's how we guessed about his condition."

There was an aching hunger in her eyes. Not for him, he knew, but for those remnants of her old life. He swallowed. "How I wish I could go back and undo all the things that went wrong. I'm sorry."

She blinked hard, and her lips trembled as she spoke. "What do you have to be sorry for? You, Wally, were always my gentle sound. My father was the tumultuous sea."

Walt smiled gently. "And you were a barrier island caught in between. Immovable."

She gave a humorless laugh. "Immovable? More like slowly washed away until I didn't know who I was anymore. Nothing has a shorter memory than sand on a seashore. Reshaped every time a whitecap rolls in."

He shifted in his seat. "We found something else, Cay. In between the stones of that old light."

She gasped. How he wanted to offer some sort of comfort to the stark fear in her eyes. "No one was ever supposed to know. But . . . but I felt like if I didn't write it down, I'd lose myself. I should've used them for kindling." She gripped the armrest of the rocker, white-knuckled like she was trying to hold herself in place.

He covered her hand with his own. "I wish I'd tried harder to reach you. To understand. You deserve the highest commendation for the way you loved your father, trying to hold back the tides of his disease all on your own. A disease that neither you nor anyone else understood back then. I know the world doesn't know what you've done, but I do. And your courage astounds me, Cay. Even if I didn't know the full extent of what you faced, you were never forgotten. Not by me. Not by God. He kept a record of every tear. Every fear."

She turned to him, moisture gathering in her gray-green eyes. "I wasn't brave. I was a coward who cost people's lives because

I thought I could handle it. Hold together what little of him remained. But it was wrong of me." She pulled her hand away from his, and her posture curled, the picture of a soul-crushed child.

"So you've spent the rest of your life punishing yourself for the decisions made by a sixteen-year-old girl who was trying for all the world to protect her father. We can't live life looking backward, Cay. You'll torture yourself to death living like that.

"I thought buying your island and fixing it up could fill the hole I created in my heart when I left you. But it didn't. I've had to forgive myself for things I did when I didn't know any better. And I'm just thankful to God that I've been given the chance to tell you how sorry I am."

She wrapped her arms around her middle. "I don't know why I fought so hard to keep Dad's post. No matter what, it was never going to be mine to keep."

He shifted in his seat and removed the thick envelope from his back pocket. "I can't believe how blessed I am to get the chance to hand you this."

She stared at the envelope in his hands. "What is it?"

"The deed to Bleakpoint Island. Although if you look up the property records, it's been given a new name." He wiggled the envelope. "Go on. Take it. Saint-Mae Island is yours."

Her mouth dropped open. She shook her head.

He smiled. "Though the official maps will always retain the old name, it's not the one I'll call it by."

She pushed the paperwork back toward him. "I can't accept that."

"I'm only returning what was rightfully yours all this time. I just ask that you wait another week before you come see her. My friends and I have been working on a little surprise for you."

Worry creased her face.

"Don't fret. My friends are of the best sort. Discerning. Discreet. Your secret is safe with us, Cay. For as long as you want us to keep it."

She searched his eyes. "I need to know something first, Wally. Can you really ever forgive me for not telling the truth? To you. To anyone. I . . . I caused—" Her gaze found the scar on his hand.

"I forgave you a long time ago. Can you forgive me for running away when I got my feelings hurt?"

She nodded.

He slapped his knee. "Good. We're way too old, and we've missed way too many years to hold grudges."

She gave a soft laugh, then gestured to the car. "Someone waiting for you?"

"My grandson. He'd love to meet you."

Her chin trembled a little. "Okay."

Cathleen lived alone. Existed alone. She ventured out to church each Sunday. But her relationships never reached beyond polite hellos, goodbyes, and God bless yous as she dropped off casseroles for potlucks she never stayed for. And now there was a man and his grandson sitting on the sofa that, though it was twenty years old, still looked like it was fresh from the furniture shop.

A man who happened to be her childhood best friend. And his grandson. *Grandson?* How was it possible that Wally O'Hare had a grandson? Just yesterday they were a couple of kids tooling through the sound as though they owned it.

She'd held onto that time capsule image of him so long, she struggled to believe the man sitting on her sofa was the same person.

She glanced across the room. Walt sipped the unsweetened peppermint tea she'd scavenged from the back corner of her pantry. He attempted to hide his slight grimace of distaste at the flavor behind his mug while his grandson good-naturedly ribbed him for his apparently inflated description of his "gorgeous" sailboat. That twinkle in Walt's eye as he defended his boat was the same Wally she remembered though.

He always had a way of seeing beauty and worth in things others didn't. Like the way he'd overinflated his memories of the girl she'd been.

Cathleen had been trying to pay attention to the conversation at hand, but all her mind wanted to do was scour the past for memories—to look back on those last days. The misunderstandings. The false information that had made them believe they were forever lost to each other.

"Cathleen?" The way Finn said her name, with that tinge of concern, clued her into the fact that that wasn't his first attempt at getting her attention.

Heat rose to her face. "Yes?"

"Do you mind if I ask you a question? We've pieced a lot together about the days leading up to the night you disappeared, but there are some things I still have questions about. Would you be willing to share, to fill in some of those blanks?"

"Finn." The warning in Walt's voice made even her sit at attention.

She raised a hand. "It's okay. I don't mind."

"We didn't come here to call you to accounts, Cay. You don't owe us anything," Walt said.

"Really, it's fine." She looked to Finn. "What would you like to know?"

"A lot of things." He chuckled. "But how did the misunderstanding happen? What really happened that night?"

She pressed her hands to her stomach, trying to still the churning. There was so much of her story she'd kept back, even from Kit, the one woman she'd entrusted to be the keeper of her story. Maybe it was time to reveal what really happened. She closed her eyes, letting years rewind. Soon the scene played in her mind like she was a spectator instead of the one who'd lived it.

Wind whistled and the door smacked in its frame, jarring Cathleen fully awake. She blinked hard and shifted in the rocking chair by the fire where she'd started to sleep after her father had taken to nighttime wanderings. She hadn't intended to fall asleep, but there were days lately when her body refused to cooperate with her constant vigil. She wasn't sure if she'd spent more time peering over the water looking for signs of scouting U-boats or studying her father's revolving moods.

She dragged her exhausted body from the chair and peered out the window. Looked like it was going to be a bit nasty out. Rainy and low visibility. Though the weather was ugly, the ships would likely find safer passage on a night like this. She'd planned to be up long before now, patrolling the coast from Bleakpoint's darkened tower. She slipped into her rain slicker and boots, ready to climb those many steps even knowing there was little use playing lookout on a night like this. She tramped into the rain and dark, the path so engrained into her muscle memory that she didn't require a lantern to guide her. When she reached the lighthouse, the door stood ajar.

She stepped inside, heart thudding. The solid stone structure instantly muffled the wind and the rain. But now another sound pinged against her eardrums. An unintelligible voice from the top of the lighthouse. She attempted to sound in command of the situation, but the tremor in her voice betrayed her. "H-Hello? Who's there?" The muttering ceased. Should she go back for her father, a father who could no more defend her against a German invasion than tell Cathleen her name?

She grabbed the handle of the push broom she stored behind the stairs and traversed the steps quiet as a cat. It was little use sneaking since she'd already announced herself, but maybe she could still count on an element of surprise. The intruder had heard a girl's voice. A girl they'd expect to scurry on back to bed after no reply. She kept her breathing shallow even though her heart was beating out of her chest, demanding oxygen to fuel its frantic pulse.

The muttering resumed as she drew closer. A voice she knew.

She tightened her grip on the broom handle. If she was wrong, she was about to reveal her position. But if she was right, she had no time to lose. "Da? Are you up there?"

His scowling face appeared, leaning over the rail. His eyes, clouded and suspicious, belonged to a stranger. "Who are you?"

She attempted a tremulous smile and propped the broom against the wall. "Just a fellow keeper of the light, here to assist. Tonight's your night off, you should get back to bed."

"Why have you let the light go dark? Lives could be lost because of your neglect." Guilt roiled in her gut. Fatigue had caused her to neglect her duties, just not in the way he proposed.

She continued climbing toward him at a slow and steady pace. "We're waiting on some things to be repaired so that we can get her going again."

He disappeared from the rail and his footsteps clomped overhead. "I see nothing amiss aside from all this disconnected wiring. Why have you done this?"

Cathleen sprinted up the stairs. Rattles and clanks sounded. And then the whole room was flooded with light.

"No!" She gasped as she reached the landing. "There's U-boats out there hunting ships. We have to shut it off."

Suspicion and anger clouded his face. "Lies." He stepped to block her from the instrumentation.

"We've got to turn it off. Now." She attempted to shove him aside, but emaciated as he'd become in comparison to his once-strapping build, she still was no match for his strength. "Listen to me." She begged God to restore his mind, if only long enough to convince her father of the reality in which he lived.

She sent a furtive glance out of the glass. A ship silently slipped into view. In the next instant, an explosion rent the night sky and vibrated the ironwork beneath her feet. The tranquil silhouette had been swallowed by a wall of flame.

Her gaze darted back to her father. Chest heaving with his hands limp at his sides, he stared, eyes haunted orbs inside his skull. She took advantage of the moment and performed the necessary operations to shut off the light.

But it was too late.

The damage had been done.

A ship burned off the coast of Bleakpoint, betrayed by the very people committed to keeping her from danger.

She took her father by the hand and led him down the stairs. He followed like a child who had been found sleepwalking. Once she got him inside, she poured him a cup of tea, moving calmly though urgency thrummed in every nerve ending. "Here you go. Have a cup of tea by the fire. I'll be right back." She led him to a chair, and he sat holding the mug, an odd look in his eye. She offered a gentle smile and nod and then turned for the door.

"Right back from where, Cathy?"

She gasped and turned. His eyes were lucid and earnest. Afraid.

How long had it been since she'd heard her name on his lips. Everything inside of her wanted to run to his feet and lay her head on his lap. Let him stroke her hair like he had when she was a girl. Even while a ship sank to the ocean floor. Because this would not last. For one fleeting instant, she'd like to remember what it was just to be this man's daughter. Not his keeper.

"Just . . . just an errand." She stepped closer to the door, praying for a way to prevent him from following.

He pressed his lips tight, and water leaked from the corner of his eyes. He put the mug on the table, his hands shaking so much that tea lapped over the rim and spilled onto the wood. "I saw the ship. I . . . I did that."

She shook her head and rushed to him and grasped his hands. "No, no, you didn't." If anyone was guilty, it was not him. "It was just an accident."

"I can't let you go, Cathy."

"I must."

"I'll go," he rasped.

"You're not well. It has to be me."

He stared at her like he was memorizing her and then he nodded.

"You'll be here when I return?" She craved so much more than just his physical presence.

He nodded once more. She turned on her heel and ran for his boat, praying the entire way that God would somehow let his clarity remain until she returned. She unmoored the boat and motored for the damaged ship. As soon as she got back from rescuing any survivors, she and her father had to go. No one could find out what had happened here and why. This destruction could not be what he was remembered for. She couldn't let him be counted as a madman. A criminal.

She looked back once more to Bleakpoint Light. Her skiff bobbed on the waves, the sound of the outboard motor lost in the wind.

Her heart sank to the bottom of the sea.

Cathleen lifted her chin, taking in Walt and Finn who listened in rapt attention. "I could either go back and try to take my father on the run. Or I could go out there and see if there was any way I could help the poor souls I'd doomed as best I could and pray my father would be okay until I could get to him. By the time I found Walt and got him back to shore on Ocracoke, I'd long lost sight of him. As soon as I sent a gawking kid for help, I went back for my father. In the morning hours I found my skiff overturned but largely unharmed on a shoal, but no sign of him no matter how long I looked. I scuttled his boat and took the skiff."

Walt looked like he was ready to spring from his seat, but he stayed in place. "I'm so sorry."

She dropped her chin and whispered her thanks. She'd tried to go back a million times and rethink it all. Rewrite history that didn't leave her without her father. In these imaginings, she'd had superhuman strength that didn't flag. Or after she'd returned him to the house, she'd somehow had the power to convince him to stay and not leave. She sighed. "I wish I had been there for him in his last moments. I wish I had had more wisdom. More strength."

Walt smiled gently. "He remembered you at the end. That's something."

"The sound of my name on his lips that night still visits me when I dream."

Finn scooted to the edge of the seat. "And after that night?"

Cathleen clasped her hands, squeezing tight. "I hid in the shadows waiting for news of Walt by day. Searched for my father by night. When I saw Walt's mother run out crying from that makeshift hospital, I knew." She swallowed hard. "And then I saw that paper. Like a feral thing, I stayed on our island for over a month, surviving off fish and anything I could forage. I scoured those surrounding salt marshes for any sign of my father. Like an empty broken shell of something that used to be alive, I slept and ate just enough to not die."

Walt shifted. "After I healed up, I came back. The tin can in our tree was empty."

She raised her brows. "It must have been while I was still there, then. I remember one time thinking I'd heard someone but thought I'd dreamed it. Because before I left, after I'd found your mouth harp, I wrote you a farewell letter. I almost left it in the tree, but I found I couldn't part with it. When I gave up hope that my father survived, I sank my own skiff and then stowed away on the mailboat."

Finn pulled something from his messenger bag and walked it over to her. The old coffee can. She took it in her trembling hands. "Kit?"

Finn nodded. "She's the one who told us how to find you."

"I left it to her. I guess because she was the only person I'd ever trusted my story with," she said. "That might be the one right move I've ever made with my life."

"That was a good move but not your only," Walt replied. "I hope I can convince you of that."

FORTY-SEVEN

Joey blew out a slow breath to steady her nerves. Today was the day Cathleen McCorvey would return to Bleakpoint Island or, rather, Saint-Mae Island, as it was secretly called by the people who knew the true history behind the legends.

Joey turned a slow circle, taking in the work she'd facilitated. She hoped that when Cathleen looked upon what they'd done, the updates would fade to the background and all she'd see was the home she loved and memories that were sweet.

Jerry and Renee exited the keeper's house after a final walkthrough to make sure everything was staged and polished to a shine. They gave her hugs in turn and told her they'd be in touch to see how things go.

"You're not staying?" Joey asked.

"We'd love to come visit later on, with Cathleen's blessing, but we don't want to overwhelm her. We're riding back on the workboat with all the cleanup supplies."

"Sounds good. They should all be arriving soon." Finn and Peter were on their way to retrieve their secret guest of honor in a borrowed boat. Walt should be there in minutes with Cathleen, ferrying her across on his sailboat, which he'd been buffing for a week straight in preparation for the event.

Joey watched as the workboat departed. This island had been

the catalyst on her journey to find herself again, reminding her what she really wanted out of life. To be surrounded by people she loved and who loved her back, living her own adventure with only a side job of orchestrating the celebrations of others. And this celebration was one she could wholeheartedly dive into.

She sighted Walt's sailboat coming her way, and headed to the dock to meet them. Joey stood a little ways back so Cathleen didn't feel pounced upon and could take in her old home unhindered.

Walt took a wobbly step off his boat and then held out a hand for his guest. Her eyes drank in the island like a person who'd wandered in the desert for decades and had just stumbled into their longed-for oasis.

Joey approached with a small wave. "Hi. My name is Joey Harris. I had the joy of restoring your property. It is an absolute honor to meet you."

Walt grinned. "Joey here was like a dog with a bone trying to find out what had become of you. I'm forever indebted to her for bringing you back to me and making my dreams for this island a reality." He gave Cathleen a beseeching look. "I hope you like what we've done with the place."

Joey stepped back. "I'll leave you two to it. Peter and Finn will be here in a little while."

They'd timed things carefully to give Cathleen a little time alone with her island before they brought their surprise guest. Joey followed along at a distance trying to imagine what it would be like to experience this place from Cathleen's point of view. From the family photos they'd found among Callum's hidden things displayed prominently to the restored and newly furnished keeper's cottage. Thanks to Renee's careful curation, every item was in keeping with the time period in which Cathleen lived there.

Joey pictured Cathleen taking the freshly washed mugs from the cabinet, holding the very vessels she and her father once drank from. She and Walt left the cottage and strolled to the lighthouse that she would find polished to a high shine, displaying Cathleen's lightkeeping logs as she climbed the stairs. A history no longer hidden but celebrated. Though Cathleen McCorvey had been an imperfect heroine, she deserved to be seen and known by those who loved her, out of hiding.

Joey looked at her watch. In exactly three minutes, the timer would turn on the gently glowing lantern, now housed in the top of Saint-Mae's light. No longer a beacon warning of dangerous shoals ahead but a warm symbol of people coming together, finding a place they belonged.

The light came on. A few moments later she saw the form of Cathleen McCorvey standing on the galley walk, looking out over the rolling waves, the wind sweeping her chin-length gray curls back from her face. It wasn't hard to imagine her as a sixteen-year-old girl again, looking as though she had the ability to sprout wings and fly down to Walt's boat where he'd waited, longing to be closer to her.

Joey's radio crackled to life, carrying Finn's voice. "We made it."

"Be right there," she radioed back. She gave a final glance to Cathleen, who seemed to have spotted the new arrival from her lighthouse vantage point. Joey hurried to lend a hand to their newest guest as she navigated the now wheelchair-accessible dock.

When she reached them, Kit waved from her chair. "Hullo there, Joey. They busted me out of the joint and fixed me up a new set of wheels made for the sand. Reckon Cathleen knows it's me yet?"

"She knows someone is here. She was watching from the lighthouse tower."

Kit clapped her hands like a giddy schoolgirl. "Oh boy. I hope I shock her socks off." Peter wheeled his great-grandmother down the widened path to the lighthouse.

By the time they'd reached the structure, Cathleen had made it down the stairs. Her eyes glittered with new life and a girlish pink colored her cheeks. She walked slowly to the gathered group with Walt in her wake. Her mouth parted and she stared.

"Well, aren't you going to hug my neck, you renegade girl?" Kit asked.

Cathleen closed the gap between them. "I can't believe it's really you."

After several long moments enveloped in her friend's arms, Cathleen straightened and pressed her hands to her cheeks. "I simply cannot believe this." She caught each of their gazes in turn. "Thank you all for giving back to me so, so many things I'd lost. Many of it by my own foolish choices. I simply do not deserve this."

Walt put an arm around her shoulder and squeezed. "On that point we disagree. But that's the beauty of love and grace, Cay. The real kind. We don't have to earn it."

Epilogue

Joey and Finn strolled down the beach of Bleakpoint. Finnegan Walter O'Hare IV walked between them, his small hands tucked in theirs. But, like his great-grandfather, the four-year-old found the moniker a little stuffy, and he preferred to go by Wally.

They came every year on this date, a commemoration of the day Walt returned the island to Cathleen McCorvey.

The boy wriggled his hands free from his parents' and skipped ahead. It was such a gift that Walt had had the chance to meet his great-grandson, but it broke Joey's heart knowing that Wally wouldn't remember him. But they'd forever tell the boy the adventures of young Walt and Cay roaming these marshlands like they owned them.

As it had turned out, Cathleen had never married, so she didn't have family to occupy the guest cottage as Walt had planned. Eventually, Walt had moved into the spare house. The two friends kept each other company on the quiet island for as long as their health allowed.

Then they'd moved in with Joey and Finn.

Cathleen passed on first, with Walt to follow within that same year. It had been heartbreaking and yet somehow hopeful watching the two of them support one another through the final trials of this life.

Joey would count herself forever blessed to witness Cathleen and Walt finding their way back to the friendship that had been so dear to them.

Finn's charter flights had proven far more lucrative than he'd originally foreseen, allowing Joey to take on select restoration projects that piqued her interest. Namely those with a little hidden history. She was always sure to call up her favorite young historian to help her solve any mysteries she encountered.

Finn put his arm around her, pulling her close as they walked.

She smiled up at him. "Peter's coming with his wife. Tomorrow, I think."

"And then your family the next week? Both houses are ready?"

"Of course," she replied and then grew quiet as she listened to the crashing waves. "Missing him today?"

He nodded. "Every day."

"Me too."

He pulled her to a stop. She watched their little boy kick sand and peer down crabholes out of the corner of her eye. Finn turned her chin to him. "Thank you. I know I have told you a million times, but you're the reason I was able to enjoy those last years with him. It yanks the breath from my lungs knowing how close I was to missing out on even a moment of it." He pressed a kiss to her forehead.

She pulled back and looked into his eyes "I'm grateful to have played a role, but I wasn't the planner orchestrating this event. This one was in the hands of One far more skilled than I, gently guiding even when we were all half certain we'd lost our way."

You saw me before I was born.
   Every day of my life was recorded in your book.
Every moment was laid out
   before a single day had passed.

Psalm 139:16 NLT

Author's Note

While the other Outer Banks locations mentioned in the book are real geographical places, Bleakpoint Island and its lighthouse are works of my imagination. Likewise, the command for Bleakpoint Light to go dark is this author taking a bit of artistic license for the sake of the story.

During Operation Drumbeat, in which hundreds of Allied freighters were torpedoed by German U-boats along the United States' Eastern Seaboard, there is no record that the lighthouses were asked to go dark or to dim their lights, unlike some US lighthouses on the West Coast and in Europe. In fact, there wasn't even an official blackout order for civilians in the Outer Banks until April 1942, after the tides of the battle had shifted and the U-boat bombings had all but ceased.

There is documented communication between German officers commenting on what easy targets the unescorted merchant ships were because of the light coming from the shoreline and the absence of military protection. Lack of resources and coordination between the Army, Navy, Coast Guard, local government, and air forces is cited as the reason behind the lack of blackout regulations and ongoing loss of merchant ships. Around four hundred Allied freighting ships were lost during Operation Drumbeat, eighty-two of which were sunk along North Carolina's coast alone. Almost none of the mariners aboard those torpedoed ships survived.

The people of the Outer Banks were quite nervous about German invasion as well as spy operations. While there were many rumors and tales about spies traipsing about stealing chickens and livestock, there is no official record that spies were discovered or captured in the Outer Banks.

Though the legends of Saint-Mae are my own creation, the Outer Banks is steeped in folklore and ghost stories. If you'd like to get a taste of the real deal, check out the many compilations written by Charles Harry Whedbee.

I hope you enjoyed the nuggets of Outer Banks history woven into this story.

Turn the page to read an excerpt
from another captivating tale
by Amanda Cox

Prologue

Callie's ears filled with the sound of windshield wipers slapping and Momma's incessant muttering. Prayers or curses, Callie couldn't tell. She wished Momma would turn the car around—that for once in their lives they could just stay.

The feeling that had clenched Callie's chest while they shoved their few belongings into duffel bags early that evening hadn't let up an inch in the hours they'd traveled.

Her mother had tried to hide behind smiles and promises of adventure, even in the dark of night. Didn't she know by now that Callie knew the difference between the truth and a lie? Momma's smiles were as dependable as the flimsy dress-up costumes from the bargain store that ripped halfway through trick-or-treating.

She studied the back of her mother's head, wishing she could crawl inside and see what lived there.

Sometimes she wondered if Momma was like the neighbor's cat that had gotten hit by a car. It lived, but it was never right again, given to darting wildly about the yard but not escaping. Running and running until it fell over.

Callie pushed out a heavy breath and leaned forward to pick up the canary yellow teapot resting by her feet.

Her mother glanced over her shoulder. "Go back to sleep, sweetie. When you wake up, we'll be at our new place," she said with too-bright sunshine in her voice.

Callie cradled the teapot against her middle and shut her eyes.

Instead of sleeping, she imagined Ms. Ruthie's round kitchen table, sliced by a ray of sunlight, with the bright teapot at its center, warm next to the robin's-egg blue walls.

Momma had swiped it from the apartment before Ms. Ruthie's real relatives arrived to sort through her belongings. She'd pressed that cool, ceramic vessel into Callie's hands as though a teapot could compensate for a living, breathing human being. Momma promised tea parties and a lot of other things. But the only thing Ms. Ruthie's teapot held since the day she died was air.

Ms. Ruthie. The tea party queen. Her pretend parent at Open House at school. The baker of cookies so Callie hadn't come to bake sales empty-handed. The drier of tears when Callie cried for a mother who too often disappeared without warning.

She stared out the window and sniffled. Headlights reflected off the droplets jittering across the panes, and Callie pretended they were squirming slugs racing for safety. Some made it across. Others grew heavy from the weight of water and dropped into the deep darkness beyond her car window. She silently cheered the droplets on, even those that struggled, doomed to fall.

Callie was sucked into repetitive dreams in which she fell in unending dark alongside the plummeting raindrops, never reaching the ground. Windshield wiper slaps. Ms. Ruthie. Water droplets.

A jarring motion woke her. The round teapot slipped from Callie's sleep-laxed hands and hit the floorboard with a sickening crack.

The car jerked again, and Callie's mother cursed at potholes and rainstorms and the absence of streetlights on the winding road.

Momma slowed. Rain drummed against the pane at a frantic rate.

Moments later, the car turned. The scratchy slosh of deep, wet gravel met Callie's ears as the single beam of Momma's one working headlight shone on a wooden sign.

Walsh Farm.

One

TWENTY-TWO YEARS LATER

The field dotted with white boxes hummed a song Beckett Walsh had tuned her life to. Arms loaded with black cloths, she tramped through the field, the tall grass thwacking against her rubber boots. At the center of the apiary, she set down her burden. Though she'd never believed in these superstitions, she'd made him a promise.

One by one she unfolded the repurposed tablecloths and draped each hive. Every time, she said the same thing.

"He's gone. He's not coming back. It's just me now."

She swallowed and blinked her dry eyes. The bees' capacity to understand this loss was probably about as good as hers.

The early summer fever broke as the sun lowered behind the distant hills. Thank goodness for that. She wanted to keep her promise, but wouldn't these cloths overheat her bees? Her bees. They were supposed to be their bees. They'd always been theirs.

He'd brought home their first package of bees twenty-three years ago, when she was only five. She could still remember stretching her hand up to the mesh that made the sides of the small wooden box. The tight cluster of bees clung to the top, the power of their delicate wings stirring air against her palm.

At the memory, the ache inside her swelled, cutting away her

319

breath. The days, hours, years they'd spent in this field. Working side by side. Checking queens. Diagnosing hive issues. Collecting liquid gold. Talking.

He'd always been a quiet man, but being out among the bees changed him. Here, his pent-up words flowed freely, like the gentle brook that formed the border between their field and the woods.

Mere days ago she'd listened to those low tones for the last time. Had she known it, she might have paused her work, leaned in, and let his talk of bees and their mysterious ways cradle her like an embrace. She clenched the black shroud in her fists and swallowed hard as she draped another hive. "He's gone. He's not coming back." The words scraped past the knot in her throat.

"Hey! What are you doing?"

Beck turned, searching for the small lilting voice that had jolted her.

A slender girl emerged from the brush at the edge of the field. She pulled a bramble from the end of a honey-colored plait.

"This is private property."

But the girl traversed Beck's invisible boundary in her shorts and mismatched knee socks. She marched up to Beck, picked a bur from the flower-patterned sock, tugged the striped sock higher, and swiped at the angry red scratch on her thigh.

"This is private property," Beck repeated more slowly this time.

The girl plucked a long piece of grass and stuck it behind her ear. "I'm sorry. I didn't know. Where I come from there is no such thing as private property. We are all one people. One land." The girl pulled a small notebook and a nub of a pencil from a neon fanny pack at her waist. She scrawled something on it and stuffed it back into her pack. "I am learning so many interesting things on your planet."

Beck sighed. This child had to be at least nine. Maybe ten. Beck didn't know much about kids, but surely the girl was too old to pretend to be a life-form from another planet. Too young to be wandering by herself all the way out here. Beck put her hands on her hips. "Here on Earth we frown upon things like trespassing." She motioned to the hives surrounding them. "You could get yourself hurt if you don't know what you're walking into."

The girl edged away from the nearest bee box. "They'll sting?"

"They're bees. Of course they'll sting." Beck pursed her lips. She'd never been one to instill fear in people about her beloved bees, but the last thing she needed was an unchaperoned child hovering about her hives.

The girl shivered and rubbed her bare arms despite the soft blanket of heat lingering in the early evening air. "But you're not even wearing one of those suits."

"My bees know me. It's strangers they don't like."

The girl stuck out her hand.

Beck eyed her skinny, briar-scratched arm.

The girl tilted her head. "Is this not the customary earthling greeting? My name is Katya Amadeus Cimmaron. I hail from the planet Zirthwyth of the Vesper Galaxy."

Beck crossed her arms over her chest. "You look like an earthling to me." She glanced to the descending sun. "You'd better head home. I'm sure some other earthling is looking for you."

Katya shrugged and dropped her waiting hand. "I only look like an earthling. I am a shapeshifter. It is my gift. To you, I look like a mere child. But to my people, I am two hundred of your Earth years old. How old are you?"

Beck did not have time for this nonsense, and yet this imp of a girl had a gravitational pull that tugged Beck into her fictional orbit. Or maybe she was simply a convenient delay from facing the painful things beckoning her back to the farmhouse.

Beck propped her hands on her hips. "I am twenty-eight in Earth years, if you must know."

"What's your name?"

"Beckett Walsh, but everyone calls me Beck."

Katya scrunched her nose in animated concentration. "Beck,

why are you covering up the bees? Does it protect them? I hear there is a crisis of dying bees on your planet. And if bees die out, human life will become unsustainable. Funny how such a tiny thing can keep the earth going." The girl pulled out the notebook again and poised her pencil at the ready position. "How do these black cloths save your bees?"

Beck raised an eyebrow. This kid was some piece of work. "Why the interest? Do you have a bee crisis on your planet too?"

Katya shook her head, her expression somber. "I am not here to find out how to save my planet. I am here to see if there is still time to save yours."

Something about the solemnity of this child in her jester's attire made Beck's reservations fade. Or maybe it was the way deep down she wished someone would swoop in and save her, so much so that even the words of a wayward child served as a life preserver. "How kind of you to make the attempt. You can help me cover the hives if you'd like."

Katya chewed her lip. "But I am a stranger. You said they don't like strangers."

Beck took a deep breath and projected her voice. "Hey, bees. This is Katya. She's an alien, but I think she's all right." She smiled. "There. Now they know you. Truth is, honeybees rarely sting unless they feel threatened. When they sting, they die. They prefer to avoid that if they can help it. Just promise me you won't come around here without a grown-up."

With her index finger, Katya drew an X over her chest. "Cross my heart. I won't bother your bees."

"Take this end of the cloth, and we'll drape it together."

Katya pinched the hem between her fingers and edged toward the nearest hive. "You never told me. What do these cloths do?"

"Absolutely nothing."

"Then why do you do it?"

"It's an old superstition that if the beekeeper dies, you must tell the bees of his passing or the bees will die too. The cloths are supposed to help them properly mourn. The keeper made me promise I'd do it if anything ever happened to him."

"I thought you were the beekeeper."

"I'm just the apprentice. Well, I was." Beck bit down on the inside of her cheek, focusing on that ache instead of the one welling in her chest.

Katya stared at the hive in front of her, eyes wide. "What happened?"

Beck swallowed hard. "Heart attack."

"Oh." Tension left the girl's body, and she tugged the fabric until the wrinkle on the top of the hive disappeared.

Beck placed a hand on top of the box. "He's gone. He's not coming back. It's just me now."

The notebook reappeared from the fanny pack. Katya peered at her over the top of the spiral wire and scrawled as she spoke. "I don't think it's just superstition. If your whole world is getting turned upside down, then someone should tell you to your face. The bees have a right to know."

Beck picked up another cloth from the pile. "Their world isn't getting turned upside down. Nothing changes for bees. The world just keeps spinning, and they keep on doing their thing."

"Humans never count what the little things in the world notice." By the look in Katya's eyes, Beck would almost believe the child was two hundred Earth years old.

"We've got two hives left. You cover one and I'll cover the other." She motioned to the waiting UTV. "And I can give you a ride to . . . to wherever you're staying during your visit to Earth." She stooped, picking up the remaining shrouds, and turned back to find herself alone again with her hives. "Katya?"

She scanned the uncleared land, looking for sounds and sights indicating movement in the brush, but it was as though the child had vanished into thin air.

Beck finished covering the hives and called for the girl a few more times before climbing in the UTV. She rolled her shoulders to shake off the tension resting there. The girl was probably a guest at the neighboring farm. A few years back, the Baileys had started renting out the loft apartment in their barn for the summers. With a little hand-holding, they let suburbanites and city slickers try their hand at farm life. Surely her mismatched sock alien had just wandered back to where she belonged.

Beck cranked the engine and rambled back to the house, giving one final glance to the shrouded hives, the wind toying with the edges of the cloths, lifting and waving them. A silent farewell. Her father really was gone. He wasn't coming back. It was just her now.

Acknowledgments

Thank you to the entire Revell team for the opportunity to publish another book with you. I am eternally grateful for the time and talent you have invested into my work. Kelsey and Robin, I count having the opportunity to work with you on these past four books as one of the greatest privileges of my writing journey.

To my agent, Tamela Hancock Murray, I am so thankful for your guidance and encouragement. I'm blessed to have you in my corner.

Patti Stockdale, thank you for always being willing to be my first reader. Your words to me completely embody Proverbs 25:11: "A word fitly spoken is like apples of gold in pictures of silver" (KJV). They are full of good judgment on areas I can tweak and full of encouragement in the places I need it.

Huge thanks to Kevin Duffus for taking the time to reply to all of my emails about Outer Banks history in the 1940s. Your book *War Zone: World War II Off the North Carolina Coast* was such a fantastic resource as I wrote this book.

Phillip Howard, I appreciate our shared emails about Ocracoke history as well as your blog articles. They truly helped me imagine what it would have been like to live on those islands during Walt and Cathleen's time.

Caleb, Ellie, and Levi, as much as I love writing, nothing compares to the awesome privilege of getting to raise and teach you three. Thank you for your patience and grace when I'm on a time crunch. Thank you for always insisting that whatever I'm writing is going to be "the best book ever" when you notice I look a little worried about whatever I'm working on.

To my husband, Justin, thanks for making a big deal about my accomplishments when it's my tendency to shrink them. I attempted to infuse a smidge more romance in this one as requested, but you're the romantic one, not me! Thanks for your help in that department.

Jesus, my Savior and faithful friend, thank You for meeting me each morning at my writing desk. As I shaped words on the page, You shaped me. Thank You for being my constant, the One in whom I can always trust.

Amanda Cox is the two-time Christy Book of the Year Award–winning author of *The Edge of Belonging*, *The Secret Keepers of Old Depot Grocery*, and *He Should Have Told the Bees*. She holds a bachelor's degree in Bible and theology and a master's degree in professional counseling, but her first love is communicating through story. Her studies and her interactions with hurting families over a decade have allowed her to create multidimensional characters that connect emotionally with readers. She lives in Chattanooga, Tennessee, with her husband and their three children. Learn more at AmandaCoxWrites.com.

A Beautiful Exploration
of the Complexity of the
MOTHER-DAUGHTER
RELATIONSHIP

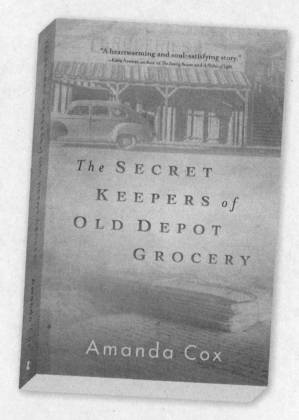

"Luminous and lyrical ... storytelling of the finest sort."

—AMANDA BARRATT,
Christy Award–winning author of *Within These Walls of Sorrow*

MEET AMANDA

FOLLOW ALONG AT
AmandaCoxWrites.com
and sign up for Amanda's newsletter to stay
up-to-date on exclusive news, upcoming
releases, and more!

AmandaCoxWrites